M000042525

ANY LUCK
at all

Other books by A.R. Casella and
Denise Grover Swank

Asheville Brewing Series
Any Luck at All
Better Luck Next Time
Getting Lucky
Bad Luck Club

ANY LUCK
at all

A.R. CASELLA AND
NEW YORK TIMES BESTSELLING AUTHOR
DENISE GROVER SWANK

Copyright © 2020 by A.R. Casella and Denise Grover Swank
Cover: Design: Okay Creations

All rights reserved.

No part of this book may be reproduced in any form or by
any electronic or mechanical means, including information
storage and retrieval systems, without written permission
from the author, except for the use of brief quotations in a
book review.

To the Franceses: two strong women, generations
apart

—ARC

To my girls: never settle

—DGS

CHAPTER One

"How much longer is this going to take?" Prescott Lee Buchanan said in a condescending tone, his fingers drumming on the conference table.

Georgie Buchanan knew that drumming all too well. She'd lived with it for her entire childhood.

"The attorney said we're waiting on something," she told her father.

"I don't understand why we're even here for the will reading," Georgie's baby sister, Adalia, moaned. "I can count on one hand the number of times I've seen Grandpa Buchanan. The last time was over a decade ago. He's not going to leave us anything. I heard his brewery's basically worthless."

Georgie's brother, Lee, who was the middle child but always acted like he was the most important one, shot Adalia an irritated glare. "Unfortunately, *Adalia*, life isn't a free-for-all. Sometimes there are duties and obligations, and they're not always fun and games."

Adalia slapped her ink-stained hand on the table and leaned forward. "I know you don't think much of my life, *Junior*, but at least I'm not Dad's puppet."

"That will be enough, Adalia," Prescott snapped. Then he turned to Lee. "Junior, go and see what's taking so long."

Irritation flickered in Lee's eyes. Georgie knew how much he hated to be called Junior, and if he jumped up to do their father's bidding, he'd be proving Adalia's point.

Lee's girlfriend, Victoria, stood with a grace that made Georgie feel like a backwoods hick, which was saying something since Georgie had created and built a company that she'd just sold for five million dollars. Of course, her father would argue that a company that sells *feminine products* was nothing to brag about.

Victoria gave Prescott a smile that suggested a comradery Georgie had never shared with her father. "*I'll* get answers," she said in a commanding tone that probably reassuring to her clients but was grating on Georgie's nerves. "Professional courtesy."

The woman, a corporate attorney who was tall and skinny enough to be a supermodel, walked out of the room, her gray pencil skirt so tight Georgie wondered how she could walk at all.

"They have high-priced call girls here?" Adalia asked in a dry tone.

One of the men sitting at the opposite end of the table covered his mouth with his hand, but Georgie could tell he was trying to hide his laughter. He'd walked in after she was seated and she'd let her gaze linger on him for longer than was polite. Tall, dark, and handsome was definitely Georgie's type, and it had been far too long since her last boyfriend. Still, the reading of her grandfather's will hardly seemed like the place to pick up a guy.

"Have you no impulse control at all, Adalia?" Lee demanded, the veins in his neck bulging.

8

"There's something to be said for saying how you feel instead of keeping it all bottled up inside," Adalia said with a smirk. Then she glanced back at Mr. Tall-Dark-and-Handsome and the people around him. "Am I right?"

There were a handful of people Georgie didn't recognize at the table. A man wearing jeans and a button-down shirt who looked to be in his late fifties. A middle-aged Latina woman wearing a simple floral dress. The smirking man, who looked to be in his late twenties or early thirties, wore a black suit that was obviously off the rack and not tailored like Prescott's and Lee's. The man who sat next to him was around the same age, dressed in khakis, a button-down shirt that still had creases that hadn't quite been ironed out from the packaging, and a cheap black tie. He sat stoically in his chair, mostly watching her father but occasionally sneaking glances at her and her siblings. And in the center of them all, at the head of the table opposite Georgie's father, sat the one non-Buchanan person Georgie recognized, an elderly woman with short, curly lavender hair, who had on a bright pink business suit that looked like it was straight from the 1980s, shoulder pads and all. Dottie Hendrickson was dressed just as colorfully as she had been when Georgie had met her a few weeks ago at her grandfather's brewery.

When Georgie had asked the legal assistant about all the nonfamily newcomers who'd shown up for the reading of the will, the woman had said, "He bequeathed a few odds and ends to them."

They'd all sat at the opposite end of the room, as if Prescott had sectioned off a kids' table for them. Of course. Prescott was flanked by his three children in their finest black attire: Georgie and Adalia on one side—with an empty chair between Georgie and her father—and Lee and Victoria on the other, Lee glued to his father's side, of course, and Victoria's vacated seat next to him.

Of the Buchanan contingent, Georgie was the only one who'd seen Beau at all in recent years. She'd paid him a visit a few weeks ago, at his request. He'd called to congratulate her on the sale of her company, something her own father had still not done, and invited her to come to Asheville in the near future. Something in his voice had told her the visit should come sooner rather than later, and with no new project yet in the works, she'd made an impulsive decision (not her usual) and hopped on a plane. He hadn't looked like the picture of health, but then again, he'd been in his late eighties. Still, she hadn't expected him to die so *quickly*.

During her two-day visit, he'd taken her on a tour of Buchanan Brewery, the oldest brewery in Asheville, North Carolina, a city which had become a hotbed for beer brewing...and apparently left Buchanan Brewery in its dust. The equipment was old, some of the staff even older, including the woman currently holding court opposite Georgie's father. Dottie was the tasting room manager.

Dottie smiled at Georgie now, her eyes twinkling as though she was privy to an amusing secret.

Georgie's back stiffened. *Wait. Was she?*

She was about to say something to her father, but Victoria and an older man with salt-and-pepper hair— Georgie's grandfather's estate attorney—walked in arm in arm, smiling and laughing as though they'd been close for ages.

Georgie wanted to gag.

She'd been in the business world long enough to know a woman could get ahead either by flirting her way to the top or becoming a hard-ass who took no crap.

She'd gone the latter route.

So why did she still let her father and brother walk all over her?

Georgie didn't have time to think about it because the attorney walked in with Victoria and escorted her to her leather chair, pulling it out for her to sit down.

"Thank you for your patience," the man said as he moved to an empty seat in the middle, standing behind the chair. "For those of you who don't know, I'm Henry Manning, Beau Buchanan's attorney, and everyone present has been mentioned in the will. Again, thank you for your patience, but we had to be certain we had everything in order before we began."

"I still don't understand the need for all the pomp and circumstance," Prescott grumbled. "Just hand us a copy of the will and be done with it."

The attorney gave Prescott a tight smile. "These were the wishes of your father, Prescott. I am merely his instrument."

The way he held Georgie's father's gaze suggested the two men had already made an acquaintance and it hadn't gone well.

The assistant Georgie had spoken to earlier walked in, carrying a legal box with a lid. She set it down on the console table behind Mr. Manning.

"Before we begin," the attorney said, "can I get anyone anything to drink? Water? Coffee?"

"*Will you just read the damn will already?*" Prescott demanded.

To his credit, Mr. Manning ignored him and turned to the people at the opposite end of the table.

"Water sounds like a good idea," Dottie said, getting to her feet. "Everyone needs water."

"We don't need water," Prescott said, tugging at his tie. "We need to find out what the old man said, and then get out of here so I can start making arrangements to sell off the brewery."

Dottie's smile momentarily froze, then got bigger. "Nonsense. You've all had a *very* long day, what with your mourning at the funeral and all. Water's *just* what you need."

The mourning comment was a not-so-carefully concealed jab. Georgie had been the most upset, but to be fair, none of her siblings had really known the man. Their father had made sure of that.

For some reason, her gaze shot to the handsome man in the ill-fitting suit. His jaw had a firm set, and all vestiges of humor had fled from his face. Their eyes met for a moment, and Georgie shifted her gaze, unnerved by the judgment she saw there.

Dottie turned to face the attorney. "Henry, I'll just go fetch some glasses."

Henry, Georgie thought. Interesting. She clearly knew him as more than a passing acquaintance. Either that, or she was at an age where she didn't stand on ceremony. Georgie suspected it was some combination of the two.

"We don't need water!" Prescott shouted, his face turning red.

"Just let the woman get some water," Lee groaned, pushing his chair back from the table.

Dottie headed for the door but stopped and pinched Prescott's cheek. "Patience, my boy. You never really understood the concept, but you're not too old to learn it now."

She walked out of the room as every member of the Buchanan family stared at her in shock. She'd dared to touch *the* Prescott Buchanan.

Georgie couldn't remember the last time she'd physically touched her father, and she struggled to hide a grin at the woman's outrageousness.

"This is ridiculous," Prescott sneered. "No one needs water!"

"I need water," Adalia said, tilting her head and giving her father a mischievous look.

"I could use some water," the Hispanic woman said in a small voice.

"Who are you again?" Georgie's father demanded.

"You'll find out soon enough," Mr. Manning said, a fine sheen of perspiration covering his forehead. He pulled out a handkerchief and dabbed at the sweat, then stuffed it back into his pocket. Another second ticked by, and he lifted his arm to look at his watch even though there was a clock on the wall next to him.

Georgie's father glared at everyone while Lee was visibly annoyed, and Adalia looked like a cat who'd not only eaten the canary but a couple of chickens too. Victoria appeared bored, but she arguably always looked that way. Georgie just wanted this over with. Her family was definitely showing the rest of the room how they put the *fun* in dysfunction.

Dottie returned a couple of minutes later carrying a pitcher of water, while a woman trailed behind her with a tray full of glasses.

"Now, give everyone a glass," Dottie instructed. "*Everyone*, whether they say they want one or not."

The woman began to set them in front of people, starting with Georgie, then Adalia, and moving around the table. Dottie followed her, pouring water into each glass. She'd gotten halfway around the table and was just about to run out when a man walked in with another pitcher.

"If you had to *insist* on water," Prescott sneered, "couldn't you at least have gotten water bottles?"

"Water *bottles*?" Dottie asked with a chortle. "Well, aren't you the funny man?"

Georgie burst into laughter, drawing shocked looks from both of her siblings. But she couldn't help it—she'd never once heard anyone refer to her father as funny.

"See?" Dottie said, taking the pitcher and continuing to pour. "Even Georgie knows how silly that was."

Georgie continued to laugh. The idea of someone calling Prescott Buchanan both funny and silly was too preposterous to bear.

Or maybe the stress of it all was getting to her.

"Georgie," Adalia said in a concerned tone as she rested her hand on Georgie's forearm. "Are you okay?"

She nodded as she wiped tears from her face.

"Look what you've done, Prescott. Now the poor girl's crying." Dottie tsked, continuing to move around the table. "She's grieving over the damage those bottles do to the earth." She stopped and shot Prescott a glare. "Plastic is the devil's mischief. Don't you *forget* it." Then she gave Georgie a knowing look. "Georgie girl gets it."

"Georgie girl?" Lee asked. "Just what were you doing down here to earn a nickname, Georgie?"

"You were down here?" Adalia asked. "In Asheville?"

Georgie cringed. "Grandpa Beau asked me to come visit."

"When?" Adalia demanded.

"A few weeks ago."

The hurt look on Adalia's face said she was upset Lee had known and she hadn't. Not that she ever picked up any of Georgie's calls.

"Now, now," Dottie said, pouring water into Lee's glass. "All this squabbling isn't healthy." She set the pitcher down on the table, then reached into her pocket and pulled out a crystal. Setting it on the table, she began to wave her hand over it, as if wafting its essence toward Prescott. "Let's get rid of some of that negative energy."

"What the hell are you *doing*?" Prescott demanded, rolling his chair back so hard it hit the wall. The clock overhead fell off and landed in his lap.

Dottie pursed her lips and shook her head as she eyed him with a worried look. "That's a bad omen. I told you that you should learn more patience."

Then she walked back to the end of the table and resumed her seat, leaving the pitcher on the edge of the table between Prescott and Lee.

Prescott picked up the wall clock and stared at it as though intimidating it to give him an explanation for daring to jump off the wall and into his lap. Pushing out a breath of frustration, he put the clock on the conference table. "Can we please get this going?"

Mr. Manning's entire face was red and covered in sweat, but he nodded to his assistant.

She opened the lid and handed the attorney several pages stapled together.

"Beau had a trust," he said, loosening his tie, "but he thought it might be easier for some of you to digest the terms if they were delivered in his own words."

That suggested the will might not be as straightforward as her father expected. Georgie wasn't sure whether to be thrilled or horrified. Her father's narrowed eyes suggested he wasn't expecting good news. The excitement in Dottie's suggested she was fully aware of what was about to happen.

Oh mercy. Had her grandfather gone and given everything to his employees?

A little voice in the back of her head said they were probably more like family to him than his own family had been. She'd seen it herself when she'd toured the brewery. They'd loved Beau Buchanan, and it had made Georgie acutely aware of how much she didn't know about him. She'd spent the rest of her visit asking him everything—about the brewery, his late wife, raising his only child. He'd shown her photos and told her stories that had made her sides ache with laughter. He'd been a charming man, and she'd found herself wondering how she had gone thirty-three years without getting to know him better. His conflict with her father was theirs, not hers, and despite not knowing all of the details, she suspected she knew who was at fault.

When she'd left, she'd promised to keep in touch and return soon. She'd called him last week, and he'd told her that he had a cold but not to worry. He'd be fine.

Three days later he was dead. Her heart ached with the loss.

Mr. Manning pulled a pair of reading glasses from his jacket pocket and perched them on his nose. He shot Georgie a forced grin. "Eyesight's not what it used to be."

She gave him a tight smile, her stomach doing flips.

"*If Henry's reading this to you, that means I'm dead, but don't mourn me. I've lived a long, full life with few regrets, and those few I do have I'm hoping to rectify with this will.*" Mr. Manning picked up a glass of water and swallowed several gulps.

"Good boy," Dottie said. "Flush away the bad karma."

Bad karma? That didn't bode well.

He set down the glass and continued to read. "*I'll start with my work family first. To Tom Magee, my plant manager, my fishing buddy, and dear friend, I leave my fishing equipment. You won't be able to tell me any more whoppers, old boy. I'll be watching over you, keeping you honest."*

The middle-aged man grinned and nodded his acknowledgment.

"To Rita, you were a joy and a treasure. I've left you fifteen thousand dollars for not only cleaning my house but watching over me. Now I've finally gotten my way and can buy you a decent car."

Tears ran down Rita's face and Dottie pulled another crystal from her pocket and put it in the woman's hand, whispering something into her ear. Idly, Georgie wondered how many crystals she had in there.

"To River," Mr. Manning continued. *"You've become like a son to me. To you, I leave my father's pocket watch. It should go to someone who appreciates the meaning of such things."*

The man in the off-the-rack suit looked stunned at the announcement. His eyes turned glassy and he cleared his throat before he said, "Thank you."

Dottie reached over and patted his arm.

"And now on to Prescott," the attorney said.

Georgie noticed that the letter hadn't yet addressed two of the people at the end of the table—Dottie and the young man with dark hair and brooding eyes. What was the significance of that?

Dread filled her gut.

The attorney dabbed his face again before continuing. *"Dear Prescott. We've had our differences, son, some of them my doing and some of them yours. I wish I'd spent more time with you when you were a boy, and I wish you'd corrected my mistakes, rather than following my lead when it came to raising your own children."*

Georgie's gaze shot to Lee, who was already giving her a questioning glance. Did he think she'd spilled the family secret during her visit with her grandfather? Although it wasn't much of a secret that Prescott Buchanan had devoted far more of his life to his business than his family.

The attorney continued. *"You built your own life, and I confess that was partly my doing, but now I want to give your children the chance to make different choices."*

Adalia perked up at that, turning to Georgie with a questioning look, her short blond curls bouncing around her shoulders.

Georgie made a face that suggested she was just as clueless.

Mr. Manning took a deep breath, as if he were a soldier preparing for battle, then enunciated each word carefully. *"The brewery, the house, and everything in it, other than what's already been stated, goes to Prescott's four children."*

Mass chaos broke out, everyone shouting at once.

"This is outrageous!" Prescott shouted as he got to his feet. "I will fight this!"

Lee jerked his gaze to the attorney. "How could this happen?"

Victoria was already patting Lee's arm. "Don't worry. We can fight this."

Georgie just stared at them in shock. Was Lee such an ass-kisser that he'd give up his inheritance to placate their father?

Adalia sat back in her seat and turned to Georgie. *"Four* children. Why did he say that? Dad only has *three* children."

Because it turned out Beau Buchanan *had* somehow known Prescott's dirty little secret.

Horror filled Georgie as she turned to face the young man at the end of the table. And she wondered why she hadn't seen it before. He shared her father's cheekbones. And dark eyes. His hair was the same dark color her father's had been. Georgie and her siblings' coloring had come from their mother.

"Georgie?" Adalia demanded.

"There are four," Georgie said quietly, unable to take her eyes off her younger brother. While she'd known of him, she'd never seen him. Not even a photo.

"What?" Adalia screeched. "How?"

"Come now, Adalia," Victoria sneered. "You're a grown woman. You know how these things work."

Adalia turned to Georgie. "You *knew*?"

"We both did," Lee said quietly. "We found out a few years ago by accident."

"And no one thought to tell me?" Adalia asked, her voice so full of pain it hurt Georgie's heart. She wanted to reach out and comfort her sister, to tell her they hadn't meant for it to go so long. Adalia had been going through a bad stretch, and she and Lee had decided it wasn't a good time to tell their baby sister. And then there had never been a good time after that. *Oh, by the way, Lee and I found out that Dad cheated on Mom, and we have a brother only a few months older than you. How's the weather?*

But now this was a huge mess, and Adalia's hurt feelings were entirely justified.

"Addy," Lee said, his voice full of apology.

"Don't you even try to explain it!" Adalia said to her brother, then turned her icy stare on Prescott. "And you! How *dare* you cheat on our mother!"

"Here, dear," Dottie said, getting up and putting yet another stone in front of Adalia.

"I don't think a crystal's gonna fix this, Aunt Dottie," River said in a dry tone.

"Nonsense," Dottie said, her eyes burning brightly. "Nothing's broken that can't be put back together."

Georgie wasn't so sure about that.

CHAPTER Two

Watching the Buchanan family made River feel like a rubbernecker checking out an accident by the side of the road. It was more uncomfortable than the suit he was wearing, which was saying something.

He caught the eye of the pretty blonde again, the one with her hair pulled back in a bun so tight it looked like it hurt. Georgie. Beau had told him a little about her visit, although he hadn't mentioned a damn thing about passing over his son and giving the brewery to his grandkids. Prescott had been pretty upfront about wanting to pawn Beau's legacy, and probably Beau had expected that. Maybe the kids wouldn't sell, although he suspected four strangers could run a business together better than this crew.

He doubted any of them knew jack about beer.

There were tears in Georgie's eyes, which made his stomach wrench a little. Beau's son and grandson were obviously blowhards—well, Junior, at least—but the granddaughters seemed okay. Still, he felt worse for the guy sitting next to him. The secret son. For everything that had been said around and about him, he hadn't said a word. He'd just soaked it all in like he was used to listening, to reacting rather than acting.

River knew what it felt like to be the kid who got left behind—literally, in his case—and it sucked. Now, this guy had become the sideshow in this hoity-toity circus, through the mere act of being born. The look in his eyes said he could take it, though—that maybe this was something he'd been waiting for, his chance to claim whatever piece of the Buchanan pie he felt he was owed.

In this case, a fourth of Beau's estate.

It was time for the rest of them to leave.

"Maybe we should get out of here," he said, to which all of the other non-Buchanans eagerly nodded. "Give the family some space. You've already addressed the parts of the will that relate to us, right, Henry? Any reason for us to stay?"

Henry gave him a panicked look. His handkerchief was as wet as if he'd soaked it in one of Aunt Dottie's water pitchers. He clearly didn't enjoy the thought of being left with the Buchanans, and really, who could blame him.

"Good idea, dear," Aunt Dottie said. "But if I remember correctly, I'm supposed to stay until the end."

Adalia had picked up the crystal his aunt had given her and was turning it around in her hand as if she might hurl it at someone—who the target would be was anyone's guess—but her eyes flew up at his aunt's comment. "You knew I had another brother before I did!"

Her tone was shrill, and Prescott picked up his glass of water, untouched, of course, and banged it down on the table. "You will stop acting like a child this instant, Adalia. We've had enough of your display."

She'd been saucy enough earlier that River expected her to throw back a comment, but she didn't. She just sat back in her chair, her mouth in a thin line, like she was forcing herself to hold back all the things she wanted to say. Or maybe she was just trying not to cry. With her short curly hair, she looked every bit the part of the little sister. Somehow that made it worse. He didn't think much of men who intimidated women.

The door closed, and River realized Rita had already left the room. Smart lady.

"See," Aunt Dottie said brightly, although River knew her well enough to see beyond it, "aren't you glad I got the glasses? A plastic bottle would never have made such an authoritative sound. You would have *crushed* it."

"Who *is* this woman?" Prescott asked Henry. "Is there any reason for her to stay?"

The words were said with such distaste, River felt the urge to bite back, but this was his aunt's moment too, and if anyone knew how to stand up for herself, it was Dottie Hendrickson. A man had attempted to mug her once, and she'd reduced him to tears in the space of five minutes, and not because she kept a can of mace in her purse. She'd engaged him in conversation, and he'd spilled his life story to her. She'd invited him home for tea, and he still sent her a card every Christmas. That was Aunt Dottie for you.

"Dad…" Junior said, likely the first time he'd done anything to stand up to his father, but he needn't have bothered.

"Oh, bless your heart," Aunt Dottie said. "I'm the woman who's shared your father's bed for the last twenty years."

And *that* was his cue.

As voices rose on the other side of the room, River nodded to the guy next to him, whose name he still didn't know. "Good luck, man. You're going to need it."

For a second, he wondered if maybe he'd pissed the guy off, but then a corner of his mouth lifted up.

"Thanks, I guess."

River got up and slapped Tom on the back. "Ready?"

They walked away, River closing the door behind them, but as they left the room, he felt compelled to look back. He met Georgie's eyes again, drawn to her despite himself, but she looked away as if embarrassed. He couldn't blame her for that. He had a feeling everyone in that room would be talking about this will reading for years to come.

Once they left the office and stepped onto North Market Street, River turned to Tom. "If they sell to one of the big companies, let me know, man. I can put in a word for you with Finn. No one wants to work for the corporate overlords."

Tom gave him a weird look. Had he overstepped? They'd always gotten along well, so the possibility hadn't occurred to him.

Before he could ask, Tom shook his head. "I'll see how it plays out. I guess we know why Beau never talked about his family much. I feel like we just walked out of a reality TV show."

River went home to change out of the suit, something he was grateful he had time for before he met up with Finn. Finn had gone to the funeral too, but he'd ducked out afterward, saying something about a business meeting. Although they'd worked together for five years, River was happy to leave that kind of stuff to him. The business angle wasn't something that spoke to him; brewing was what he loved. There was a certain kind of magic to brewing beer—you never knew exactly how it was going to turn out. Small differences could end up being big in the end. A little more of this, a little less of that, and suddenly you had a new flavor, the kind that kept people coming back.

River didn't have any official training—he'd never taken any classes—but he'd started when he was a teenager, schooled by Beau, who maybe should have known better. And Finn had taken a chance on him after they met at a local beer festival. Together they'd made Big Catch Brewing the go-to craft brewery in Asheville. And that was something to be proud of.

About a month ago, Beau had invited River over for a drink. They'd sat on the back porch with a couple of brews—some of Big Catch's stuff River had brought over—and shot the shit. It wasn't so unusual for Beau to ask him over, even if Aunt Dottie wasn't around, but something about Beau's energy had seemed off—and wouldn't his aunt have had a field day if he'd told her that—so it hadn't surprised him when the tone turned serious.

Beau had set his beer down and turned to look River in the eye. "Son," he said, "you're happy, aren't you? Working with Finn? I didn't know what to think of a man named after a fish appendage, but he seems like a good enough sort of fellow."

A little uneasy about where the conversation was going, River had nonetheless fallen into the joke. "Sure, once I got used to the smell."

But Beau's expression had stayed serious, and so he'd responded in kind.

"Yeah, Beau, I'm happy there. Who would have thought I'd have all of this after...well, you know." He tapped the bottle in his hand. It was their Lake Trout Lager. Given their respective names, River and Finn, they'd gone in hard with the whole fishing theme—a joke that probably seemed funnier after a couple of drinks.

"Good, good," Beau had said distractedly.

River sat up straighter. "Are you having trouble with the brewery?"

Beau swatted the air, although they both knew Buchanan Brewery needed a major overhaul. The equipment was outdated, and it had been at least three years since the brewmaster, Lurch, had come up with anything new. Five years since he'd come up with anything good. Still, Beau was nothing if not loyal, and Lurch had once helped him out of a lurch (hence the nickname). He refused to replace the man, even though they were both far past the normal age of retirement. With as much competition as there was—a new brewery popping up every few months like a mushroom— they couldn't keep skating by forever.

"Don't you worry about that," Beau said. "I was considering some plans for the future, and I want to be sure you're taken care of."

"We've talked about this before. You've already given me everything I could possibly want. As far as I'm concerned, the only plan you should be making is when you're getting a haircut, because you're starting to channel a serious Einstein vibe."

"Consider the source," Beau had said with a smile. "Before long you'll be able to pull *that* into a ponytail"—he winced—"and then one of those man buns."

"Oh, don't worry, I'll never let it go that far. Now, will you stop being morbid?"

"Only once I die," Beau had said, picking up the beer again. He took a long sip, looking off into the distance, and then said, "I'm thinking of asking my granddaughter to visit. It's time."

Beau's family had always fallen on the do-not-discuss list, or rather the do-not-discuss-unless-Beau-brings-it-up list. Not because he was the sort of man who kept secrets, or at least not until this whole will disaster, but because it had broken his heart. That was something River understood. He didn't talk about his mother either.

So he'd just nodded.

Now, he wished he'd asked more questions. He wished a lot of things.

After a stop at his loft on North Lexington—the suit went into the back of his closet until someone else died or got married, and he checked on the fermentation of his new test batch—he walked to Buchanan Brewery, feeling a whole hell of a lot more like himself in jeans and T-shirt. The South Slope location, which had been kind of iffy fifteen years ago when they'd first moved to this spot, was now ideal. They had the street, just not the street appeal. There was a kind of hominess to the tasting room, though, like your grandparents' somewhat mildewy basement. But maybe he just thought that because Beau had been the owner, and Aunt Dottie was the tasting room manager.

The place was packed tonight, with so many people standing he couldn't edge his way to the bar. Annoying from a logistics perspective, but it made him proud of Beau. Everyone wanted to raise a glass to him. A few people waved at River and slapped him on the back, some of them mutual acquaintances with Beau, others locals who patronized Big Catch, and then he caught sight of Finn sitting at a small two-top, chatting with a couple of pretty tourists, a blonde with pigtails and a brunette drinking a hard lemonade. Leave it to Finn to wheedle his way into a seat—and female company.

"Over here, buddy!" Finn called. "Already got you a beer."

He wrestled his way over to the table, nearly tripping over a Chihuahua in an emotional support vest—his friend Maisie was so hearing about that—before he finally grabbed the seat across from his buddy.

Although River had ditched his suit the first chance he got, Finn was still wearing his. Of course, Finn was the kind of guy who wore suits well, just like Junior from earlier, only not an asshole.

"I'll call *you* later," Finn said to the blonde with the pigtails, and the two women took off, Finn's date looking over her shoulder.

"Let me guess," River said, waiting for them to be out of hearing, "you told her you're a big catch."

"Ha. Ha," Finn said. "Very funny. You're lucky that, loss of Beau aside, I'm in a very good mood." He slid a pint across the table to him. "Beau Brown. I thought it only appropriate." He picked up his own drink, a pint of the same, and they clinked glasses.

"To Beau."

River's throat felt a little thick at that, but he took a swig. Beau had been eighty-seven, for God's sake. They didn't have much reason to complain, did they?

Somehow that didn't matter like it should.

"Sorry, buddy," Finn said, some of his good humor deflating. "He was one of a kind."

River's mind shot to the will reading again, to the spectacle of it. Part of him wanted to tell Finn, who would surely laugh at the Buchanans. Joking around was what he did best. But he didn't want to talk about it yet, and in a weird way, he didn't want to laugh about it either. Which was why he changed the subject instead. "So the meeting went well, I take it?"

Finn's grin would have been answer enough. "Better than well."

"What was it about, anyway? Wider product placement? I know you've been chasing that down lately."

"No, man. It was a rep from Bev Corp."

Bev Corp, as in the largest multinational beer company in the world.

Bev Corp, as in where creativity went to die.

"Why the hell did you meet with *them*?" he asked, already bristling.

"Now, River, I know how you and Dottie feel about big corporations and all that noise, but wait until you hear what they offered me. Us. They want you too. They're going to give you a huge bonus once I sign."

Once I sign. He'd already made the decision.

This meant Big Catch wasn't theirs anymore, except the fact that Finn had made this decision without even talking to him first—hell, he'd accepted the meeting without telling him—meant it had never been his at all. This likely wasn't the work of one meeting either. How long had Finn been talking to them?

All of the emotions River had been trying not to feel since Beau died seemed to pour into him at once, only he felt pissed off instead of sad.

"Was I the last one to know about this?" he asked, not caring that his voice had risen. Hadn't Tom acted weird earlier? As if he knew something River didn't?

"It's not like that," Finn said. "I wouldn't agree to anything that wasn't in your best interest too. You know me better than to think that. Come on, just hear me—"

River stood up then, pushing his chair back a little harder than he'd intended. The emotional support

Chihuahua yelped and jumped into the arms of its owner—a huge tattooed man with a bald head.

"Hey, back off!" the man shouted. "You scared Princess Leia!"

"Dude," he said, staring the guy down, "we all know that's not an emotional support dog. The little vest isn't fooling anyone."

The guy took a step toward him, a threat that was somewhat undermined by the Chihuahua cuddled in his arms. She was wearing a pink tutu beneath the vest.

River burst out laughing at the absurdity of it, at the absurdity of *life*, which apparently offended the guy because he came barreling toward him. At first he thought the dude would try to punch him, which he'd maybe even welcome, but Princess Leia was still cradled in his arms. Instead, Baldy tried to kick him in the shins, and River jumped over his huge feet as if he were a girl playing double Dutch, which was when Finn intervened.

"Leia's not much of an emotional support dog if you're kicking my friend while you're holding her, now is she? Why don't you sit down before I find Dottie. I have a feeling she won't be too pleased with your behavior. You do know River's her great-nephew, don't you?"

The fear on the guy's face indicated he was a local because he obviously knew better than to piss off Aunt Dottie. Not that she'd rage at him or bonk him over the head or anything like that—violence wasn't her style. But he might find himself suckered into an hour-long meditation session in the back room, which smelled like dank hops and stale bread. Her cleansing tonics were also infamous. Although not on the menu, she offered them to guests who seemed unduly upset or angry. No one made that mistake twice.

Baldy set down Princess Leia with an affectionate pat, then lifted his hands palm up. "Sorry, man. I had no idea you were related to Dottie. Only good energy here. Namaste."

As he turned away, looking over his shoulder as if he feared Aunt Dottie might be onto him, Finn gave River a tentative smile. Normally, he would have smiled back and they would have laughed about all of this later. But the trust they'd had was broken, and for River, trust was everything.

He shook his head and said the one thing he'd never imagined saying. "I quit."

CHAPTER
Three

Georgie watched as the cute guy—River—got up and made his escape. She couldn't remember the last time she'd felt so envious. He cast her a sympathetic glance on the way out, but she looked away, too embarrassed to meet his eyes.

Talk about a train wreck.

She was half tempted to jump up and run after him, and not just because she found him attractive.

Instead, she was left with her over-the-top family and Dottie, who was pulling even more crystals out of her purse and stacking them on the table as if creating her own miniature Stonehenge. Apparently desperate times called for desperate measures. It was probably no accident that the stack appeared to be pointed toward her father, who was seething. "What the hell is going on, Manning?"

Mr. Manning's face looked like he'd just stepped out of the shower.

Georgie had never realized one person could produce that much sweat, but then Prescott Buchanan could make the most confident of men shake in their boots. How many of her boyfriends had taken off running after meeting him?

Okay, only two had made it to that stage—one in high school and the other in college. Maybe that was why she was single now. She'd yet to date a man who could stand toe to toe with her father. She also knew it was an impossible bar to hold men to.

Terror filled the attorney's eyes. "Uh…"

The legal assistant, who'd been standing behind him, stepped forward and handed him a napkin.

Mr. Manning started to dab his face, but he must have realized it was a lost cause, because he gave up halfway through and tossed the soaked napkin onto the table with a sickening splat.

Adalia turned and gave Georgie a theatrical look of disgust. At least she was willing to put her anger away for a moment, even if it was over their mutual disgust for the attorney's overactive sweat glands.

Dottie seemed oblivious to it all and pulled out a skein of yarn and some knitting needles from her apparently bottomless purse. Georgie couldn't tell what she was working on, but it looked like it had tiny armholes.

"Perhaps I should just get to the reading of the trust," Mr. Manning said.

"Yes," Georgie's father sneered. "I think you should."

Mr. Manning's voice wavered as he started reading the thick document produced by his assistant. It was all dry legalese at the beginning, but when he got to the part saying everything Beau Buchanan owned would be passed on to his grandchildren, Adalia put her hand on the table and leaned forward. "In English, please."

"It means you four children own it all," Dottie said, her needles clicking. "Every last bit of it."

"So we sell it," Lee said. "Dad has to leave tonight, but I'll stay a few days and find a commercial real estate agent."

Adalia turned to her brother. "Who says I want to sell?"

His mouth dropped open. "What the hell would you do with a brewery?"

"I don't know, Lee, but *you* can't just decide to sell it. We should all be part of that decision."

"With all due respect, Addy," Lee said, softening his tone. "Stick to what you know."

Adalia jolted in her seat. "*Stick to what I know?*"

"It has to be a unanimous decision to sell," Mr. Manning said, then winced as he snuck a glance at Prescott. "One person refuses and you keep it. All of you. But you have to decide to sell or keep it by noon tomorrow, or it will be sold to the highest bidder, with the profits going to an animal shelter called Dog is Love."

Prescott leveled a glare at his youngest daughter. "Agree to sell, Adalia."

She flinched and sat back in her seat. Georgie resisted the urge to reach over and give her a pat of reassurance. Or her father a swat.

"I've heard enough," Prescott said, getting to his feet. "Lee, clean this mess up." He cast one final withering glance at all of them and strode out of the room.

As soon as he left, half the tension in Georgie's shoulders faded. Adalia's body seemed to relax too. The only one who still looked on edge was Georgie's secret half-brother, who eyed them all as though they were an alien species, and it hit her how awkward this had to be for him. While she wasn't thrilled her father had carried on an affair with the man's mother, it wasn't his fault. In fact, she suspected he wasn't thrilled either.

"I'm Georgie," she said, offering him a tentative smile. "You must be Jack."

Adalia turned to her in outrage. "You knew his name too?"

"Not now, Addy," Georgie said, keeping her gaze on Jack.

He nodded slightly. "Guilty as charged."

"I'm sorry we had to meet under these circumstances."

He didn't respond.

Georgie turned back to her other siblings. "Obviously, we need to figure out how to sell the brewery and the house."

"Agreed," Lee said in relief.

Now that their father had left, it was natural for Georgie to fall back into the take-charge mode she'd assumed when their mother had become sick her sophomore year of high school. Their father had never been around and their mother had quickly become too ill to run the house. That responsibility had fallen on Georgie's shoulders, and her siblings still let her jump back into that familiar role in times of crisis.

"I don't want to sell," Jack said in a firm tone.

Georgie turned back to face him, sure she'd heard wrong. "What?"

His dark eyes held hers. "I don't want to sell."

"Now, look here," Lee said, his face turning red. "If you think you can just waltz in here and start pilfering from my grandfather's carcass—"

"Our grandfather," Jack said in a calm voice. "He's *our* grandfather. And I'm only here because I was told to be here. I've known about all of you for years and never once tried to make contact."

Lee sat back in his chair, the fight draining out of him.

"Because you were biding your time," Victoria said in an icy tone.

Jack cracked a slight smile, neither a denial nor confirmation.

"Why are *you* here?" Adalia asked, turning her wrath on Lee's girlfriend. "You aren't any part of this."

Shock covered Victoria's perfectly chiseled face. (Georgie would bet money she'd had work done. Surely, no one was so lacking in emotion naturally.) "I'm here to support Lee."

"You're his *girlfriend*," Adalia said. "You have no business here."

Georgie was inclined to agree. The two had only been dating eight months. "She's right."

"Georgie…" Lee cringed as he snuck a glance at his girlfriend.

"I have every right to be here," Victoria said, her gaze pinned on Georgie. "How *dare* you suggest I don't."

"You're not married," Adalia said. "You're not even engaged, which means this has nothing to do with you."

Victoria squared her shoulders as though preparing for a fight. "We are eight months into our three-year plan."

Dottie, who'd been steadfastly focused on her project, lifted her gaze. "What's that, dear?"

Lee's girlfriend scrunched up her nose as if she smelled something disgusting, giving the older woman a look that suggested it was none of her business, so Georgie was surprised when she said, "Our three-year plan. First year is a committed relationship, the second year we get engaged, and the third we get married and buy a house. We'll have our first baby at the end of year three."

"Let me guess," Adalia said in a dry tone. "You've not only got the wedding venue booked, but you've already picked out your first child's name and commissioned monogrammed bibs."

Victoria let out a huff. "You have no idea how far ahead you need to plan to book the Brookside Country Club for a reception, but I have *not* had bibs monogrammed."

"No, but you did commission that tapestry," Lee said, his mouth twitching a little.

Victoria shot him a look so cold Georgie couldn't believe he hadn't turned into a block of ice. Why did Lee always go for women like that? Their own mother had been nurturing and sweet—funny too—an odd fit for Prescott, or so everyone used to say. But Lee's girlfriends always looked like they'd just as soon stab you with a stiletto heel as look at you.

"Nevertheless," Georgie said in the motherly tone she took on when bossing her siblings around. "You can't stay for this discussion. We can vote on it if you insist, but I suspect that's a waste of time."

"You have no authority to do that, Georgie!" Victoria snapped.

"No, but I do," Mr. Manning said. "You have to go."

"Henry!" Victoria protested, as if a dear friend had betrayed her.

"He's right, dear," Dottie said as she leaned over her knitting, concentrating on her next stitch. "You have no reason to be here."

"But you *do*?" Victoria asked. "You don't even know these people."

Dottie's face lifted. "I know Georgie, and I'll be getting to know the rest of them soon enough. Your bad energy is clouding my chi." She made a waving motion. "Off with you now."

"Lee!" Victoria protested.

He shrugged. "Sorry, Victoria."

She got up and slung her Louis Vuitton handbag over her shoulder, then stomped out. Georgie could swear her brother looked relieved as the glass door closed behind her.

"Dottie's right," Mr. Manning said. "*She is* supposed to be here. Beau specifically requested she stay the whole time."

Lee pushed out a breath, then leaned both arms on the table. "Look…Jack. I don't know what you're up to, but none of us know squat about running a brewery. Do you?"

"No, but—"

"The practical thing to do is sell the house and the brewery. We can get an estate company to sell off the furniture, then the four of us will split the profits." He gestured toward Adalia. "You can use the money to pay off your art school student loans, and maybe have enough to pay for a studio for a few years." His expression softened. "It's the smart thing to do, Addy. If you think about it, after our phone call last week, this is a godsend."

Lee and Adalia had talked last week? Georgie hadn't talked to either one of them in over a month. Not even after the sale had gone through. Part of her had hoped they'd call to congratulate her, but it hadn't happened.

Adalia sighed, which Lee must have taken as an agreement because he turned to Georgie next. "Georgie. You can take this money and add it to your pot and do…what are you planning to do now that you sold your business?"

Something bristled in Georgie, and she couldn't keep herself from snapping, "*Now* you ask what I'm planning to do?"

Lee groaned. "Georgie…"

She shook her head. "No. We're not deciding this now." Her grandfather had asked her to visit for a reason, and there had been so much pride in his eyes when he'd shown her around the brewery. Beau had known Prescott would sell the place, and instead he had willed it to his grandchildren. That *meant* something. "We need to think about this before we make a decision. Jack doesn't want to sell, and I've got nothing going on right now. Maybe Jack and I can run it."

Lee's eyes bugged out of his head. "You can't be serious. You were the first one to suggest selling it."

She lifted her chin. "Maybe I am serious. It's *Buchanan* Brewery. It has our family name in it, and obviously Grandpa Beau wanted us to take over."

"What? You have one visit with the old guy and suddenly you want to assume the family mantle?" Adalia asked.

"I don't know, Addy," Georgie said, overcome with exhaustion. "But I *do* know I'm not making this decision right now. We should at least consider it."

"Be practical, Georgie." The condescension dripping from her brother's words made her cringe. He sounded just like their father.

"I *am* being practical," she said, getting to her feet. "Just like I was being practical when I started my company ten years ago. The one that started in my kitchen and ended up employing fifty people. The one I just sold for *five million dollars*. So forgive me if I don't buy into your idea of practicality, *Junior*." She sucked in a breath and turned to Jack. "Obviously, we need to talk, but I'm not in the frame of mind to discuss business right now. Get my cell number from Mr. Manning, and we'll talk in the morning."

Surprise filled Jack's eyes, and there was a one-second delay before he shook his head. "Yeah. Okay."

She nodded. "Okay, then." She started to walk out the door, then glanced over her shoulder. "Oh, and Jack? Welcome to the family."

CHAPTER
Four

River didn't know where he was going at first. He just started walking and didn't stop. Finn shouted something after him, but he didn't respond. He didn't respond when his phone started ringing either. Everything that needed to be said had been said. The path he'd been walking on had ended. Now he needed to figure out what the hell he was going to do next.

After a while, he realized where he was headed: Beau's house. It felt right, so he kept walking, and when he got to the Victorian in Montford, he let himself in using the key hidden in the hanging planter Aunt Dottie had made for Beau last Christmas.

The house still smelled like Beau. Like Old Spice and hops and a hint of vanilla. Maybe it was because he spent all day thinking about things like flavor profiles, but he always took note of a person's scent. It saddened him to think it would fade away. Probably the Buchanans would want to sell, and they'd get a realtor to show it to people—someone who'd use that fake cookie scent to lure people in.

"Shit," he said out loud. He really didn't like the thought of this place going to strangers. Although the

Buchanans were strangers too. Part of him wanted to hate them—they'd ignored Beau, hadn't they?—but he knew how complicated relationships could be, and from what little he knew, the neglect had gone both ways. He hoped for Beau's sake they'd give it a chance. The house. The brewery.

I want to be sure you're taken care of, Beau had said to him.

Part of him couldn't help but wonder what would have happened if Finn had made his decision a month ago. Would Beau have entrusted his legacy to him?

A stab of envy and grief made him feel even worse. Beau and Aunt Dottie really had given him far more than he'd ever deserved. It was only right that Beau's real family should get his inheritance. But damn, he could have done great things with that place. He could have turned it around without tossing out all the things that made it special.

He'd offered to help often enough, but Beau had been stubborn in his own way. He'd always refused.

Beau's cat Jezebel, fondly known as the Creature of Evil by her former owner, wound her way around his legs and back, and he stooped to pet her. She tipped back her head, closing her pale green eyes in pleasure—and then promptly hissed and bit his hand. Any affection was on her terms, and those terms changed at a moment's notice. Strangely, it had made Beau more fond of the cat. Aunt Dottie had been stopping in to feed her since Beau had died, although she insisted no one should remove Jezebel from the house. Jezebel was tied to the place, she insisted, as if the cat were some sort of wayward spirit. Which might not be too far off. The one time Beau had attempted to board Jezebel at a pet spa, she'd scratched three attendants and a fourth man had quit.

If the Buchanans had inherited everything in the house, did that mean Jezebel was theirs too? He had to smile at the thought of that Victoria woman attempting to pet the cat. No, she'd never make nice with an animal. She looked like the type who'd adopt a French bulldog after seeing one on some cutesy TV show, only to bring it to the shelter the next day after realizing she'd have to wipe its butt after it pooped—a little known fact all those IG posts neglected to mention with all their cute photos. He had Maisie to thank for keeping him up to speed on strange pet trivia.

He let himself down into the unfinished basement, shutting the door behind him because the smell of hops made Jezebel as crazy as if she were rolling around in a field of catnip. A few glass carboys were still down here, fermenting from when River, Beau, and Finn had agreed to a competition to determine who could make the best beer incorporating three discordant ingredients. Aunt Dottie was the one who'd chosen them: cinnamon, jalapeño, and watermelon. He wasn't overly excited to try that one.

He headed to the back of the basement, to the fridge where Beau had stored beer—a variety of local stuff plus some bottled home brews—and grabbed something at random, cracking it open with the bottle opener magnet.

Lifting it up, he said, "I miss you, Beau. Things already suck without you."

He took a sip of the beer—an amber—and remembered the watch. Maybe he should take it while he was here so he wouldn't have to bother the Buchanans.

He started back up the stairs, beer in hand, and was on the third stair from the bottom when he heard the front door creak open. Aunt Dottie. It had to be.

What was he going to tell her about his confrontation with Finn?

The truth. She knew how he felt about Bev Corp, and he had no doubt she'd agree with him. Even if it meant he was back to square one.

He opened the door at the top of the stairs, and a hunk of crystal flew at his head.

Everything happened at once after that. In dodging the crystal and trying not to fall down the stairs, he dropped the beer, which exploded into glass shards and liquid foam, and Jezebel, who'd been perched in her armchair—literally hers, since no one else was allowed to sit there—shrieked as if she'd been scalded with hot water. She leapt into the air, back arched, and Georgie Buchanan, the person who'd thrown the crystal, screamed and jumped backward.

Aunt Dottie was nowhere to be seen.

Jezebel made another leap for Georgie, and when Georgie jumped back again, the cat yowled and scampered away, leaping onto the cabinets in the open kitchen to watch them warily from the wide opening.

"Dottie gave me the key," Georgie said in a burst, holding up her hands as if she were the one trespassing. "I'm so sorry. I...I thought you might be a thief or a vagrant. The crystal was the only hard thing I had in my purse. Your aunt gave it to me."

For some reason, that struck him as funny—not the part about the crystal, although really, was Dottie buying them in bulk?—but the word "vagrant." It was the kind of word someone from a big city might use for a homeless person. In a way he kind of was a vagrant, or rather he'd been one as a teenager.

"I...I didn't know Beau had a cat," she continued. "I never saw it when I visited him here at the house."

"Well, you can see why he didn't brag about her," he said, sweeping some of the broken glass aside with his shoe.

He stepped out of the doorway and shut the door behind him. "She's an unholy terror. Half the people in the neighborhood are terrified of her. The other half should be."

"I really am sorry. Your aunt gave me the key. I wasn't planning on coming tonight, but…"

She was flustered, and he felt bad for making her uncomfortable, even though he kind of liked seeing her like this—some of her hair had fallen out of that bun, a couple of wavy pieces, and her cheeks were pink.

"Hey," he said, "it's okay. It's your house, after all. I shouldn't be here. I just…"

Just what? Part of him wanted to unburden himself, but surely she was dealing with enough drama of her own. He didn't need to add his personal issues to the pile.

"You came for the watch?" she asked.

"Yeah," he said, happy to latch on to the easy excuse.

Her eyes shot down to the puddle of beer and broken glass on the floor before rising back to meet his gaze.

He laughed, unable to stop himself. As Aunt Dottie would say: *no grass grew under her feet.* "Well, okay, and I figured maybe I'd have a beer while I was here. For the watch. I guess I kind of needed a drink after today."

Georgie heaved a long sigh that made him wonder what, exactly, had happened at the rest of the will reading. Would she tell him if he asked? He found he wanted to know, and not just because he was concerned about the future of Buchanan Brewery. He wanted to get to know Georgie. Find out if he'd see in her what Beau had seen.

Speaking before he could talk himself out of it, he suggested, "Why don't I clean this up, and we can have a drink out on the porch? Maybe Jezebel will stop glaring at us, although I won't guarantee it. She's been known to lurk by the screen door."

She huffed a laugh. "He named her Jezebel?"

"You better believe it, and she's earned it every day of her life." He paused, and then added, "I'm pretty sure she's yours now. Comes with the house."

Her eyes widened, and even though he shouldn't have been looking, he found himself noticing the golden specks in them. "Oh, no, I'm not very good with animals. I've never had a pet."

"Anyone else in the family you can pawn her off on?" he asked, heading into the kitchen to grab some paper towels and cleaner from under the sink. She padded after him, carefully eyeing Jezebel's perch atop the cabinets. Probably wise. She'd been known to leap down on unsuspecting people.

"No. Lee's girlfriend's allergic to anything with fur, although I think she just says that because she doesn't like getting the hair on her clothes." He glanced back at her, and she flushed, as if realizing she'd said something that could be interpreted as disloyal.

"Don't worry," he said. "I didn't take her for the animal lover type. How about your sister?"

"Adalia does like animals," she said, brightening a little, "but we still have so much to figure out. We'll have to talk about it. I...I'm Georgie, by the way. I guess you know that, but it felt weird not to introduce myself."

She held out her hand, all business-like, and he couldn't help but smile. Her hand felt soft and small in his grip as he shook it.

"River Reeves. Nice to make your acquaintance, although I'm sure the circumstances aren't ideal for either of us."

"River," she said, musing. "That's an interesting name."

"Not around here, it isn't. Half the kids in this town are named things like Arbor and Leaf."

"Huh," she said, as if it were a foreign concept. He supposed it probably was. He knew the Buchanans had been raised in Connecticut, outside of New York City, and likely the guys at their prep schools had all had names like John and Edward III. "So you're from here, then?"

"Sort of." Which was the short answer. He didn't like giving people the long one.

She quirked her brow, as if waiting for more, but Jezebel picked that moment to hiss threateningly, swishing her tail, and Georgie wisely flinched.

"Let's see about getting that mess cleaned up before Jezebel gets any ideas," he said.

He stooped down to grab the supplies, plus a bag for the glass, and she reached out a hand for them.

"I'll do it," he said. "My mess."

She balked a little, as if she wasn't used to people disagreeing with her, or maybe she was thrown by the whole situation. Which was understandable. But she didn't say anything, just followed him back to the mess and helped by picking up the larger pieces and putting them in the bag while he scrubbed. Before he threw the broken glass and soaked towels away, he handed the crystal back to Georgie.

"Better put it back in your purse," he said. "Apparently it's a good thief-repellent device."

She grinned. "Your aunt sure likes these, huh?"

"Whatever you do, don't ask her about them. You'll never leave that conversation. Seriously. Never."

"Well, I don't think I'd mind so much. She seems like a really special person. She has a way of making people listen to her that isn't rude or demeaning."

His throat felt a little thick again, and he forced himself to swallow.

She has a way of seeing to the heart of things, Beau had said about Georgie. And didn't she ever. He'd figured the Buchanans would write his aunt off as an old eccentric.

"So about that drink," he said.

"Yes," she said, still smiling. "I'd like that."

So would he. Which made him worry. He should *not* be letting Georgie Buchanan affect him like this. There was exactly zero chance a woman like her would stick around in Asheville for any longer than it took to dispense with the inheritance she'd been given by the only man who'd cared enough to mentor him. Best-case scenario was they'd sell it to someone local, although he wouldn't be in the running. He'd saved up some money but nothing like what Buchanan Brewery would need to become competitive again. In the meantime, he needed to focus on what, exactly, he was going to do with his life now that he was suddenly jobless. Maisie always needed more help at the animal shelter, but that wasn't going to pay his bills.

"Me too," he admitted. "What's your poison?"

She pursed her lips, then asked, "Do you think Beau had any wine?"

Good lord.

CHAPTER
Five

River stared at Georgie like she had grown horns.

"I take that as a no?"

His mouth lifted into an amused grin. "There might be a bottle in the basement, although I can't guarantee it won't be dusty. I can go check."

She eyed the door he'd emerged from when he'd scared the bejesus out of her.

She'd been a championship-winning softball player in the sixth grade. River was lucky the cat had messed with her aim.

After the reading, Dottie had followed her out of the room, knitting still in hand. Close up, the hot pink sweater was obviously intended for an animal, not a baby. Jezebel? No, not even Dottie would attempt to dress up that cat, let alone in something like that. The cat would surely think it beneath her dignity.

"Here, dear," Dottie had said, handing over a key ring boasting a single key and a tarot card keychain. The Wheel of Fortune. "You'll need that. I imagine you'll want to see the house before you make up your mind."

49

Before she could even get out a thank you, Dottie had pulled out the big hunk of pink crystal from her bag. "Something tells me you'll be needing this too."

The power of suggestion being what it was, her thoughts had jumped to that crystal and the "something" Dottie had warned her about the moment the door creaked. Hence her leap to violence.

While she'd hoped to be alone, to have some time to think everything over before she met her siblings for the breakfast she'd arranged by text after storming out of the lawyer's office, she'd been surprisingly glad to see River, and not just because he looked better in worn jeans and a T-shirt than he had in his ill-fitting suit. She wanted to know the man who'd inspired her grandfather to give him that watch.

"I can go down with you. I might as well take a look. Beau invited me to stay with him when I came to town a few weeks ago, but I didn't want to be any trouble. I've only seen a bit of the house."

He started to say something, then stopped. "Yeah. It might be a good idea to introduce you to Beau's world."

She was about to ask what he meant by that, but he'd already turned around and started down the dimly lit stairs. She followed him, and he called over his shoulder, "Be sure to close the door or Jezebel might come down."

"And that would be a bad thing?" What was she thinking? If she left it open, the cat might descend into the basement, looking for her portal to hell.

She shut the door, making the staircase even darker. The smell of yeast hit her nose, reminding her that she hadn't eaten for hours.

"I think the light bulb's burnt out," River said. "I'll change it before I go."

"And here I was about to ask if you were a serial killer luring me down to your killing room, but the light bulb offer has me second-guessing."

"No self-respecting serial killer would offer to change a light bulb," River joked. "Not very intimidating."

Georgie reached the bottom of the steps and came to a halt when she saw a worktable covered with multiple glass bottles the size of watercooler jugs filled halfway full with pinkish liquid. It looked like a homegrown science experiment.

"Grandpa Beau wasn't making meth down here, was he?"

River chuckled. "No, it was a beer competition."

"Really? I thought he made beer at the brewery. He showed me the tanks and everything."

"This was a competition between me, Beau, and Finn."

"Who's Finn?"

His smile faltered, making her regret asking. "My partner." He shook his head, and when he spoke again his tone was darker, angrier. "My boss. Or used to be."

He walked past the table toward a fridge so old it looked like it had come from the set of a period piece, but he didn't open it, instead looking in a cabinet above it.

"No wine, dusty or otherwise. I take it you're not a beer drinker?" He closed the door and turned to face her.

She scrunched up her nose. "I haven't had beer since I went to a kegger in high school. I suppose I should be ashamed to admit to that, my situation being what it is. Beau did offer when I visited, but he didn't seem to mind too much when I declined."

He snorted, but his eyes lit up with mischievousness. "Then I guess tonight's your lucky night."

Georgie couldn't help laughing. It sounded like a pickup line, but she could tell that it wasn't. River really was that excited about beer.

"What kind of wine do you like?"

"Whites—Pinot Grigio, Riesling."

He opened the fridge and pulled out two bottles. He popped off the metal tops and handed one to her. "Try this. It's an amber. It's what I was drinking before. A good entry-level beer."

When she took the bottle, her fingers brushed his, and she tried to ignore the flutters in her stomach. She remembered what it had felt like shaking hands with him earlier, his grip so strong around hers. What did he do to get those muscles? Something told her he didn't belong to a CrossFit gym. River's gaze held hers, and even though his face didn't give much away, she thought she saw something in his eyes. Like maybe he felt that spark of attraction too.

She lifted the bottle to her lips, but her attention was still on River and that little spark between them, and when the beer filled her mouth, the taste caught her by surprise. She started to cough, spewing a mouthful of the brew on his chest and face.

He instinctively leaned backward, and she reached for him in horror. "Oh! I'm so sorry!"

A grin spread over his face. "If you didn't like it, you could have just said so."

Even though she was still horrified, laughter burst from her throat. When was the last time she'd had a good laugh, let alone with a man she found attractive? Her last boyfriend had been far too serious. He never would have teased her, and he would have had a heart attack if he'd gone longer than six weeks without a haircut, let alone allowed it to grow as long as River's.

He grabbed a kitchen towel from the worktable and wiped his face.

"River, I'm *so* sorry."

He laughed again. "Try it again, only this time sip it slowly." He took a couple of steps toward the refrigerator. "And I'll stand back here."

Georgie laughed despite her mortification, then took a sip of the beer.

"What do you taste?" he asked, the task of cleaning himself up seemingly forgotten as he watched her.

"It's sweeter than I expected. And a bit citrusy." She took another sip, a bigger one this time. "And maybe a hint of caramel?"

"Come on," River said, gesturing toward the stairs. "It's a nice night. Let's go sit on the porch."

She cast a glance at the glass jugs. "You said that was a competition?"

"And an experiment," he said, tossing the towel on the workbench. "Beau and I used to come up with new flavors in small batches like this, but you'll never see this particular one on a line," he said with a chuckle. "I doubt the special ingredients would fly."

Georgie had heard of people brewing beer in their basements, but it hadn't occurred to her that Beau or anyone else who ran a brewery might do so. It seemed so old school.

"So how does this work?" she asked, gesturing to the table.

Surprise filled his eyes. "You really want to know?"

"Well…yeah. If I'm going to help run a brewery, I guess I should know how it works."

His jaw dropped and he blinked. "You're not selling?"

She shrugged in an attempt to look nonchalant. "I haven't decided yet, but if I—I mean *we*—keep it, will we have to do this?"

He grinned. "No… I mean, you can if you want, but you don't have to. Finn is capable of making beer, but he's not good enough to create really interesting and layered flavors. That's where I came in." Some of his easygoing attitude faded.

"And Finn was your old boss?"

He took a long pull from his bottle—his first, she realized—then said, "Yep."

Obviously, he didn't want to talk about it, and although she was curious about what had happened, she didn't know him well enough to pry. She really needed some levity, at least for tonight. She suspected he did too.

"So you create beer recipes?" she asked, narrowing her eyes as she studied the bottles and tried to put it all together. "This is a test kitchen like you see on those *Bon Appétit* videos."

His brow shot up. "I don't know what those are, but yeah." His back straightened. "This was Beau's testing ground."

"And where is yours?"

He took another drink, then said, "At Big Catch. We had our own testing area." He flashed her a tight smile. "A testing kitchen, but I work on some at home too."

Georgie resisted the urge to ask him what had happened. "You said Finn used to be your boss. Where are you now?"

He sucked in a breath and turned his attention to the table. "I'm currently exploring my options." When he looked at her again, she saw a flash of pain in his dark eyes, but he covered it with a grimace. "Let's head out to the porch. I'm getting a little claustrophobic down here."

He headed toward the steps but waited for her to go up first. When she reached the top of the stairs, she gingerly cracked the door open to make sure the cat wasn't about to pounce on her. Jezebel was still on top of the cabinet, surveying her kingdom, a good ten feet away, although she let out a little hiss to tell Georgie she was watching her.

Georgie hurried across the kitchen to the door leading to the porch, where she and her grandfather had sat and talked less than a month ago. It was hard to believe so much could change in such a short time. She sat in the same wicker chair with the faded and flattened cushion and waited for River to take the seat next to her.

He hesitated before he lowered himself into it, then gave her an awkward grimace. "This was Beau's chair."

"Oh." She sat up. "Would you rather not sit there?"

"No," he said, sitting back gingerly as though still getting used to the idea. "So…" He let his voice trail off, then said, "So you're considering keeping the brewery. Before I left the meeting, your family seemed adamant about getting rid of it."

"Yeah, call me crazy, but I'm thinking about it." She took a tentative sip of the beer, and the flavor slid over her tongue more easily than before.

River was right; it tasted rich and malty, and about a million times better than the light beer she'd had at that college party.

"Beau called me last month to congratulate me on the sale of my company." She turned to him. "I don't even know how he found out. We weren't close, and truth be told, neither one of us had ever contacted the other before. We only saw him when we were kids. But he was so gracious and complimentary. He knew that I'd started it from nothing and helped revolutionize feminine hygiene products, and he wasn't even embarrassed by it, not like my father." She took a sip of the beer. "He asked what I planned to do next, and when I told him I was still figuring it out, he invited me to come visit for a few days. So I did. I'm guessing he changed his will after that."

"He never mentioned his plans to me specifically," River said, his gaze on the patchy grass in the backyard as he sipped from his bottle. "I knew he was getting older, but I'll admit I didn't want to think about it. I was surprised when I was invited to the will reading. I'd presumed everything would go to your father."

"All of us did." She took another pull, enjoying the taste more and more. "But my visit with him was special, and I talked to him on the phone after I got back to Boston." Tears stung her eyes. "He was encouraging me to relocate to Asheville. He told me the city was booming and there were plenty of opportunities here for an entrepreneur." She paused. "I think he just wanted a relationship with me, and call me crazy, but I was starting to consider moving."

In a few weeks' time, Beau had given her the love, support, and attention she'd always wanted from her father, and the prospect of having him so close had been enticing. But now he was gone and she found herself rudderless again—a businesswoman without a business, or even the inspiration for one—not that she would admit any of that to River.

"The brewery meant something to him," she said quietly. "And he meant something to me, albeit belatedly. I can't help thinking that he wanted me to do it. Maybe he was hoping it would bring my sister and my brothers together too."

She turned to face him, surprised that he was watching her with so much intensity. So much…hope.

"I think you're right," he finally said.

They were silent for several long seconds before Georgie said, "Obviously, you know Beau through your great aunt."

His mouth tipped up with the hint of a smile, and Georgie wondered if some memory had popped into his head.

"I met Beau when I was thirteen. I came to stay with Aunt Dottie and never left. Beau's the one who taught me how to brew beer and encouraged me to perfect my craft." He grinned. "I was making beer before I could even drive a car."

Her eyes widened. "Is that legal?"

Laughing, he took another pull from his bottle. "Probably not, but in fairness to Beau, I wasn't really drinking it. Just sampling. And Aunt Dottie being Aunt Dottie…well, let's just say she didn't put up a fuss. In fact, she encouraged it. Believe it or not, it helped me stay out of trouble."

"Did you work for Beau when you got older?"

"I knew my way around his operation, but I never did anything other than scut work at Buchanan. I guess you could say I wasn't sure what I wanted back then." He glanced at her as he spoke, and she saw her own uncertainty reflected back at her. "I ended up having a lot of jobs. But thanks to Beau, I learned how a brewery works, so when I got the opportunity to work with Finn, I was ready to land on my feet and take off running." He shot her another glance. "We started with nothing and placed third at the Brewfest Competition in our third year."

"What's the Brewfest Competition?"

"It's where you go to prove you're somebody in the world of beer. Last year Big Catch placed first...and caught the eye of Bev Corp." He said the corporation's name with more than a hint of attitude.

"Where did Buchanan place?"

He grimaced. "They didn't. They haven't placed for years."

"Oh." She wasn't sure what to make of that, so she moved on to her next burning question. "And who is Bev Corp?"

A storm of emotion filled his eyes. "The devil."

CHAPTER
Six

Georgie looked taken aback, and well, okay, he *had* sounded a bit melodramatic.

"What do you mean?" she asked.

"It's the biggest beer company in the world," he said, "and they like to buy craft breweries so they can put other craft breweries out of business. Nice trick, huh?"

Her expression didn't change, and it struck him that she'd just sold her company. Some big corporation had probably snapped it up, and they likely didn't care about her vow to be eco-friendly.

Okay, maybe he'd looked her up after her visit with Beau. Moon Goddess still had information about her up on their website. She'd started the operation out of the kitchen in her small apartment in Boston, and it had grown into a company she'd sold for five big ones.

Menstrual cups, period panties, they were the kind of things that made most men cringe, but he admired her guts. She'd seen an opportunity to grow something—and she'd succeeded. Kind of like Beau when he'd opened Asheville's first brewery years before the town became mainstream. No wonder the two had gotten along so well.

Still, the kind of person who'd sold out once might sell out again. Maybe she was just trying to buff Buchanan Brewery up so she could find a better deal.

But the thought refused to stick. He could tell meeting Beau had changed something for Georgie, just like it had for him. He could honor that. He *would* honor that.

"Sorry, Georgie," he said, reaching out to touch her arm before he realized what he was doing. Her skin was soft beneath his fingers in a way that made him want to keep his hand there—or maybe stroke her—but he forced himself to pull away. Her lips had parted a little, and he found himself telling her everything. "I didn't mean you. I'm just pissed because of what happened with Finn. Tonight, after the will reading, he told me he's selling to Bev Corp. He's throwing away everything we built together for a paycheck, and he didn't even talk to me about it first. He made it out to be like he was doing me some big favor, because they wanted to keep me on and throw some money at me too. But he knows how I feel about staying local."

"He told you tonight?" she asked, putting the emphasis on *tonight*. "That's awful. He should have talked to you, first of all, and he definitely shouldn't have landed this on you right after you lost Beau."

He noticed she hadn't said anything about Finn's decision to sell, but it would be rude to comment on it. She was being sweet, and he liked it.

"Thank you. I think I needed to hear that." He lifted his beer to clink it with hers, and realized it was empty. "How are you doing on beer?" he asked.

She gave her bottle a little shake and looked at it in surprise. "Empty. You know, you were right. It was pretty good. Do you have anything else we can try?"

"About six or seven something elses come to mind," he said with a grin. "I have what's almost assuredly a bad idea, but I'm hoping you'll like it."

Beau had about a dozen tasting cups from various beer festivals, souvenirs he'd kept in the way people hoard things they like, and River had arranged them in two rows on the dining room table—one tasting cup each for each of the beers he'd picked out. A few fruity ones since she liked wine and cocktails, plus a lager, a gingerbread Christmas beer, and a chocolate cherry porter he'd made for Valentine's Day. She'd never experienced everything that was possible with beer, so he'd figured he might as well offer a wide selection to show her.

They'd made it through all of the fruity ones, which she'd liked more than the amber, plus the lager, which had made her scrunch her nose in a cute way, and the gingerbread. The chocolate cherry was the last one he'd chosen, and he did a drumroll on the table as she lifted it to her lips.

She held it back from her mouth, laughing a little. "If you're not careful, you're going to make me laugh when I'm drinking, and this one's going to end up on your shirt too."

"Maybe I want it to," he said. "It might balance out the smell of the other one."

She made a face and then sipped it, and from the way she kept drinking, he knew they had another winner.

"What do you taste?" he asked as she pulled it away from her lips, which glistened a little from the liquid.

"Mmm. That one was maybe my favorite, even better than the peachy one. Chocolate and cherries but not too sweet."

"That's what I like to hear," he said, making a plus mark next to it in the little chart she'd made. Leave it to a businesswoman to carry around a notepad and pen in her purse. A *monogrammed* notepad.

"Only one minus and five pluses," he said. "Guess you like beer more than you thought."

She grinned at him, a wider, looser grin than earlier. "I guess maybe I do. Although you're being a little generous with those plus signs. I said the mango sour was *interesting*. That was a nice way of saying *I'm not going back for seconds*."

He hammed up a dramatic frown as he scribbled out the plus sign and added a minus sign next to it on the chart. "Demoted! Does this mean I have to be suspicious of anything you call interesting?"

"No, just the mango sour." She paused, meeting and holding his gaze. "*You*, River Reeves, are quite interesting."

Her eyes sparkled as she said it, and he felt warmth pulse through him. He found her interesting too, and he was running out of reasons why he shouldn't. She planned on staying, on restoring Beau's brewery, and he had no doubt she had the brains and means to do it.

But this woman had been to business school—she'd formed a business from nothing—and he was almost thirty and still a few community college classes short of a degree. He'd fumbled his way into the job that he'd quit a few hours ago. He doubted he was Georgie Buchanan's type, or at least her type for more than one night. And for some reason, that wasn't what he wanted from her.

"I like the porter too," he said, clearing his throat and reaching for his tasting cup. The moment shattered, like he'd meant it to. "We sold out at the brewery, but I brought a six-pack over to Beau's. This one's all that's left."

"I'm glad you did," she said, reaching for the bottle the porter had come in. "I think I'm going to claim the rest of this one for myself."

Her phone buzzed again, about the fifth time it had— he'd set his on silent mode after getting yet another message from Finn—and she glanced at the screen before setting it down on the table with a little more force than necessary. She took a big sip of her beer.

"Anything you want to talk about?" he asked. Not to be nosy, or at least not just to be nosy. He'd confided in her, and he wanted her to do the same if she needed to unburden herself.

"Just my brother Lee trying to talk me around. He wants to sell, or at least his girlfriend and my father have convinced him he does. But I think this could be good for Adalia, even if she doesn't agree, and for Jack too." Her face twisted up a little when she said it, and he felt sorry for asking. The last thing he wanted was to upset her. Tonight was about having fun, forgetting a few of their worries. "Maybe especially for Jack," she added.

"You'd really never met him before?" he asked, because despite himself he was interested.

"No," she said, taking another sip from the bottle, pausing a little to savor the taste in a way that made him smile. "Lee works with our dad in the real estate firm. I'd say the family firm, but I'd argue it can't really be called that when it's just the two of them. Anyway, he was looking for some files in my dad's office, and he found a nondisclosure agreement. My dad made Jack's mother sign it in exchange for a big one-time payout. My half-brother's name was in there, but I had no idea where he lived or anything."

She paused, looking into his eyes. "Truth be told, I didn't look very hard. I wanted to meet him, but I wasn't sure what I'd say. I was ashamed of our father—of being one of the kids he acknowledged. Lee thought it best for us to both forget the whole thing, although he did tell me so we could decide together."

She glanced down, as if embarrassed, and he found himself staring at the freckles on the bridge of her nose. They almost looked like a constellation.

"I shouldn't be laying all of this on you. I'd blame the beer, but it's my fault we kept Jack a secret. Well, Lee's too. We could have sought him out and we didn't. So I want to make sure he gets plenty of say in what we do. Although, I'll be honest with you, I don't know the first thing about running a brewery. I'm not even sure there's even room for four of us if we'd just be replacing Beau."

"You'd find a way," River said, believing it. He reached out to touch her arm. "Beau had zero social media presence. Someone can handle that, maybe Adalia. And if you grow the brewery, there'll be new jobs. Things like event management or opening a new location. Beau, he liked doing things the old-fashioned way, but he knew it wouldn't last forever. He knew things would have to change. That's why he trusted you to do the changing for him."

Something flashed in her eyes, and she smiled at him— a smile so bright he had to pull his hand away to keep himself from pulling her to him.

"You're right. And maybe they'll have ideas for how they can contribute. I always think I need a plan for everything, but sometimes I need to be reminded to ask other people for help."

"I think we all need that," he said. It was something Aunt Dottie had told him often enough in the days he'd struggled.

"You know," she said, setting down the bottle. "I came over here partly because I wanted to avoid talking to Jack. I know I need to do it, but I feel so guilty I can hardly stand it."

"Why don't you ask him to come over?" he suggested on impulse. He didn't really want to end their tête-à-tête, but he had a feeling he wouldn't be able to hold back much longer. If someone else was added to the equation, he wouldn't have the opportunity to make a fool of himself. Besides which, he remembered the way Jack had sat in that meeting, his back rigid as he looked at the father who refused to acknowledge him and the siblings who didn't know him. He'd felt sympathy for him—no, more than that, *empathy*. If Georgie wanted to talk to him, she should, and there was no time like the present. Waiting on something like that would likely only lead to more regret. "If you don't sell, this is his house too," he added. "He might as well see it before he makes his vote."

"He did text me earlier," she said. "Said he was getting a drink at Buchanan, and I could join him if I felt like it." She shrugged one shoulder. "At the time I didn't."

"Tell him to get a car service," he suggested. "Or walk. It's not too far."

She lifted the beer again, took a drink, and nodded. "You know, River Reeves, I think I just might do that."

He picked up her phone and handed it to her, letting his fingers linger on hers longer than was needed. "I'm holding you accountable."

"I'd expect nothing less," she said, smiling up at him before she leaned down to send off a text.

Her stomach grumbled then, a loud sound that hung between them. He wouldn't have laughed except for the look of open horror on her face.

"What kind of a house-squatting host am I? You're hungry. When was the last time you ate something?"

"It's been a while," she acknowledged, her cheeks flushing an adorable pink. "Should we go get something?"

"Let me see what Aunt Dottie has in the kitchen. She spent some time getting the place cleaned up before you got here. I'll bet she wouldn't leave the fridge empty."

Her phone vibrated again, and she looked up at him, her eyes full of hope, before she glanced down at it. "He's coming," she said. "He's going to meet us here."

"Good," he said, opening the refrigerator door. Just as he'd expected, there were a few labeled glass Tupperware containers inside.

Georgie joined him, leaning in close to look at the labels. He caught a whiff of her scent, something he'd been noticing over the course of the night. She smelled a little like the lemon bars Aunt Dottie liked to make, sweet but tart. It suited her.

She laughed a little, low and husky, as if she noticed how close they were standing. "She didn't label any of these for what's in them. They're all labeled with a mood."

And so they were. A large square container filled with what looked to be homemade mac and cheese was labeled "sorrowful." Another container, which looked to hold some sort of red sauce with sausage and peppers, was labeled "aggrieved"—*that* one would be punishingly spicy, he knew from past experience. The "exuberant" Tupperware contained a fruit salad (nothing said happy to Aunt Dottie more than nature, and he'd bet some of the fruit was from her own trees), and then there was a final Tupperware with a label that read "wanton." That one held a huge piece of chocolate cake. *Sinful*, as Aunt Dottie would say with delight. She'd likely wink to accompany it.

"What will it be?" he asked, raising an eyebrow.

Georgie grinned, and was it his imagination, or was she leaning closer?

"Would you think I was being greedy if I said I was feeling a little bit of each?"

Had she just told him she was feeling wanton?

But before he could ask, or even pull out any of the containers, he heard a yowl from the basement.

Georgie's eyes widened, and she pulled back from the fridge. "Oh no, River, I forgot to shut the door last time!"

It sounded like Jezebel had found Beau's stash of hops.

CHAPTER
Seven

"I take it that's bad," Georgie said, her head fuzzy from all the beer she'd consumed. It hadn't seemed like a lot while she was partaking in River's beer flight, but her lack of coordination suggested otherwise.

River didn't answer—he just bolted down the stairs. Georgie considered following him, but she wasn't sure descending stairs in the dark was a good idea, and she wanted to be upstairs when Jack arrived.

Jack was coming over.

She was second-guessing her decision to invite him over. She was in no condition to discuss business. What was she thinking? Obviously, she hadn't been. River had given her copious amounts of beer and weakened her with his charm. And his warm brown eyes. And the way his hair curled at the nape of his neck, making her want to reach out and smooth it with her fingertips.

No. Stop. She couldn't think of River like that.

Right?

River appeared at the top of the stairs, pinning Jezebel's back to his chest while the cat took wide swipes at his hands and wrists, drawing blood as she hissed and yowled.

"Oh my goodness, River! I'm so sorry!"

He closed the door to the basement and dropped the cat, who took off running to the living room. She worried he'd be pissed at her—her last boyfriend would have been; he'd been all about accountability—but River gave her a lopsided grin. "I'm told women admire war wounds."

"Not this one. Especially not when it's my fault you got them. We need to clean those up," she said, feeling almost guiltier because he didn't seem to blame her. "You could get cat scratch disease. Do you know where Beau kept his first aid kit?"

"Probably in the hallway bathroom."

"I'll be right back." She rushed down the hall to the bathroom and started opening cabinet doors, looking for bandages, antibiotic ointment, and antiseptic. She found a white plastic box shoved behind a half-used roll of toilet paper, and after confirming that it held what she needed, she stood, catching her reflection in the mirror. Her hair was falling out of her bun, tendrils brushing her cheeks. Her cheeks were pink and her eyes bright, but what caught her off guard was how happy she looked.

When was the last time she'd felt truly happy?

She turned at the sound of some rather aggressive meowing. Jezebel was blocking her exit from the bathroom.

"Uh, River…" she called out, holding the first aid kit to her chest.

The cat hissed and batted a paw at her.

She started to call for River again but then decided she could deal with it herself. If she ended up staying in Asheville, the logical thing to do would be to live in this house—a house that Jezebel clearly saw as her territory. Now that she was better acquainted with the cat, there was no way she would attempt to saddle her little sister with the beast. The thought of Victoria dealing with the cat was funny, but she suspected Lee wasn't about to adopt her.

"Jezebel," she said sternly, "we might end up becoming roommates, and this will go much better if we can reach an understanding. I follow a *live and let live* philosophy, so how about I leave you be and you let me live?"

For a moment, the cat just stared at her, her green eyes glowing with an almost human understanding. Then she arched her back and hissed again, spun around, and slunk off.

"Okay," Georgie said, her heart racing. "I'll take it."

She eased her way out of the bathroom and found River washing his wrists in the kitchen sink while talking to someone on speaker phone.

"You're sure Jezebel will be okay?" he asked.

A woman answered, "I suspect she didn't eat many hops, if any at all, but keep an eye on her. If she starts to act strangely...well, *more* strangely...you should call an emergency vet."

"Okay, thanks, Maisie." He hesitated, then said, "Are you free for breakfast tomorrow? Something big happened today, and I need to get your opinion on finding another job."

"What?" she screeched.

He must have sensed Georgie standing in the doorway because he said, "I've gotta go. I'll explain in the morning. Text me when you're ready."

Then he pressed his phone with his wet finger to end the call.

Georgie started to ask him why he was looking for a job. Sure, he'd mentioned the situation with Finn, but it felt wrong to pry. If he'd wanted to talk about it more, he would've...right? Instead, he'd called someone else—

someone he knew. For all she knew, the woman on the phone had been his girlfriend, a thought that made her feel surprisingly jealous.

River wasn't hers—she'd only met him hours ago—and she'd do best to remember that.

"I called my friend Maisie to make sure Jezebel's okay," he said, tucking a lock of hair behind his ear. "I'd read somewhere that hops are poisonous to some cats and dogs. She might be an ornery old thing, but Beau loved her."

Georgie gasped in horror. "I had no idea…"

"Oh, I'm sure she'll be fine," he said, waving her worry away. "That cat is the terror of the neighborhood. A few hops aren't going to bring her down."

She gave him a wry grin. "She did just corner me in the bathroom."

He grinned back, his eyes twinkling as he turned off the water and grabbed a couple of paper towels. "You survived a face-off with Jezebel, huh? I'm impressed." Nodding to his arms, he said, "I figured I'd wash the scratches with soap and water."

"Good idea," she said. "How about we sit down at the table, and I'll put some bandages on them?"

"I'm sure I'll be fine," he said.

She pointed to a chair. "I risked my life defying the devil cat to get these supplies, so you're gonna sit in this chair and let me put antibiotic ointment on your scratches to keep your hands from falling off."

He laughed and sat down.

She turned a chair so she could sit facing him, then set the box on the table and opened it up. After uncapping the antibiotic ointment, she grasped his hand, pressing her thumb against his open palm. A swarm of butterflies unleashed in her stomach, and her gaze lifted to his face. She liked staring at him. He had beautiful eyes, his black hair was thick and just the right kind of long if you asked her, and his skin was a warm bronze.

His gaze lowered to her lips before rising to meet hers again, and his fingers closed around her thumb.

Her butterflies intensified, something she couldn't remember feeling since she'd crushed on Brian Whitby her junior year of high school, and her breathing turned shallow as she leaned closer. Something about this man had a powerful draw, but while she was usually good at cutting to the heart of things and making lists, she couldn't pinpoint what it was that made him so compelling. It was more than his indisputable attractiveness, or the way he teased her, or his genuine goodness. It was all of the above rolled into this man named River, and she realized she wanted more than just a beer tutor. She wanted *him.*

The look in his eyes suggested he wanted her too. He leaned forward, his hand lifting to her face. She held her breath, wanting him to kiss her more than she'd ever wanted a first kiss, when a sudden knock at the door caught her by surprise.

River sat back in his seat, his face unreadable. "I suspect that's Jack."

Georgie couldn't tell if he was relieved or disappointed. "Yeah."

"You go let him in. I'll take care of these scratches."

She hesitated, then stood and headed toward the front door. She paused in the threshold to the living room, casting a glance over her shoulder. River was concentrating on smearing ointment on his wrist. Jezebel had resumed her post on top of the cabinets, and had hopefully stayed her vendetta against them for the night.

She closed the distance to the front door, her heart racing for a different reason now. She was worried she'd already blown things with her half-brother. They'd had a very limited interaction at the will reading, and then she'd turned down his invitation to get a drink at the brewery. Would he hate her? Would he be aloof? She deserved it and more. How would she have felt if she'd been the odd one out?

Steeling her back, she opened the door. "Jack. Thanks for coming."

He nodded, his back as stiff as it had been that afternoon at the attorney's office. "I figured we should discuss this tonight…before the noon deadline tomorrow."

"Yeah," she said, taking a step back. "Come on in."

He glanced around the entryway and living room as he crossed the threshold, taking it all in.

"This is Grandpa Beau's place…obviously," she added, feeling foolish, but the alcohol had weakened her filter. "We figured you should see it before we make our decision."

Surprise filled his eyes. "The others are here?"

It took her a second to grasp what he meant. "No," she said, shaking her head a little too vigorously, to the point where she had to catch herself to keep from falling over. "Just River."

He looked puzzled. Then understanding washed over his face. "The guy at the will reading. I didn't realize you two knew each other."

"We don't. Didn't," she said, then scrunched her eyes shut and slowly opened them. "Sorry. It would seem I've had a few too many beer samples. We didn't know each other, but we do now." She gestured toward the entryway to the kitchen. "Why don't you come this way and we can talk."

He headed into the kitchen without comment, walking several feet into the room to give her space to enter.

Jack held out his hand to River, who was closing the first aid box. "We didn't get formally introduced earlier. I'm Jack Durand."

River stood and clasped his hand. "River Reeves. Things got a little crazy this afternoon." He glanced at Georgie, as though cueing her to take over.

It took her a second to catch on to what he was doing. Then she broke into a too-big smile. "Jack. Why don't you sit down?" She gestured to the table. "We've been sampling beers."

Jack took in the multiple beer bottles and empty glasses. "I can see that."

He probably thought she was a lush. "I'm not much of a beer person, and River thought it would be a good idea to introduce me to the world of…"

"Beer?" he finished, his lips quirking into the hint of a smile.

"Yeah."

"I had a couple at Buchanan," he said. "I guess you could say I was sampling them myself. Getting a feel for our grandfather's place."

That made her feel a little better as she crossed to the sink and reached for a glass to get some water, but River stood and moved behind her, resting a hand lightly on her hip. An electric buzz shot through her, stealing her breath.

"I'll get you some water," he said in a low tone that didn't help the buzzing. "Why don't you sit with Jack and talk?"

"Yeah…thanks." She whirled away from him, nearly toppling over again, but River grabbed her elbow and held her steady.

"You okay?"

She was fully aware of every pressure point of his fingers and thumb, and also the fact that she was definitely drunker than she'd realized. She'd lost control of herself. And Georgie was *always* completely in control. This was not acceptable.

Slowly pulling away from him, she sat in a chair opposite Jack, who was studying her every move.

Talk about a poor first impression. No, poor second impression.

"So," Jack said, taking the lead, "you said you were considering keeping the brewery. Does the fact that you're sampling all this beer mean that you're still leaning in that direction?"

"Yeah," she said, resting her hand on the table. River set a glass of water in front of her, and she picked it up and took a long sip. When she finished, she said, "I suspect that Grandpa Beau changed his will after I came to see him. I think he asked me here because he was already considering it. He really wanted to keep the brewery in the family, and for whatever reason, he decided not to give it to our father. He probably knew Dad would sell it."

That felt strange, saying *our father*. She couldn't help wondering if it was weird for him to hear it, but it seemed inappropriate to ask.

"And I get the impression Beau didn't like Prescott and vice versa," Jack said.

"That's an understatement," Georgie said. "I'm not sure why they had a falling-out, but whatever the reason, we didn't see much of him when we were growing up."

"Prescott or Beau?" Jack asked with a snide look.

That stung. "Both, I guess."

Jack picked up a discarded bottle cap and twisted it between his thumb and forefinger, studying it. "So...about the brewery... what changed your mind?"

"I really liked Grandpa, Jack, and I'm disappointed that I won't get the chance to know him better. I feel like I wasted so much time. I can't help but think that keeping the brewery is another way to get to know him."

"Just like that?" Jack asked. "You can drop everything in your life and run a brewery?"

"As you probably heard, I recently sold my business, and I've been trying to figure out what to do next. This might as well be it."

Jack gave her a deadpan look. "Even though you know nothing about beer?"

Her back stiffened. "What I lack in beer knowledge, I make up for in business knowledge. I know how to launch a product."

"This isn't the same as starting from scratch," Jack said. "It's rebuilding an established brand. One that people see as a relic of the past, judging from what I heard tonight. People loved Beau, but they don't see Buchanan making it. To succeed in brewing, you'll need to make it hip. Trendy."

"You keep saying *you*," Georgie said. "I thought you wanted to keep it too."

"I do, but I want to be a partner, Georgie. I want to help run it, not just collect the profits, not that it has any. It's been running in the red for a couple of years."

Georgie flinched. Why hadn't she thought to look at the books? But did it matter? The business was established. Fully furnished with equipment and employees. They just needed to figure out how to freshen up its image. Make it competitive again.

"You want to help run it?" Georgie asked. "Last I heard, you live in Chicago." Yeah, she'd stalked him on social media for a week after learning about his existence, but it would have been stranger if she hadn't. All she'd found was a little used LinkedIn account with no photo and no job history. She'd only known it was him because there was apparently only one Jack Leopold Durand in the United States, and also because the man with the LinkedIn profile had the same birthdate and year: March 8. "You'd have to quit your job and move here. And if the company's really in the red, you won't get a paycheck for some time. I can live off my savings. What about you?"

A hard look filled his eyes, and Georgie wasn't sure if he was upset that she'd known where he lived but never attempted to contact him or insulted that she'd questioned his ability to live without a paycheck. "Let me worry about my finances. You've never been concerned with them before. Why start now?"

"Hey," River said, sitting up in his seat. "That was uncalled for."

"No," Georgie said softly, overcome with shame. "He's right. I never reached out, but can you imagine how awkward it was for me—and Lee? I didn't know if you even knew we existed. What if your mother had told you that another man was your father? I didn't want to destroy your world too."

"Too?" he asked with plenty of attitude.

"Look," Georgie said, running a hand over her forehead. "My father was *far* from perfect. He only cared about having a son, so I was a disappointment from the start. That's why he named me Georgie—not Georgia or Georgina, just Georgie. I never, ever measured up for him, even if he pretended otherwise to the world. But he loved my mother. And I trusted in that. Finding out about you meant the one thing I'd believed my father and I had in common was a lie too." As she finished the last sentence, she realized she'd said too much, and her face flamed with embarrassment. She'd never even told any of her previous boyfriends any of that, let alone a stranger. No, *two* strangers. She cast a glance to River, who was giving her a sympathetic look.

Then she saw the look on Jack's face—the gleam in his eyes—and realized what she'd said. *He only cared about having a son.*

Just not this son.

She wanted to say something to him, but she doubted he'd want sympathy from her. Not after everything. So she took a deep breath and did what she did best: focus on the task at hand. "All of that is neither here nor there. We're here to discuss the future of Buchanan Brewery. You say you want to be a full, working partner. How soon can you be here?"

His eyes widened slightly. "A month. Maybe a week on either side."

"Okay. We'll need to figure out what to do to update the brewery."

"I've already been talking to Dottie and some of the staff," he said, his shoulders relaxing. "First, you need to know that Lurch quit tonight."

"Lurch?" she asked in confusion.

"The brewmaster. He told Dottie he had no desire to work for stuck-up pricks—his phrasing, not mine," he said with a grin.

She grimaced. "He's not far off."

Jack's grin spread, and Georgie couldn't get over how much he resembled Lee in the rare moments when her older brother actually looked happy. She hadn't seen it before because of their different coloring, but it was there in his smile. Something she hadn't seen Lee do in a long, long time.

"So we'll need a brewmaster," she said.

"Not just any brewmaster. We need a good one," Jack said. "No, a *great* one. Our brewmaster will be the key to making Buchanan Brewery great again."

"So where do we find a brewmaster?" Georgie asked, then immediately recalled River's phone conversation with his friend.

Had he really quit?

She turned to him, about to say something, but Jack beat her to it. "Dottie happened to mention that the best brewmaster she knows is currently unemployed." His brow lifted, and he shot a look at River. "Our first executive decision should be offering River a contract to pull us into the twenty-first century."

Georgie wholeheartedly agreed, even if her heart sunk a little at the thought that he'd become off-limits.

CHAPTER Eight

"Will you do it, River?" Georgie asked, her eyes glowing.

About a hundred different thoughts ran through his head, but strangely, the one he settled on was disappointment. Turning Buchanan Brewery around would be the achievement of a lifetime—not to mention an homage to Beau—but it would mean he couldn't date the owner.

He'd be stupid to even think about it.

Of course, he'd already reached the conclusion that Georgie Buchanan wouldn't want to date him anyway. Hadn't he?

Sure, but there'd been that moment when he'd almost kissed her...

Both of the Buchanans were looking at him now, silently pleading with him—hell, even Jezebel was giving him a dirty look from atop her perch on the cabinets—and he couldn't help but think he'd be dumber than mud to turn them down. Even if Georgie and Jack probably shouldn't be making a decision like this without discussing it with their other siblings first. Maybe they wouldn't want to play an active role, but they were still partial owners.

But hell, maybe the other two were used to Georgie making decisions for them. She wasn't the type to hesitate—something he liked about her.

His mind was already spinning as he thought through all the changes he'd want to make—the brews he'd keep and the ones that would go off the roster. Seasonal beers they'd need to get started on now if they wanted to have them ready for fall. Truthfully, it would feel good to innovate again. Success made life slower in some ways—his job had become more about damage control than about creativity, but now he would have a whole new drawing board.

He took a deep breath and let it out. "I'll do it," he said, looking Georgie in the eye, "on one condition."

She bit her lip, as if thinking he might ask for a kiss, and God he wanted to, but he just smiled and said, "I didn't forget the way your stomach was growling earlier. You should eat something. How about you, Jack? Care for any food? My aunt's a fantastic cook, and she stocked up the fridge."

"Yeah," Jack said, "thanks. Don't mind if I do. She mentioned there was some chocolate cake in there with my name on it."

Georgie looked at him then, and when their eyes met, she burst into laughter. The sweet sound of it, and the way it made his stomach flutter—almost like he had butterflies, for God's sake—told him all he needed to know: he was in trouble.

<hr />

When River's phone beeped the next morning, he slapped it like it was a mosquito in his ear, something that hadn't happened much since he'd done all that camping with his mom when he was a kid. It took a minute for everything to filter back in: in the space of a few hours, he'd quit his job and maybe found a new one.

But he knew it probably wouldn't be that easy. Georgie and Jack might want to work with him—they'd spent another hour or two discussing his plans and their ideas—but Georgie was meeting Lee, otherwise known as Junior, and Adalia for breakfast this morning. And Lord knew, Junior was going to push hard to sell. Still, he didn't figure Georgie or Jack as the type to budge.

But did he really want to sit in the middle of a sibling feud?

Yes, he decided—it would be worth it if he could make Buchanan Brewery competitive. It wasn't the kind of opportunity that was likely to fall into his lap again.

The question of whether he was ready to keep things professional with Georgie was a whole lot less simple. His mouth twitched into a grin as he remembered the way she'd shouted a warning to Jack when Jezebel leapt down to snatch a piece of sausage he'd dropped in his lap. "Careful, she scratches!" she'd said, and given the cat had landed inches away from his junk, Jack had done the logical thing and tried to shoo her off. Normally, that kind of thing would have thrown her into a rage, but she just batted at his hand as if he was playing, and curled up on his lap.

Turned out Jezebel had a soft spot for the younger Buchanan brother.

River checked his phone, saw another three missed texts from Finn, one from Maisie, and another from Georgie. He skipped to that one first: *Thanks for being there last night, River. Without you, I'm not sure how it all would have worked out. I hope you really meant you'd work with us, because we'd be lucky to have you.*

He grinned and shook his head a little as he noticed the time stamp: 5:45 a.m. Leave it to Georgie to be awake and writing in full sentences at 5:45 after downing the equivalent of four high-gravity beers. She'd told him her breakfast date with the others was at 8:30, in an hour, so he wouldn't hear anything else for a while.

He ignored the messages from Finn, although from the few words he caught, Finn was still deeply in denial. He knew he couldn't avoid him forever. There'd be some hoops to jump through for the HR employee, Gladys. He'd need to get that settled before firming things up with the Buchanans. Still, he didn't feel like eating bullshit for breakfast. He'd much rather get Maisie's opinion on everything that had gone down.

They'd been friends since he first moved to town—sixteen years, as she'd recently reminded him, and he trusted her more than anyone other than Aunt Dottie. And Beau, but Beau was gone.

Awake, Maisie's text said, *although I didn't sleep great wondering WTH happened yesterday. I WANT TO KNOW EVERYTHING. Come over to the shelter, STAT. I'd meet you somewhere, but we had seven puppies come in last night. Chaos. Bring coffee and danishes. Dustin's been here since 7, so please show some love for him too.*

He responded with the thumbs-up emoji and added, *Seems like a fair price to pay for your advice. And playing with puppies.*

Forty-five minutes later, he knocked on the locked door of Dog is Love. They didn't open the doors until ten.

Dustin, one of Maisie's regular volunteers, peered through the glass before opening the door. A man with a mane of long white hair and a short, trimmed beard, he'd come to Asheville for retirement after spending forty years selling life insurance in Florida. He still talked about the frigid winter weather in Asheville, even though most winters were mild. Any annoyance that might have caused was offset by the fact that he so regularly donated his time to the shelter. He was one of about a dozen regular volunteers who worked for Maisie. She only had one other full-time employee, Beatrice, who worked on fundraising. It was a small shelter, but they'd saved a lot of lives, something Maisie was rightly proud of. She'd inherited the land from her parents, and the rest had evolved from there. River had helped her in the beginning, back when he was lost. They'd fenced up the outdoor enclosures together.

"Come on back, River," Dustin said, beaming at him. "She's in the playroom with the puppies, but I know she'll be happy to see you."

"Thanks, Dustin." He reached into the paper bag he carried and pulled out a blue cheese Danish. The very idea of it put him off, but Dustin was extremely vocal about his love for them. "Got something for you too."

"Don't mind if I do," Dustin said. He grabbed the Danish and headed off to sit at the front desk, leaving River to find his way back. They both knew he didn't need directions or a guide. The Danish served a dual purpose, actually—it was a nice gesture that Dustin deserved, and it would keep him busy enough that he wouldn't linger outside the door to listen to their conversation. Maybe it was retirement-induced boredom, but the older man was a known gossip.

Reaching the small playroom, he did the secret knock he and Maisie had made up when they were teens.

The door burst open at once.

"Thank God," Maisie said, "I needed that coffee like yesterday."

She did look tired, although he was wise enough not to say so. Her curly red hair had been scooped back into a fuzzy ponytail, and her eyes had circles under them.

"This isn't just because of my news, is it?" he asked. A little sound—to call it a bark would be an exaggeration—drew his gaze to the bottoms of Maisie's pants. A tiny little multicolored furball was toeing at her leg. Behind it, there were six more, a few of them chasing each other, one gnawing at a toy, and the final two snoozing in a dog bed.

"Oh yes, River," she said dryly, "every moment of my life is dependent on yours. Look at these little monsters. I took them home last night because we couldn't round up volunteers quickly enough. They're too young to be around the others dogs. Now, give me that coffee." He handed her one of the coffees and the paper bag, which she immediately opened.

"Thank God, you got the right one," she said, pausing to use the industrial-sized bottle of hand sanitizer anchored next to the door before she pulled out the blueberry muffin. She eyed it as if it were of equal importance to the coffee. Knowing that she regularly forgot to eat on rescue days, he figured it probably was.

"I only got the banana nut once," he complained.

"And you'll never live it down."

He rolled his eyes as he set his coffee down on the table against the wall. The little puppy was still clawing at Maisie, even as she sat down, so on impulse he used the hand sanitizer and bent down to scoop up the little puffball.

The response was several tiny, enthusiastic licks. The dog's little face looked up at him, the eyes so full of excitement that he didn't want to put him down. He started petting him instead.

"Oh, come on," Maisie said through a mouthful of muffin. "Get going! Talk to me. What the hell happened with Finn? He's not an idiot. He wouldn't fire you even if you screwed his mother."

"Language," River quipped, covering the puppy's ears. In response to her fierce look, he shrugged. "Okay, maybe I quit. Finn told me last night he's selling to Bev Corp. He didn't even talk to me about it before he made up his mind."

"Seriously?!" Maisie said, her face falling. "Just when I was starting to think he wasn't such a bro after all."

"Uh-huh," River said. "You don't need to pretend you don't like him for my sake. But that's not actually what I wanted to talk to you about. Something interesting happened last night."

He'd meant interesting as in *I got the job offer of a lifetime...maybe*. But the image that flitted through his mind was of Georgie Buchanan, her hair tumbling out of that immaculate bun, her cheeks pink with laughter.

And it occurred to him that he didn't just want advice on whether or not to take the job.

Maisie tilted her head. "Really, River, there's no need to be tall, dark, and handsome, *and* mysterious. Give the rest of us something to do."

He snorted a laugh just as the puppy gave him a little nip on his finger. He set him down, and the little dog scampered off to steal the toy his brother or sister was still chewing.

"Duly noted. I got another job offer last night. It turns out Beau didn't leave the brewery to his son—he skipped over him and gave it to his grandkids. Two of them have decided to keep it, although I'm not sure what the others will do. Anyway, we got talking last night after the whole thing with Finn, and they offered me a job on the spot. We haven't talked salary or benefits or anything, but I'm inclined to take it."

"Obviously," Maisie interjected, giving him a play punch to the arm. "This is freaking awesome! You know Beau would have wanted you to be involved."

"Well," River said, playing with the lid of his coffee, "there's one possible snag."

The thing was, he wasn't quite sure how to bring it up. Which was weird, since he and Maisie usually told each other everything. But he wasn't the kind of guy who got this tied up over a girl after one night, especially if that one night hadn't involved anything other than conversation.

"What could possibly get in the way of you accepting an offer like that?" she asked, glancing down at the puppies. The little multicolored one now had full ownership of the toy, and the one it had displaced looked like it was pouting. Maisie reached into the play bin and tossed it a rope toy.

When he still didn't say anything, she glanced back up at him.

"Oh," she said, her eyes widening. A moment passed, and then her usual wise-ass smile slid into place. "Let me guess. One of the grandkids in question is a woman. Riverrr has a crushhhhh."

Which was the exact same thing she'd said when he'd told her about liking the girl who sat behind him in English junior year.

"Shut up," he said, somewhat serious. "Dustin's going to hear you, and I'll never live it down. You know that man thinks we're destined for each other." And he refused to accept the fact that they were like brother and sister. Dustin was firmly of the *men and women can't be friends* camp.

"Well?" she said. "Am I right?"

Abandoning the toy, the little puffball puppy raced back over and started nibbling at River's shoelaces. It was adorable, so he let it happen.

"You're giving him bad habits," she tsked. "Plus, you still haven't answered me."

"Okay," he said, meeting her gaze. "Yes, Georgie, Beau's granddaughter, and I spent a lot of time together last night. I felt like we had a real connection. I've never experienced anything like that before, not so quickly."

A strange look passed through Maisie's eyes, but she waved him on. "Continue."

"Well, I'm not sure I should accept the job. If I do, there's no chance anything will happen between Georgie and me. She's way too professional to consider it. Which is the problem, I guess. I'm not sure what to do. It's the job of a lifetime, but she might be the girl of a lifetime too."

Maisie paused for a second, as if considering. "And did you get the impression she feels the same way about you?"

He remembered the way she'd looked at him as he leaned in to kiss her, the sparkle in her eyes. "Yeah, she's interested," he said, "but she also seemed adamant about hiring me. I'm not sure what to make of it."

"River," she said, "I say this as your best friend of an astronomical number of years…take the job. You'll regret it if you don't. What'll it feel like if they bring someone else in to transform the brewery? It'll never be right. It'll never be the way you would have made it. Don't blow that for a maybe romance. This is too important."

It felt like his heart dropped in his chest, although he wasn't really sure what he'd expected her to say. Maybe he'd come here because he'd known she'd say this. It was true. He couldn't turn down the offer, if the offer still existed after the breakfast meeting with Georgie's siblings.

"Thanks," he said, nodding. "I guess I needed to hear that."

"You can tell me all about it at movie night later."

He nodded again, although he'd almost forgotten. So much had happened in the last few days. So much was still happening.

She gestured down to the puffball still gnawing away at his shoelace. "Now, how would you like to foster a puppy? I daresay you've been chosen."

CHAPTER
Nine

Georgie was nervous. A lot hinged on this breakfast. Lee was pissed and Adalia was being standoffish. She didn't need their permission *or* their blessing to keep the brewery—the will had said they could only sell if all four of them decided to do so by the noon deadline—but she still wanted their approval. She also wanted their help, although she knew that was beyond a long shot.

She was the first to admit she'd drunk too much beer before making her official decision—in fact, she'd had to get an Uber back to her hotel—but in the light of day, she stood by it. She was sure she and Jack could make a go of this, especially with River making the beer.

River.

While she was utterly sure about keeping the business, she was having second thoughts about offering him a job. Not that she didn't think he was capable. Her gut told her he was the linchpin to making Buchanan Brewery successful— no, *more* than successful—*great*. She'd learned to listen to her gut. It was what had made her previous business, Moon Goddess, such a success. But in this instance her gut and her heart were at war. The spark she'd felt with River was instantaneous and strong, but she couldn't let that matter. Every man who'd wandered into Georgie's life had proven to be unreliable and temporary, her father included, but a solid business offered security and fulfillment. It created the kind of satisfaction that lasted. Part of her suspected that River was different, but she couldn't make a hasty decision based on one night of attraction that had involved a possessed cat and multiple samples of beer...and one almost kiss.

She hadn't imagined that, right? They'd almost kissed.

In hindsight, it was a good thing they hadn't. It would have complicated everything. Hiring River Reeves meant there could never be anything romantic between them.

Why did that thought cause her heart to ache so much?

Standing in front of the full-length mirror in her hotel room, she appraised her appearance. She was wearing a gray dress with flats, but she'd left her hair down in loose blond waves rather than securing it in her usual bun. Asheville had a more casual vibe, she told herself. Even her dress was probably too fancy, but she knew deep down that wasn't why she'd chosen to wear her hair down. River had mentioned that he liked it loose around her face.

You're playing with fire.

Was it wrong that she felt gratified by a handsome man appreciating her appearance?

It is if he's your employee.

With a heavy sigh, Georgie grabbed her purse and headed out the door to the stairwell. She was on the fourth floor, but she was too antsy to wait for the elevator, not to mention she needed to expend some nervous energy.

Once she was outside the building, she put on her expensive sunglasses to shield her eyes from the bright sunlight, then started walking toward the hip organic restaurant the hotel concierge had recommended. In hindsight, she realized it would drive the meat-and-potatoes Lee crazy, but it was likely to win her some points with Adalia.

Georgie needed all the help she could get, but perhaps she'd pandered to the wrong sibling. Too late to change it now.

She was a few minutes early, but she spotted Lee as soon as she entered the restaurant lobby. To be fair, he was hard to miss. At six foot two, he stood half a head over almost everyone else, and his short, stylish blond hair and bright green eyes had always garnered attention from women. It wasn't until Georgie was within a few feet of him that she noticed Adalia next to him. If she'd shared that thought—something she couldn't imagine doing—she could anticipate her sister's response. *That's because I'm always overlooked. It's what happens when you're the afterthought kid.*

"Good morning, Lee, Addy," she said, keeping her voice light and cheery as she took off her glasses. "I hope you both slept well."

Adalia simply frowned, but Lee looked irritated. "Maybe it would have been better if you'd actually called me back last night."

"Sorry," she said, genuinely meaning it. "I needed some time to process everything."

"Thank God," Lee said in a breath of relief. "I knew you were logical enough to come to your senses."

His comment pissed her off, but she needed to keep him relatively happy, so she let it roll off her back as she walked up to the hostess and checked in for her reservation.

The hostess led them to their booth, and Georgie gestured for Lee and Adalia to slide in first. She didn't want to risk being flanked by them; she needed to see them face-to-face.

Adalia scooted in first and Lee sat next to her, leaving Georgie the side opposite them, and she felt a sense of relief that things were already going well.

She was truly desperate if she was calling the seating arrangement a win.

"What did you both do last night?" she asked as she picked up a menu.

"Are you really resorting to chitchat?" Lee asked in a snide tone. He'd always been a touch bossy, but this seemed over the top, bordering on their father's level of high-handedness.

"Don't mind him," Adalia said as she opened her menu. She beamed when she saw the choices. "Victoria left with Dad last night, and it wasn't pretty."

Lee frowned and picked up his menu.

Adalia leaned over the table a few inches and mouthed: *She was pissed.*

Georgie could only imagine, and she had to wonder if Lee partially blamed her for his almost fiancée abandoning him. Georgie wasn't sorry she'd voted for Victoria to leave the meeting. That woman held far too much sway over Lee and their father, particularly considering she'd known neither of them a year ago—or maybe that was her own bitterness speaking. After all, neither man ever seemed to listen to *her*.

"My flight is early this afternoon, so I won't be able to sign the papers at the attorney's office," Lee said. "The attorney says you can sign for all of us. Addy got her flight changed so we can go back to New York together."

Georgie couldn't hide her surprise. Lee and Adalia had never been particularly close. She was usually the bridge between them, although she'd be the first to admit it was a shaky wood bridge with a few loose planks. Was this his attempt to sway their sister to his side?

"That's fine," Georgie said, pulling herself together. Once her business got off the ground, she'd gotten herself a present: a good therapist. The doctor had helped her understand that she'd shifted from trying to gain her father's approval to seeking her brother's, an equally impossible task. Logically, she knew she only needed one person's approval—her own—but knowing it and living it weren't always the same thing. "The business side of things won't take long, but we haven't all been together in at least a couple of years. I thought it might be nice to share a meal, just the three of us."

The way Lee pursed his lips as he studied the menu suggested he didn't feel the same, and Adalia seemed unsure of how to react.

"Addy," Georgie said enthusiastically. "What are you working on right now?"

A war played out on Adalia's face, but excitement won out. "A gallery wants to display some of my work next month, so I've been busy prepping for that." She held up her stained hands. "Hence the reason I look like I have the nail beds of a mechanic."

"You're working with ink now?" Georgie asked in surprise. The last she'd heard, her sister had been working on mixed media sculptures.

"I've been dabbling with screen printing," Addy said, becoming even more animated. "The gallery owner saw one of my prints hanging in someone's home and reached out."

"You should see her pieces," Lee said, his gaze still on the menu. "They're amazing."

Lee had seen her screen prints? Her siblings only ever saw each other at family events—like funerals—or when

Georgie arranged it. What had happened to draw them together? And why hadn't they included her?

But she shook off her hurt feelings, telling herself that she should be happy Lee and Adalia were making an effort. Even if they weren't making an effort to spend time with *her*.

"That's so exciting!" Georgie said, truly meaning it. She'd be the first to admit that her younger sister's waywardness had worried her. She had no doubt that Adalia was talented—she'd seen plenty of her work—but she also had a tendency to float from one art medium to the next. And while Georgie hated to agree with their father about anything, one of his favorite sayings about Adalia made a sad sort of sense: talent didn't pay the bills, and a successful career in the art world was just as difficult as an actor making it on Broadway. There were plenty of uber-talented actors waiting tables across the city. "Does the exhibit have a theme?"

Addy's smile wavered for a moment, then became more serious, but now pride filled her eyes. "Yeah. Isolation."

The theme hit Georgie in the face. Art was an expression of the artist's psyche. Adalia always seemed so happy with her life and her friends. Had things changed? Regardless, it sounded like she was doing well professionally, which probably meant she wouldn't want to move to Asheville. Adalia and Lee would probably remain remote partners.

The waitress appeared with a carafe of coffee and a small creamer container. "Coffee? It's our special organic Bolivian blend."

Lee turned his cup over as though it was a race to see who could get coffee first. "Bolivian. Columbian, North Carolinian...I don't care where it's from. As long as it has caffeine, I'll take it." Then his eyes narrowed as he scanned the menu. "I think I have the wrong menu. Where are the breakfast items?"

"Oh, they're on there," the perky waitress said, pointing to one side of his menu. "See?"

"That says bean sprout toast," Lee said in a deadpan voice.

"It's one of our most popular dishes," the waitress said.

"Where's the bacon?" Lee asked. "And the eggs?"

"We have tofu bacon and egg substitute," she said. "We're vegan."

Lee looked up at Georgie, his mouth gaping.

Oh dear.

Adalia leaned forward and held the waitress's gaze. "We're gonna need a moment to look over the menu, but we'll take coffee while we're looking."

"No problem," the waitress said, setting the creamer dish on the table as she poured coffee into Adalia and Georgie's cups.

"Is that half-and-half or heavy cream?" Lee asked.

The waitress laughed as if he'd made a hilarious joke. "It's almond milk."

Then she left to check on the next table.

"Vegan?" Lee asked, staring at Georgie in disbelief.

"I'm sorry," she said. "I knew it was organic, but not vegan. We can go if you want."

"No way," Adalia said, pouring almond milk into her coffee. "I've heard this place is great."

"You've been in Asheville less than forty-eight hours," Lee said in disgust. "How in the hell did you hear this restaurant was great?"

"Everyone's talking about it," Adalia said with a mischievous grin. "We're staying."

"We can pick up a muffin from a coffee shop after we finish," Georgie told her brother.

"They have muffins here," Adalia said.

Lee made a face. "Chia rhubarb agave muffins."

"And blueberry," Adalia said. "And also pancakes. Try them. I'm sure you won't even notice the difference."

Lee shuddered.

Georgie couldn't stifle a laugh. "Okay, I'll not only get you a muffin but also an Egg McMuffin."

"Deal." He grinned, and some of the tightness eased from her chest. She liked it when he let himself lighten up. It reminded her of how things used to be, before Lee followed in their dad's footsteps and became his clone in training.

When the waitress returned, Georgie ordered a fruit plate and Adalia ordered strawberry pancakes. Lee stared up at the waitress, looking hopelessly lost. "What's the tofu bacon taste like?"

She made a face. "I can recommend the egg substitute." When he didn't seem impressed, she said, "Or the banana almond pancakes. They're my favorite. With the egg substitute scrambled on the side."

Lee handed her the menu. "Yeah. Okay," he said, but he sounded like he'd just committed himself to a three-day fast.

Then again, Georgie supposed it did feel like that to her brother, whose favorite breakfast had always been eggs over easy and multiple pieces of bacon.

"I'm sorry, Lee," Georgie said after the waitress walked off with their order. "We really can go someplace else if you like." She needed him in a good mood for the conversation they were about to have.

"No, it's okay." He sucked in a breath, then let it out. "Sorry I'm being such an asshole. It's just that when Victoria and I fight…" He shook his head, offering her a puppy dog smile. "Congratulations on the sale of your business, by the way. After the mess at the attorney's office, I realized I'd never touched base with you after you emailed and told us all about the deal…" He grimaced. "I'm sorry, Georgie. I really was—and still am—proud of you. I just got busy."

"Yeah, Georgie," Adalia said less enthusiastically. "Congrats."

"Thanks," she said, feeling a little hurt over Adalia's response, and more thrilled than she should be by Lee's acknowledgment. "I keep wondering what Mom would have thought."

"She would have been so proud," Lee said, his smile wavering, but Georgie knew it wasn't because of her. Their mother had been gone for more than fifteen years, but the pain of losing her sometimes felt like a fresh wound.

Adalia nodded, swiping a tear from her cheek. "So proud."

"I miss *us*," Georgie said before she realized what she was saying, but now that she'd opened the door, she decided to walk right through it. "We used to be close. What happened?"

"We were kids," Lee said. "We grew up." She could always count on Lee to be the voice of reason, but the look in his eyes told her he didn't totally buy his own words.

"But we're still siblings," Georgie said, and when defensiveness tightened his jaw, she held up a hand. "I'm not laying fault on anyone. I'm just as capable of picking up a phone or hopping on a train. It's just…I can't help but think how disappointed Mom would be." She took a breath and pushed it out past the lump in her throat. "Remember what she always told us?"

"Friends come and go, but family is forever," Adalia whispered, looking close to tears.

"We let that go," Georgie said. "We're practically strangers."

"We have lives of our own," Lee said, defensively. "We live in different cities. Running a business"—he gestured to Adalia—"or working on art takes time and dedication. That time has to come from someplace. We know we're always there for each other when it counts." He gave Adalia a warm smile. "Right, Addy?"

Adalia smiled back. "Yeah."

Georgie swallowed the prick of jealousy she felt for her sister. Although Adalia had picked on Lee in front of their father, they'd clearly become closer, and they'd left her out. But Lee was right, they'd all been focused on their projects, be it business or art, leaving little time for each other. They needed something to work on together.

Maybe Grandpa Beau had known what he was doing after all.

"Is everything okay, Adalia?" Georgie asked.

"Yeah. Things are good." But her hand encircled her cup and she stared into the light brown coffee.

"So, about the brewery," Lee said, taking a sip of his almond-milk-doctored coffee, then grimacing. He traded his cup for Georgie's currently untouched mug of black coffee, and she shrugged her acceptance. "Mr. Manning says it's just a matter of signing the document. In fact, he already has a buyer lined up. Someone called Bev Corp. We'll need to talk Jack around, but I'm sure he'll see sense."

Horror raced through Georgie. River had called them the devil. He'd be so upset if Buchanan Brewery sold out to them too. It would be like a double betrayal. Steeling her back, she said, "I know you and Adalia want to sell, but I spent some time at Grandpa Beau's house last night, talking to River, and I've decided I definitely want to keep it."

Lee stared at her in disbelief. "You can't be serious, Georgie."

Georgie tilted her head and held her brother's gaze, almost as though in a dare. "Why is that so inconceivable, Lee?"

"You know *nothing* about running a brewery, Georgie. You don't even like beer."

"I do so," she said, feeling like a teenager as soon as the words left her mouth. She cleared her throat, then said, "I didn't know the first thing about new-age feminine hygiene products when I started Moon Goddess, but I'll do the same thing now that I did then. I'll learn." Then, because she wanted to put it all on the table, she added, "And Jack's going to help me."

Adalia blinked. "You've been planning this with our father's *illegitimate son*?"

She put particular emphasis on those words, and a few people turned to look at them. Georgie shot her sister a glare. "Our *brother*, Adalia."

"He is not my brother," Adalia spat out in contempt.

Her attitude toward Jack hurt Georgie, but she'd deal with Adalia's feelings about him later. Right now she wanted them on board with her plan. And if she couldn't manage that, well, at least they'd be informed.

"Does *Jack* know anything about running a brewery?" Lee asked.

"No," Georgie said, "but he's the manager of a bar—"

"Running a bar and managing a brewery are two different things. This is harebrained," he said in disgust, "not to mention Dad wants us to sell it. He already has plans for the money."

"Are you *kidding* me?" Georgie demanded. "Grandpa Beau gave *us* the brewery and his house, not Dad." When Lee looked away, Georgie narrowed her eyes. "I suspect he'd want all four shares of the money, or at least the three from us."

Adalia gaped at her brother. "You're really planning on giving everything to Dad?"

Lee put a hand on her arm. "It's for an investment, Addy."

Her face hardened and she jerked her arm away. "No."

Confusion washed over Lee's face. "What do you mean no?"

"I mean no. I'm not giving him a dime." She turned to Georgie with fire in her eyes. "But I still vote to sell. You have to get rid of it, Georgie."

Get rid of it. The words sent a pang of pain through Georgie's chest. Because despite her initial trepidation, she had seen the brewery through her grandfather's eyes. And River's. It was a living, breathing entity, just waiting to spring back to life. The brewery wasn't a building full of equipment to sell off. It was her grandfather's legacy. It was the Buchanan siblings' future, whether they recognized it or not.

"Grandpa Beau wanted us to keep it," Georgie said. "He wanted us to run it together."

"Then he was a fool," Lee said. "I have a high-six-figure job. I live in New York City. I'm not moving to Asheville to make beer."

"I have a life too," Adalia said. "And friends. And my art. What is it you expect me to do?"

"You don't have to live here if you don't want to," Georgie said. "Jack and I will run it."

"You don't know the first thing about running a brewery, Georgie," Lee pointed out again. "And from the sounds of it, neither does Jack. And you're going to give up your life in Boston and move to *Asheville?*" He said Asheville as though it were a trash dump.

"If you knew anything about my life, you'd know that I have nothing to do at the moment, and I hate standing still. I've been looking for my next project, and I've decided this is it." She leaned closer to the table. "But most of all, Grandpa Beau thought I could do this, and I don't want to disappoint him."

"News flash," Lee said. "You can't disappoint the old man because he's dead."

She cringed at him calling their grandfather *old man*. "He trusted me with his brewery. And Jack and I are going to make it great." Her brow lifted. "Plus, we hired a brewmaster who's going to put Buchanan Brewery back on the map."

"You already hired someone?" Adalia asked. "Without consulting us? You can't do that, Georgie. We're *selling*."

"We're *not* selling," Georgie said, infusing authority into her tone. "And yes, Jack and I hired him together. You and Lee can be silent partners, and we'll work out how we'll deal with the profits when we start making them. For now, Jack, River, and I will work on rehabbing it together. And Lee, when we start paying you your share of the profits, if you want to give your share to Dad, be my guest, but I'm keeping mine and so is Adalia."

Lee looked like he was about to have a stroke. "You can't do this, Georgie."

"I can and I will." She was so furious with her brother it took everything in her to not wring his neck. "You say you're proud of me because I built Moon Goddess from nothing and sold it for five million, but you never thought I could make it work." She stabbed the table with her index finger. "I took an idea and made it into a multimillion-dollar business. I can do the same with our grandfather's brewery." Tears burned her eyes. "For *once*, Lee, I wish you'd have just a *little bit* of faith in me."

Regret washed over his face. "Georgie."

She sucked in a breath and gave him the best resting bitch face she could muster. "Jack and I both want to do this, and Grandpa Beau wrote his will so that only one of us had to want it. I don't need your blessing or your help. Call me stupid for wanting it anyway."

"It's going to take a lot of work, Georgie," he said, his voice soft.

"I'm not afraid of hard work," she said. "If you'd seen any part of me building Moon Goddess, you'd know that."

He grimaced. "Ouch." Then he added, "but I suppose I deserve that."

"I can do this, Lee," she said earnestly.

He studied her for a moment. Then a soft smile spread across his face. "If anyone can, it's you."

"You're giving her your blessing?" Adalia asked in disbelief. "What about Dad?"

Something flickered in Lee's eyes, but it was gone too quickly for Georgie to register what it might have been. "Dad should know by now how headstrong Georgie is. He'll just have to get over it."

"You're really agreeing to this?" Adalia asked.

Lee's face broke into a huge grin. "Yep. The Buchanan siblings own a brewery. What would Mom think of us now?"

Georgie wanted to cry with happiness. Their mother would be so proud.

CHAPTER Ten

It's on. Will you meet Jack and me after our meeting with the lawyer? One o'clock. We can do a walk-through of the brewery together.

There was a pause after Georgie's text came through. Then she added, *Thank you again for last night. I'm excited to do this with you.*

River gusted a sigh, and lifted the little animal carrier Maisie had given him. "Well, pup, there goes that. I guess I should be happy."

He wasn't, not totally, but he'd decided to accept anyway.

He went to unlock the door of his loft, but it was already open. The only two people who had keys were Maisie and Aunt Dottie, so he wasn't terribly surprised to see his aunt sitting at the table opposite his open kitchen. What *did* shock him was that Finn sat across from her. His hand fisted around the handle of the animal carrier, his knuckles turning white. Part of him wanted to turn around and leave, but he wasn't a coward, and he didn't run away. He was the type of person who established roots rather than broke them. He'd promised himself that a long time ago.

As soon as Aunt Dottie saw the animal carrier, she cooed and hurried over. She went to take it from him, and he let her, eliciting a little whimper from the dog.

"Goodness, Maisie finally broke you, and none too soon," Aunt Dottie said. "I made a sweater for Jezebel, but wouldn't you know it, she refuses to wear the darn thing. It'll look perfect on your pup."

"Don't get too used to him, Aunt Dottie. He's just a foster," River said, but his gaze was on Finn.

Finn looked terrible, like he'd stayed at Buchanan Brewery for the whole night and staggered home. He had on a Big Catch T-shirt and jeans, which was like someone else wearing pajamas out of the house. Maybe it was foolish of River, but it made him feel a little better. At least Finn cared about selling him out, not that it changed anything.

"You know, I didn't give you that key so you could let in anyone you want," he said, shifting his gaze back to Aunt Dottie. She'd already lifted the puppy out of the carrier and was fitting him into a bright pink sweater with pom-poms. He knew better than to dissent, and from the way the puppy was wagging his tail, he didn't seem to mind. Part of him wanted to share a look—and a silent laugh—with Finn, but he couldn't bring himself to do it.

"Well, dear, I was under the impression you gave it to me to be used at my discretion, just like Beau and I told you where he kept his spare key." She gave him a wink as she said it, which made him wonder just how much she knew, or thought she knew, about what had happened last night.

Of course, Jack had seen her at Buchanan, hadn't he? So she at least knew Georgie might make him an offer.

"I just want to talk, River," Finn said. He ran a hand through his hair, which was almost too short to be messy, but it was messier than River had ever seen it. Again, it made him feel a little better, although the part of him that was still Finn's friend weirdly hated to see it. "I know you're pissed, and you have every right to be. I should have talked to you first."

"Damn straight, you should have," River growled. He set down the things Maisie had given him for the dog and moved toward the table, staying several feet away. Even if Aunt Dottie had brought over fresh cinnamon rolls. "It was something we built together. You always said that. Shouldn't I have had some say?"

"Yes," Finn said. "Of course. And I would have, but then Beau got sick, and I knew you'd feel—"

"Betrayed."

Because he did. In a way he'd only felt one time before and had never wanted to feel again. What was worse, he'd expected it the first time, at least a little—he'd thought he could trust Finn.

Finn's face lost a little more color, and he looked to be just this side of puking.

"Did Aunt Dottie make you any of her hangover cure?" he asked. He told himself he was just asking because he needed to get this conversation behind him, the sooner, the better, but again there was that awful feeling of caring. You couldn't just shut it off, even if you wanted to.

"How's something with a raw egg in it going to make me feel better?" Finn asked dubiously.

"You're questioning the wisdom of my aunt?" he asked, feeling the corners of his lips twitch up a little in spite of himself.

"Exactly what I said," Aunt Dottie offered. "His color is so peaky, and the energy in here… You fixed that right up, though, didn't you?" she cooed to the puppy, who was literally eating something out of her hand.

"I know," Finn said, drawing River's gaze back to the table. "I guess I'm making all sorts of dumb calls lately." He rubbed his nose. "The thing is, River, I was always going to walk at some point. I wanted to build the biggest brewery in the state, and we did that. Where else is there to go from here?"

"We could have become an anchor in the community," River said. "The kind of place people can count on." The last words sounded a little sharp, like some of his hurt was leaking out, and he patched it back in. "And yeah, maybe I knew you'd walk at some point, but I didn't think you'd sell to the devil. And I definitely didn't think you'd do it *now*."

They both knew what *now* meant, and he saw a flash of pain in Finn's eyes. Yeah, he knew he'd messed up good.

"Like I said, I made some bad calls. But selling to Bev Corp was the right move."

River started to say something, but Finn cut him off. "I know what you and Dottie think about them, and hell, maybe you're not altogether wrong, but they offered a good deal to you, and to the rest of my people. That's what mattered to me. I don't want to screw anyone over. I'm just... I got bored." Finn met his gaze then, and he held it. "And be honest with me, River, because I got the impression that you were getting bored too."

River's first instinct was to rage at him again, but then he found himself thinking of how he'd felt last night, sitting with Georgie and Jack, talking about their plans for the future. He'd felt more excited about work than he had in at least a year, maybe two. And it wasn't because he lived for challenges—he and Finn weren't alike in that. It was because Buchanan Brewery was a different kind of place. It was a family business with deep roots. It wasn't a flashy new thing, but something well loved that had been pushed to the back of the drawer. And he and Georgie and Jack could polish it up and make it new again. There was something special in that, something sacred.

"Yes and no," he said, his tone softer than it had been, "but you let me down by not talking to me. And I still quit. I'll give Gladys a call to work out details and pick up some of my stuff today or tomorrow."

"Okay," Finn said, "I accept that." He got up from the table and pushed his chair in, then shot a longing look at the cinnamon buns.

"Go ahead," River said with a wave. His aunt had brought a good dozen.

Finn nodded and scooped one up with a napkin. "So where does this leave us?" he asked. It wasn't the kind of question Finn usually asked—to the point where River almost wanted to tease him about it, but he wasn't ready for that yet.

"I don't know," he said honestly. "But I don't trust you right now, and I don't know if I ever will again."

He saw the hurt on Finn's face, but he didn't back down. Couldn't. They both knew he meant it.

"Well, I heard something about you working with the Buchanans."

River just nodded.

"Word to the wise. Bev Corp wouldn't be opposed to buying them out as a second location for Big Catch."

And he'd thought calling them *the devil* was putting it too strongly?

"Thank you, Finn. But I think it's time you leave," he said flatly, stepping aside.

Finn walked past him, Aunt Dottie calling out, "Lovely to see you, dear! Consider what I said about seeing Lola. I've never had such a spot-on reading. No better time to go than when you're at a crossroads."

"Thanks, Dottie. I'll keep it in mind," he intoned. He looked back at River once before he left. "Cute dog."

The as-yet-unnamed puppy was humping a discarded sandal.

Then the door closed and Finn was gone, probably out of River's life too. Which hurt more than he would have liked.

Focus on the new job.

So why did he find himself thinking of Georgie? Wondering if she'd like the puppy better than she did Beau's mostly evil cat? Wondering if he was making the right call even if he needed—and really, really wanted—the job?

Because you're an idiot, that's why. And Finn knows it too. That's why he didn't talk to you about this while Beau was dying. He thought you'd fall apart.

"I recognize that look," Aunt Dottie said knowingly. "Beau's granddaughter is quite lovely, isn't she?"

"Really?" he said, stooping to pet the dog—and remove the sweater. It was, after all, the beginning of June, but Aunt Dottie did love her knitting. "I hadn't noticed."

"You know how I feel about lying, River."

He glanced up at her and smiled. Something told him everything was—currently—going according to her plans. But she had to know he couldn't, or at least really, really shouldn't, notice how beautiful Georgie Buchanan was if he intended to accept her job offer.

"You asked a rhetorical question. Anyone with eyes can see she's beautiful. It's only after talking to her for a while that you realize she's also brilliant, kind, and funny."

Aunt Dottie's eyes lit up. "I knew it! The pink crystal wanted to go to her. It sensed there was something between you."

"Well, Aunt Dottie, you might want to rethink your interpretation. That pink crystal nearly ended up smashing my brains in."

He told her about the way he and Georgie had officially met last night. They relocated to the table, and he ended up telling her a whole lot more, ending with the offer she and Jack had made.

"I guess I'm going to take it," he said, "although I can't say it doesn't suck."

"What makes you think you can't romance her if you work with her?"

Leave it to his aunt to put it like that.

"Well, there are rules about that kind of thing," he said.

"Not at Buchanan Brewery," she said. "I started working there before Beau and I began courting. Indeed, it's how we got to know each other. You really learn the make of someone when you work with them."

"Well, I'm not so sure about that," he said, gesturing toward the door even though Finn had left a long time ago. "Besides, even if it's not in the HR manual, surely it's not encouraged. And trust me, Aunt Dottie, she's nothing if not proper. Even if it's not unheard of, it would be for Georgie."

His aunt shook her head knowingly. "That pink crystal tells me differently. There's a lovely energy to that girl. Nothing like that dry husk of a father. She's the type who'll stand up for what she believes in—and for the people she believes in." A sad look crossed her face. "And I'm not so sure you misjudged Finn, either. Sometimes you expect too much from people, dear, and it can only end in disappointment."

He shrugged it off, although it was the kind of comment that had barbs, and he already knew he'd be thinking about it later.

"We'll see, I guess."

"Indeed, we will," she said, shifting her gaze to the puppy, who'd fallen asleep on the sandal he'd been humping earlier.

"Hope he didn't imprint on it," River said.

"What are you going to name him? He looks an awful lot like a Flavius to me."

River just shook his head. He was used to Aunt Dottie coming up with ridiculous names for things. "I was thinking I'd call him Hops. The last time I spoke to Beau, he told me he thought our…Big Catch's new beer was too hop-forward." He shrugged. "I bet he'd find it funny."

She smiled at him. "I bet he would. Now, about Lola. Finn's not the only one who'd benefit from having his cards read. You're at a crossroads too."

"No thanks, Aunt Dottie. I'll find out what happens when it does."

Which was how he always responded, but she still hadn't given up. Part of him liked that. He liked knowing he could count on things—because for much too long he hadn't been able to count on anything.

But could he count on Georgie Buchanan?

CHAPTER
Eleven

Georgie walked into the law offices of Gramble and Manning at 11:57, ready to start the next phase of her life. After she and Jack finished with the paperwork, they were meeting River at the brewery at one. While Georgie had toured the space with her grandfather, she needed to see it again from an owner's perspective, not to mention Jack hadn't seen it at all. River had spent plenty of time at Buchanan Brewery, so he would make the perfect tour guide.

Sure, and that's the only reason you want to see him.

Mr. Manning's assistant met her as she walked through the door. "Jack is already in the conference room and Mr. Manning is readying the documents for you to sign." She gestured down the hall to the room, then said, "Can I get you coffee or water while you wait?"

"This should only take a moment, right?" Georgie asked. "I won't need anything."

The assistant didn't answer, just gestured for her to enter the room where everything had gone down the day before. "He'll be here in a moment."

Jack was standing next to the wall of windows overlooking a parking lot, wearing a pair of khakis and a short-sleeved button-down shirt. He turned when she entered the room, and she gave him a soft smile.

"Hey," he said, appearing unsure of his standing with her. Georgie understood. They'd both been drinking last night, which called the decisions they'd made into question. Georgie had no regrets... Did Jack?

"How was breakfast with your siblings?" he asked, his body tense.

She stopped herself from saying they were his siblings too. "Good." She brushed a loose strand of hair behind her ear. "Actually, great. Lee's on board and plans to be hands-off, which means we can run it how we see fit."

"And Adalia?"

She made a face. "Not so eager, but I think she'll come around once it starts doing well and making a profit."

He nodded, then turned back to the view.

Georgie eyed the table, reluctant to sit down. The emotions of the previous day still hung in the air, but she was also antsy. She wanted to get this done so she could head to the brewery and get down to business, not because she was eager to see River again. Okay, a partial lie. She was eager for both.

"Ah, Georgie," Mr. Manning said as he walked into the room, holding a stack of papers. "And Jack. Thank you for coming in."

"Of course," she said with a smile. "Lee said it was okay for me to sign for him and Adalia."

"Only one of you has to sign that you want to keep it," the attorney said. "So the two of you signing is more of a sign of solidarity and not a legal necessity." He set the stack of papers on the table and Georgie took a seat. Jack sat next to her, resting both his hands on the table.

It looked like Mr. Manning had more than one document for them to sign. He flipped the pages until he reached one with two signature tabs.

"Let's start with the reason you're here. This document says that you both agree to keep the brewery. Sign next to the tabs."

Georgie grabbed a pen from a cup in the center of the table but stopped with the pen hovering over the signature line. "Lee said you had a buyer lined up for the property?"

Jack's body jolted.

The attorney's smile wavered. "That's right. Bev Corp, a national company, is very interested."

"How much did they offer?"

"Four-point-two million for the brand, the recipes, and the facility."

Georgie couldn't help wondering if Adalia needed the money. A quarter of the sale price would be enough to completely change her sister's life. Was she being selfish? But then she thought of the determination in Jack's eyes. He deserved to be part of the Buchanan legacy. And Lee believed in her, for once, something she'd always wanted. And then there was River. He'd been important to Beau, and he wanted—needed—to make this work as much as she did.

Jack shot her a questioning look. Even if Georgie decided at the last minute to sell, she knew he would never agree to it.

Ultimately, she trusted her gut, and it told her this was the right decision. She leaned over and signed her name, then passed the form to Jack. The attorney produced several other papers for them to sign, one naming Georgie the executor of her grandfather's trust—which included the brewery and the house—and giving her control over Beau's business and personal bank accounts. "Grandpa Beau named me as executor? How did he know I'd agree to do this?"

"As you've likely guessed, he changed his will after your visit. Originally, the house went to your father, and the brewery went to someone else."

"Who was it supposed to go to?" Jack asked.

Instead of answering, Mr. Manning pursed his lips and handed Georgie the bank account statements.

Had Beau originally planned to give the brewery to Dottie? He hadn't left her anything in the will, although Georgie had assumed that was because he'd passed along everything he'd wanted to her before dying.

She considered pressing Mr. Manning, but she was more interested in the financial state of the brewery. She slid the papers between her and Jack, and they quickly scanned the business account documents, which proved the business was indeed in trouble.

When they both finished signing nearly everything in the stack, Mr. Manning gave them an apologetic smile. "Now that you've finished most of the official paperwork for keeping the brewery, I need to tell you both about the strings."

She gaped at the attorney, sure she'd heard him wrong. "Strings? What strings?"

"Beau wanted to make sure that you and your siblings didn't make this a side project. He was worried the others might be uninterested."

Her heart skipped a beat as she waited for what she was sure would be terrible news. "Excuse my language, Mr. Manning, but I have no intention of half-assing this."

"And neither do I," Jack said with a firm resolve.

Perspiration began to dot the attorney's forehead. "They aren't *my* rules. Trust me, I tried to talk Beau out of it."

Her stomach turned to a dead weight. "What did Grandpa Beau do?"

Mr. Manning handed her an envelope. "Perhaps you should read this first."

She broke the seal, pulled out the page, and read the shaky handwriting.

Dear Georgie,

You have no idea how much I loved your visit. You have your father's drive for success, but you also have something he never possessed. Sure, he has ambition, but he doesn't have heart. You, my girl, have it in spades.

I knew after our visit that you wouldn't sell Buchanan Brewery. I could see the fire in your eyes—the same fire that led me to found my business so many years ago. I'm ashamed to admit that I got tired. I lost my drive and I let things slide. I considered passing BB on several years ago, but the successor I'd named wasn't ready. He had to pay his dues, just like you and your siblings will have to pay yours if you fail to meet the challenge I've set for you.

I know this will seem harsh, my dear, but I assure you that I would never ask this of you if I didn't think you were up to it. We all need a little fire under our britches. Remember I do this out of love.

If anyone can turn Buchanan Brewery around, my dear, it's you. My love, Dottie, is there to help you. Now go make me proud.

Love,

Grandpa Beau

Georgie stared up at the now-drenched attorney in horror. "What challenge?"

"What does it say?" Jack asked.

She handed him the paper and his head moved slightly from side to side as he read. Mr. Manning pulled yet another paper out of his stack. "I could read the legalese, or I could get to the heart of it."

"I'd rather just hear the bad part," Jack said, setting the paper on the table in front of Georgie.

"Yes, please cut to the chase," she said, trying to keep the fear out of her voice.

"Well, there are two stipulations. The first is that Dottie Hendrickson cannot be fired. She can only retire of her own volition."

"Well, that's no problem," Georgie said, puzzled. Why would her grandfather have thought it was even necessary to put that in writing?

"Like I said, let's hear the bad part," Jack said.

The perspiration on Mr. Manning's brow confirmed he'd told them the easy part first. He cleared his throat, then said, "Buchanan Brewery has to place in the top five of the Brewfest Competition."

She shook her head. "Brewfest Competition... River told me about it last night. It's a beer contest."

He nodded, pulling a handkerchief from his pocket and dabbing his forehead. "It's usually held at the beginning of March."

March...it was early June, so they'd only have ten months.

Her mouth gaped. "River told me that Buchanan Brewery hasn't placed in years."

"Let me get this straight," Jack said, leaning over the table while his eyes bored into the attorney's. "We have less than a year to take a below-average brewery and make it nationally competitive?"

Grimacing, Mr. Manning wiped his handkerchief over his forehead. "I'm sorry. I really *did* try to talk him out of it."

Georgie's head swam and she sat back in her seat as she tried to soak this in. Was it even possible to create a winning beer by then? From what River had told her about brewing, it took weeks just to create one batch. Trying not to panic, she said, "What if we realize we'll never win and we want to sell it instead?"

He shook his head. "I'm sorry, Georgie. By signing those papers, you agreed not to sell."

She'd been a fool not to read the fine print. She knew better than that, but she'd been caught up in the moment, thinking about the future. About the look on her father's face when he learned his children had chosen Beau over him.

"And what happens if we lose?" Because Georgie's father had taught her at a very young age that there was no point of a challenge if a dastardly threat wasn't dangling over her head.

Now she wondered if her father had learned his tactics from Beau. That sweet old man she'd met had had some bite left in him.

"The brewery goes to the person originally named in the will."

"And who is that?" she forced out past the lump in her throat.

"River Reeves."

CHAPTER
Twelve

River stood outside of the brewery, tapping his foot while he waited for Georgie and Jack. The whole nervous energy thing wasn't usually his jam, but he'd left Hops at home in his crate, so he didn't have a puppy to fuss over. Maybe he was overthinking it, but it felt like a lot was riding on this moment.

What if the walk-through didn't go well, and Georgie and Jack changed their minds? Sure, Georgie had seen the brewery before, but she probably hadn't been looking at things critically—like she would be today—and he was well aware most of the equipment was old. If Bev Corp was waiting in the wings with an attractive offer, it might be hard for them to say no.

He didn't think they'd cop out, he really didn't, but so much of his life had changed in a blink. So much of what he'd counted on had slipped away.

He'd expected them to take a car—although it wasn't a long walk, it wasn't terribly short either—so it took him a moment to notice them across the street. His heart thumped faster in his chest at the sight of Georgie, her hair bouncing around her face. Jack strolled beside her, and they were deep in conversation.

He'd been thinking of seeing her again too—wondering if it would feel the same, or if the magic of the previous night would slip away.

But it hadn't, or at least not for him. And she'd worn her hair down. Was that a message?

It wasn't until they came closer that he realized they were arguing, and Georgie had a stricken look on her face. Jack's expression veered closer to pissed.

Well, shit, that couldn't be good. If breakfast had gone well, what could have happened since? Had something happened with the father, maybe?

Except...hadn't he already left?

Georgie made a *shut up* gesture to Jack, and they crossed the street in silence.

"Hey," River said, stepping toward Georgie. He went in for a hug, because that's how they'd said goodnight, but she flinched away.

Definitely not good. Although maybe she was being a consummate professional, just like he'd told Dottie she would be. It was one instance in which he did not relish being right.

Georgie nodded to him—*nodded*—and then Jack did the same, although he looked like he'd rather punch him instead.

"Um. Okay," he said. "Everything go all right at the lawyer's office?"

Georgie opened her mouth to answer, but her gaze shot to Jack, and something like regret passed through her eyes.

"Yes. Fine," she said, her tone not matching her words. But one look at Jack told River he'd do best not to press. If he was going to get her to talk, he'd have to do it alone. He'd gotten along with Jack last night—hell, he liked the guy—but now Jack was looking at him like they were blood-sworn enemies.

"Ooookayyy," he said. "They gave most people the day off after yesterday, but Aunt Dottie said Josie, kind of a jack-of-all-trades assistant, would be able to show us around." Jack-of-all-trades was a nice way of saying she didn't really do anything but was still on the payroll, but he wouldn't be the one to point it out. Nor was he about to mention the fact that Aunt Dottie had once described her as a bit peculiar. They'd soon figure both things out for themselves. "Did Henry give you the key?" When he was greeted with blank looks, he added, "Henry Manning. Beau's attorney."

Jack pulled it out of his pocket. "Yeah, we have it."

He pushed his way past River and opened the door. The tasting room, a madhouse last night, had been restored to immaculate order. Knowing Aunt Dottie, she'd stayed late into the night, stacking chairs and rinsing glasses right along with all of the other employees—and reading their energy and commenting on their love lives while she was at it. Her work ethic had always impressed him. When he was younger she'd run a little business on the side, making energetic necklaces and selling them at fairs. He'd even helped her a time or two, although that wasn't something he'd advertised to his friends. If he hadn't had her as an example, he wasn't sure where he would have ended up.

So he was smiling a little as he led the Buchanans into the other half of the building. He knocked on the door, then knocked again when Josie didn't answer. She should have been expecting them, but then again, she had the mistaken belief that she had a deeply ingrained sense of time—one that required no watch or alarm.

One more knock, and Jack shook his head impatiently.

"Let's just open it. It's ours now. No sense in waiting." He sent a look of gloom Georgie's way as he said it, and she bit her lip. Part of River wanted to tell Jack to back off, but he didn't want to interfere.

So he stepped aside, falling in next to Georgie—close enough that he could feel the heat of her—and Jack blasted the door open.

Letting out several bubbles. A sea of them, a few inches deep, covered the usually immaculate floor. The equipment might not be new anymore, but everything was usually clean.

"What the hell?" Jack said, stealing the words from his mouth.

Josie stood to one side of the door, her eyes huge behind her oversized wire-framed glasses.

One look at Georgie told River all he needed to know—she was horrified—and without overthinking it, he reached over and squeezed her hand.

She squeezed back, and instead of letting him go immediately, like he'd thought she would, she held on.

He would have enjoyed it more if only her brother hadn't been giving him the look of death. Because he'd done nothing to deserve it, he gave that look right back to him. Georgie released his hand and took a few steps toward Josie, her feet forming a path through the bubbles.

"You're Josie, right?" she asked, her tone kind but direct.

Josie just nodded mutely.

"I'm Georgie Buchanan, and this is my brother, Jack," Georgie said. "We're taking over for our grandfather, so we need to know what happened here."

"I was hoping no one would notice," Josie said, biting her lip.

Georgie glanced back at River, their eyes meeting, and he could have sworn she was on the verge of hysteria-induced laughter. Instead, she turned back to Josie, remarkably cool and collected. "Well, I'm afraid that ship has sailed. Can you please tell us?"

"Yes," Jack said sarcastically, "I'm dying for more bad news."

More bad news?

Josie flinched from him, reaching for her energetic necklace, and went to sit on her stool.

Since no good could come of them standing in the middle of this mess for what had every hallmark of a difficult conversation, River said, "Come on, let's sit at one of the tables in the tasting room while we talk. I'll grab a pitcher of water from behind the bar."

"Like aunt, like nephew," Georgie said softly, giving him a little smile even though she still looked shell-shocked, both from whatever had clearly happened before their meeting and from the mess.

"Sure, fine, whatever," Jack said, stalking off and claiming a seat at the nearest picnic-style table. Josie followed, bubbles sticking to her clogs, and took the farthest possible seat from his position. Georgie closed the door on the mess and went to sit beside Josie, probably trying to make her more comfortable, while River filled up a pitcher behind the bar (one of two in the space) and grabbed a stack of pint glasses.

He took a quick gauge of the situation, and after setting down the water and glasses—he wouldn't pull a full Aunt Dottie; anyone who wanted one could take one—sat down across from Georgie.

"…I thought they'd all pop by the time you got here," Josie was saying. "I danced around and tried to pop them, but there were just too many."

"And how'd there come to be so many bubbles?" Georgie spoke with an understanding tone, although he could see the strain on her face. Jack wasn't attempting to hide his poor mood.

"Sounds a lot like sabotage," he sneered, looking right at River as he said it.

"No," Josie said. "Or not intentionally. He was just really, really drunk. He's actually still in the back. I let him lie down on my shawl in the corner. I managed to clear that much space, at least." She fingered her necklace again, still seemingly unaware that she had yet to name who "he" was. "You see, he found the bubble machine out on the street, and he thought he was paying tribute to Beau. It's beautiful, really—he filled the brewery with bubbles because Beau had made so many bubbles in life."

Georgie's face drained of color as she looked first at River, then Jack.

"Lurch," River said.

Josie nodded sadly. "He's upset Beau's ungrateful grandchildren are taking over the brewery. Never wrote to him or called him. Only one of them paid him a visit—and even then, he had to ask her. Can you imagine? Such a nice man."

River cleared his throat, and a surprised look crossed Josie's face.

She looked from Georgie to Jack, and back. "Oh, you're his grandchildren, aren't you?"

"Can we fire her?" Jack asked Georgie.

"You're being sarcastic again, aren't you?" Josie said, shaking her head. "I've always thought sarcasm was the lowest form of humor."

Rather than break the news that Jack was obviously serious, River looked her in the eye. "Can you take me back to Lurch, Josie? I need to know what else he did."

If it was only a mess, they could clean it. Not the best first impression of the brewery, but whatever. They'd all known there would be work to do.

Turning to Georgie and Jack, he said, "I've known him for years. I can talk him around."

Jack gave him another suspicious glance, then said, "Okay, but I'm going with you."

"Do you have some kind of problem with me, man?" River said, getting kind of pissed. "If I remember correctly, this whole thing was your idea."

"Yeah," Jack said with an aggrieved sigh. "I guess it was. Don't mind me. Just woke up on the wrong side of the bed."

A massive understatement, but he'd let it go for now.

"I'll go with him, Jack," Georgie said. "One of us should go, and you're not in the right headspace."

Jack just nodded, pressing his hand to his forehead as if he had a headache.

"Are you sure you don't just want to go on the tour?" Josie asked, cocking her head. "We can take our shoes off, if you're worried about getting them dirty. Then maybe Lurch will wake up on his own."

"Wouldn't that be unhygienic?" Georgie asked, her brows pinched together.

This was spiraling out of control pretty fast.

"Josie, maybe you should go home," River said. "I'll put your shawl aside after we talk to Lurch."

"Okay," she said, already getting up. "Save the bubble machine for me too."

"I thought you said he found it on the street?" Georgie asked, although it was obvious she didn't expect to like the answer.

"He did," Josie said, as if it should be obvious. "My street."

Jack sighed again, louder this time, and poured himself a glass of water as Josie let herself out of the building.

"Okay, here goes nothing," Georgie said, getting to her feet. River did the same.

"Is everything okay?" he asked as they headed toward the back. "I can tell your brother was tense before the whole"—he gestured to the brewery—"bubble debacle. And you look…sad, I guess." *And scared.*

"Just some unexpected news about the family," she said. The way she said it told him he shouldn't pry, and so he didn't. She paused, turning to look at him. "I'm sorry about the way I greeted you before. I didn't mean to seem cold. I just…"

"We're going to be working together, and you're trying to stay professional, right?"

"Something like that," she said with a small smile.

"Look, I get it. It's a weird situation. Let's handle this other very weird situation, and then maybe we can talk."

She nodded slightly and started walking again. "I'd like that."

"Now, about Lurch…" he started, but when they got into the back, Lurch was sitting on Josie's abandoned stool, holding his head. His bald head, which had more than a few bubbles on it.

He jolted back when he saw them, nearly falling off the stool.

"Oh," he said when he saw River, "it's you." He glanced at Georgie, his eyes widening. "And this must be Beau's granddaughter, Georgie." He managed to sound not displeased about the fact, which was an impressive feat given that he currently sat in a sea of bubbles of his own making. "I'd love to talk to you, but can I steal River away for just a minute?"

That last bit had been said in pure panic.

Georgie gave River a look, and when he nodded, she said, "Sure. I'll be waiting out in the tasting room."

And wouldn't Jack love that.

But River didn't have any time to question what had happened to the Buchanans. As soon as Georgie left, Lurch grabbed him by the bottom of his shirt and pulled him forward.

"You have to help me, River. I think I peed in one of the kettles last night, but I don't remember which one."

CHAPTER

Thirteen

Georgie found Jack where she'd left him, clutching his pint glass with enough force that it looked liable to crack.

"Well?" he asked with a dark scowl.

"Lurch had something he wanted to discuss in private, so I told River I'd wait out here."

Jack groaned. "I bet he did."

Georgie sat across from him and lowered her voice. "What's that supposed to mean?"

"You know what it means, Georgie. How do we know that River and Lurch aren't making plans to sabotage us? After last night, we know that beer is River's life. Beau gave him his start. This place is nostalgic for him, and he obviously has more fond memories with the old guy than you do."

While Jack had absolutely none.

All of that might be true, but it didn't mean River was out to get them. "We spent several hours with him last night," Georgie argued gently, "and granted, we were drinking, but River didn't strike me as the kind of guy who would use subterfuge to get what he wants." She leaned closer. "Not to mention that I doubt he even knows the terms of Grandpa Beau's will. Before *or* after."

"We can't count on that. We need to find someone else for the job."

She was surprised at the shiver of fear that sent through her blood, not only for the business, but for her. She wanted to see him every day, even if they couldn't have a romantic relationship. They could still be friends…well, as friendly as a boss and her employee could be. "We can't do that, Jack. We *need* him."

"What if he finds out?"

"All the more reason to tell him!" she whisper-shouted.

This had been the root of their argument on their walk to the brewery. Georgie wanted to tell River so there wouldn't be any secrets. She figured it would be better to put it all out in the open. But Jack was vehemently opposed to it.

Normally, Georgie might have agreed with her half-brother. His arguments were sensible, but she had a good sense of people, and she couldn't believe River would act so duplicitously. "There's not a vindictive bone in his body. I think he'd be touched to know that Beau had considered him."

"Or pissed that Beau had planned to give it to him until you showed up a month ago." Jack took a breath and glanced out the window to the empty courtyard, and when he turned back to her, his face had softened. "Georgie, I actually think you're right about some of it and wrong about the rest. I think River is a good guy—a *great* guy. But if we go through with hiring him, which I'm still not convinced we should, we absolutely can't tell him. Even a saint would have second thoughts about saving this place if *not* saving it means he gets to keep it."

Georgie started to protest, then stopped to reconsider. Her gut told her that River could be trusted, but it was a tough call. She couldn't let her personal feelings get in the way. "If we don't keep him, then what do you propose we do? River said that Beau came up with all the best recipes for Buchanan, not Lurch. Lurch quit anyway, and even if he hadn't, this whole mess would have twisted our arms. We'll have to hire someone, and I have no idea who we'd go to next."

Jack leaned closer. "River can't be the only brewmaster around."

"I'm sure he's not," Georgie admitted, "but he's available. And he's won awards." Hadn't she spent half an hour before bed researching him on her phone? She'd been tipsy enough that her predictive text function had been wildly off-kilter. River had somehow been corrected to "ride her," which had made her blush, even alone in her room. Shaking the memory off, she placed her hand on the table. "Jack, let's not forget that we'll lose the brewery if we don't come in fifth or higher at Brewfest. We can't just hire any brewmaster, we have to hire a *great* one."

Sitting up, Jack tilted his head slightly. "Don't you find it odd that River lost his job the very day of Beau's funeral?" His gaze leveled with Georgie's. "The day River found out he didn't get it."

"There wasn't a single ounce of bitterness in him last night," Georgie said. "He didn't know about the provision. I'm sure of it."

Jack pursed his lips. "We need to call his former employer."

"What?"

"If we're hiring him, then we should talk to his former employer and get a reference." When she didn't respond, he cajoled, "Come on, Georgie. You're the experienced businesswoman. Why aren't you thinking about this stuff?"

He was right. And normally she would have, but she was letting her feelings for River cloud her judgment. Again.

"We'll call him together," she said, getting to her feet. "Come on. Let's go outside and I'll put him on speaker."

She headed for the door and didn't stop until she was partially down the street, Jack trailing her like a puppy. She'd already pulled out her phone, looked up River's former employer, and placed the call.

"Big Catch Brewing," a woman said in a friendly voice.

Georgie stood next to the side of the brick building and put the phone on speaker, holding it up between her and Jack so he could hear. "I'd like to speak to Finn, please."

If River had told her Finn's last name, she'd forgotten it. In hindsight, she should have looked it up. She should have done more homework *period*, but it was too late now.

There was a moment's pause. "May I ask who's calling?"

She could lie, but the direct approach had always worked best for her, one more reason she wanted to be upfront with River. "Georgie Buchanan. It's in regard to River Reeves."

The woman gasped, then said in a shaky voice, "One moment, Ms. Buchanan."

An elevator music rendition of "Another One Bites the Dust" filled the air.

"She knows who you are," Jack murmured. "I'm not sure if that's good or bad."

"It means the brewing community in Asheville is small...or Big Catch has already caught wind that River's going to be working for us."

The music ended mid-chorus, interrupted by a friendly male voice. "Ms. Buchanan, this is Finn Hamilton. I have to say I'm surprised to hear from you so soon."

She was surprised he'd expected to hear from her at all. "Pleasantly surprised, I hope," she said with a little laugh. "And please, call me Georgie."

Jack's expression was grim.

"It's just that most employers get references for employees *before* they make an offer, Georgie." He sounded perfectly reasonable, but she caught the slight bite in his words.

"This is just a formality," she said, still keeping her upbeat tone. "Dotting all the I's for HR."

He laughed. "Last I heard, Beau didn't believe in HR departments. He let Dottie handle anything employee-related."

After meeting Josie and seeing Lurch, that explained so much.

"Welllll…" Georgie said in a slow drawl, "that will probably change after we get everything settled, so, you know, formalities."

"What do you want to know?" Finn asked. He sounded friendly but guarded.

"Finn, this is Jack Durand," Jack said in a direct tone, giving Georgie a look of challenge. "One of the Buchanan siblings."

Finn chuckled. "Dottie said there was a bit of drama at the will reading, and from the sound of it, your mere existence was one of them."

Dottie was friends with Finn? She wasn't sure why she was surprised. Finn was River's friend, and he was close to his aunt.

Jack made a face that suggested he was about to go off on the man, but instead he asked, "How long has River worked for you?"

Finn chuckled again. "We've been friends for about five years now, and business partners for one day less than that."

"Partners?" Georgie said before she could stop herself. "River said you sold Big Catch Brewing and told him after the fact. That doesn't make it sound like you were partners."

Finn was quiet for a moment. "Okay, you have me there, but truth be told, Big Catch wouldn't be what it is without River." He paused, then said under his breath, "Damn, I really screwed that one up."

Jack's eyes widened as he caught Georgie's gaze.

"If you want a reference," Finn said, sounding resigned, "here you go—if you're looking for a man dedicated to the craft of making beer, River's your man. And if you're looking for a loyal friend, he's your guy too. The man's only fault is his idealism, which some would say is one of his best traits. The only reason he left was because I screwed up and left him out of the loop. He wasn't fired and Bev Corp wanted him as part of the package. You'll be damn lucky to have him." Then he hung up.

Georgie lowered the phone. "River didn't know anything about the will."

Frowning, Jack said grudgingly, "Agreed."

"Jack, we *have* to keep him."

Jack gave her a long look. "Okay, but only if we don't tell him about the will."

Georgie hated to keep it from him, but she had to wonder if River would see Beau's decision as a betrayal. Maybe it would be too much for him to handle after what had happened with Finn. Besides, if they failed, he'd get the brewery anyway, and while she suspected River would never give less than 110%, this way he'd never have to ask himself if he'd subconsciously held back. Keeping it from him was for the best. For them, and for him.

"Fine," she said, "but let's get back in there and see what needs to be done. We've got a hell of a mess to clean up." She didn't just mean the bubbles. Everything pointed to Buchanan Brewery being more than she'd bargained for, both in terms of commitment and money.

As they headed back to the door, Georgie asked, "You said you could move within a month or so, right?"

"Six weeks at the most. Is the offer still good to stay at Beau's house?"

"Of course, it's your house too. There are four bedrooms. Plenty of room for both of us." But she couldn't help thinking that meant an awful lot of togetherness for two virtual strangers. Then she moved on to the uncomfortable question, one she had to ask even if she already suspected the answer. "Do you have any money to help finance bringing the brewery up to speed?"

His face paled. "Georgie…"

That was a fat no. Which meant it was going to be up to her. She had the money, but this whole thing was starting to scare the crap out of her.

You have River.

He had the knowledge and talent to create award-winning beers, the kind of brews that would bring in tourists and locals. That restaurants and bars would want on tap. They could do this. Together. The three of them. Yet it wasn't lost on her that she and Jack were the most replaceable parts of the equation. River was the essential part.

Which made her feel even guiltier about keeping their secret.

They found River in the tasting room. She found herself reaching up to brush back her hair. River made her feel nervous and scared and excited and hopeful for the future all at the same time. She just had to keep in mind that any future with him was strictly business.

She gave him a warm smile, hoping Jack treated him better after talking to Finn. But River wasn't returning her smile. In fact, he didn't look happy at all.

"Georgie. Jack." He took a deep breath, then said five words that brought fear to her heart. "We have a major problem."

CHAPTER
fourteen

"He *what?*"

Georgie, quite rightfully, had a look of horror on her face. A quick glance at Jack revealed he looked pissed again—whatever brother-sister pep talk they'd had outside had already been forgotten—and not a little suspicious. Like maybe he thought River had given Lurch a boost up that ladder.

Stupidly enough, the *how* of it had been River's first question to Lurch.

"How the hell did you get up there if you were drunk enough to douse this place with bubbles?" he'd asked.

Lurch had just shrugged, the movement dislodging one of the bubbles on his scalp, and said, "Where there's a will, there's a way." A pause, then he'd added, "And I was drunk enough to think the bubbles would catch me if I fell."

Then he'd leaned over and vomited, giving them something else to clean up.

Jack shot Georgie a look—lots of silent conversations going on here—and said, "I'd like to talk to Lurch." His fierce gaze shifted back to River. "*Alone.*"

Part of River wanted to say *be my guest*. Lurch deserved it, didn't he? The man had pissed in a kettle of beer, which was beyond a cardinal sin for a brewmaster, and worse, he didn't know which one it had been.

For all they knew, it had only been the fever dream of a very drunk old man. But it didn't matter. If the Buchanans were any kind of honest, this meant they had to throw out the contents of every single kettle.

Georgie's panicked expression said she knew it.

"I told him to leave out the back," River said. "He's in no shape to talk. But I suggested he come by Monday morning to apologize. Just fair warning that morning to him is noon, earliest."

"Of course it is," Jack muttered, rubbing his brow. "What kind of sideshow is this?"

"The Cesspool of Sin," River said with a grin, shifting his gaze to Georgie. Her eyes had a faraway look, like her mind was hard at work, reaching for a solution. Or maybe trying to figure out a way to rewind the last hour so she could tear up those papers instead of signing them. "Or so some politician called us. We wear it as a badge of pride." His grin slipped. "Look, you might want to go easy on him."

"Go easy?" Jack said, raising his voice. "And why the hell would we do that?" The accusation in his tone was obvious. He leveled a glance at Georgie, cutting River out, and said, "We should take legal action against that idiot."

Georgie's mouth firmed like she was considering it.

River understood the sentiment. Here Jack had probably thought he'd hit the jackpot—and now someone had literally pissed in it. And he didn't need Georgie to tell him that this wasn't the kind of ship she usually ran. Didn't matter. He couldn't let that happen.

"Look," he said, keeping his tone flat and calm. "You could do that. You'd be well within your rights. But consider this—you're two outsiders taking over a local brewery. Lurch is part of this town. He might be an idiot half the time"—at least three-fourths, he mentally corrected—"but he knows basically everyone who lives here, and most of them actually like him. Your grandfather certainly did, and it wasn't for his brewing skills. Besides which, he doesn't have much money, so you'd be paying through the nose to make a point. Do you really want to start out here like that?"

Georgie laughed, but this wasn't her natural laugh from last night—this one held a razor's edge of panic. "I'm starting to think I don't want to start out here at all."

"Hey," he said, meeting her eyes, "I get that. This"—he gestured back to the brewery—"isn't exactly a great impression. But we can come back from it. Think of it as a clean slate."

"I'm listening," Jack said, catching River off guard. He'd been looking into Georgie's eyes still, and he'd somewhat forgotten Jack was there.

"Everyone thinks Buchanan's flatlined, right?" River said, forcing himself to look back and forth between them. "That the creativity's gone? Well, here's our chance to make it new. Now. I suggest we make a couple of the flagship brews, the classics, but the rest should all be new. Why wait?" He paused, then added, "Of course, we should definitely wait for everything to be professionally cleaned. Maybe twice." This he added with a hint of a smile for Georgie's sake.

Georgie didn't smile back, but she reached for him, something that made his heart race in his chest before she realized what she was doing and let her hand drop. Her cheeks pinkened a little. "Will we have to close for a while?

What are we supposed to do if there's no beer to sell? Or to bottle?"

"There's got to be a reserve," River said. "Enough to last us for a while. Probably a couple of weeks. Maybe more. But any beer we brew now won't be ready in time to fill the gap. So, yeah, we might have to close for a while."

Georgie's mouth pressed into a worried line, and he wanted nothing more than to span that gap between them and take her hand. To comfort her the way he wanted to. Instead, he forced himself to shift his gaze back to Jack. "Did you hold any events at that bar you manage?"

"Sure," he said, caught off guard. He hadn't been expecting that. "St. Patrick's Day in Chicago is a pretty big deal." His mouth twitched with a hint of humor. "The fact that I'm still alive should count for something."

A glint entered Georgie's eyes, and she tilted her head to look at River. "You think we should do a grand reopening."

"Look at you," he said with a grin. "You've only known my aunt for one day, and you're already reading minds. Must be that pink crystal."

"This'll take a lot of planning," Georgie said, but she didn't sound so dejected anymore. She sounded like she was actually looking forward to it.

And so was he—because he'd get to plan it with her. She probably had a special pen she used for planning launches and the like. And if she didn't, maybe he'd get one for her.

"I've got to hand it to you," Jack said, shaking his head. "It's a great idea. Five minutes ago, I didn't know if we'd be able to turn this around. But this might just do it. This place needs a total reset." His glance darted to Georgie, as if silently asking her opinion, and she gave a small nod. That was good—it meant they were forming a mutual respect, something they'd need for a successful partnership. He had a feeling he'd have a harder time winning Jack's trust.

Jack's phone rang, and he pulled it out to look at the caller ID. A pained look crossed his face, and he nodded to them. "I've got to take this."

Then he was gone, and it was just Georgie and River in the empty tasting room.

He nodded to the table they'd abandoned earlier. "I think it's about time for that water, don't you? Everyone needs water."

She laughed, and this *was* the laugh from the night before, which felt like a victory. "You're right about that. They say up to sixty percent of the body is water."

"Except for Lurch," he said as he followed her back to the table. "It sounds like he was at least twenty percent beer last night."

She shook her head as they reached the table. "I still can't believe he did that."

Because she'd run a professional outfit, and truth be told, Aunt Dottie had influenced Beau in a lot of ways these last years.

She sat down, and River sat opposite her.

"Lurch was nice earlier, but I guess he must really hate us," she said. "Will a lot of people feel that way? Like we're outsiders prying this place away from Beau?"

"Maybe some of them. There are foolish people everywhere, no escaping that," he said. And because he really was his aunt's nephew, he poured her a glass of water and slid it over. "But I think you, Georgie Buchanan, are the best thing to ever happen to this place. And so did Beau. That's why he left it to you. He knew you'd be the one to turn this ship around."

Her lips parted slightly, and a little smile tugged at her lips, but the next moment it was gone, and she was looking down.

"Thank you. For everything. I don't know what we would have done without you. Or maybe I do." She bit her lower lip, drawing his attention to it. He'd come so close to kissing those lips last night—just like he wished he could now. He shifted forward a little, drawn toward her despite himself. "I probably would have let my brother and sister convince me to sell. Jack would have wanted to keep it, but I don't know how he would have managed on his own. And I would have gone on knowing about my brother but not knowing him. So thank you."

"You don't need to thank me, Georgie," he said softly, letting himself put his hand next to hers on the table but stopping short of taking her hand. "You did this all on your own, but if I can guide you in any way, it would be my pleasure." He lifted an eyebrow. "And I suppose it'll also be my job."

He thought again of the way Georgie and Jack had acted before the whole bubble extravaganza. Jack had been strangely accusatory even before everything had fallen apart.

"That is, of course, if the offer is still on the table."

She'd been sipping the water, and she snorted a little, choking on it. He was about to get up to pound her back, but she finally did take his hand, stopping him. A zip of awareness shot through him, much stronger than it should have been from such an innocent touch.

"I'm okay," she said through coughs. "I was only laughing because not even five minutes ago I was thinking you were the irreplaceable one in this equation, not Jack and not me. We're lucky you want to work with us." Her lips pursed in a worried look. "From what I can tell, Beau was paying Lurch a lot less than the average salary for a brewmaster."

"Don't you worry about it," he said, feeling the heat of her small hand over his. She must have noticed too, because a horrified look filled her eyes and she snatched it back so fast she toppled the water pitcher, the water splashing all over his shirt and lap.

"Oh no! I'm so sorry, River!"

"It's okay," he said. And because he wanted her to erase words like "replaceable" from the vocabulary she used about herself, and he still couldn't shake the feeling of her hand, he found himself saying, "A little beer on my shirt yesterday, a little water today. It's almost like you want me to take my shirt off."

Her cheeks went bright pink at that, and she stopped what she was doing, feverishly grabbing napkins from the holder in the middle of the picnic table. His shirt was soaked through, and those napkins would do nothing to help. The downward glance she gave her hands told him she knew it.

"I'm just teasing," he said softly. "But I think I will grab some of the merchandise, if you don't mind." He nodded to the counter of the bar, where a few of the brewery T-shirts were on display, and headed over to grab his size. The only design left was one Aunt Dottie had put together last year. *Do it the Buchanan Way!* it said. The image was of a beer can in the center of a starburst, which he'd always thought made it look like it had just exploded. Maybe not so inspiring.

He pulled off his shirt to change into the fresh one, which was, of course, when Jack came back in.

He did a double take—which, fair enough, River had just taken off his shirt during what had to be one of the strangest business meetings of all time. "I'm gone five minutes, and now River has his shirt off."

"Little accident with the water," River said, nodding to the table. He was about to pull on the brewery shirt, but his gaze shot to Georgie. She'd taken a seat again, but her eyes were fixed on his chest, and the heat in them shot straight below his belt. Well, shit, he'd better get sitting again.

He pulled on the shirt and returned to the table, but instead of sitting opposite Georgie, he sat next to her, telling himself he could use the water as an excuse. She didn't move away.

Jack sat opposite them, avoiding the water spot.

"I think we might need to design new shirts too," Jack said wryly.

"Too bad Adalia's not much interested in the business," Georgie said. "She's an amazing artist."

"Oh?" Jack said, tipping his head. There was genuine interest in his voice, and River could tell that Jack had spent time thinking about his sisters and brother, wondering what they'd be like. He put on a tough front, but he wanted to know his family, that much was clear.

"Maybe she'll change her mind if it's something that interests her," River suggested. And having a joint project could help draw the siblings together to do something other than argue.

Although what did he know? Maisie was the closest thing he had to a sister, and he'd met her for the first time when he was thirteen.

"I hope you're right," Georgie said, turning to him with a smile. "I'll talk to her." Happiness shone in her eyes, and he was grateful to have put it there. It had seemed impossible just a half hour ago.

"Good plan," Jack said. Some emotion passed through his eyes, but River couldn't pin it. "Georgie, something's come up in Chicago. I wanted to stay in Asheville for at least a few days longer so we could get things moving, but I have to go back immediately."

Based on what little he was saying, it was obvious it was personal—and even more so that he wasn't going to tell them who'd called or what was said.

"I hope everything's okay," Georgie said after a moment of silence, and River could hear a hint of hurt in her voice.

Jack ran a hand through his hair. "It's not," he said bluntly. "But it will be. I'd rather not think about it, though, and I'm even less in the mood to talk about it, if that's okay. But we can figure some things out over the phone and email while I'm away. I still plan on being back in about a month. Plenty of time to plan for the reopening."

River admired him for being direct—too many people would have lied and given the all clear. At least he hadn't blown her off. That was something.

"Sounds good," Georgie said. Another pause. "But I'm here to listen if you ever *do* want to talk."

Jack just nodded, but he seemed almost embarrassed.

Since one of the new owners was about to leave the state, River figured it was as good a time as any to talk direction for the brewery.

"We'll probably need to move forward with putting together our first beer list, Jack," he said. "Any ideas you wanted to add? I was thinking we'd make some changes seasonally. So we might want to focus on fall right out the gate."

"Actually, I was thinking about this last night," Jack said, his tone brightening. "Before I was a manager, I spent years making drinks. What do you say we do a line of beers inspired by classic cocktails?"

"That's a great idea!" Georgie said, catching his excitement, and River could tell it was a mix of genuine appreciation for the idea and her desire to bolster her brother. She turned a little to River as if to say, *Is it?*

"It is," River said. "We can have one or two specials a season." He told them a little about his own thoughts—the beers that had worked best at Big Catch, which he could mimic without copying, plus a couple of more experimental ones he wanted to try. Some of the barrel-aged ones would take months.

Jack's phone made a buzzing noise, and he flinched. "My car's here," he said. Georgie's eyes rounded with surprise, and she shot another look at River. Whatever that phone call had been about, it had lit a fire under Jack, enough so that he'd summoned a car immediately.

They all got up, and River shook Jack's hand. Georgie and Jack had an awkward moment where she went in for a hug, and he tried for a handshake.

"I'll be in touch soon," he said, and then he left. Georgie's gaze followed him as if he were a puppy running off and she wondered if he'd ever find his way home. Once the last of him disappeared from view, she turned to River.

"So what now?" she said. "What needs to happen first?"

A slow grin stole over his face. "Let's hire some cleaners. Then it's time for you to make your first batch of beer."

CHAPTER
fifteen

"This is it," River said as he put his key into the lock of his heavy wooden front door. He looked relieved when the lock turned. "Well, at least I know that Aunt Dottie won't be here waiting to ambush us."

"What?" Georgie asked, wondering if she'd heard him wrong.

They'd called an outside cleaning crew to come clean up the bubbles and empty and sanitize the tanks. Georgie hadn't had the stomach to stay and watch, but Aunt Dottie, who had shown up in response to a call from Josie, had insisted on supervising the cleaning. She'd assured Georgie that everything would be okay—Mercury was rising and the stars were aligned for a change. Georgie was nervous about leaving the task to the older woman, especially since she'd shown up with her pink sea salt lamps and started some chants to disperse bad energy with a sage stick. But River had assured her that while his aunt had some odd beliefs, she was a stickler for cleanliness. They would be better served working on their new brews.

Now, standing in front of his front door, he gave her a wry grin that held a playful look. "Nothing. Go on in."

He pushed the door open, and she took a hesitant step over the threshold, surprised at the smell of fresh bread, but then she recognized it from Beau's house and realized it was the smell of brewing beer. She was surprised, and more than a little bit pleased, to discover that she liked it. She associated it with River now.

Her gaze wandered around the open living room and dining area, curious about River's home. You could tell so much about a person from their personal space, and she was relieved to see that River's loft was warm and homey...and littered with shredded toilet paper and pillow stuffing.

"Oh shit," River said, coming up short behind her.

She was about to ask him if he had a rat infestation when a tiny bundle of fur came bounding out of the kitchen and slammed into River's feet. He bent down and scooped up the furball, holding the cutest puppy she had ever seen up in front of his face.

With a mock scowl, he said, "Hops, how did you get out of your kennel?"

She laughed. "I didn't know you had a puppy." But then she felt foolish. How would she have known he had a puppy? She barely knew him, yet for some reason, she felt like it would have come up in conversation during their multiple discussions about Jezebel the night before.

A grin lit up his eyes. Had she ever met a man with more expressive eyes? His were always so full of humor and kindness, even at the brewery today when everything had gone to hell. But she shouldn't notice things like that. Especially given their professional relationship. She told herself that good bosses made sure their employees were happy, but she knew that was a stretch.

No good boss made her employee happy the way she wanted to make him happy.

Boy, was she in trouble.

"I didn't until this morning." River balanced the fluffball's belly on his palm and turned the puppy to face her. "Georgie, meet Hops; Hops, this is Georgie." The puppy's feet began to paddle as though it were swimming. River laughed and held the puppy close to his chest. "Hops is a foster. Maisie caught me at a weak moment this morning and twisted my arm into taking him." But as Georgie watched him rub the puppy's head, she wondered how much arm twisting had really been involved.

"And you named him Hops?" She couldn't help grinning. Somehow it fit.

His gaze darted to the puppy's head, and he looked slightly embarrassed. "It's kind of a tribute to Beau."

Guilt nipped at her momentary happiness. It felt like she was stealing River's inheritance. Still, she'd made a promise to Jack, and that was important to her too. She didn't want to break her word to him, particularly not when things were still so fragile between them.

"Hey," he said, misinterpreting her sudden somberness. "I didn't mean to upset you about Beau. After this afternoon..." He grimaced, then gave her an earnest look. "It's going to be okay, Georgie. I won't let you fail. I promise."

His words and his tone, so earnest, brought tears to her eyes. How could she keep this from him? "Um...can I use your bathroom?"

"Of course," he said, worry crinkling the bridge of his nose. "But I'm concerned about what you'll find there. If he pulverized all of the toilet paper, there's some under the sink. I'm going to take him out anyway, so that will give you a moment to yourself." River grabbed a leash off the kitchen table and headed out the front door, the puppy still cradled in his strong arms.

Like she wanted to be.

Don't be a fool, Georgie. She went to the restroom, smiling a little as she changed out the toilet paper, and when she washed her hands, she stared at her reflection in the mirror. If she could see the guilt in her eyes, would he?

When she returned to the living room area, River still hadn't come in, so she took a moment to survey the space. He definitely couldn't be accused of buying his pieces from a furniture showroom floor, but while his furniture was obviously older, each piece looked well-worn and loved. He was a man who found value in things others might discard, and she sensed he had a deep loyalty to those he cared about. More guilt washed over her.

She needed to get a handle on that or she'd never make it to the Brewfest Competition next March.

Torn, she ran her hand over a cracked leather side chair, letting herself think about River sitting there, reading one of the books from the case. Multiple photos lined the fireplace mantel—Dottie and Beau with a mountain view behind them. River with a man around his age, both beaming. They stood in front of a banner that said Brewfest Competition, and River was holding a blue ribbon. An older photo of a beautiful woman with long blond hair and River's eyes, only hers looked troubled, taken in what appeared to be a jungle. But it was a photo of River with a cute woman with curly red hair that triggered an unexpected surge of jealousy.

Georgie was falling for him, something she could *not* do. Coming here had been a bad idea.

The living room and dining area were strewn with the puppy's mess, so she started picking up the ripped tissue and fluffy batting. She had a good portion of it scooped up when the door opened.

"Georgie, you don't have to do that," River said apologetically as Hops trotted in next to him on the leash. They were a funny sight—the six-foot-tall River walking a puppy who was all of nine inches tall. He looked all kinds of adorable…and the puppy was cute too.

"I was just standing around," she said, giving him a nervous smile and a shrug, her hand full of stuffing and damp toilet paper. "Figured I might as well help."

River squatted next to Hops and unhooked the leash. The puppy bolted for Georgie and zeroed in on the bow on her right shoe.

"Apparently he has a thing for shoes," River said with a chuckle.

Georgie picked him up with her free hand and giggled when he nibbled on her fingers.

River quickly took the trash she'd picked up and then cleaned up the rest and dumped it. After he examined the carrier, he declared it defective and murmured something about Maisie setting him up. Georgie wasn't sure if he was teasing or not, but he seemed good-natured about it, so she supposed it didn't matter.

She loved that about him. He'd found the place a mess, and instead of blowing up or getting frustrated, he'd taken it in stride. She could only imagine the reaction her father or brother would have had. Or even her past two boyfriends.

Turned out all of the men in her life had perpetual sticks up their asses. Maybe Asheville had more men like River. Only when she thought about dating men other than River, a heaviness settled on her chest. An overall wrongness.

That wasn't good.

"So," she said, stroking the puppy. "About making beer. You're gonna teach me?"

"Sure am," he said, washing his hands at the kitchen sink. "How about we head back to my office, and I'll start gathering what we need to make our first batch."

His office? That had her intrigued, but for some reason, it also made her think of Jack. Maybe because Lee had found out about him in their father's office.

What had that phone call been about, anyway? It was none of her business, but it had her worried. What did she really know about him other than that he was a bar manager in Chicago and half of his DNA belonged to her father, which wasn't exactly a positive tick in the character column? Still, she'd gotten the impression he was fairly trustworthy, albeit slightly intense. She'd only just met him the day before, but it was obvious something had upset him. She wasn't surprised he hadn't opened up to her. He barely knew her, and on top of that she was a full-fledged Buchanan kid. He probably resented the hell out of her.

"I keep wondering about Jack's phone call," she said as she followed River through the door across from the bathroom. When he'd called it his office, she'd imagined a desk with a computer, but instead she found a futon pushed against a wall with a window and a wall of shelving on the opposite side. The wooden shelves were lined with bottles and tubing, and all sorts of equipment that looked like it belonged in a laboratory instead of a spare bedroom, as well as multiple containers of grains and pellets, all neatly labeled.

"I'm sure he's okay," River said, his eyes focused on her. Hops made a little sound as if in agreement, or maybe support.

The tension in her shoulders eased at the tenderness in River's voice, and she made herself take a mental step back.

A romantic entanglement with him was a very bad idea, professional reasons aside. He was the person who inherited the brewery if it failed. It was hard enough to keep that secret without the added guilt that would come with dating him.

"Yeah," she said, breaking eye contact. She gestured to the shelving with her free hand. "This looks like serious business."

"I suppose it is," he said as he stood next to her. "Like I said, I made most of my test brews at Big Catch, but it wasn't uncommon for me to work on some here. Blue Whale was created in my kitchen, and it's one of our biggest sellers." His smile dimmed some. "I guess it's not *ours* anymore." Then he seemed to shake it off. "Since *we'll* be working on an autumn line, we'll need to incorporate flavors associated with the season. What comes to mind?" he asked, grabbing a giant pot from the shelf.

"Pumpkin. Apples."

He nodded in approval. "We could make a hard apple cider. Beau never branched outside of beer, so if you're looking to freshen up the brand, a limited fall cider might be good to throw into the mix."

She liked the sound of that. "Yeah. That sounds great."

"We can start on something basic. Maybe an East Coast IPA? Beau's never had one on his menu. IPAs are usually more hop-heavy, so it might seem fitting given our new friend here." Grinning, he shot a glance at the puffball still cradled in her arms. "But the hops make IPAs bitter. Given your scorecard I think you'd like an East Coast IPA. They're fruity and have a slight kick of bitterness at the end. They use less hops and rely on yeast for a good portion of their flavor."

"Yeah, sure," she said, nodding her head. "You're the genius, River. You do whatever you think is best."

"We'll work on it together," he said cheerfully as he opened a double closet door and revealed multiple glass carboys on shelves, a couple of which were filled with dark brown liquid. "We'll focus on a few varieties of malt I know work well together, and then we'll play with variations of hops. We'll finish it off with a British yeast."

"Okay."

She set the puppy down and helped him carry all their equipment and containers of grain into the kitchen. First River told her the importance of sanitizing every part they would use, starting with the stockpot. Next he weighed the grains on a scale and put them into a cheesecloth bag, then measured out multiple pellets and put them into small glass bowls, explaining why he chose those specific blends and amounts to create a subtle play of flavors. "I went a little heavier on dry hops with Big Catch's East Coast IPA, but if we tweak it enough, hopefully it will be different enough to be distinctive. I hope it'll be even better. But we'll try several different versions so we can see which one we like best."

"It's like black magic," she said in awe.

"More like years and years of experience. I've made literally hundreds of batches. Some more successful than others." He laughed. "When I was a kid, Beau always encouraged me to experiment. He let me have free rein, even when he knew the outcome in advance. He was always a firm believer in learning from experience."

Was that what Beau had intended? For River to gain experience running the brewery for a year, then gain financial control? But Beau could have had no way of knowing she'd hire River as their brewmaster. That part was pure coincidence. Still, while Georgie hadn't gotten a decent look at the pots and equipment, River had said it was going to need updating. The brewery was cash poor, and it would have to be closed for who knew how many months, which meant Georgie would have to use her own money to keep it running. And if they lost the business, her money would be lost too.

But losing the brewery wasn't an option. Georgie was a Buchanan, and Buchanans didn't lose. Ever. She was going to give this her all, and if they survived after the Brewfest Competition, she'd buy Lee and Adalia out so she could offer River a third of the ownership, something that had been lacking in his collaboration with Finn.

Feeling better about her decision, Georgie grabbed her notebook and pen from her purse. "Okay, start from the beginning, because I want to learn *everything*."

His eyes twinkled. "There's that pen again. I've been waiting."

CHAPTER
Sixteen

They'd made three batches of IPA, each with subtle differences to the grain ratio. The first time Georgie had just watched him, the second time she'd helped with the measurements, and the third time he'd let her do it all on her own.

He'd liked watching her work. She'd had a determined look on her face the whole time, a nice change from whatever dark emotions she'd been left with after Jack's disappearing act. She had indeed taken notes while watching him earlier, extensive notes, and she'd referred to them at least a dozen times, a tiny line appearing between her eyebrows.

There was no denying Georgie Buchanan was a force to be reckoned with. Still, she knew how to cut loose when she let herself. He'd told her she could pick the music while she brewed, and straight-faced as could be, she'd turned on a '90s boy band, and proceeded to laugh hysterically at his attempted politeness.

God, he loved seeing her in his apartment, all the more so because she was making beer, his beer. The pull he felt toward her was more powerful than ever. But he wasn't going to push her. She'd had enough people pushing her every which way. He would have denied it until he was blue in the face, but Aunt Dottie had him indoctrinated just enough for him to hope that maybe the pink crystal *had* meant something. If waiting was what it took, he could wait. He *would* wait.

"All right," he said after they poured the water in— okay, so he'd helped with that part—"time for the capping. Feels like there should be a ceremony or something."

She looked up at him with shining eyes, her hair pulled back again to avoid getting anything in the brew.

"It kind of does. I can't believe I made beer. I mean, I know it has to sit for weeks, and then carbonate for weeks, but still. This is pretty awesome."

"Enjoy your drumroll," he said, tapping against the kitchen counter. "It'll have to suffice."

Grinning, she went to cap the carboy. Which was when Hops, who'd been napping in the living room, darted toward them and took a flying leap. He'd aimed himself at Georgie's arms, perhaps hoping she'd cradle him again, but she fumbled catching him, and he ended up falling onto the top of the carboy before she could grab him.

Could the dog fly? He'd never seen such a tiny animal soar so high.

Hops gave a scared yelp, snuggling into Georgie's arms. She'd scooped him up quicker than he would have thought possible.

"Oh no!"

For a second he thought she was lamenting the fate of her beer—which, fair enough, they'd dealt with enough tainted brew for one day—but then she lifted the little dog, examining him carefully for any injuries.

Damn. He really wanted to kiss her.

Instead, he stepped closer and put a hand on her arm.

"It's okay, Georgie. He didn't get hurt. He's just a little scared."

Their eyes met and held, something passing between them, but Hops gave another little yelp and pushed into River's arms. He snuggled the little puppy closer, kissed his head, feeling Georgie's eyes on him, and set him down.

"I never knew a dog could jump that high," she said, sounding a little flustered.

"Me neither," he said with a grin. "He must have some basenji in him."

Hops wagged his tail as if in agreement and proceeded to return to his favorite sandal. Maybe he *had* imprinted on it.

She cocked her head. "What's a basenji?"

"A dog breed known for jumping. I've helped my friend Maisie a lot at her dog shelter. It's given me a somewhat encyclopedic knowledge of dog breeds."

He glanced down at the carboy, and she did the same, groaning a little.

"It's ruined, isn't it? We have no way of knowing if there's any dog hair in there. Maybe I'm cursed when it comes to beer." She set the cap down on the counter, as if resigning herself to the fact that the beer wasn't worth capping. Although he knew she'd said the thing about the curse as a joke, there'd been enough actual defeat in her voice for him to realize part of her meant it.

He leaned toward the counter and started the drumroll again.

"None of that," he said. "The drumroll insists you do the honors. There's no denying the drumroll."

A smile crept back onto her face as she plugged the cap in and set up the tubing.

"But what if there's hair in it?" she persisted.

"Then you and I and probably Jack will be the only ones to ever try it. Either that, or it will prove to be the magic ingredient we want to put in all our beers."

She grinned at that. "In that case, I think I have a name for it."

"Oh yeah?" he asked, taking a step closer, telling himself he was doing it to check on the seal but knowing better.

"I hereby declare this beer Hair of Hops." She laughed, that nice warm laugh of hers, and he joined in.

He let himself touch her arm again but stopped short of leaning in like he wanted to. Like he thought maybe she wanted him to. If—no, when—the time came, he wanted her to meet him halfway. "Now, what do you say we celebrate by eating some of the cinnamon rolls Aunt Dottie left this morning and drinking someone else's beer? We can figure out what ingredients we'll need for the cider and a couple of other experiments."

"We could have been eating cinnamon rolls this whole time?" she asked with a smile. "What were you thinking?"

<hr />

As they sat there scheming over cinnamon rolls and beer, a feeling of contentment rolled over River. It felt right. All of it. The new direction they were discussing, the relaunch of the brand, and...this. Sitting here with Georgie in his home, talking and laughing with her like they'd known each other for their whole lives instead of a couple of days. When he thought of all the time he'd spent not knowing her, he felt almost robbed.

"Hops is humping your sandal again," she said, jarring him from his thoughts.

"Of course he is. When I bring him back to Maisie, he'll miss that sandal more than he misses me."

Her brows knitted together a little, her concentration look. "Are you sure you want to bring him back? He kind of seems like he fits. And we *are* naming a beer after him. Maybe he can be our Buchanan mascot."

He smiled a little, liking the thought of seeing Hops on a T-shirt—it would surely be better than their current selection—but he shook his head. "I'm not sure that's such a good idea, although it hasn't stopped Maisie from trying. She thinks everyone needs a dog, or three. Soul companions, she calls them."

"Have you fostered for her before?"

"No, but I've kept a couple of dogs here overnight in emergencies." He glanced over at Hops and couldn't help but laugh. The little guy was really going at it. "I guess something about this one just clicked."

"You said you helped Maisie at the shelter before. Was that what you were doing before you started at Big Catch?"

It felt a little like cold water had been splashed on him. He didn't like thinking of those days. The Lost Days, he thought of them.

"Sort of," he said. "To be honest, I didn't have much…direction back then. Maisie helped me. She's a good friend. She actually started the shelter from the ground up. Her parents passed away and left her the property and some money. She's always known what she wanted to do."

Unlike him.

"That's pretty amazing," Georgie said. "I wish I could say the same."

He laughed and shoved his beer back a little. "Really? You strike me as the kind of woman who knows what she wants."

His comment hung between them for a moment, heavy with possibilities, and he saw a flash of something in her eyes. Finally, she said, "Wanting something isn't the same thing as going for it. Sometimes you can't." She cleared her throat, her cheeks flushing a little. "You know, my dad had always told us kids he'd finance us if we had a good start-up idea. So after I graduated business school, I spent weeks putting together my proposal for Moon Goddess. I had a whole hour-long presentation planned. Do you know how much of it he listened to before refusing me?"

He reached across the table and put his hand over hers, needing to touch her, to comfort her. "I can tell from the look in your eyes it wasn't long."

Which made him want to pummel the stuck-up asshole for being too blind to see his own daughter.

"Seventy seconds. That's how long he gave me. He said it would never work, that he was ashamed his daughter would ask for help with something like feminine products. He thought it was a disgrace to the family name." She looked at her hand, that little crease appearing between her eyebrows, but she didn't pull away. "He gave Lee a job as soon as he graduated. I was never offered one. I've never had an interest in real estate, but for a while *that* was what I thought I wanted. Or I guess I wanted him to want it. But Georgie Buchanan stopped being his replacement son the second he got a real one."

"Well, you showed him," River said, because she had, and then some. "If Mr. Big Britches was such a good businessman, shouldn't he have recognized a multimillion-dollar opportunity when he saw one?"

"Did I, though?" she asked, looking up to meet his eyes. "I'm not going to lie, River. I wanted him to grovel at my feet. My therapist would probably have something to say about it, but I sent him the article about the sale. He never acknowledged it. Still hasn't. I'm a joke to him, and he treats Adalia even worse. The only reason he ever took any notice of us was because my mother insisted. After she died, we were beneath his notice. And Jack…"

"And Jack was always beneath his notice. It's none of my business, but do you still see your father? I mean, outside of the will reading."

Her expression held not a little bit of bitterness when she nodded. "He summons us sometimes. For family photo ops, that kind of thing, and we usually spend the holidays at the family house. I always tell myself it's just to see my brother and sister, and because my mother would want it that way, but a part of me always hopes it will be different. Even though I'm old enough to know better. I don't know if he's ever talked to Jack at all. As far as I know, he hasn't."

Because she'd told him something private about herself, something he doubted she shared with many people, he found himself wanting to do the same.

"I understand Jack a little. Or at least I think I do. I never knew my father either."

She shifted her hand, and for a moment, he thought she was pulling away, but instead she turned it around and wove her fingers through his. Her grip was firm and assured, and it felt like a lifeline.

"Oh?" she said, giving him the opportunity to talk but not insisting on it.

He squeezed her hand back. "I still don't. I don't know who he was or where he was from, but I suspect he might be Chilean. My mother was traveling through Chile before I was born."

"Is that a picture of your mother on the mantel?" She winced a little after she said it, like she couldn't believe she'd asked him, or maybe she was just mortified that she'd called herself out for snooping.

"Yeah," he said. "I can't seem to get rid of it. Funny, isn't it, how you can still care about someone after they've treated you like you're nothing?"

"No," she said, "it's not funny at all. But you, River Reeves, are not nothing."

And then she leaned across the table and kissed him.

CHAPTER
Seventeen

Georgie hadn't meant to kiss him, but everything had been too perfect. Making beer, River's eagerness to teach her, and his affection for the puppy. The way he'd opened up after she'd spilled her embarrassing truth about her father, something she'd told no one in so much detail. Her head told her that this couldn't happen, but her heart...oh, her heart. Her heart was smitten with him—no, more than that, it was enamored. Those eyes of his seemed to see the real her through the put-together image she tried so hard to maintain—not Georgie Buchanan, businesswoman, but Georgie the woman, who wanted to love and be loved. But it was more than that. Her heart recognized that River was a truly good man—loyal, trustworthy, fun. He had a way of taking a bad situation and making it better. So her heart rebelled, and for the first time in her thirty-three years, she let it take the lead, reason be damned.

Her lips pressed lightly to his—the kiss a question for him to answer. She was technically his boss, and he might think this was as bad of an idea as her head insisted, only he didn't pull away. He leaned closer, only an inch or two as his hand lightly cupped her cheek.

Her body was alive, but the tenderness of his touch, as if she was something precious to treasure, drew her to him like a magnet.

Wrapping a hand around the back of his neck, she tugged him closer and deepened the kiss, and he eagerly accepted the invitation, exploring her mouth with his tongue.

But then her stomach grumbled, and River pulled back with a grin. "It *is* pretty late. We should probably think about something for dinner other than cinnamon rolls."

Damn her stomach. She leaned back in her chair, realizing her hips were sore from leaning into the table. It wasn't very romantic leaning across the kitchen table to kiss him, yet the happiness on River's face made it clear he didn't have a problem with it.

"How about we order pizza?" he asked, already getting up to grab his phone from the kitchen counter.

"Yeah," she said, brushing a strand of hair from her cheek, her head already swooping in for damage control.

"Do you have a preference for toppings?" he asked.

She got up and grimaced as she turned to face him. "Maybe we should just call it a night. It's been a pretty long day."

Disappointment flickered over his face, but it was quickly replaced by understanding. "Of course, Georgie, but you're still staying at the hotel, right? Unless you were planning on getting room service, why don't we move to the sofa and talk or watch Netflix, or whatever you want to do to unwind before the pizza gets here?"

She had to admit that sounded ten times better than being alone at the hotel, but if she stayed…she was worried where that kiss would lead.

When she hesitated, he added, "I don't know if you're having second thoughts about what just happened, but I'm okay with whatever direction you want to take. If you want to pretend that kiss never happened, I won't deny that I'll be disappointed, but I also understand and promise to respect your decision. And if you decide it wasn't a mistake, I want you to know I won't pressure you into anything you're not ready for."

Releasing a sigh, she wondered how he could be so perfect. Her mouth twisted into a playful grin as her resolve weakened. "Surely you have some flaws, River Reeves. You're much too perfect for a mortal man."

He laughed and stepped toward her, close enough that she could feel the heat of his body, yet he didn't reach for her. "So it's my flaws you're after?"

"It might be nice to know there are a few," she said, resisting the urge to lift her hand and run it through his dark hair.

"Okay," he said, shifting his weight and moving a fraction of an inch closer while keeping his eyes on hers. His gaze dipped to her lips, and she stifled the urge to moan. "I squeeze the toothpaste tube in the middle. Um…" He rubbed his chin as his gaze darted to the puppy sleeping on top of the sandal before shifting back to her face. "Sometimes I wait too long to fill up the gas tank in my car."

She chuckled.

"And I'm not a fan of making my bed." He shrugged. "No one ever sees my bed, so what's the point?" Then, as though realizing what he'd said, his cheeks flushed with the tiniest amount of pink.

The urge to reach up and kiss him again was strong, but she resisted as she tried to wear a mock-serious face. "Those all sound like deal breakers to me."

He shrugged, his eyes still playful, but his gaze was fully on her mouth now.

She took a step back. "So, that pizza. Veggie or something with meat?"

"Lady's choice," he said, rubbing a hand over the top of his head. "I can pull up the menu for my favorite pizza place and let you pick."

She shook her head. "Get your favorite. Surprise me."

He started to place the order and she headed to the bathroom. When she emerged, he was picking up the now-awake puppy and heading for the door. "Another bathroom run."

"I can't believe he hasn't made a mess yet," she said.

Grabbing the leash off the table, he said, "Don't jinx it."

After he went outside, she grabbed her phone from the kitchen counter and checked for any missed calls or messages. There were multiple emails she could ignore, but Lee had sent her a text.

Dad's furious with you about the brewery and wants you to present a full business plan within forty-eight hours.

What? Her father didn't own Buchanan Brewery, yet he thought he was going to tell her how to run it? Not a snowball's chance in hell. She could only imagine how he'd react if he found out that the man who would inherit the brewery if she failed was now their brewmaster. And that they were becoming romantically involved.

What was she thinking? Whatever this was that she'd started between them was a terrible, terrible idea. Wasn't it?

She was scowling when River returned, the puppy trotting next to him as big as he pleased. River took one look at her and some of the happiness dimmed from his eyes.

"Is everything okay?" he asked, squatting down to unleash the dog but keeping his gaze on her.

She offered him a weak smile. "Yeah."

"I got a text that the pizza will be here in about ten minutes." He walked toward her, never taking his gaze off her. "Georgie, I know something's wrong. If it's about our kiss…"

She shook her head and held up her phone before lowering it to her side. "Lee texted me. He said Dad expects me to present him with a business proposal within forty-eight hours."

He started to say something, then seemed to think better of it and stopped.

"Go ahead," she said, hating that her father had blighted this too. "Say what you're thinking."

He slowly shook his head as he reached for her upper arms. Holding her gently, bolstering her, he said, "You don't need anyone else giving their opinion about your life. You're a beautiful, intelligent woman, Georgie Buchanan. You don't need me telling you what to do."

She stared up at him, her mouth parted in surprise, and then she smiled, blinking back tears. How many times had she longed for someone to tell her that very thing?

He wrapped his arms around her, pulling her into an embrace, and she was surprised at the rightness of being in his arms. How she seemed to fit perfectly. This man was giving her a glimpse into a life filled with love and respect, but she also knew if her brother or father caught wind that she was seeing River, they'd make her life hell. Actually, *both* of her brothers would flip.

Jack was the nail in the coffin sealing her decision. Things were already shaky between her and Jack, not to mention River and Jack. If Jack found out they had a relationship, she'd lose all of his trust and respect.

Pressing her cheek to his chest, she let herself close her eyes for a moment. If they weren't working together, perhaps it would have been different, but maybe not. She knew from starting Moon Goddess how much time, energy, and effort it took to get a business off the ground. It had killed her relationship at the time. So it probably wouldn't have been fair to start something with River anyway, knowing that their time would be limited, because one thing was for certain—River wasn't the guy you had a fling with. He was the guy you planned a future with.

She leaned back and looked up at him. "We can't do this, River."

He studied her face. "I told you, Georgie. It's your call. I won't pressure you."

"But you don't agree," she said softly, almost hoping he'd try to change her mind.

He hesitated, then said, "What I think is currently irrelevant. What matters is what *you* think. You're the owner of Buchanan Brewery now, or at least one-fourth owner. It's your business, your rules. If you think it would be a conflict of interest for us to start something, I understand."

"I like you, River. I really like you—"

"I know," he said with a sad smile. "And I like you too. But we can still be friends, right? We had fun this afternoon and evening. As friends."

She nodded. Maybe just staying friends would ease this ache in her chest. At least she'd have some part of him. "Yeah. Friends."

He gave her the sweetest smile, and she felt like crying, but she knew this was for the best.

"You have no idea how much I wish…" she whispered. Then she let her heart have its way before she locked it up again. Reaching up on tiptoes, she kissed him again, capturing his face between her hands.

He didn't hold back this time, instead slipping his arm around her back and pulling her flush to his chest. The first kiss had been a kiss of discovery and hope, but this was a kiss of desperation.

River took over, proving she hadn't imagined the chemistry they'd shared. In fact, she'd barely opened the tap. His mouth captured hers, his lips and teeth and tongue setting her body ablaze with a passion she'd never felt before and had only read about in romance novels. He was showing her the tip of the iceberg of what he could offer her, and she wanted more, Buchanan Brewery be damned.

Georgie barely registered the soft click and then the puppy's happy yips before she heard a woman say, "Uh…looks like I came at a bad time."

Georgie tried to jerk free from River's hold, caught by surprise by the redhead in the open doorway. The look on her face was pure jealousy, but she quickly covered it with a smirk as she scooped up Hops.

River froze, holding Georgie even tighter, if that was even possible. "Maisie…I forgot about our plans."

Her eyebrow quirked. "That part's obvious."

"I was teaching Georgie how to make beer," River said, still holding Georgie against him.

Maisie gave him an amused grin. "Funny, I don't remember that step from when *we've* made beer together."

"I…uh…" River fumbled.

Georgie pried his fingers off her hip and took a step back, realizing she should be grateful to Maisie for showing up when she did, otherwise things could have become even more complicated.

"If you have plans, don't worry." Georgie hurried over to the table and picked up her purse and phone. "I was just about to leave."

"But the pizza hasn't arrived yet," River said with a hint of desperation in his voice. "Maisie and I are going to watch the movie version of *Cats*." He grimaced and gave Georgie an apologetic look. "I lost a bet, but you're more than welcome to stay. Isn't that right, Maisie?"

"That's right. I've heard it's a rite of passage everyone has to experience before they turn thirty."

Thirty? Did that mean River was only twenty-nine? He was hardly a child, but the age difference made Georgie feel like her interest in him was even more inappropriate. And that look on his friend's face—he might want Georgie to stay, but it was very clear he was alone in that.

"I'm tired and not very hungry," Georgie said, plastering on a smile, but it felt like it wasn't lined up right. "I'll see you tomorrow, River." She headed straight for the door as Maisie stepped out of the way.

"Georgie!" he called after her.

She stopped at the threshold and turned back to face him. "We'll start fresh tomorrow."

The look of defeat on his face made it clear he understood what she meant. And it nearly broke her.

This is for the best, she told herself. She had too much to lose if she let things develop between them.

But if that was true, why did she feel like she'd already lost?

CHAPTER
Eighteen

"What. The. Actual. Hell?" Maisie said, her usual eloquent self, as soon as the door shut behind Georgie.

But he was still staring at that closed door, trying like hell not to think it was a metaphor for what had just happened between them. Georgie had kissed him. Twice. And somehow he'd still messed it up. Part of him—hell, all of him—wanted to run after her, to insist that they talk about this, but he'd told her it was her call, and it had to stay that way. Even if he'd never, ever felt this way about another woman.

The women in River's life had always drifted in and out of it without much of a production, either from him or from them. A therapist would probably have plenty to say about that, given what his mother had done—Maisie had always said so, at least—but it had felt easier that way. For one thing, it had helped him avoid feeling like this.

"Hello," Maisie said, waving Hops's sandal in his face as the puppy danced about excitedly, "best friend freak-out here. What happened to taking the job and keeping it in your pants?"

He groaned and ran a hand through his hair. "Maisie, as you can see, my pants are very much on."

She gave another wave of the sandal. "I hate to break it to you, but that didn't look like a job interview, unless you were trying out for a position at Skin-a-max."

"And I hate to break it to *you*," he said, forcing a smile, "but Hops has been humping that sandal for half the day."

Her nose scrunched and she dropped it, only for Hops to gleefully hop onto it.

"So you've named him, huh? We'll talk later about how that's the first step toward accepting you've found one of your soul companions. In the meantime, I'd like answers."

He headed to the couch and dropped down into the slightly worn cushions—and couldn't help but think that if things had gone differently, Georgie might have been the one lowering down next to him. Not that he didn't want to spend time with Maisie—it was just different.

Turning toward her, he saw she had on the same fierce look she wore when she went to pick up a trouble dog, the *I'm not giving up* look. That look had saved him as many times as it had harassed him, and so he sighed again and said, "I'm falling for her, Maisie."

He saw worry in her eyes, plus something else he couldn't identify. It reminded him of the way she'd looked at him this morning. Like maybe she thought he was going to fall straight into his Lost Days again. "Look, I know it's not the ideal situation, but I think she might feel the same way."

"Tell me everything," she said.

And so he did, playing up the whole situation with Lurch and Josie for laughs, not that it needed to be embellished. Midway through, the pizza arrived, and they carried slices to the couch on plates so he could continue the story.

"I take it they fired Josie?" she said, laughing so hard her body was bobbing with it. She set her plate down on the coffee table, and it was low enough to the floor that Hops immediately snagged her crust.

"Understandably," he said. "Aunt Dottie talked to her this afternoon. You can give her a call. I'll bet the puppies would like a bubble machine."

"No way," she guffawed, "she took it with her?"

"Nope, but my aunt personally dropped it off at her apartment."

Another round of laughter.

"Oh, you really can't make this stuff up," she said. And wasn't that the truth.

Maisie sobered. "I take it you brought Georgie back here after that fiasco as a mood lifter."

She raised her eyebrows up and down, but something felt forced about it, like maybe she was still worried about him.

"Not like you're thinking," he said, stacking his plate on top of hers. "We really were working most of the afternoon, but there's just something there, you know? I've never felt this kind of connection with a woman before."

She looked away, and for a second she was quiet, almost like she was trying to think of a polite way to say he'd totally blown his biggest career opportunity. He was steeling himself for it, but when she turned back, she said, "Gee, you really know how to make a girl feel important."

"Oh, you know what I mean," he said, nudging her shoulder playfully. "I obviously think the world of you, but you're basically family. It's different."

She was quiet again for a beat, and then she said, "Are you sure you're not doing this to sabotage yourself?"

Ah, there it was.

He took a moment to consider it, because *he* had sabotaged himself before. More than once. But the way he felt with Georgie—it was the opposite of self-destructive. She was one of the most extraordinary people he'd ever met, and yet she didn't make him feel like less of a person for it, or like he had to change to impress her. And even if they could only be friends, he would feel damn privileged to have a friend like her.

Even if he'd spend every minute near her desperately and painfully wanting her.

"No, Maisie," he said at last, "this is real." He paused, then added, "I think you'll like her."

"I'm not so sure about that," she said in a huff, catching him off guard. Her eyes glimmered with something like pique.

"Why's that?" he asked. Surely she hadn't gotten a bad impression from less than thirty seconds of conversation. If this was about the kiss…well, that was his bad. He genuinely had forgotten Maisie was supposed to come over.

She shrugged. "Mostly I'm worried you'll get hurt. What if she fires you over this?" She paused, thinking. "Besides, doesn't it bug you that these people are going to take credit for your work? I mean, from what you said, none of them knows the first thing about beer. Sure, Georgie knows business, but that's not one-size-fits-all. They couldn't do this without you."

He gave her a look. "Didn't you just get done saying she might fire me? Because *she* kissed *me*?"

She made a choked sound. "*She* kissed *you*?"

"Let me guess, does that somehow make it worse?" He was beginning to get a little annoyed. Sure, the situation wasn't ideal—and the fact that Georgie had just left like that made it a whole lot less ideal—but he could use a little support.

"Well, let's just say you might have a good case for sexual harassment."

"Seriously? Maybe we should table this discussion. I can tell we're not going to see things the same way." And wasn't that a twist. They were usually on the same page—and when they weren't, it was almost always River who was in the wrong. "The Buchanans own that brewery—they deserve to call the shots and hire someone who knows how to make beer. I want them to succeed, and I want to be a part of their success. From what you were saying earlier, I thought you had my back. That you realized how important this is for me."

"I do," she said, reaching out and giving his shoulder a squeeze. Warmth leaked back into her eyes. "And I'm happy for you. On both counts. I just don't want to see things go south. Sorry, River. Bad day. One of the puppies yacked all over the place, and Dustin kept ducking out of the office because he thought someone was filming a movie over the way. He was sure he'd seen Zendaya. Turned out to be some kids filming themselves skating, but he spent half the day blogging about it. I'm just tired. Why don't we watch the movie?"

"Yeah, good idea," he said, although the thought of the CG cats made him want to shiver.

They got some more pizza, settled into the couch with Hops tucked between them and started the movie, just like they'd watched a hundred other movies through the years. But their conversation didn't sit well. What did Maisie have against Georgie and her family? She was usually the most accepting person he knew. It didn't seem like her, although he understood what she'd said about having a bad day. That could put anyone in a mood.

About ten minutes in, the horror of what he was watching stole over every other thought and emotion. Hops seemed to agree, because he gave a whimper and stole off to curl up on his sandal. A few minutes later, River looked at Maisie in disbelief.

"Did you know it would be like this?" he asked.

She gave him a look that was a little too serious to be, well, serious. "I think they were robbed at the Oscars."

He threw a pillow at her. "You chose this to punish me."

"No," she said, laughing, "I chose it because it's hilarious. This must be the most unintentionally hilarious movie of all time. Fifty years from now, you'll be telling people where you were when you saw *Cats*."

"You do realize that by forcing me to watch this, you also have to watch it."

"Oh, it's worth it," she said.

And maybe it was, because they spent the next agonizing hour and a half laughing and joking as if nothing had happened between them.

When Maisie left, she gave him a hug. "Sorry again about earlier," she said. "I know I got all weird and mama dog on you."

"No need to apologize," he said, and meant it. "Everyone's entitled to their moods, and their opinions."

"I'll check in about Hops tomorrow."

"Sounds good. Maybe he'd like to see his brothers and sisters again soon."

"Sure, as long as the rest of them don't start yacking. I don't want to leave you with a sick puppy on your hands."

After she left, the apartment felt aggressively empty, even with Hops, and River found himself staring at his phone. Maybe he should text Georgie. Not to pressure her or confront her about anything. He could keep things light, tell her about the movie. Warn her away from it, as it were. It would be an excuse to reach out, and he found he very much wanted one.

He was reaching for the phone when the text alert went off. For a second his spirits lifted, like he was Hops when presented with a bowl full of food, but a quick glance revealed it was Aunt Dottie, not Georgie. Because of course it wasn't Georgie.

He unlocked the phone to see it was a text message, and was taken aback to realize it wasn't just to him—she'd also sent it to Georgie, Jack, and two other numbers.

Please join me at Beau's house on Sunday at 7 p.m. for a séance. I sense Beau has a very important message for you, my dear Buchanans. I'll set up video conferencing for those of you who are unable to join us in person. I fear you'll be unable to partake in the thematic meal I'm preparing, but we'll be sure to show you everything on the video feed. Until then. Namaste, your friend Dottie.

What in the world was she planning now?

CHAPTER
Nineteen

After returning to her hotel on Friday night, Georgie got an alert reminding her to check in for her flight.

Damn it. She'd meant to change the flight to next week, but all of the space in her mind had been occupied with the brewery debacle and River, and she'd completely forgotten. Something that was quite unlike her. But after a few moments' reflection, she decided to fly home after all. She only had a few changes of clothes, and if she was moving to Asheville, she needed more of her personal belongings. Besides, after the way her evening had ended with River, a couple of days away seemed like a good idea. So instead of canceling it, she booked a flight back to Asheville on Sunday afternoon, early enough that she could get a good night's sleep before (hopefully) having a fresh start on Monday.

But when she landed in Boston early Saturday afternoon, she turned her phone on and found a string of texts between her siblings.

Lee: *Does she really expect us to "attend" this thing on Sunday night?*

Adalia: *Relax, Junior. It'll be fun*

Lee: *Victoria and I have dinner reservations at Geoffrey's.*

Adalia: *Of course you do*

Lee: *What's that supposed to mean?*

Adalia: *That you're too pretentious for your own good. Mom would want you to "attend"*

Lee: *That's bullshit and you know it.*

Adalia: *Do I? ...do YOU???*

Adalia: *Georgie, is Jack going to this thing?*

What on earth were they talking about?

She was about to ask them when she scrolled down and saw Dottie's text. She could have sworn it hadn't been there that morning when she'd texted her friend Meredith saying she'd be home for less than twenty-four hours for the last time in who knew how long. Meredith had texted that she and her newest boyfriend had left for Nantucket the night before. She wouldn't be back until late Sunday night, she'd said, but Georgie owed her an explanation on Monday.

There were no texts from Jack, not even in response to Dottie's message. He hadn't tried to contact her since his abrupt departure the day before...had it only been a day? So much had happened since their short-lived tour of the brewery.

She texted back, *No. Jack went back to Chicago to wrap up some personal things so he'll be able to devote his attention to the brewery.* No need to tell them he might be gone for a month or more. She was sure Lee would give her flak for that. Or tell their father.

Thinking about the brewery made her think about River. Why had she gone and ruined everything and kissed him? Twice. Now there was the potential for things to be mega awkward between them, not to mention it could prove to be an HR nightmare. If she had any HR employees. But even though Lee would leap to the possibility of some sort of complaint, she knew it wasn't an issue. River was no liar, and she hadn't made an unwanted pass at him. In fact, his response proved he'd felt no obligation to respond. But respond he had, and in a way she would never forget.

The heat of the kiss filled her again, as powerful as if she'd just left his apartment, that inner fire fanned by the thought of where things might have gone if they hadn't been interrupted by Maisie, making her entire body flush as she flagged down a taxi to take her to her condo.

"You need me to turn down the a/c?" the middle-aged driver asked once she was settled on the back seat with her purse and her overnight bag. "You're looking a little hot."

Getting caught thinking naughty things about River made her flush even more. "Um…no thanks, I'll be fine."

"You sure?" he asked, cocking an eyebrow as he watched her in the rearview mirror. He pulled a small photo from his visor and held it up for her to see the middle-aged woman. "My Nina gets hot flashes all the time, and I'd rather turn the car into an icebox than have you strip off your clothes."

Georgie's mouth dropped open, unsure which part of his statement to take offense at—his supposition that she might be menopausal, something that especially chafed given she'd discovered she was at least three years older than River, or his worry that she'd strip in the back of his car. "I think I'll be able to restrain myself."

"You sure?" he asked again as he pulled away from the curb. "They hit my Nina right out of nowhere, and boom, the next thing you know, she's taking off her clothes. Last weekend at Mass, Nina was walking down the aisle to take Communion when a hot flash hit her. One minute, she's standing there, her head bowed and her hands folded together in silent reflection as she contemplated receiving the Body of Christ, then the next thing you know, she was standing there in her bra and granny panties and fanning herself with the church bulletin. We had a devil of a time trying to explain it to Father Timothy." He shot her a serious look in the mirror. "She had to say six Hail Marys and promise to run bingo for the next six weeks."

"Um..." she stuttered, trying to figure out how to purge the image of Nina stripping in church. Having seen her face made it more difficult. "Sure. Turn it down." The way she'd been behaving recklessly and out of character...perhaps she *would* do something as crazy as take off her clothes.

But River's kiss stayed with her, and she reached her fingers to her lips, savoring the memory. She'd never been kissed like that before. And of course, it had to be the one man who was off-limits.

Of course, she couldn't let it happen again. On Monday morning, she'd take River into her office and apologize, telling him she regretted her behavior. It was unprofessional and the brewery would be in a world of hurt if they went forward with a romance and things ended badly.

When she got back to her apartment, she drowned her sorrows in too much wine, telling herself she was drinking it because she had no idea when she'd be back, and the bottle was too good to go to waste. But she found herself comparing it to the beer flight River had set up at Beau's house...and thinking about the moment he'd almost kissed her that night. She hadn't imagined that, right?

No more thoughts about River. You need to focus on saving that failing business, not finding a boyfriend. Because business always trumped personal, a lesson her father had taught her at an early age.

Despite her copious wine consumption, she managed to pack three suitcases of clothes and personal effects and made arrangements with the management of her condo to have someone drop by her unit to check on it from time to time and notify her if her mail wasn't being forwarded. The building manager had also agreed to hand her car keys over to the transport company she planned to hire on Monday. She'd have to figure out what to do with her condo and her belongings, but Beau's house was fully furnished and she didn't want to put so many things in storage. She'd let it sit for now, and figure it out later.

She took occasional breaks from packing to take a deeper dive into the accounting for the brewery, which was what her sister Adalia would mockingly call a Georgie kind of break. It was not necessarily a good idea given how much she was drinking, but she didn't have to be sober to see the brewery was genuinely in trouble. It wasn't the employees' fault they were closing temporarily, and Georgie didn't want to start from scratch, which meant she'd have to come up with enough cash to pay their salaries, even if at a slightly reduced rate, until they reopened.

Her flight on Sunday was delayed, and she sat next to a screaming baby from Boston to Charlotte, which didn't help her raging hangover headache. Then she was put at the back of the plane to Asheville, next to a toilet that became clogged about five minutes after takeoff.

So by the time she drove her new rental car to Beau's house, she was bordering on cranky and considering another night at the hotel to avoid dealing with Dottie's nuttiness. Only Adalia had texted during her Boston flight that she was really looking forward to the séance and she was 93.4% sure Lee would be there too.

93.4%? Georgie texted in reply on the tarmac at Charlotte.

Don't question it, Georgie. Just trust me. I can't wait for you to taste the specially planned menu and describe it to me

Georgie was so hungry, she was looking forward to it too. Everything Dottie had left in Beau's fridge had been delicious. It was the séance part that worried her.

Her other concern—being alone with Dottie—was quickly overshadowed when she saw River's car parked on the street. There were a bunch of other cars too, but in the short time she'd been in Asheville, she'd learned that parking came at a premium and it wasn't unusual to see cars parked on the street. But it was River's car that had her on edge. Had Dottie invited him too? Once she parked the car in the driveway, she opened the text, and sure enough, River's number was at the end of the list.

After she put on the parking brake, she got out and wrestled all three suitcases out of the trunk. She could wait and ask River for help, but it didn't seem like a good idea—or very fair—to ask him for favors, so she decided to try to carry them to the front porch herself. She backed the two slightly smaller bags together, one pressed against the other, and grabbed the handles in one hand while balancing her overnight bag on top of them, her purse slung over her shoulder. Her other hand maneuvered the bigger suitcase. It might have worked out if the driveway hadn't been on a hill.

She'd made it to the porch steps when her purse slipped around and knocked into the hand holding the two suitcases. Her fingers flexed as pain shot through her knuckles, and the bags broke free, rolling down the driveway. She tried to chase after them, while still holding the other suitcase and overnight bag, but the wheel of the big suitcase caught on a small rock and overturned, sending the bag flying into the yard.

Georgie heard a crash and turned just in time to see one of the smaller suitcases get smashed under the wheel of a large Buick that looked like it came straight out of a '70s police show. The other was nowhere to be seen. At least one of them had made it.

The car tried to back up, but the tire was stuck on the suitcase. It rocked back and forth, trying to work itself free.

"Georgie?" she heard River call out behind her. She was surprised at the panic in his voice. "Are you okay?" he asked as he stopped beside her.

She ignored the flutters in her stomach when she saw him. "I'm okay, but my suitcases..." she cried out in dismay. "I lost two of them. One of them is under that car, but I don't know where the other one is."

"Don't worry, we'll find it," he said. She presumed he was trying to sound reassuring, but he hadn't quite hit the mark. Not that she blamed him. The bag under the tire was nearly completely smashed flat. No coming back from that.

That was the bag holding her cosmetics, her blow drier, and curling iron.

The car's engine revved and the vehicle finally broke free, shooting backward. A loud crashing sound filled the air. The smashed suitcase had been freed, but the car appeared stuck again.

"I think we found your other bag," River said with a grimace, sneaking a glance at her.

They walked down the driveway together, their view of the mess partially obscured by a car in the street, but when they reached the edge of the driveway, Georgie gasped. Underwear and bras were lying on the street, on the parked cars, on the side of the road. A blue bra hung from a tree branch on the side of the road.

Josie got out of the car and stared at the mess with a look of wonder. A breeze kicked in and a silky pair of black panties blew up off the road and hit Josie smack in the face. She peeled it away, beaming as though she'd just won the lottery. "When my horoscope said good fortune would rain on me today, I never suspected it would be underwear."

Georgie stared at her in shocked silence. Every piece of lingerie she owned—other than what she was wearing—was scattered all over Flint Street. In front of River.

"I know this is bad," River said in a calm voice. "I'm sure not everything is ruined."

Josie left her car door open and squealed as she started picking up clothing off the bushes. "It's like an Easter egg hunt!"

Georgie looked up at River. "Josie was invited to the séance."

It wasn't a question since the answer was so obvious.

Hesitation filled his eyes. "Aunt Dottie said she and Lurch had unfinished business with Beau."

"Lurch is here too." She shook her head as her gaze shifted back to Josie, who was looping her arms through Georgie's panties like they were bracelets. "Of course he is."

"Georgie..."

"Is there alcohol at this séance?" she asked. "Because I need lots and lots of alcohol."

River turned to stare at Josie, then back to Georgie. "Well, there's beer, of course, and my aunt's elderberry wine." He hesitated, then added, "And she said she was making punch."

"Punch?"

"Pineapple and orange juice, champagne, and beer." He hesitated again. "Fair warning... Aunt Dottie's calling it Lurch's Pee Brew."

Georgie stared up at him and the absurdity of it all hit her head-on. She began to laugh, breaking out into hysterical giggles that put a stitch in her side.

River watched her first in horror, then in concern, and then finally his mouth twisted into an amused grin.

"I won!" Josie exclaimed, waving both arms—one lined with panties and the other with bras.

Georgie stopped laughing.

River's smile fell. "I'll deal with this, Georgie. You go on inside."

She didn't respond, just headed for the front door, leaving her other suitcase and overnight bag in the yard. They weren't going anywhere...unless Josie decided to plow through the yard with that monster car of hers.

Georgie had no idea what to expect when she walked through the door, but nothing could have prepared her for the sideshow in front of her.

"I need some of Lurch's Pee Brew," she called out on the way to the dining room. "Stat."

CHAPTER
Twenty

It had been no more than forty-eight hours since River had last seen Georgie, but what a forty-eight hours. Since sending him an invitation to the séance, Aunt Dottie had followed up with no less than thirty texts asking him to do various tasks in preparation. A few of them had seemed to have no obvious connection to the event, and he feared the moment when their usefulness would come into clarity. In between brainstorming recipes for the rest of the Buchanan beers, he'd done his aunt's errands, all of them, because even if she was a little, well, dotty, he loved her with all that he was and she was mourning in her own way.

The first and easiest of the tasks had been to set up the video conferencing. Apparently she did not, in fact, know how to do that and had been relying on him to make the arrangements. Maisie had a big flat-screen computer she'd donated to the cause, large enough for all of the Buchanans to take part. Maisie had gotten an invitation too—because apparently his aunt had been feeling pretty free with them—but she'd declined. The way she'd done it, averting her eyes, had made River wonder if it was because of the awkward moment they'd had on Friday night. He'd tried to encourage her to come anyway, but he hadn't tried too hard, truth be known. And not just because she'd agreed to puppysit for Hops to ensure he didn't destroy the entire apartment.

Truth was, he was hoping for a chance to talk to Georgie. Privately. In the midst of what was sure to be a madhouse.

Scratch that, it was already a madhouse. Georgie's plastic suitcases had broken open like piñatas, and some of the sexiest yet classiest lingerie he'd ever seen was strung on Josie's arms.

Good God. Why couldn't he have seen them on Georgie instead?

Although he'd barely had a free minute to breathe all weekend, he'd found himself remembering the feel of her every night.

"It's a sign, River," Josie said confidently once Georgie disappeared inside the house.

"That you need a new car?" he murmured, his eyes lingering on the door. "Any one of us could have told you that."

"No, I mean it's a sign Beau changed his mind." He turned to her in annoyance, and she gave him a serious look through her oversized glasses.

"Is this because they fired you?"

She tilted her chin up, as if to say she wouldn't deign to respond to his question. The gesture drew attention to her hat.

"Are you wearing a witch's hat?" he asked in disbelief. It was mostly a normal size, but it came to a slight point, marked by a sequined star.

"Yes," she said, reaching up to touch it. "Thank you for noticing. But consider this. On Friday, the whole brewery was full of bubbles, and the tanks were contaminated. Today, Georgie's suitcases exploded in front of the house. What does that mean to you?"

He sighed deeply. "Josie, you were directly responsible for two of those things. If it's a sign of anything, it's that the Buchanans should stay away from you."

He reached out for the underwear and bras, and she handed them over with a bit of a pout.

"Just wait," she said, "Dottie knows Beau has something to say, and I think he's going to surprise us all."

God help him.

She made her way to the house, and River headed down to look at the damage, Georgie's panties and bras cradled in his arms.

The bags were both unsalvageable, and one of them was full of goop from what looked like a bunch of burst bottles, but he gathered together what he could from the "Easter egg hunt" and put it in a couple of cardboard boxes he had in his trunk. He stowed the busted bags in the back seat, cleaning up the mess as much as he could with what he had on hand. While he knew Georgie would be staying at the house, he had a feeling she wouldn't want everyone gawking at her things. It wasn't until he finished that he let himself look at one of the silk panties. Printed into the silk was Moon Goddess. Huh, so they made underwear too. Sexy underwear. It was all kinds of hot to think of Georgie wearing panties made by her own company.

His phone vibrated in his pocket, and he dropped the panties like he'd been caught snooping—because he sort of had.

His heart leapt when he saw it was from Georgie.

Forget the suitcases, River. PLEASE come back!

Well, shit. A quick glance at the time told him he'd been gone longer than he'd intended. It was almost seven.

As soon as he walked through the door, he sucked in a breath. He'd been by earlier to set up the computer for the video conferencing, but his aunt hadn't decorated for the party yet. His attention immediately shot to the far wall, which was covered in the oversized sheets of cardboard Aunt Dottie had requested. She'd painted it with the letters of the alphabet, all in caps, aligning each with the unplugged Christmas lights tacked to the wall.

He had to get his aunt to cancel her Netflix subscription.

The big-screen computer sat directly across from it, on a table high enough to ensure the Buchanans had a good view, both of the wall and the horrifying sculpture beside it. Horrifying not because it wasn't artistically sound but because it was a life-size model of Beau—nude. Only his anatomy appeared to be carved from a crystal.

A pink crystal.

His aunt had never told him she was working on that.

The dining room table had been pushed to the side of the room, and on it sat a huge bowl of alarmingly yellow Lurch's Pee Brew, served in a white bowl he'd acquired for Aunt Dottie, which was uncomfortably reminiscent of a toilet. The food she'd prepared was all dark brown or black—"like the earth where he should be at rest" she'd said. His aunt had always been a wonderful cook, but everything other than the brownies looked pretty unappetizing. It didn't help that each dish had been labeled with the name of the type of dirt that had inspired it.

He'd urged his aunt not to use real candles—the last thing they needed was for the house to go up in flames—and she'd reluctantly agreed, but the tea lights he'd picked up were arranged everywhere, adding to the glow of her pink salt lamps. There were at least four of those. He even saw a pink salt night-light in the corner. A big box crowded with crystals had pride of placement on a side table constructed from a repurposed barrel. God, maybe he should talk to Aunt Dottie about seeing a therapist.

He glanced around the room, nodding to a few people he recognized, Tom and Rita and one of Beau's golfing buddies, pretending all of this was normal, until his gaze found Georgie. She had a glass of the yellow punch in her hand while she talked to Lurch, of all people, overlooking the Ouija board arranged on the coffee table. Perhaps Aunt Dottie was hedging her bets by using every spirit communication method on record.

Georgie looked up just then, and when they made eye contact, she mouthed, "Help."

A strangely buoyant feeling rose in him, and he made his way toward them.

"It was my idea," he heard Lurch say proudly as he gestured to the yellow punch. "Figured it'd be better to drink it all down rather than let it turn to vinegar, don't you think?"

Georgie set the glass down, looking like she was just this side of vomiting. Before River could interject, someone tugged on his shoulder from behind.

He turned to look at his aunt, who had donned a long black dress that trailed across the floor and a necklace with a huge crystal pendant. It was pink like the one in Beau's statue, and he didn't want to think too hard about what it had been carved to resemble. She had a worried look. "Do you think it's enough, River?"

He suppressed a laugh, because she was obviously in earnest. "Aunt Dottie, I'm pretty sure a tenth of this would have been enough. But Beau would have loved every bit of it."

And it was true, because Beau had loved Aunt Dottie. He'd always said she kept him from taking life too seriously, something he'd described as a Buchanan trait.

"Well," she said worriedly, "we'd better move forward with the crystal selection. We'll all need to choose one to better communicate with Beau."

He glanced back at Georgie, who was now listening to a story about Lurch's prostate problems with a pained expression. She met his eyes, giving him a *get me out of this* look. Although he had no idea what this crystal selection entailed, it had to be better than being cornered by Lurch. "Maybe Georgie should go first," he suggested. "We can pick some for her sister and brothers too."

That ought to take a while.

"Wonderful idea," Aunt Dottie said, brightening. "I worried they wouldn't feel included. Should we conference them in now so they can watch everything?"

"We gave them the number to call," he said. "I'll open the meeting and make sure the volume's high enough, but they'll dial in when they're ready." Although he couldn't imagine why they'd want to watch their sister pick a few crystals from a box. It seemed like the New Age equivalent of watching paint dry. He'd be surprised if Lee called in at all—the guy didn't strike him as a good sport, or someone who had a sense of humor.

He turned around just as Lurch was saying, "Anything can be a toilet if you're really desperate, is what I'm trying to get across."

"Sorry to interject," he said, "but we need you, Georgie. We have to set up the conferencing so your brothers and sister can call in, plus my aunt's ready to start…" He paused, working on his straight face. "…the crystal selection."

He'd never seen someone jump to their feet faster. "Sorry," she said back to Lurch, "duty calls." But she paused and added, "You know, I'm pretty sure there are prescription medications that can help you with that. I'd suggest talking to your doctor."

Lurch lit up like one of Aunt Dottie's lamps. "You know, that might not be a bad idea," he said, as if no one had suggested it to him before. And maybe no one had. Most people would have probably run out on the conversation right after it started.

Georgie gave River's arm a little squeeze when she reached them—a silent *thank you* that sparked a warm glow inside of him.

Her hand lingered there, making him wonder where her mind was at after the weekend. Did she still think kissing him was a mistake?

Did she want to make that mistake again?

"My stuff?" she asked.

He pulled a face. "Sorry. I tried to save everything I could, but the suitcases themselves are basically shrapnel. I folded your things into a couple of boxes I had in my trunk. I'll help you bring everything in after the…" He stopped short of calling it a party. "…thing."

"Oh, thank you," she said, her face flushing. She had to be thinking about just what he'd folded—which made him think about it too. Not that he'd really stopped. He felt his ears burning, and his aunt shot him a knowing look.

They headed toward the computer together, but Tom waylaid Aunt Dottie.

He held out his arm, which sported angry-looking scratches. "Dot, that cat's guarding the bathroom. Won't let anyone in."

"Oh dear, that won't do. We don't want Lurch to get any ideas and use the punch bowl," she said with a wink at Georgie. "I'll be right back, my dears. Can you make sure the computer's all set?"

"Will do, Aunt Dottie. Let me know if you need any help wrangling the beast." Not that River had a particular talent for that. If Jezebel had been pissed that he and Georgie had intruded on her territory the other night, she had to be a thousand times more on edge tonight. No one had ever accused her of being social. Still, he wasn't worried about his aunt. She had enough of a way with animals, even *that* animal, that she'd once convinced Jezebel to wear a Christmas sweater. No one had been able to get it off her, not until it essentially fell off from wear and tear, but the initial accomplishment was still impressive.

Georgie pulled away her hand, as if only then realizing it was still there. "Thanks, River." She paused. "For dealing with the mess, and for saving me with Lurch back there."

"Don't thank me just yet," he said. "We still don't know what the crystal ceremony entails."

Her mouth quirked up. "Just how much were you involved in the preparations for this?" She waved a hand, indicating the insane display in what was now her living room. Yeah, he probably should have warned her.

"Directly? Not much. But enough to know she'd gone a little over the top." His eyes combed the room again. "Okay, massively over the top. I'm sorry, Georgie. I should have called or texted you about this, but I figured you wanted space. I honestly didn't mean to encourage her. I just thought all of this might help her feel better."

Sadness welled in her eyes, and she touched his arm again, in that same spot. He wondered if her touch would be seared there, if he'd feel it always from now on. He hoped so.

"You don't need to apologize for being a good nephew. Besides, my sister said there's a 93.4% chance Lee will call in, and I absolutely want to see his face when he gets a look at all of this."

His smile spread wider. "Will you think less of me if I say I feel the same way?"

"You may be perfect," she said softly, "but you're only human." Then she smiled at him again and made her way to the computer, leaving him with the glow of having been called perfect—again—by a woman like her. Even if it was far from true.

When he joined her there, he started up the meeting, something that only took a matter of clicks given he'd already set everything up. Adalia connected instantly, so she must have been waiting on them. She had on a paint-splattered black T-shirt, and her hair had been pulled back in two short French braids.

Her face stretched into a huge grin when she saw them—only she wasn't really looking at them, but at the statue of Beau and the insane wall of letters behind it.

"Hi, Georgie. Hi, River. Oh, this is even better than I thought," she said. "Did Dottie make that?" Her expression had been teasing, but she tilted her head a little, studying it— her attention drifting up to Beau's sculpted face. Some of the humor dripped away. "Wow, she's really good! I had no idea your aunt was an artist."

"And I would be thrilled to create art with you one day, my dear. I see it in our cards," Aunt Dottie said, joining them. River wasn't sure whether she meant it literally. With her, there was simply no way to tell. "Soon, I think." Her gaze darted around the screen before landing on River. He shrugged, indicating the other two hadn't yet called in. "I'm afraid we'll have to start the crystal ceremony without your brothers," Aunt Dottie said, "but you can tell them all about it."

"Oh, I will," Adalia said, grinning again. "You can be sure of it."

River was about to ask about Jezebel's whereabouts, but he caught sight of her on the food table, eating a dish of something brown. The people who'd been standing around the table had backed up in a protective circle, and it was obvious no one intended to stop her.

Neither did he. He had too much to live for.

Aunt Dottie picked up a bell she'd set beside the computer and rang it, and all conversation in the room trickled to a stop.

"It's time for us to begin. I know you're all as excited as I am to reach across the curtain and commune with our dear Beau. Please help yourself to the refreshments, if you haven't done so already," she said, gesturing to the table. The people closest to it flinched, as if worried her gesture might startle Jezebel, who'd moved on to what looked like a black dip.

"To start, we'll each choose a crystal to put us in tune with Beau's psychic energy."

Aunt Dottie left her spot at the front of the room and walked up to the statue. Georgie let out a gasp as she reached for the crystal shaped like Beau's dick. At that exact moment, River heard a chime, indicating someone else had joined the video conference. Lee stared in openmouthed disbelief as Aunt Dottie removed the crystal from the statue. "We'll use Beau's crystal as a tuning rod to lead us to the crystals that will best allow us to communicate with him."

Oh shit. He'd volunteered Georgie to go first.

"Georgie," Aunt Dottie said with an expectant grin as she turned and held the crystal out to her. "Would you do the   honors?"

CHAPTER
Twenty-One

"Uh…" Georgie stared at the phallic crystal Dottie was offering, then took an involuntary step back. Could this night get any worse?

A third box had popped up on the screen and Jack stared out into the room with a look of horror, obviously regretting his decision to call in.

"What are you waiting for?" Adalia's voice crackled from the computer speakers. "Go get yourself a crystal."

"Is that what I think it is?" Lee asked with a shocked look on his face.

"If you're thinking it's a pink crystal replica of our grandfather's penis, then yes," Jack said in a dry tone, "I believe it is."

Georgie Buchanan was a put-together woman who had handled herself with integrity and professionalism in a wide variety of situations, but this…she had the urge to run home and hide under the covers, only *this* was her house now and she was stuck.

Oh, mercy. Dottie might be hosting this séance, but Georgie was the location host, which meant she was stuck here with Dottie and Lurch and Josie and all the craziness that seemed to accompany her grandfather and his business and the people associated with him.

Well, everything but River. *He* seemed relatively normal. She took it as a good sign that he hadn't treated her any differently tonight than he had in their previous encounters. The kiss—kisses, she mentally corrected—hadn't made things awkward or rendered him standoffish. As long as he was here, she wouldn't be alone. She could handle anything.

Well, anything besides touching her grandfather's crystal penis. *That* was a step too far.

She gave Dottie a forced smile as she moved toward the box containing multiple small crystals. "You know, I can already feel Beau's energy with us." She held her hands up and waggled her fingers, then lowered them as though mimicking rain. "And it's telling me to choose *this* one."

She hastily picked another pink crystal and held it up in triumph.

The frown on Dottie's face suggested she wasn't particularly happy with the way Georgie had chosen, but she didn't put up a fight. "Now the other Buchanan grandchildren need to pick a proxy to select their crystals. Children, who do you choose as your proxy?"

"Oh! Oh!" Adalia shouted, raising her hand in the air and bouncing around like she was a kid in class desperately trying to gain the attention of their teacher. "Let me go first! I choose Georgie!"

Georgie shot her sister a glare, but it was obvious Adalia was having too much fun with this to back down. She looked to be losing a fight to keep a straight face. "And I'm going to need you to use Grandpa Beau's tuning rod to pick mine."

Lee's face turned beet red, and Jack stared at them with wide eyes from the screen, looking like he was having major misgivings about not only attending the séance but having anything to do with the Buchanans period.

Which was fair, considering Georgie was having major misgivings herself.

"I really don't think that's necessary, *Adalia*," Georgie said through gritted teeth. "I assure you that I'm already in tune with Beau's energy."

Adalia tilted her head, still trying to look serious, but the evil glint in her eyes gave her away. "See...*you're* in tune with Grandpa Beau's energy, but *me*? Not so much. I'm worried your connection will cross over to my rock choosing."

"She has a point," Dottie said earnestly.

"See?" Adalia gave Georgie puppy dog eyes. "I'm going to need you to use the *tuning rod* to make sure you pick the right one."

"Really, Adalia?" Lee protested in disgust. "Is this séance not bad enough? You have to stoop to juvenile games?"

"Juvenile games?" Adalia countered, quick to anger as always. "This was Dottie's idea, and she's well into her seventies."

"Eighties," Dottie corrected, her head bobbing.

"Well, there you have it," Adalia snapped. "She's *much* older than me."

"Well, I'm not sure about *much* older," Dottie muttered to River. "I'd like to think I'm young at heart."

"Of course you are, Aunt Dottie." River was speaking to the elderly woman, but his gaze was fully on Georgie and everything about him screamed, *I'm so, so sorry.*

"I think I should go first," Jack said with a bit of a glare, but it was hard to know who it was directed toward since he wasn't there in person. "I choose River to be my proxy, and I'm gonna need him to use the tuning rod too." He held up a fist in front of his scrunched-up face and twisted it. "Like really grasp it tightly to feel the energy. Since you were so close to him and all."

Dottie perked up. "Oh, that's a good idea. Especially since Jack didn't know Beau at all, and you did."

River's face froze and his eyes flicked from Georgie to the large crystal in Dottie's hand.

Georgie moved next to the monitor, banking on the hope that Dottie was electronically clueless. "Maybe River and I should flip for it," she said. "Does anyone have a coin? Dottie?"

Dottie glanced down at her hips, as though looking for pockets in a dress that obviously lacked them. Georgie took advantage of the moment and blindly reached behind the monitor, ripping a cord out of the back at random.

The screen went black. Maybe her luck had changed.

"Adalia?" Georgie called out in mock concern. "Jack? Lee?" She turned to Dottie wide-eyed. "I think Beau disconnected them."

Dottie frowned, her lips thinning as she studied the screen for a moment.

"She's right," River added. "One minute they were there and the next they were gone. This must be Beau's doing. I don't think he wanted them here for the séance."

"Hmm…" Dottie said, deep in thought.

Josie's brows knitted together. "But didn't Georgie—"

"I think it's obvious that Beau's spirit is already here," River said, picking up the basket and grabbing a black rock. "I say we just pass this around." He shoved it at Lurch.

"Pick the one that speaks to you and hand it to the next person." When no one was looking, he snuck a glance at Georgie and winked.

An odd mixture of emotions pooled in Georgie's chest. Gratitude. Comradery. Appreciation. None of the other men in her life, past or present, would have handled this situation like River just had. Her father and Lee would have made withering comments and then started bossing people around (which Lee would have gotten around to if Georgie hadn't pulled the plug), and her previous boyfriends would have stomped off or acted disgusted. Granted, Dottie was River's aunt, but Georgie knew the respect and concern he'd shown for her feelings wasn't limited to her. He'd shown it to Josie and to Lurch. He didn't jump to conclusions or shoot off his temper. His kindness and empathy made him even more appealing.

No. No. No. You're supposed to be thinking about him less. Not more!

He still hadn't looked away, and the warmth in her chest shifted, now igniting her body, and she released an involuntary laugh. She must have it really bad for him if she was getting turned on in the middle of all of this.

Jezebel let out a loud screech as if to concur.

Several people scampered out of the way as the cat jumped off the table and shot into the kitchen, but the basket of crystals continued to make its way around the room until it reached Josie. She dumped them all onto her lap and began to sort through them.

Georgie was starving and there was no way she was eating anything on that table after Jezebel had wandered through it. She half-considered running into the kitchen to see if Dottie had any comfort food in the fridge, but she worried it would be rude. Plus, while she didn't like admitting she was afraid of a cat, she was pretty sure anyone with half a brain was afraid of *that* cat. How much longer was this thing going to take?

"Dottie," Georgie said. "What's next?"

"Well, after everyone has their crystals, we're going to communicate with Beau."

Oh dear. Was Dottie going to use the Ouija board? Georgie wasn't particularly superstitious, but after everything else that had happened, the last thing she needed was to open a demon portal in Asheville, North Carolina.

Dottie asked everyone to gather in a circle. River slid next to Georgie, his arm inches from hers. She felt the heat of his body seeping into hers, and found herself edging slightly closer.

"Okay, now," Dottie said. "Holding the crystal in your right hand, take the hand of the person next to you."

River glanced down at Georgie as his hand tentatively sought hers, as though he feared she might pull away.

She stared up at him, telling herself that holding his hand was a bad idea—the *worst* idea—yet she found herself linking her fingers with his, the smooth rock in his hand pressing into her palm.

This felt too right, too natural. Other than the rock, of course, and the absolutely insane scene around them.

He squeezed, holding her gaze, and she knew he felt it too.

She'd lost herself in the moment, so she wasn't prepared when someone snatched her right hand. A quick glance revealed it was Josie. She swung Georgie's hand back and forth as if they were schoolkids on a playground.

"I can't wait to talk to Beau." Then she sobered, letting their arms hang. "I know he wasn't my grandfather or anything, but I really miss him."

Georgie squeezed Josie's hand and offered a reassuring smile. Josie was infuriating, but as far as Georgie could tell, her intentions were good. "I hope you get a message from him."

"I *am* sorry if this doesn't go well for you," Josie said. "You're not sarcastic like your brother is, and you have really nice underwear."

Georgie heard a muffled sound from her left—River stifling a laugh, if she had to bet. Although she had no idea what Josie was talking about, she figured it would be best not to ask.

Her gaze shifted to Dottie, who was edging her way behind the sofa.

"Aunt Dottie," River said. "Do you need help with that?"

"Don't worry," she said with a grunt, holding the plug at the end of the lights she'd strung up around the hand-painted letters on the cardboard taped to the walls. Thank God she hadn't painted directly on the plaster. "I just need to get the lights hooked up so Beau can communicate with us." Still holding the end of the lights, she bent over, feeling for something on the floor.

"Maybe I should help," River said with a slight edge of concern.

"Don't be silly," Dottie said, still bent at the waist and fumbling around on the floor. "It's here somewhere. I put it here myself this morning."

"What are you looking for?" River asked, his hand loosening its hold on Georgie's.

"That extension cord. I found it in Beau's basement on a shelf... There it is!" Beaming, she stood upright and produced the end of a fat electrical cord that looked like it had come straight from the 1940s.

"Um… Aunt Dottie…" River released Georgie's hand and took a step forward. "Maybe you shouldn't use—"

But Dottie wasn't paying attention as she shoved the plug from the light string into the extension cord.

The smell of ozone hit Georgie's nose and an electrical buzzing noise filled the room. Light burst from the bulbs on the wall, far brighter than it should have been, and multiple bulbs shattered, sending flying glass into the air.

Which was when several of the light sockets caught fire, along with the connection between the light plug and the extension cord.

Georgie let out a cry of shock, then covered her head to protect herself from flying debris, while several of the other attendees shrieked and ran out of the house.

A smoke alarm began to blare.

The rest of the lights went dim—or rather dimmer—and the light in the kitchen went out. The only thing lighting the room was the burning light cord, the cardboard underneath, and a curtain next to the sofa.

Jezebel let everyone know she didn't approve of this nonsense by releasing several loud shrieks of protest from the kitchen.

"It's so pretty!" Josie exclaimed in awe. "Beau's really putting on a show!"

"Everybody out!" River shouted, grabbing his aunt by the shoulders and escorting her halfway across the living room. "Georgie, can you get Dottie and Josie out of here?"

She didn't answer, just snagged both women's arms and started dragging them to the door, but she turned back to see River running into the kitchen. As she pushed the women out onto the front porch, he was hurrying back to the living room with a small fire extinguisher.

Georgie followed the women outside to take a quick head count. Pulling her phone out of her pocket, she called 911, letting the dispatcher know there was a house fire and to send a fire truck.

The front windows opened while she was on the call, and gray, then black, smoke billowed out.

When she hung up, she was already running through the front door, searching the living room for River, but most of the fire was out and the darkened room was filled with smoke. She heard the sputtering of the fire extinguisher, which sounded nearly empty.

"River!"

"Georgie! Go back outside!" he shouted, something like panic in his voice.

She wasn't about to leave him to fight this alone.

She nudged a large crystal someone had dropped on the floor over to the door to prop it open, then ran to the back door, nudging a kitchen chair into the opening before she headed back to River. As she ran back into the smoke-filled room, she could hear River coughing, but the haze kept her from seeing him.

"River!" she shouted. "Come on! The fire department's on the way!" The faint sound of sirens punctuated her statement.

"It's almost out!" he shouted, stomping flames on the floor.

The punch bowl caught the corner of Georgie's eye, so she scooped it into her arms, surprised at how heavy it was, then rushed over to River. The sloshing punch soaked her shirt, but she managed to toss most of its contents toward the flames.

River shifted to the side as she dumped the liquid, but the weight of the bowl threw off her aim and most of it ended up on him, drenching his chest and legs. What liquid did hit the flames made the fire flare even higher.

Well, crap. She forgot there was alcohol in the punch.

The sirens got louder. Help was on the way, but Georgie had just made River a human torch.

"River! I'm sorry! Leave it!"

But then she was hit with a spray of cold water from behind. She turned to see Dottie standing behind her holding a garden hose and wearing the fierce expression of a warrior headed into battle.

The flames sputtered out, and River rushed over and wrapped his arms around both of them, sweeping them toward the front door despite Dottie's protests that she still needed to talk to Beau.

A fire truck pulled up as they went outside, and the firefighters rushed in to assess the damage. The first responders called an ambulance to check River for smoke inhalation. They arrived quickly, and they told him his oxygen levels were good, thank God. Their official advice was that he should go to the hospital to be fully examined, but he'd assured them he felt fine. Thankfully, he had gym clothes in the car, so he'd been able to at least switch out his T-shirt for a clean one.

Georgie felt grimy and her clothes stank of smoke, but the house hadn't been officially cleared yet, and she didn't want to swap her shirt in front of everyone.

While River talked to a firefighter, Dottie stood in the front yard, staring up at the house in dismay. Several people had gathered around the house, although they hung back at a slight distance. A small group of them surrounded Josie, who was talking with a lot of hand gestures. Sighing, Georgie went over to check on Dottie. "Are you okay? Are you sure we shouldn't have the ambulance crew check you over too?"

"I'm fine," the older woman said, more subdued than Georgie had ever heard her. "But now I'll never get to talk to Beau."

Shame washed through Georgie. While she had seen the séance as a joke and an inconvenience, she realized this whole thing had been orchestrated by a woman who had lost the love of her life. If she'd had a marriage license or wedding ring, she would have been seen as Beau's widow, and as such, granted more respect and sympathy. But from what she'd gathered, Dottie and Beau had been together for decades. She might not have the legal status of widow, but Dottie's pain ran just as deep as if they'd been married.

"That's not true," Georgie said softly as she slipped her hand into the older woman's. "You can talk to Beau any time you like."

"But he won't talk back." Her voice quavered with tears.

Georgie turned to face her. "Oh, Dottie. From what I can see, Beau's voice is everywhere. It's in the brewery. In his house. It's in River. And it's in you. He's here. You just have to search a little bit for him."

The older woman nodded, a tear escaping and running down her cheek.

Georgie grabbed her other hand and turned the woman to face her. "You lost someone very dear to you. Perhaps you should take some time off to grieve."

Her face fell. "You're firing me."

Georgie squeezed her hands. "*No!* I most definitely am not. I *need* you." And to Georgie's surprise she meant it, and not because the will had stated she couldn't be fired. "Just like I need River. I can't do this without either of you."

"But I just nearly burned down your house," Dottie said, her gaze darting to the house.

"Nearly. Which means you didn't. The house isn't important, Dottie. What matters is that everyone is safe. That *you're* safe. I'm sure Grandpa Beau would have hated it if you'd gotten hurt trying to talk to him. You have River. And now you have me. We'll get through this. I promise."

"Oh, Georgie." Dottie threw her arms around Georgie and held tight. "I wasn't so sure at first, but everything's unfolding the way it was supposed to. Beau knew what he was doing when he picked you."

Georgie's body stiffened. Had Dottie known that River was supposed to get the brewery? Before she could ask any questions, the older woman dropped her hold and walked away.

CHAPTER

Twenty-Two

For a moment there, holding Georgie's hand in the séance circle, River had felt pretty good about what the future might hold for them—and he'd gotten the impression she felt pretty good about it too, complications aside. And then his aunt had set her house on fire.

How did you even apologize to someone for that? He would insist on paying for the repairs (even if it wiped him out), but that didn't seem like enough. And nothing could atone for that disaster of a crystal-selection ceremony.

He'd failed Georgie, and Aunt Dottie too. He should have put a stop to the séance back at the idea stage, before everything had spiraled out of control. But he'd gone along with it, in the way he went along with most of his aunt's crazy plans, because he'd thought it would make her happy. Because he didn't know how to talk to people who were grieving, even when he was too. But he'd made a mess of everything.

His aunt wasn't happy.

One glance at her, talking to Georgie, was enough to tell him that. She looked like Beau had just died all over again. And then Georgie took his aunt into her arms, and something in him loosened.

"I'm sorry about the pictures," the firefighter said. "He's erased them, of course, and we'll make him do a hundred push-ups back at the station."

River had witnessed one of the guys taking phone pictures of the pink crystal dick, sadly disconnected from its statue. In her haste to get him out of the house, Georgie had unwittingly used it to prop open the front door.

"It's fine," he said. "I get it. Do you have any recommendations for local companies to clean up this mess?" Although, it occurred to him that they could use the same people who'd taken care of the brewery.

God, it would be a miracle if Georgie didn't sell the company just to get away from them all.

The firefighter gave him a couple of cards and told him they'd be wrapping up soon. River glanced back at Georgie and saw his aunt walking away from her. He needed to talk to Georgie—hopefully he'd open his mouth and suddenly know what to say—but not before he made sure his aunt was okay.

He hurried after her, calling, "Aunt Dottie, wait!" and she turned to face him just as she reached Josie's boat of a car.

"Are you okay?" he asked. "I don't want you to be alone tonight. Will you stay in my spare bedroom?"

"No, dear," she said, reaching up to cup his cheek. "There's no need for that. Josie is coming to stay with me tonight. I'm a little too shaken to drive, but she's agreed to chauffeur me as well."

"We're going to meditate about what happened tonight," Josie said brightly, joining them. She'd been talking to a circle of people by the front yard, and from the looks on their faces, she'd told them enough that he wouldn't be surprised to see an article about it in the local papers.

Meditation wasn't dangerous, was it? Of course, he hadn't thought a séance was dangerous either.

"No old extension cords or open fire, okay?" he said to his aunt. "And absolutely no mind-altering substances." This time he leveled a look at Josie. She had an edibles habit, and on one memorable occasion, she'd sat cross-legged on the bar at Buchanan Brewery and declared herself a fortune-teller—only she'd cursed the love lives of anyone adventurous enough to ask for a reading.

"If you're attuned enough to the world around you, anything can be a mind-altering substance," Josie said airily.

"Oh, you know what I mean."

She opened her mouth to reply, but Aunt Dottie cut her off. "Josie, go ahead and get in the car," she said. "I want a word with my nephew."

Surprisingly enough, Josie complied.

"I'm sorry things went down like that," he said, "but Aunt Dottie, you really freaked me out in there." He toed the grass a little with his shoe, and flinched when he saw an incredibly sexy green lace thong that had blended in with the grass. Stooping a little, he grabbed it and pocketed it. "I need to know you're going to be okay," he continued. He had to grit the words out past his vulnerability, but he forced himself to say it. Because he loved her. Because he couldn't lose her too. Because she wouldn't turn that vulnerability back on him like his mother might have. "Even though Beau's not here anymore, there are people who need you. *I* need you. And everyone who came here tonight did it as much for you as for Beau."

A smile spread across her face, sweet and real, and he felt reassured. Whatever Georgie had said to her had helped turn things around. He'd have to thank her for that. After he apologized at least a dozen times. "I know, dear boy, and you won't be rid of me yet. I have plenty of work left to do. Speaking of which, did you notice the crystal Georgie picked tonight?"

"Don't even get me started on the crystals," he said, shaking his head. Still, he couldn't help but smile back. "But yes. Of course I noticed."

"You might want to offer *her* your spare bedroom." She glanced up at the smoking house, and at Georgie on the sidewalk, bent over her phone with a grim look on her face. "She won't be able to stay here, and she might have a tough time checking into a hotel this late."

If he hadn't known better, he might have wondered if she'd planned the whole thing, down to the faulty cord.

"I will," he affirmed.

A sad look crossed her face again. "And find Jezebel, if you would. Beau loved that cat."

River repressed the urge to say, *He's the only one who did.* Even if it was true, it wouldn't make her feel better, and he still wanted that.

"I'll do my best. But even if we don't find her tonight, I'm sure she'll come back. She haunts that house like a poltergeist, and the people in the neighborhood know better than to mess with her."

Someone tapped him on the shoulder, and for a moment he thought it might be Georgie, but when he turned around he saw a slightly familiar-looking woman with wavy brown hair and glasses. A small group of people stood behind her, a few of them known to him, the others vaguely familiar in that same way as the woman in front. The neighbors.

"Did you say Jezebel is on the loose?" she asked.

"Um, yeah," he said.

She flinched as if he'd physically struck her. "What are you going to do?" she asked. "Is someone from the fire department going to apprehend her?"

"Apprehend her?" he asked in disbelief. "She's not a criminal."

She just gave him a flat look, which was when he remembered where he'd seen her before. A couple of years ago, he'd been hanging out at Beau's place with his aunt when this woman had come by, fundraising for her kid's school softball trip to Henryetta, Arkansas. Jezebel had leapt on the box of cookies in her arms. The woman had thought it was cute—until she'd attempted to remove her. Needless to say, they'd bought the whole case.

The others started murmuring their assent, and he figured he'd better say something to pacify them. The last thing he wanted was for Georgie to be chased out of the neighborhood with pitchforks because of him.

"Look, I'll give you guys my number, and you can text if you see her, okay?"

"Day or night?" someone asked.

"Sure," he said, "day or night. And I'll canvass the neighborhood looking for her."

Not that he thought it would do any good. Their best bet was to put out cans of sardines, or whatever brown and black food she'd been scarfing down with such relish tonight.

They all whipped out their cell phones to take down his information. Then they started to disperse. Aunt Dottie gave him a hug, murmuring something along the lines of, "Oh, all this fuss over a harmless little cat," and got into the car.

River glanced back at the sidewalk leading up to the house and caught Georgie staring at him. Although her shirt

214

had patches of soot on it, and there was a smudge of it on her chin, she looked beautiful. She immediately glanced away, as if embarrassed, and her cheeks flushed a little. God, she'd be terrible at poker, but he loved her openness. He liked knowing he could trust her.

The fireman he'd spoken with earlier stood beside her, and he felt a little stab of something when he noticed the way the man was looking at her.

"Thanks again," Georgie told the guy.

"I'm Jake," he said, handing her a card with a handwritten number on the back. "Please give me a call if we can do anything to help. Like I said, the house should be safe once it's clean and aerated, although you'll still need to replace the plaster on the interior walls and repaint."

"Will do," she said, but her eyes were on River again. She didn't look judgmental or pissed. If anything, she looked worried about *him*.

"My personal number's on there too," Jake said. Persistent, wasn't he? But River found he didn't care anymore. Georgie wasn't interested in this guy—he knew it like he knew beer. Somehow he'd gotten lucky—big-time, he-should-play-the-lotto kind of lucky—and she was interested in *him*. Even now, with Lurch's Pee Brew crusted in his hair and on part of his jeans, and with every bit of him smelling of smoke. The only question was whether she'd give him a chance.

"Thanks, Jake," she said with a smile. "I love that everyone's so friendly here." River noticed she hadn't promised to contact Jake, but judging by the triumphant grin on the guy's face as he headed down to the truck, it didn't appear he'd caught on.

Everyone else started to leave too, and River took Georgie's hand and led her around to the backyard. There was a bench there, nestled in the bushes, and it would be private enough for them to talk.

She didn't object or try to pull away, and he took that as a good sign.

He gestured for her to sit down first, which she did, and he sat beside her, not as close as he wanted but a good deal closer than he would have sat if it had been Lurch next to him.

"So," he said, feeling awkward suddenly, "I was hoping to talk to you alone tonight, but this wasn't how I saw it going down."

She laughed at that, longer and louder than it warranted, and he found himself laughing too. When their laughter started to wind down, he said, "Georgie, I'm so, so sorry for this. For everything. My aunt's usually harmless, and I figured…"

He stalled out, but she gave him a bright smile. "You wanted to help her. That's honorable, River. You don't need to apologize for that. Dottie's lucky to have you, and you her. It's rare to find a connection like that, even with family."

"Well, needless to say, I'll pay for all of the damages. It doesn't make up for"—he waved a hand at the house, temporarily at a loss for words—"but at least it's something."

"That's not necessary," she said. "I'm sure I can work things out with the insurance company."

God, he hoped so. The damage was fairly extensive.

"Well, then I'll cover the deductible or whatever." She looked like she might object, so he shook his head. "Look, it'll make me feel like slightly less of a failure. How about that?"

"We'll see," she said. Her phone buzzed in her pocket, and he remembered the way she'd been looking at it earlier, on the sidewalk.

"Your siblings blowing up your phone?"

"Yeah," she said with a frown. "Adalia's over the moon about your aunt, but Jack's on a bit of a warpath. Lee's just generally pissy. He doesn't like that I ignored my father's request for a business plan, or maybe he doesn't like that Dad won't leave him alone about it."

Huh. Jack had been weird with him a few days ago, but he'd been straight-up hostile tonight. Whatever mystery problem had drawn him home clearly wasn't going well. Or maybe that wasn't the problem. Maybe...

Hell, might as well come out and ask.

"Does he have a problem with me because he knows I'm interested in you?"

She looked him in the eye, and the attraction he saw there had him thinking about that kiss again—the sounds she'd made against him, the way the sparks of color in her eyes had danced.

But there was something else in her gaze too, an inner conflict he could guess at all too well. The work situation still stood between them.

"Maybe part of it is that he knows *I'm* interested in *you*," she said softly, "but I don't think that's all of it." She opened her mouth as if on the verge of saying something else, only to close it again without uttering a sound.

He wanted to reach for her, but he couldn't until they got past this. Somehow. "He wants me out," he guessed, "and after tonight, I'm guessing Lee feels the same way."

Her mouth twisted, but she didn't deny it.

"I've been working on a plan for the fall beers all weekend." He paused, glancing back at the house. "In between helping Aunt Dottie with this fiasco. But it occurs to me that I haven't actually signed any papers yet, and two of the owners are against it happening."

A look of horror crossed her face. She took his hand and turned to face him, her knee knocking into his leg. "Oh, River, I don't want you to think I'd take your work and then go with someone else. I'm going to get the paperwork sorted out tomorrow. You're the one who made me realize how great this could be. Restoring Grandpa Beau's legacy, working with Jack." She held his gaze, her eyes intent. "Working with *you*. I started Moon Goddess by myself, and while I hired a lot of great people, I didn't have anyone to brainstorm with. To collaborate with. I want that with you."

"But we don't work together *yet*," he repeated.

Her eyes widened with understanding. The conflict from earlier was still there, unresolved, but she leaned toward him. "No, I guess we don't."

She took out her phone, and for a second he thought he'd been reading her wrong, but she turned it off without looking at the texts. Tucking it back into her pocket, she looked up at him, her lips parting.

He reached up to wipe the spot of soot off her chin, smiling a little when he saw her skin was tinged pink again, and leaned in to kiss her. Her lips were as soft as he remembered, and the kiss was gentle at the start—as if their lips were reacquainted with each other—but it turned fierce as quickly as it had that last time. She wrapped her arms around his neck, bringing him closer, and he lifted her into his lap, eliciting a little gasp from her that was muffled as she changed the angle of their kiss.

She pulled back to look at him, her eyes bright and intense. She looked on the verge of saying something—like maybe they should get out of Beau's somewhat public backyard, or suggest that they both take a shower, hopefully together—but then her gaze lowered, and her nose scrunched. For a moment, he thought she was staring at his obvious arousal, but then she reached into his pants pocket and pulled something out.

"Why are my panties in your pocket, River?"

CHAPTER
Twenty-Three

The look of horror on River's face was almost too much for her to take with a straight face, especially when he started to fumble over his answer. "I...they were on the ground... I thought Josie and I had gotten them all, but then I saw these in the yard, and I—"

"So you were being chivalrous?" she whispered with a playful look.

The tension eased from his face. "Yeah."

"I think it's kind of sexy that you have my panties." She slowly tucked them back into his pocket. "You can keep them for now."

His body tensed, but she was sure it was for a different reason this time. The growing bulge pressing against her thigh was proof enough.

He stared up at her in wonder. "How the hell are you so forgiving after everything that's happened tonight? Hell, the last few days."

Her smile softened, settling into contentment. "You have a good heart, River Reeves. From my limited observations of the male species, that's somewhat of a rarity." Her grin brightened again. "And it buys you a few passes."

Warring emotions flickered in his eyes. "I'll make it up to you, Georgie."

Her hand fanned against his cheek as she studied his warm brown eyes. If she wasn't careful, she might lose herself in them.

"Um...am I interrupting something?" a man asked from a few feet away, his surprise obvious.

River's arms tightened around her, the sudden tension in him coming in his voice. "What are you doing here, Finn?"

Finn? As in Finn Hamilton, the owner of Big Catch?

Just when Georgie was sure this night couldn't get any worse, it kept on coming. It might not have been so bad if she hadn't called Finn for a reference on Friday, and now...

Good Lord. What did he think of her?

She scrambled off River's lap so fast she almost fell onto the ground. River grabbed her arm and pulled her to her feet as he stood.

"You didn't answer my question." The anger in River's voice caught Georgie by surprise. They'd encountered their fair share of messes over the past seventy-two hours, and he'd never once raised his voice to anyone. But River felt betrayed by Finn, so she couldn't say she blamed him.

"Maybe I should go," she murmured, wondering where she'd left her purse. Somewhere in the kitchen. Assuming it had survived the fire. Although why was she so concerned about her purse? All of her worldly belongings in Asheville were either in the house, the back of River's car, or smashed on the street.

"No," River said, putting out an arm to stop her. "Finn was just leaving."

"Come on, man. After I heard about the fire, I raced over to check on things," Finn said, running a hand over his short hair in frustration. His hair was somewhere between brown and blond and looked like it might be curly if he let it get long enough, and he had ocean-colored eyes—blue and green—fringed with lashes darker than his hair. The fact that she wasn't attracted to him at all was only further proof of how hung up she was on River.

"How did you even find out?" River asked in a cold tone.

"The neighbors," Finn said sheepishly. "I could see the smoke, plus Gertrude from down the block is going door to door warning everyone that the devil cat is loose after a fire, and, well…there are a lot of cats in this neighborhood, but only one Jezebel. I figured they had to be talking about Beau's house." He paused, looking at them with eyes that seemed to see everything. "I was about to ask if everyone is okay, but I'd say it looks like everyone's doing better than fine."

"We were until a few minutes ago," River muttered.

Finn's gaze shifted to Georgie, and she felt like she was being examined under a microscope. He took a step forward and extended his hand. "Finn Hamilton, River's friend." There was no missing the insinuation that she was the intruder, the odd woman out. He certainly didn't lack for confidence—while he was right in a way, this was still her house. One-fourth hers, anyway. "You must be Georgie Buchanan, the new owner of Buchanan Brewery. I recognize you from your photos online."

"You researched her?" River asked, incredulous.

Finn grinned, but it didn't quite reach his eyes. "I had to see who hired you out from under me."

"You mean from under Bev Corp," Georgie said as she took his hand. "And yes, I'm one of the owners."

"You and your two siblings," he said, still holding on.

She cocked an eyebrow, ready to take on whatever challenge he threw her way. She hadn't gotten where she was by backing down to blowhards. "Three, actually, but I'll be the one running things."

Which was true enough. Jack would come back at some point and help, or at least that was the idea, but she was in charge for now.

He gave her an appraising look, and she would have thought he flat out didn't like her if she didn't also see the worry in his eyes. Before the fallout of the Big Catch sale, Finn had been one of River's closest friends, and it was obvious he still felt that way. Finding Georgie and River in a compromising situation like this was bound to make him worry that she was taking advantage of his friend, and damn if that didn't burn, because in a way, she was.

Taking a step back, she said, "I'll let you two chat while I go inside and grab my things. River, I'll meet you out front."

She was prepared for him to stop her, but instead, he glared at Finn.

Once she was in the already-open back door, she heard River light into his former partner. "What the hell, Finn? Why did you treat her like she was the enemy?"

"What the hell did I just walk into?" Finn countered. "Are you sleeping with her?"

"That is none of your business," River countered.

"River, look. I'm worried. We both know Buchanan Brewery wasn't very solvent before Beau's death, and after the fiasco on Friday...yeah, I heard about it. Everyone heard about it. Lurch himself has told two dozen people. You'll have to close down for at least a couple of months, I expect. Can you survive that? What if the Buchanans don't make it? What will you do then?"

"This isn't Big Catch, Finn. What happens to Buchanan Brewery is none of your concern. That's for Georgie and her siblings to decide."

"But where are they getting their advice, River?" Finn paused. "Do the Buchanan siblings know anything about running a brewery, let alone making beer?"

River shook his head, sounding exhausted. "Go home, Finn."

"River, listen…"

Georgie heard the frustration in Finn's voice. She wondered if she should stop eavesdropping, but the cold hard truth was that this concerned her too. So she stayed in the kitchen, watching them through the open window, hoping the darkness concealed her.

"No, *you* listen," River said. "You know how much this brewery means to me. How much it would kill me to see it sold off to the devil too."

Neither of them spoke for a moment, and Georgie held her breath, sensing they were on the cusp of something. Then Finn said, "Are you sure you're not holding on to it because Beau was like the father you always wished you had?"

"What is the matter with you?"

"River, please," Finn pleaded. "This is all coming out wrong, but if you'd just listen—"

"Listen to you insult me?"

"I'm not *insulting* you, River. We both know you have blinders on at times, and I think between Beau's death and the bad timing of the sale of Big Catch—"

"Bad timing? You think I'd feel differently about the sale if it had happened *a few months from now?*"

"No, I think you'd be just as upset, but it's a lot, River. A whole lot. Your life was just turned upside down on multiple fronts, and I'm asking you to *take a breath* and think this through." Then he added, "And that includes whatever it is you have going on with Georgie Buchanan."

"Excuse me?"

"She called me for a reference on Friday, River. After you and I talked."

"Did she? Good. Unless you bad-mouthed me to her too. Did you warn her I'm emotionally damaged?"

"No," Finn said, outrage on his face. "*Of course not!* I gave you the glowing recommendation you deserve, but think this through, River. Do you really think it's a good idea to start a romantic entanglement with one of the owners? You don't exactly have a great track record of staying with your girlfriends for very long. What's going to happen when you end things with her? Haven't you ever heard that you don't shit where you eat?"

Georgie sucked in a breath. She'd never gotten a player vibe from River, but surely his best friend would know better than she did.

"How much is she paying you?" Finn asked. "It can't be much. The brewery was in the red, and with no income for the foreseeable future…"

"There's a reserve," River said. "Not that it's any of your business."

"*Of course* it's my business if it directly affects you. You're like a brother to me, and this disagreement isn't going to change that."

River glanced down at his feet.

Finn pushed out a groan, running his hand over his head as he took a few steps away. When he turned back, he wore a look of determination. "Look, promise me this—don't let your personal relationship with Georgie get in the way of what she pays you. Bev Corp was going to top what you were making at Big Catch and then some, and you could go just about anywhere else and make more than you're likely to at Buchanan."

River started to say something and stopped. Was he having second thoughts about working for her? She had to admit that Finn had some very valid points. She already knew she was going to have to dip into her Moon Goddess profits to cover the employees' salaries during the closure, and she'd be a fool not to modernize the facility and the equipment while they were closed. River had indicated he'd accept less than he was worth, but she wouldn't agree to that. She refused to make Finn right. Which meant she'd need to dip a little deeper for his salary.

Georgie grabbed her purse off the kitchen table, then hurried up to the room she'd chosen to stay in, gathering the items she'd left there on Saturday morning. When she headed back down, she used the flashlight on her phone to survey the damage in the living room. While the ceiling and walls were black from smoke, it looked like the majority of the fire had been contained. Still, she had no idea how long it would take to repair the mess.

Perhaps she should look into staying in a short-term residence.

When she brought her things out front, Finn was gone and River was standing in the yard, staring at the house with a look that broke her heart. Like he'd lost his best friend, his father, and his job, which wasn't far from the truth.

She walked straight to him, dropped her things on the ground, and took both of his hands in hers. Not a great place to start given what she'd decided, but she needed to touch him. Needed to comfort him. Right now, nothing else mattered.

"I heard a good part of your conversation with Finn." Cringing, she forced herself to continue. "It was wrong to eavesdrop, and part of me is sorry, but the rest of me isn't. I want you to know I'd never take advantage of you or your talent. I'll pay you every cent you're worth, River."

He lifted a hand to her cheek, a pained smile spreading across his face. "Georgie, I never once thought you would take advantage of me, but there is some truth to the rest of what Finn said. I do want to make it work because of Beau. There's no denying I have an attachment to the place."

"And so do I. It doesn't hold the memories for me, but I see it and think of all the time I missed with my grandfather. He trusted me to bring it back to life, and I don't want to disappoint him." She paused. "And I don't want to disappoint you. We'll make this work. Together. But Finn's right." Her voice broke. "Once you're my employee, we can't have a romantic relationship. Finn already thinks the worst of me, and my brothers…"

"I know," he said, the disappointment on his face weakening her resolve.

Part of her knew this was a huge mistake. Once she opened this door, it would be hard to close it again, even if River really did shun long-term relationships. Still, her heart wanted this, and she was tired of letting her brain take charge all the time. In her heart of hearts, she knew that if she didn't give herself this night with River, she would regret it for the rest of her life.

She playfully lifted an eyebrow. "But as I reminded you earlier, you're not officially an employee at Buchanan Brewery. Which means we have tonight…"

Before she realized what he was doing, River swept her into his arms and kissed her so thoroughly she wondered how she was still standing.

CHAPTER
Twenty-Four

River couldn't get Georgie back to his loft quickly enough.

One night. He could work with one night. It was better than nothing, and although he wouldn't say so to her, his heart hoped they could still figure things out. They'd let everything come together with the brewery, allow the dust to settle, as it were, and then maybe things would be different. Then maybe they could try in earnest.

But good God, he wanted her. It was painful, the wanting.

He opened the trunk to put the rest of her things in with the boxes, and her mouth quirked into a little smile when she saw her neatly folded clothes in the cardboard boxes.

"No wonder you were out here for so long."

He felt his ears heat. "Well, I know you're going to wash them anyway, but I figured it would soften the blow of seeing your suitcases in the back seat."

She leaned over to look and flinched a little. "Ouch. They didn't stand a chance."

Neither do you, said an inner voice that sounded suspiciously like Finn.

Damn it. Why had he needed to show up out of the blue to stir up shit? Finn could say he was concerned until his voice went raw, and maybe it was true, but there was more to it. He couldn't accept that his actions had reactions. Finn hated it when anyone was mad at him, whether they had a legitimate reason or not—and so he'd turned things back on River, making some big pep talk about the mistakes River was making. The risks he was taking. Turning himself into the big hero who'd save him, like he had before.

And now he was thinking about Finn when Georgie—sexy, smart, beautiful Georgie—was about to come home with him.

"Ready?" he asked, closing the trunk.

"Yes." That one word had hidden layers, and the sound of it stirred him as much as her touch. Her brow furrowed. "You know I'm thirty-three, right?"

She said it so seriously, he almost laughed. He *had* known. He'd done the math after seeing her bio on the Moon Goddess website. And while he didn't care in the least, he'd wondered if she would.

"Oh, are we exchanging birthdays?" he asked with a grin. "My thirtieth birthday's in a month, if you're planning on enforcing the whole awkward cake tradition."

She smiled back. "Mine was last month. I'll admit I'm relieved that you didn't just turn twenty-nine. I know it doesn't matter, but—"

"But it sort of matters."

She shrugged self-consciously and then glanced back at the house, very obviously trying to change the subject. "It just occurred to me. Was that your computer in there? I think it probably has water damage."

"Shit," he said, running a hand through his hair. "It's Maisie's. I think it was an extra from the shelter, but even so. Yet another reason why tonight was a bad idea."

Which reminded him. Maisie was still at the apartment, and he needed her not to be.

"Let me just text her before we get going," he said, opening the passenger door for her. She got in, and he pulled out his phone.

Thanks so much for watching Hops. Now, scram. I'm bringing Georgie back to the loft. Also, my aunt kind of, sort of started a fire that probably damaged the computer. I'm really sorry, but I am 100% buying you a newer, nicer one. Oh, and Jezebel is missing. I'll tell you everything tomorrow.

He paused a second before adding, *And buy you lunch. Okay, signing off.*

He circled around to the driver's side and slipped behind the wheel. Bringing his phone up so Georgie could see it, he turned it off.

"Fair is fair," he said, tucking it into the console beneath the radio. "Like I said, I did a bunch of brainstorming over the weekend, but I think we should table that too, as much as I'm dying to tell you everything."

She did the mouth quirk thing again. "And I agree, as much as I'm dying to hear it. A clear delineation between work and…not work."

"From the bags, I take it you went back to Boston this weekend?" He'd intended to ask her earlier, and then everything had gone up in flames. Literally.

"Yeah," she said as he pulled away from the curb. "I forgot to change my original ticket, which is completely unlike me, but someone's been distracting me." She shot him a look that was somewhere between accusatory and playful, which he took to mean that while it had been a good distraction, she also didn't like the hiccup in her thinking. "I figured I should grab the stuff I'd need right away and make arrangements for the rest."

"You know," he said, "I think Josie would tell you this is a sign a shopping trip is in order."

She laughed. "I suspect she would say that. So she's staying with Dottie tonight? I saw you guys talking in front of the house."

"Yeah," he said, taking a turn, "Josie is another of what you might call my aunt's adoptees. Aunt Dottie met her when she was panhandling downtown. They got to talking, and within a half hour, Aunt Dottie had offered her a job and a temporary place to stay."

Georgie gasped. Her voice laced with horror, she said, "She was homeless? Jack fired her. Is she going to be okay?"

"Georgie," he said, "Jack was right to fire her. And I wouldn't say she was homeless so much as drifting, looking for a place to call home and people to call a family. I think maybe she reminded Aunt Dottie of my mother." A little twist of pain made itself known in his abdomen. Why had he said that? He never talked about his mother willingly, and yet he'd mentioned her to Georgie twice now. He swallowed. "You don't need to worry. My aunt would never let anything happen to her. She'll find something else, probably something better suited to her."

"Still, I feel bad," Georgie said. "I feel like we're coming into your house and messing everything up."

"Like we did to your house?" he said, glancing at her with a grin.

"Yeah, exactly like that. Speaking of which, should we be putting up posters for Jezebel, or canvassing the neighborhood or something? I'm sure Dottie's beside herself with worry."

"I'll put up some posters tomorrow," he said, "but trust me when I say word of mouth will be more powerful than any poster. It took Finn all of five minutes to come over." His mouth flattened at the thought.

"True," she said, "and I can't imagine it would be easy to spot a black cat in the dark." She paused, as if weighing her words, and said, "I feel like we should talk some more about Finn…"

He grimaced. "If we're turning off the rest of the world off tonight, Georgie, I especially want to turn off Finn."

It had become dark suddenly, as if night were a blanket that had been lowered on them. Or maybe it only seemed sudden since his attention had been so fixed on Georgie and the horrors unfolding around them.

He parked in the alley, grateful his usual space was open, something that had become increasingly rare as Asheville became a more popular spot for tourists. No sign of Maisie's Jeep.

They both got out, and he looked at Georgie over the hood of the car.

"What would you like to bring inside?" he asked.

She smiled. "Just the fully intact one will do," she said. "In fact, we can probably go ahead and throw the other two away." She nodded at a dumpster midway through the alley.

He rubbed the back of his neck. "You might want to go through them yourself to make sure there's nothing you want in there. One of them had a bunch of burst bottles of shampoo or something inside, so I didn't poke around too much."

"I'm feeling impulsive," she said. "Let's throw them away. Boston is done."

The finality with which she said it surprised him, and it rubbed him the wrong way a little. Like someday she might

233

say that about Asheville and her chapter at Buchanan Brewery. About him.

But his mind was running away from him again, and the excitement shining in her eyes was infectious, so he opened the back seat and pulled out one of the bags, the green one, its plastic corpse jutting out in jagged angles.

"Let's do it," he said.

She grabbed the other bag, and they hauled them to the dumpster, which smelled like hot garbage always smelled, except maybe riper. Like it had been left to ferment. Of course, River wasn't sure he smelled a whole lot better. Smoke and sickly sweet punch did not make for a good combination, but it hadn't repulsed Georgie yet.

"Maybe this wasn't the best idea," she said, laughing a little as they came to a stop in front of it. "That smell is wilting my sails."

"No," he said as he set down the green bag on a clean patch of concrete. "We have to do it now. We've come too far." Scrunching his nose dramatically, he lifted the lid of the dumpster and flipped it open.

The smell instantly became ten times worse.

Georgie shoved the bag in her hands at him. "I think you should do the gentlemanly thing."

"I opened the dumpster, didn't I?" he said, but he took it from her anyway, hefting it up and in. It landed with a squishing sound, sending up another waft of stink.

"Hurry," Georgie said, lifting the green bag and handing it to him, "here's the other."

He hefted that one in too, and it landed on the first. But before he could close the lid of the dumpster, a foot-long rat scurried out of the opening, almost running across his hand.

He jumped back, making a sound of alarm—his ego prevented him from thinking of it as a scream—and Georgie did the same. They hurried toward his building without shutting the dumpster, running as fast as if the rat were chasing them, and when they got to his doorstep they exchanged a look and burst out laughing.

"Did that feel as inspirational to you as it did to me?" he asked.

"You bet," she said as he got out his key, glancing back to make sure the rat hadn't actually followed them, "but we're both going to need to wash our hands at least twenty times before I let you touch me."

"Deal." He turned the key in the lock, his mouth ticking up at the thought that surfaced. "Good thing I don't need to touch you to kiss you."

Opening the door, he leaned in to do just that, his lips finding Georgie's as they stumbled into the loft together. He instantly felt the energy, the connection he always felt with her.

Except Maisie was sitting at the table with a couple of takeout bags, and Hops ran up to him with a frantically wagging tail and started to sniff his pants in an overly interested way that confirmed he very much needed a shower. As soon as possible.

He pulled away from Georgie, mood deflated by Maisie's sour, disapproving expression as much as by the fact that she had clearly ignored his message. What was it with his friends today? Why did everyone but his aunt want to stand in his way?

"We've got to stop meeting like this," Maisie said in an airy tone that probably didn't convince Georgie and certainly didn't convince River.

"Didn't you get my message?" he asked. He studiously ignored Hops, who had started licking his shoe.

"Well, yes, plus about ten texts from Finn. And Beau's neighbors have started a group on Nextdoor for citizens concerned about Jezebel's escape."

Which was exactly why he'd made a point of turning off his phone earlier. He didn't want to deal with any of that tonight, or ever really.

He shot an apologetic look at Georgie. She smiled at him, but this wasn't her natural, warm smile. She was struggling for this one. Plus, she was clearly embarrassed they'd been caught. Again.

"I told you I'd go into all of the gory details tomorrow, Maisie. Georgie and I have had a long night, and we're both tired."

Maisie gave him a look that said she knew exactly what *tired* was code for. "I know, which is why I brought you takeout. Surely you're both hungry after your ordeal."

He glanced at Georgie again. "Hey," he said, "you want to go wash your hands in the bathroom? I'll use the sink out here."

He could have invited her to take a shower, but he still hoped to do that with her. And he also didn't want to embarrass her in front of Maisie.

"Yeah, that sounds like a good idea," she said. "Nice to see you again, Maisie." Then she took off almost as fast as they'd retreated from that rat. It wouldn't take her long to wash her hands, but from the look in her eyes she knew what he really wanted—a moment to convince Maisie to leave, or to shove her out the door if she wouldn't go peacefully. She'd give him the time he needed.

River headed to the kitchen sink and washed his hands thoroughly before stooping to pick up Hops—still going at his shoes—and carrying him over to the table.

"What gives?" he asked. "I get that you and Finn don't approve, but I'm not some lost puppy or project. Not anymore. You guys don't get to decide for me. I've finally met someone I like—really like—and it feels like everyone keeps thinking of reasons I shouldn't be happy."

Her stubborn expression slipped, and a stricken look took its place. Almost as if she was on the verge of crying, and Maisie hardly ever cried. Even after she lost her parents. Shit, maybe he'd been too harsh.

He softened his tone and said, "Look, I'm sorry about the computer, and if you're up for it, we can go computer shopping at lunch tomorrow, and I'll tell you the whole sordid story. But I need to be alone with Georgie tonight. I'm asking you to understand."

"River," she said, reaching out to touch his arm, "I do understand. I just don't want you to get hurt. You're clearly in this, but is she?"

He smiled, looking down at Hops because he didn't want Maisie to see his eyes. He felt the vulnerability there. The doubt. "I guess I aim to find out."

CHAPTER
Twenty-Five

Georgie washed her hands for long enough that she likely would have been clean enough to perform surgery, yet she still wasn't ready to leave the bathroom. Not while River was dealing with his friend.

Other than Dottie, it seemed like everyone in his life hated her. Or at least the important people. First Finn, now Maisie. Except she supposed Maisie had shown her disapproval first. Georgie couldn't help thinking Maisie disliked her because she herself was in love with River. But even so...

Josie would have taken it for a bad sign, and she couldn't help but wonder if there was something to that. It didn't help matters any to know that at least two of her three siblings would have a coronary if they knew what she was up to.

Georgie sat down on the toilet lid, surprised when tears stung her eyes. She wasn't much of a crier—her father had made sure of that—but damned if this didn't sting. The connection she felt with River was so much stronger, so much more alive than anything she'd experienced with another man. Her body flushed just thinking about the electricity in his touch. Had she ever blushed more than in the last few days? But with so many people against them...

One night. Just one night. You owe it to yourself.

She was a logical person, though, most of the time, and she knew it would be so much harder to resist him if they slept together. Once she walked through that door, could she really walk back out?

Would she want to?

But Georgie Buchanan had a resolve of steel when the situation required it. She knew she could resist him. Was the same true for him?

She got up and opened the bathroom door, deciding that while the discussion between River and Maisie was very much between them, it would be cowardly for her to keep hanging out in the bathroom. Steeling her back, she headed down the hall to the living room, prepared for Maisie's icy glare, but all she found was River holding Hops in the middle of the room, staring at the closed front door.

He turned to look at her, his eyes troubled, and guilt quickly slid into her head. The last thing she wanted to do was come between him and his friends, even though she had a pretty strong suspicion he and Maisie were not on the same page. It wasn't her place to say so.

"River..."

He set the puppy down and walked toward her. "Georgie. If you changed your mind, you don't have to explain yourself to me. After Maisie and Finn, I can't say I would blame you."

"They're your friends. They're worried about you."

A wry grin twisted his mouth. "They like to butt themselves into my business."

"Because they care about you." Her heart tightened, and she found herself saying, "I wish I had friends like yours."

He stared at her for a moment, then burst out laughing. "Are you drunk? Did Lurch's Pee Brew take an hour to kick in?"

She smiled up at him, lifting her hands to rest on his shoulders, and flutters filled her stomach. "My friends in high school weren't the lifelong type, you know? And my college friends too. Let's just say that I became so focused on Moon Goddess, I let a lot of my friendships die. The few I have aren't that close."

Why was she telling him this? She was making herself sound like a driven asshole, but then again, maybe it was good he knew the truth. Maybe it would help him realize they really could only press pause on reality for so long. He had commitment issues, apparently, and she was too committed to work. A nonstarter.

"I didn't make Moon Goddess what it was without personal sacrifice," she continued. "Buchanan Brewery will likely be the same way."

He studied her for a moment. "I'm not sure what you're trying to tell me. That after tonight you're going to be so driven you won't have time to see me?" His eyes twinkled a little. "I expect we'll be seeing a lot of each other—in a professional capacity—but I understand the rules, Georgie, and I respect them. What happens tonight won't have anything to do with our working relationship. We're both grown-ups. We can set boundaries."

"I'm a fair boss, but sometimes I'm—"

He kissed her lightly. "No work talk."

"But I just want—"

He kissed her again, letting it linger this time, sending shivers all the way to her toes. "We'll compartmentalize. Tomorrow you'll be the boss and I'll be the employee, but tonight..." He kissed her again, slowly slipping his arm around her back and pulling her closer so her body was flush with his. This kiss wasn't as fiery as the one behind the house, but it was full of seduction and promise. "Tonight, it's just the two of us, River and Georgie, two people who find each other irresistible."

The puppy yipped at Georgie's foot, tugging on her shoelace.

She laughed. "You mean the three of us."

River made a face as she glanced down at the interloper.

"Do you need to take him out?" she asked.

"No, Maisie did before we got home. Let me put him in his kennel with a chew stick and his sandal, and he'll be sufficiently entertained."

"Okay," she said, bending down to pick up the fluffball. "Good thing he's so cute."

She glanced at him and caught him looking at the two of them as if he wanted to memorize the image.

He took the puppy from her and headed into the kitchen. Georgie suddenly felt awkward. Should she wait for him here? She still needed a shower. Would it be best to take one now? Or maybe wait and ask him to join her?

Her past relationships had been different, more perfunctory. Men who had required little from her yet failed to hold her interest. Men her father and brother would have approved of—if they could be bothered to meet any of them.

Was that why she was so attracted to River? Because he was everything her father and Lee would object to? Was this an act of rebellion?

But even as she thought it, she knew it wasn't true.

He returned and frowned when he glanced at her face. "Having second thoughts?"

Was she? Her head was starting to protest again, but her heart—and her body—needed this. She needed to know that there could be heat and passion. That she could *feel*.

She slowly shook her head.

"It just occurred to me that you never ate," he said. "Are you hungry? Maisie got—"

It was her turn to quiet him, closing the distance between them and placing the tip of her finger on his lips.

"The only thing I'm hungry for is you," she whispered.

River's dark eyes turned even darker. He lightly kissed her fingertip, and then his tongue darted out, barely touching her skin, sending a bolt of heat down to her core.

Releasing a soft moan, she slid her hand down his neck to his chest.

He wove his hand into her hair and kissed her deeply.

She melted into him, needing to be closer, needing more. Her fingers spread across his chest, feeling the hard muscles she'd gaped at when he'd changed his shirt on Friday, and now that she had that image in her head, she wanted to see them again. She wanted to know the feel of him without any barrier between their skin.

Reaching for the hem of his shirt, she tugged up, and River quickly caught on, taking a moment to pull it over his head and toss it onto the floor.

He leaned over to kiss her again, but she backed up a step, giving him a sexy grin. "Let me look first. I've been thinking about your chest since you ripped your shirt off in the tasting room. I might or might not have peeked earlier too."

His eyes hooded as his breath hitched. "And I've been thinking about those sexy bras and panties spread all over Flint Street." Then he added with a shake of his head, "About them *on you*. Not on the street."

She laughed, loving that she knew he wouldn't be offended, that he was laughing with her…and she stripped off her own shirt to reveal the lacy navy-blue bra underneath.

"God, Georgie. You're even more beautiful than I'd imagined."

Her own breath caught, realizing that no man had ever told her that before and meant it. She could tell he did. Would she really be able to walk away from him and go back to business as usual? She wasn't sure, but she had two options: stop things right now or see this through, and now that she'd had a taste of this, she wasn't stopping.

"Let's shower together," she said. The thought of him wet and naked, his skin slick against hers, made her knees shake.

He grinned. "I was hoping you'd say that. Because I intend on learning every inch of your body."

CHAPTER
Twenty-Six

The first thing River did when he woke up was reach for her. He could still taste her, could still feel her moving against him. It had never been like this with anyone else—it was almost as if they'd anticipated each other's movements, as if they were perfectly in sync. They'd moved seamlessly from the shower to the bed, and there'd been no first-time awkwardness (or second or third time). He hoped to hell she would consider a quick round four since it was still sort of, kind of dark outside.

But he didn't feel the curve of her next to him anymore, didn't hear her soft breathing or smell the shampoo she'd used in the shower. That meant she'd been gone a while.

A hollowness formed in his chest, a familiar ache that made it no less painful. The pain of being left.

You idiot. You knew the deal.

Yes, and he'd known it would feel like this, but he'd decided it was worth it. And it was—or rather it had been— but knowing her in that way had made him want her more. Of course it had.

He turned to look at the empty pillow next to him and saw a crisply folded note.

His mouth ticked upward just a little as he opened the paper and saw the embossed monogram.

I'm sorry I left, River, but I thought it would be easier this way. Last night was—

The pen trailed a little, as if she'd thought about writing something different but had changed her mind.

—amazing. But it's time to put it in that box we talked about. We didn't discuss your usual hours yet, given it certainly qualifies as work talk, but I'd appreciate it if you'd come at 9. We have a lot to discuss.

As a love letter, it left a little to be desired, but he found himself smiling. Because it was so Georgie, and because he hadn't totally given up, not really. He hoped they'd find a way. Because two people who fit like this?

It was kismet. And that didn't come along more than once in a lifetime.

⊷⊷

When River turned on his phone, twenty notifications instantly popped up.

He took a fortifying sip of coffee before he started scrolling through them. The majority were from unknown numbers, but he'd received a text from Maisie at 5:30 a.m.

Either puke bugs are transferable between dogs and humans, or you should consider this a retroactive warning about the food I brought over tonight. I won't be able to do lunch. You'll have to give me the crazy story later, although the accounts on Nextdoor really do paint a picture. ;-)

Huh. Maisie sounded like herself, not like she was pissed or anything, but what was the likelihood she'd come down with a bug the same night he threw her out of his apartment? He and Georgie had eaten the takeout Chinese sometime around midnight, and his stomach still felt fine.

He couldn't shake the thought that Maisie was upset he hadn't followed her advice about Georgie. But he didn't want to make assumptions.

I'll check in later, he responded. *See if you need some soup.*

Her only response was the yacking emoji.

Sorry you're sick, he added, *and sorry about last night. I hate that we don't see eye to eye on this.*

He saw the three dots that indicated she was writing something, but the message never materialized. More proof that she wasn't over it. Well, he'd swing by to see her later. Make sure she was okay.

He checked the time—8:00—and glanced through the rest of the messages.

Half were from a woman named Pat, who was apparently the head of the Nextdoor group, which she'd titled CONTAINING THE CAT MENACE ON FLINT STREET in all caps. She'd last texted to ask for a status update at three in the morning. Several other messages were from people who'd supposedly seen Jezebel, although one described her as a portly ginger cat and another admitted to being partially blind. Perhaps he should have thought twice about giving out his number so freely.

Hops pawed at his pants, reminding him that he needed to be taken out. Would Georgie be okay with him coming back to the loft a couple of times to do that? He couldn't imagine she'd say no, but he was thinking about Georgie, the warm, wonderful woman who'd crept into his heart and lain in his bed, not Georgie, the businesswoman.

A sense of disquiet crept up on him—what would it be like when he saw her?—but he swallowed it down and continued with his morning routine. He arrived at the brewery at a little before nine and headed straight to the back, making his way to Beau's old office. The place looked cleaner than he'd ever seen it, down to the beer rings on the tables, so at least they'd gotten that sorted. Hopefully Georgie had been able to book the company to take care of Beau's house too.

He knocked on the door, his heart thumping powerfully in his chest, and heard Georgie's crisp "Come in."

He did, and his eyes instantly found her. Her hair had been unbound last night, loose and wild, like she herself was a moon goddess—a notion he'd shared with her while he was still inside her, making her laugh…and then gasp. "Why do you think I named it that?" she'd asked afterward. "I'm a goddess by moonlight."

This morning her hair was pulled back into that tight style of the first day they'd met. Not a hair out of place. She was wearing an immaculate gray skirt suit that was much too fancy for Asheville, let alone for a brewery, plus a shirt buttoned up to her very chin.

As a message, it was clear, but something flashed in her eyes—like maybe she was remembering everything too—before she pointedly glanced to his left. Which was when he realized other people were present. For some reason, he'd thought they'd be alone—Georgie and River, planning what came next together, but Tom and Aunt Dottie were both seated in chairs in front of her desk, and although Georgie's monitor was angled away from him, he heard Jack say, "Is *he* there?"

It punctured a little of his positivity, but he merely lowered himself into the empty chair next to his aunt's. She winked at him, and he couldn't help but wonder what she knew. Or what she'd guessed.

"Hi, Jack," he simply said. "Do you need any crystals this morning?"

Georgie's mouth twitched—he'd be generous with himself and call it a smile—and Jack said, "Your aunt already offered. I'm starting to think you have stock in some New Age company." Georgie eyed the screen, and Jack sighed audibly. "Let's just move on, okay?"

"Yes, let's," Georgie said. What had been said between them before the start of this meeting?

"Now, to get you up to speed, River," Georgie said. For a second, he considered apologizing, but she'd told him to come in at nine, and he'd shown up a few minutes early. "I've spoken with Tom and Dottie about our existing stock, and they think we can stay open for two weeks. Jack and I love your idea of doing the big reopening with new beers, and we figured it might be a good idea to take it one further. We're going to have a closing party too."

Something flashed in her eyes, and he realized she was enjoying this. She was good at organizing things—scary good—and he was seeing her in her element. He was grateful for it. In a weird way, he liked this side of her just as much as the unbound Georgie from last night.

"That's smart," he said, grinning at her. Maybe it was an overly friendly grin for an employee to give his boss, but you could box up the past all you liked, there was no erasing it. "It can be a kill-the-keg party. A celebration of Buchanan Brewery the way it was, and an invitation for customers to be part of the future. We can hold a naming contest for one of the new brews. And if we still want to go with Jack's idea of having one cocktail-inspired beer for each season, we can take votes on that too."

Georgie's whole face lit up—and damn, did he feel good about being the one who'd made her smile like that.

"That's great," Georgie said. "And you said you already have a few more beers planned. We can go over that after this meeting."

"I do," he said, grinning back at her. "I'd love to walk you through it."

Their gazes held for a moment, River feeling that invisible connection between them, binding them even as they sat apart, untouching, but Aunt Dottie cleared her throat.

"I've been thinking," she said, her tone very serious. "I'd like to donate my statue of Beau to the brewery. Beau *belongs* here. I'm not ready to part with him yet, but he should be at Buchanan for the grand reopening."

Georgie's face leached of color, as if the takeout had in fact been tainted, and the effects had only just kicked in.

"Um, that's really generous of you," she said, at the same time Jack said, "Are you talking about the statue with that giant crystal...?" Another look from Georgie silenced that last word, at least, but Tom shuffled a little in his seat, uncomfortable.

"You should keep the crystal, Aunt Dottie," River said. "I think Beau would want you to have it. And you could maybe put some of his old clothes on him? Or some of the new merch once it's redesigned?"

Georgie immediately grasped on to the idea. "Yes, that sounds great! I agree. We definitely want to celebrate the full history of the brewery."

"With clothing," Jack added.

"What's your plan for the employees?" Tom asked, speaking for the first time since River had entered the room, not that he'd been given much of a chance. "Some of them can be assigned different tasks, especially since you talked about rearranging the tasting room, but redesigning the labels and merch will probably have to be done by a contractor."

"I've been thinking about that a lot," Georgie said. She picked up a pen and started tapping it. "We'll need a full staff when we reopen. Like you said, some people can take on different functions. For those who can't, I'll offer them 75% of their salary during the closure *if* they sign an agreement to come back. They'll be free to work elsewhere in the interim, of course."

Tom's eyes widened, and River didn't need to ask to know what he was thinking—it was generous to the point of surprising. Most employers would have laid them off, especially since there were plenty of people looking for jobs in the area. It was the honorable thing to do, but it bothered River to know the vast majority of that money would come straight out of Georgie's profits from Moon Goddess. So would whatever salary she offered him, and it was bound to be more than he wanted or needed after Finn's big talk. How long would her savings last? And what if Buchanan Brewery still flopped after everything they were doing to save it?

"I think they'll be pleased to hear it," Tom said, rubbing the back of his neck. "There's been a lot of talk of people losing their jobs."

"Which is why we ought to throw an after-party for all the employees," Aunt Dottie said. "At my house."

Would any of them survive it?

"Aunt Dottie," he said, turning to her, "I'm not sure that's such a good idea."

"Actually," Georgie said, catching his eye for a brief moment, "I think it's a good plan. The employees need to know they're valued. Jack and I will help you plan it, Dottie." She glanced at her brother on her computer screen. "I'm not sure what your timeline is like, Jack, but it might be a good idea for you to plan on being back in time for the closing parties. I'm going to invite Adalia and Lee too, although I doubt they'll both be able to come. It'll be a chance for everyone to get to know us."

Assuming it didn't end with another fire.

"I'll try" was all Jack said, and River couldn't help but wonder if he'd told Georgie anything else about why he'd left town.

"All right," Georgie said, clapping her hands together. "I'm pleased with where this is going. For now, we'll carry on with business as usual, but we'll have to announce our plans soon. Jack and I can work on that, and I'll address the staff before we open for customers at 12:00." She smiled at them each in turn, but this was her professional smile, her business smile. "We've got a lot to do, but I'm confident we can do it." Her gaze shot to River, and something passed through it—regret maybe—before she said, "River, can you stay for a minute? I need to speak with you about something."

His heart started pounding too fast again, and he felt both excitement and panic—did she want to talk about last night? In a quiet moment, as they lay together in bed, their bodies cradled together, he'd whispered to her, "Georgie, if you change your mind, you need to be the one to tell me. I promise I'll never try to press you." She'd just tipped her head to kiss him. But maybe she had rethought things.

Or maybe her brothers convinced her to get rid of you, a voice in his head countered.

Recognizing their dismissal, Tom and Aunt Dottie got up and left, River's aunt pausing to squeeze his shoulder on the way out.

River had almost forgotten Jack was still there, remotely, when he said, "Make sure to tell him about what we discussed, Georgie."

The way he said it, still with a bit of attitude, meant it wasn't good news, but it clearly wasn't *you're fired* kind of news either.

"I will," she said, a little pique in her voice. "Goodbye, Jack." And she clicked the call off without giving him the chance to say anything else.

"Georgie…" River said, but truth be told, he wasn't really sure where he was going with that. And he didn't have the opportunity to find out. She slid a document toward him from across the desk.

"Here's your official offer, River, like we discussed." She licked her lips in a way that brought his attention to her lower lip—and made him remember sucking on it. And God, this was so much harder than he'd told himself it would be. "You can have a few hours to look it over, if you'd like, or have a lawyer, or even Finn, review it, but I'd appreciate it if you could give me your official answer sooner rather than later. I know we still have to discuss the new beers, but we'll want to get started immediately on the Buchanan ones we're keeping."

There were so many things he'd like to say, but most of all, he wanted to take her hand. To reassure himself he hadn't been dreaming everything. Instead, he took the document.

It was more than he'd made at Big Catch. Which meant she was definitely paying him from her savings. It was wrong, and he opened his mouth to say so when he realized there was a second paper behind the first. He flipped to it and frowned.

The heading read: *Addition to the Employee Manual.* And beneath it, it said: *Fraternization is strictly prohibited between employees of Buchanan Brewery.*

CHAPTER
Twenty-Seven

The look on River's face sent a bolt of pain through her gut. It seemed like the ultimate insult to present it to him like this—not that she'd wanted to present it at all—but she'd woken to a group text between her siblings, Jack included, with Lee insisting she present the addendum he'd already prepared.

She'd nearly told him to go to hell. He hadn't expressed the slightest interest in helping her run the business, and it wasn't his money on the line. How dare he—they, because Jack had obviously played a part in this—think she would be anything less than professional. Hadn't she been willing to give up River for that very reason?

And yet, it was a moot point anyway, wasn't it? She and River had made a deal, an arrangement. They'd given themselves one night—last night—and now it was over. Georgie had known it would be hard to go about her business as though nothing had happened, but in the cold light of day, she realized how naïve she'd been. Or, more accurately, she'd discovered how amazing sex with River had been. Tasting heaven would make it difficult to go back to the way it had been before…because she knew that her life would now be *before* River and *after*.

She'd still thought about chucking the addendum. It had been on her mind all morning, pricking her like a bramble bush. She could say no. That's all it would take. But something had held her back. At first she'd thought it was the part of her, the small part she hated, that still craved her father's and brother's approval, but now that she was with River, she realized what it really was.

One look on his face when he'd walked into her office had made it clear he'd be more than willing to pick up where they left off very early in the morning. And she wanted that. She wanted him almost enough to say the hell with their ridiculous deal and reach for him.

And that was why she slid that damned piece of paper toward him. Because her hesitation didn't have anything to do with her family. Not anymore.

She knew she could lose herself in River if she allowed it to happen, and she'd never given any man control over her heart. Now wasn't the time to start. She'd seen what had happened to her mother. She'd had a promising career as an art history professor, but she'd never gotten beyond the associate professor stage. Her interests, her drive, her ambition—they'd always taken a back seat to Georgie's father. His whims had controlled everyone in the family, and the wisdom of retrospection told her they'd all but crushed her mother. Georgie had vowed to never let the same thing happen to her—to never let a man become her be-all and end-all—and she'd never been tempted before. It had never been an issue. But she'd only known River for a matter of days, and she was already thinking about him far too much. It scared her. Last night was fine…more than fine…but she stood behind her original decision—it couldn't happen again. Which meant no River in her bed, or her in his, as the case may be.

"I know…" Her voice was rough, so she paused and cleared her throat before starting again. "I know we've already agreed to this, but my brothers insisted that all the employees sign it."

His gaze was on the paper for several seconds, and for one brief moment she was terrified he'd get up and walk out of the room, leaving Buchanan Brewery. Leaving her. Not that she could blame him given the way her family was treating him.

Given the way *she* was treating him.

Finally, he released a short laugh and tilted his head, still not meeting her gaze. "That's good. For a moment there, I was about to take it personally."

"I didn't write this up, River," she said just a little too quickly.

That was what prompted River to raise his eyes to hers, a sad smile lifting the corners of his mouth. There was a novel's worth of messages in his gaze. Empathy. Regret. Sadness. Respect. "I know. It's okay, Georgie. You're right. This is what we agreed to."

So why did this feel so wrong? So sullied. Like making him sign that paper cheapened what had been hands down the best night of her life, with the kindest, most thoughtful…the sexiest man she'd ever known.

A lump filled her throat and she glanced down at Beau's desk…her desk now. She was in charge, which meant she had to make the hard decisions and stand by them.

"I don't need to have anyone look this over," he said, searching her desk. "The offer is more than generous. Do you have a pen?"

His willingness to sign the offer letter, which he clearly hadn't read from start to finish, put her in a panic.

"Are you sure?" she asked. "There's a noncompete clause my brothers insisted on. You *really* should seek legal advice." That had been Lee's doing as well. Last night, he had emailed her, Jack, and Adalia a draft of River's contract, drawn up by none other than the lovely Victoria. It was hard not to think it was some form of retaliation, or at least response, for ignoring her father's request for a business proposal. Jack had responded promptly, wholeheartedly agreeing with the noncompete clause. Georgie had upped the offer significantly over what Lee had proposed, and she'd planned to strike out the noncompete language, but Jack had called her at seven thirty this morning, insisting she leave it in.

"What happens when River finds out he would have gotten it all if we'd failed?" Jack had asked. "What's to keep him from jumping ship and either starting his own brewery or going to someone else's with the sole intent of running us into the ground?"

"He's not going to do that, Jack," she'd said with a sigh, her heart heavy. "He's not that kind of a guy."

"And you know this how?" he'd demanded. "Because he's obviously interested in you?"

"That's not fair, Jack," she'd snapped. "And it's damned insulting."

"We need him to sign it, Georgie. After we make it to the one year mark, we can offer him another contract without a noncompete, and he'll be none the wiser. The one Lee came up with only runs through next April anyway."

That had been another sticking point for her—the short term of the contract. It was for less than a year, which seemed insulting, but then again, she supposed it wouldn't matter if they lost the brewery. Still, River didn't know about the deadline, so she'd figured he was bound to question it. Only he hadn't. He'd almost signed without even reading it.

Because he trusted her.

She felt like she was going to be sick.

His voice tightened, as though he were being strangled. "A noncompete?"

"Just for Asheville," she said. "And a two-hundred-mile radius. You could go to the West Coast, though," she quickly added. "Or you could get an attorney to make a counterproposal." *Please, please get an attorney.*

"I take it that's your brothers' doing as well?" he asked, staring at her with so much intensity, she wondered if he was trying to read her soul. Did he see the stains of her betrayal?

"Get your attorney to make a counteroffer, River."

"Are you planning on firing me?" he asked, his gaze holding hers.

Why had she agreed to this? Jack wasn't even here. He'd run off to do God knew what, because he still hadn't deigned to tell her. "No. Definitely not."

"What about your brothers?"

"I'm giving them small concessions so I can fight for the things I really want. And I really want you, River," she said before she could stop herself. She quickly looked away, frustrated by how unnerved she felt. How she hadn't just meant she needed him for reviving Buchanan. "I need you." She glanced up at him. "They won't fire you. You have my word."

An emotion flashed in his eyes, one she didn't know how to interpret, but it wasn't anything joyful.

"Pick your battles," he finally said, the words soft but also full of disappointment.

She knew what he wasn't saying. She might be willing to fight for him, but only halfway. "Take it to an attorney," she said. "Or to Finn. Let him look it over and give you advice."

He stared at the document for a good five seconds before he rose slightly and grabbed a pen off her desk. He signed both documents with a flourish, then slid them across the desk. "Now that that's out of the way, we've got work to do. We've both agreed we should keep Beau Brown, but another popular beer is…"

Georgie tried to focus on what he was saying, but deep inside she was freaking out that he'd signed those papers so easily. She'd sworn that she would fight for him. She only hoped she could live up to it.

CHAPTER
Twenty-Eight

He'd made it almost two weeks. That was something, wasn't it?

Professional Georgie hadn't so much as cracked. Not that she'd given herself much of an opportunity—a lot of the time they spent together they had some sort of chaperone: Aunt Dottie or Tom or another employee, or Jack on whatever video app she used. Still, he'd catch her looking at him sometimes, a longing in her eyes that made him want to say to hell with it and reach for her, except he couldn't do that. And not because of some stupid piece of paper. He couldn't do it because he'd promised her.

Sometimes he wondered what he was doing. It was too hard, being around her constantly and knowing he couldn't be with her. Especially since he clicked with Professional Georgie just as well as he did with the Georgie that let her hair down. They shared a vision, and he knew that for the rarity it was.

They'd taste-tested a few beers and ciders together one afternoon to narrow down the flavor profile he was trying to achieve with the new brews—the level of hops from bottle

A, with the fruit finish from bottle B—and he'd been reminded of that first night. Of the promise he'd felt between them. Of the freedom of not having to worry about things like professionalism and paperwork.

At least they'd decided on the beers they were making, plus he'd gotten in batches of Beau Brown, Lurch White, and Donuts for Dottie. (Beau hadn't been too creative in the naming department, but it had been part of his charm.) The party planning was going full steam ahead too, both for the Kill the Keg party, which they were calling Bury the Brewery. Somewhat ominous, but the bigger launch party they were already planning for fall would be Buchanan Brewery Rises. Jack had commented that at least it was better than We Cleaned the Piss Pots, Please Come Back. Georgie had, of course, insisted on being involved in every stage of Aunt Dottie's after-party planning (in the nicest but firmest way possible). Still, he knew his aunt would have surprises up her sleeve. She always did.

The worst part of the last week was not having anyone to talk to about it. Finn would've told him he was nuts for signing that contract. Perhaps rightly so. But he still wasn't talking to Finn. There'd been some check-in texts from the other Big Catch staffers, some invitations for drinks, but he didn't feel up to it yet. They'd want to talk about the sale, about Finn, and most certainly about Buchanan. He didn't. Finn had texted him a few times too, saying he urgently needed to talk to him about something, but he'd ignored the messages—in fact, he rarely picked up his phone anymore. Every time he did, there were at least fifteen texts about Jezebel. Plenty of people had seen her, but much to Aunt Dottie's consternation, they all had a common approach: run and then text River.

Of course, by the time he got to the intersection where they'd seen her feasting on trash or chasing a child into a tree, she'd be long gone. He could have blocked their numbers, but the sadness in his aunt's eyes whenever she spoke about the cat prevented it.

Aunt Dottie talked to him, of course—she'd insisted on him coming over for dinner three times in the past week, but she always tried to hearten him, to reassure him that the stars were aligned in his favor and the tea she'd tricked him into drinking had left distinct hearts in the leaves at the bottom. Somehow her encouragement made everything harder.

And then there was Maisie—she'd been avoiding him like he had the plague, all while insisting she did. Something he wasn't so sure he believed given he'd called the shelter a few days ago and Dustin had acted surprised, and then interested, when he'd said Maisie was sick.

"Reallllly," he'd said, drawing it out, and River could practically hear the wheels turning in his mind.

He wanted to make things right, but he wasn't sure how if she wouldn't talk to him. Giving her space hadn't worked. It was Thursday afternoon, just a couple of days before the big Buchanan closing party on Saturday, and he wanted her to be there. So he'd decided to ambush her at the shelter. Something he could do since it was technically his day off. (Sure, he'd spent the morning in the office, but truth be told, he'd only gone so he could see Georgie.)

He came bearing expensive coffee and the right kind of muffins, and he felt oddly nervous. The last thing he'd meant to do was hurt her, but it seemed like he wasn't doing anything right lately.

One of the volunteers he recognized—luckily not Dustin—let him in, and pointed him toward the playroom when he asked for Maisie.

"She'll be grateful for the coffee," the volunteer said with a smile. "She's been pulling long hours with Beatrice all week on the new funding drive."

Which meant she almost certainly hadn't been sick, not that he'd really believed her story. Still, it put a pit in his stomach that she'd lied to him. That she'd gone out of her way not to see him. That she'd left him like Georgie, like Finn, like Beau. But he could still make things right with Maisie.

He had to.

He knocked on the door, using the secret knock they'd developed as teens, and instead of answering, she just opened it.

She *did* look tired. Her hair was still wet, flatter than it would be in a few hours when it finally dried and the curls sprang up, and the circles under her eyes made it look like she hadn't been sleeping.

But something inside of him eased upon seeing her. The look in her eyes told him she was glad he was here. That she didn't want him to leave.

"I come bearing gifts," he said, lifting up the cup and the bag.

She lifted an eyebrow, and before she could say anything, he preempted her with, "And yes, it is the right kind of muffin."

"Thank God," she said, taking his offerings. "Otherwise I would have had to send you back, and you're a sight for sore eyes."

She ushered him in, and he felt all the relief of being wanted.

Part of him had expected another avalanche of puppies, but the dog in the room was one he hadn't seen before, a red husky.

"A new kid?" he asked, nodding to the dog, who'd padded over and was sniffing him with interest. Smelling Hops, no doubt.

"Meet Tyrion, the escape artist. Owner was watching too much *Game of Thrones*, confused huskies for direwolves, and realized they're a lot of work."

She shrugged, but he caught the flash of righteous anger in her eyes. It would never sit all right with her that people abandoned their dogs, or their children.

"Good thing he found you," he said, and meant it.

He sat down at the table and looked up at her, feeling for all the world like that kid again.

"You were sick?" he asked.

She blew a few stray hairs out of her face and sat opposite him. Took a swig of the coffee that probably burned her tongue. "I *felt* sick, but maybe I kind of, sort of exaggerated."

"I know I was harsh last week," he said quickly. "It wasn't because of anything you did. It just felt like the world was against me." He paused, swallowed. "Or at least against me and Georgie."

She must have heard something in his voice, because her eyes softened even more, the sympathy there a welcome balm.

"And I should have listened a lot better," she said. She paused, then added, "I guess I've just never seen you go this gaga over anyone before. I was worried—I *am* worried—and I didn't know what to do. But I'm ready to listen now if you want to talk."

And he was, and he did. Of course, he didn't say anything more about his night with Georgie. Maisie knew, sort of, and the details were between him and Georgie. He also didn't mention the noncompete or the addendum to the handbook. Midway through the telling, Tyrion padded over to the table and sat, his posture regal, to listen too.

"The party's Saturday," he finished. "You'll come, right?"

"Maybe," she said, popping the last piece of muffin. "It's been a bit of a nightmare around here. We're short on funding, again, and we need to put in another big push this weekend. I'll be there if I can. And by there, I mean at Dottie's after-party." She grinned. "I'm no fool. I know where the real fun's at."

"Of course," he said, a return grin tugging at his face. "And if you need any help with the fundraising, just let me know. Maybe we can do some sort of event or drive for you once the brewery reopens. I'll talk to Georgie about it."

"Thanks. And while we're talking about Georgie..." Maisie leaned over, giving Tyrion a pat, and didn't look at him. "I know it's hard, but maybe she's right. It sounds like you work well together, and it would be a shame to mess with that for something as unsure as a relationship. Especially since—"

He groaned and ran a hand through his hair. "Yeah, I know. Especially since I've never had a long one. But Maisie, this is different. Georgie's different."

"Yeah," she said, "I can see that. But all you can do is wait. Sometimes that's all a person can do." The way she said it almost held a note of bitterness. He was about to ask her if she was okay, but someone knocked on the door.

"Maisie," the volunteer from earlier called. "One of the foster families is calling. Adonis needs to go to the vet."

Genuine worry flashed on Maisie's face. "He has a heart condition," she explained. "I've got to take this, but maybe we can get lunch sometime soon." She wagged a finger in his face like a schoolmarm. "I still need that computer."

It *had* been ruined, along with a lot of other stuff. The house was still a bit of a mess, but Georgie, with her siblings' approval, had brought in contractors to update it while they fixed the damage. He couldn't help but wonder if the others did anything beyond order her around and okay her choices.

She'd shown him pictures of the downstairs in one of those rare moments they'd been alone together. Her hand had grazed his as he took her phone, sending a rush of sensation through him, and she'd kept it like that—their hands touching—for longer than needed. Their eyes had met as he handed it back, and she'd opened her mouth to say something—

Only for the video app to ring with a call from Jack.

Jack was great at getting in the way, even from Chicago, although perhaps that wasn't entirely fair.

"You got it," he said, giving Tyrion a pat as Maisie led him out of the room.

He headed back to his car, feeling restless, and found himself driving somewhere unexpected. The cemetery. Beau had a nice spot, beneath a large oak tree, and someone—he suspected Aunt Dottie—had left a bouquet of hops.

He felt a little uncomfortable being there, like it was maybe stupid of him to try talking to a dead man, communing with one. A quick glance told him no one was around, and he sat at the base of the grave and looked up at the sky, as if to see Beau's view from down below.

"I think I love her, Beau," he whispered, worried even now that someone might hear him. "I haven't told anyone else, not even Aunt Dottie, although she probably knows. I know it's too early to think that way, but I can't help it.

You'd understand. You must have seen what I see, because there's something about Georgie that just sparkles."

He swallowed thickly. "We're trying to do right by you," he said. "I think you'd be proud of the direction we're taking with the brewery, and these parties on Saturday? They'll be a celebration of everything you did. Of who you were." A grin split his face. "Right down to that statue you must have modeled for."

He fidgeted a little, fighting the sudden hotness behind his eyes. "I didn't know it was going to be this hard. I feel a little lost again, Beau, and I'm not sure what to do. I'm worried if I do anything, I'll push her away."

He sat there for several minutes, feeling the sun on the back of his neck. It started to feel a little stupid, waiting here, as if he thought he'd get an answer if he stayed long enough, when someone cleared their throat behind him, and he turned and saw Georgie.

CHAPTER
Twenty-Nine

Georgie's breath caught when she saw River sitting in front of Beau's grave, warmth spreading through her at the sight of him, just like it did every time she'd seen him since...when? Their night together? No, it had been longer than that. Since the first night at Beau's.

Why had she gone and hired him? If she'd found another brewer, she could still be sleeping with him...yet she knew that wasn't completely true. She probably would have closed the door on him forever after that night, because what she felt for him scared the crap out of her.

For the first time in her life, Georgie had found a man she was sure she could love, and the only acceptable course of action was to run. The way she'd been thinking about him—what he was doing, what he was thinking—was almost...not obsessive, exactly, but it was the kind of fixed attention she'd never given to another person. By design. She was haunted by the pain on her mother's face every time Prescott Buchanan had ignored her or demeaned her, even if Georgie hadn't understood it when she was younger...

Georgie had spent the last few years reevaluating her parents' marriage, and she'd come to the realization that her mother had known about Prescott's indiscretions. His affair—or maybe affairs. Their relationship had always been so mercurial—days of silent treatment, followed by a shower of gifts and attention. A yin and yang of happiness and despair. It was a sharp reminder that the people you thought you could love and trust *always* let you down. Her father had let down her mother. Her father and brothers had let her down. Her mother had broken her heart when she'd died.

But then, Georgie was sure she'd let down Adalia too.

Something was going on with her sister. She wasn't sure how she knew, but she knew it with certainty. Dottie would probably have told her it sprung from her womanly intuition. She kept trying to reach out, but Adalia persisted in brushing off her concerned texts, saying everything was fine, she was just busy getting ready for her show. But this morning, Georgie had video-called her to update her about the upcoming parties and ask if she was interested in helping with designs for merch, labels, and a new logo. Adalia had answered, her eyes red as though she'd been crying. When Georgie asked her what was wrong, her sister had shrugged off her concern and offered some excuse about her allergies giving her grief.

"But you don't have seasonal allergies," Georgie said.

"I'm fine," Adalia said in a tone that made it clear she didn't want to discuss it.

"Can you come to the closing parties?" Georgie asked. "Jack's still being cagey about whether or not he'll be there, and we both know Lee won't lower himself to come." Which was probably for the best. If he came, Victoria would come too, and she'd be attached to him like Velcro. She hated to admit she'd rather he not come.

Adalia had looked away. "I don't know…"

"Buchanan Brewery can pay for your trip," Georgie had added a little too quickly, suddenly overwhelmed with the need to see her sister. Seeing Adalia would help remind her there were other things to focus on besides a man. Like rebuilding her relationship with her sister, something she'd always wanted and, to her shame, hadn't found the time for. "The business can buy your plane tickets and you can stay at the house with me. I'm moving back in tomorrow."

"I still can't believe the house caught on fire."

"Yeah, neither can I." She'd told the others about the fire, but she'd described it (only somewhat accurately) as an electrical problem, the kind of thing that would happen in any old house. Equally, while Adalia and Lee knew the brewery would be closing for a couple of months so they could update the facility and brew new beers, they didn't know about the whole pee pots incident. She and Jack had agreed they were on a need-to-know basis given they'd chosen to be silent partners. And since they'd figured out how to make the most of the unanticipated delay, there was no real need for them to know.

As far as the house went, everything in the living room had been destroyed, but thankfully the damage had been localized. Georgie would be moving into a house that had an empty first floor other than a kitchen and dining room table and chairs, but that didn't matter. All she needed was a bed. She could buy more furniture after the closing parties were out of the way.

"Has that crazy cat turned up yet?"

"Not yet." Yet another reason to move back in ASAP. Jezebel was still missing, and Georgie suspected she'd be more liable to come home if someone was living there and putting out food regularly. Thinking of Jezebel made her think about River, which wasn't saying much. *Everything* made her think about River. "Can you *please* come? I really need you, Addy."

Adalia was silent for a moment. "Are you having second thoughts? Jack was so insistent we keep the brewery, but he caught the first flight out of Asheville after signing the papers."

Georgie started to say it hadn't happened like that but stopped herself because it had been pretty darn close. *Was* she having second thoughts? She'd felt plenty of fear and anxiety when she'd started Moon Goddess, but those emotions had been dwarfed by the excitement and exhilaration of doing something *new*—of making something. All of those emotions were present now, but Georgie couldn't shake the overall sadness that enshrouded her, and she was smart enough to know it stemmed from sleeping with River.

How had she been so stupid?

This was what happened when you let your heart lead you. She hoped she remembered the lesson.

But she was also smart enough to know she'd still feel this sadness if she hadn't let herself have one night with him—it just wouldn't be this deep.

Was she sorry she'd agreed to raise Buchanan Brewery from the ashes? She wasn't sure she had an answer yet.

Which was why she'd felt compelled to come here, to Beau's grave.

Except she wasn't the only one who'd felt that tug.

The look of longing and sorrow on River's face tugged at her heart, but he quickly stuffed it away and gave her a tired smile. "Looks like great minds think alike." He got to his feet. "I'll leave you to pay your respects."

He started to walk around her, and it took everything in her not to reach out and take his hand like she'd done before he signed that paper. She'd taken his touch for granted.

"Don't go," she said softly, the words almost lost in the gentle breeze, but he must have heard her because he stood stock-still, as though waiting for her to give him another order.

Order. Because she was the boss and he was the employee.

Tears stung her eyes.

He stirred, as though about to reach for her, then stopped.

"Is everything okay?" he asked gently.

His question only induced more tears. She loved that about him…how he could be so gentle and supportive. How he cared about her feelings.

Why had she agreed to greenlight that stupid addendum and the noncompete? Because part of her wanted to fire him on the spot and throw herself at him, yet she couldn't do that to him. What kind of monster would she be if she took him away from his dream job at his mentor's brewery? They wouldn't be able to be together anyway, because the noncompete clause would force him to leave Asheville and Dottie and his friends, everything that had given him the stability he'd needed after his mother abandoned him.

Dottie, being Dottie, had let that slip while they were planning the employee party, like she presumed River had already shared one of his deepest wounds with her. She hadn't told Dottie the truth—that he'd only hinted at what his mother had done—not that the older woman had given her a chance. She'd dropped it as a throwaway line—"After Esmerelda up and left River like a dress that doesn't fit anymore, he was lost for a while"—and then Dottie had moved on to suggesting they get sparklers for the party for everyone to wave around, which Georgie had gently nixed by suggesting they try mini flashlights instead.

Georgie and River had worked together for two weeks now, seeing each other for hours nearly every day, and the more she got to know him, the more she liked him as a person. Why couldn't she settle for having him in her life as a friend? A valued colleague?

Because she selfishly wanted more.

Being with River—but *not* with him—was torture, which was beyond stupid. Georgie usually had a backbone of steel. Just last year, after realizing she'd gained several pounds eating a gourmet ice cream she'd discovered and loved, she'd given it up out of sheer willpower. When Georgie set her mind to something, she did it. So why was it different with River?

This new side of herself scared her witless. She didn't recognize it, and she sure didn't trust it.

But River was standing in front of her—at her request—waiting for her to say something.

Get yourself together, Georgie.

She forced a smile, wiping a tear that streaked down her face, but keeping her gaze on Beau's temporary grave marker. "Sorry," she said with a laugh. "I had a difficult call with Adalia."

He straightened as though he was ready to spring into action. "Is she okay? Do you need anything?"

His response only drew more tears to her eyes. Why did he have to be so damn amazing? She shook her head. "No, she's fine, I think. Or at least that's what she tells me."

Because that's what Buchanans did. They stuffed all their real emotions down and told the world they were fine.

They lied to each other and they lied to themselves. Only the lies weren't working for Georgie anymore.

She took a breath and forced herself to look up at him. "I'd invited her to come to Asheville this weekend, but she said she couldn't get away. I'd hoped that she'd come for the parties." Then, before she could stop herself, she added, "So I wouldn't have to do this alone." Another tear fell down her cheek, but she left this one, because she knew more were close behind. "So I'd have *someone* here."

"You're not alone," River said quietly, his hands fisted at his sides. "You have my aunt and Tom. You have the other employees—they love you, you know. And it's because of you, not because you're Beau's granddaughter. They'd walk to the end of the earth to help you get things going again, because they see your excitement and your belief in the brewery."

He was partially wrong. While she did believe in the brewery, she believed in him more. Who was she kidding? River Reeves was the heart and soul of the new and improved Buchanan Brewery, because without the beer, what was there? Yet here he was, trying to give her the glory. She turned away, guilt eating at her. The brewery was supposed to be his. Why had her grandfather changed his mind?

She realized now that's why she'd come. To ask Beau why. She hadn't understood the pull to the cemetery, yet she'd followed her gut, because it rarely steered her wrong. Still, when she thought about trusting it to tell her how to handle River, she only felt like barfing.

Maybe that was a sign in itself.

But she realized now that River hadn't included himself on that list.

More tears fell.

"What can I do to help you, Georgie?" he asked, his voice sounding strangled.

She shook her head. "I'm sorry I kept you." Then she realized she'd interrupted his moment of reflection with Beau. *She* was the interloper. "In fact, you stay. I'll come back to pay my respects another time."

She turned to leave, but he grabbed her arm and pulled her to his chest, wrapping an arm around her back and holding her close. She sank into him, needing his comfort. She wrapped her arms around his back and held on for dear life.

His rapid pulse pounded in her ear, the only sign that this was affecting him as much as it was affecting her.

They stood like that for nearly half a minute, not saying a word, not making any movement except for Georgie's soft cries.

Tell him you'll tear up the addendum. But she couldn't. If she felt this much pain denying herself a relationship with him, how much more would it hurt if he left her one day? If their one night was any indication of what was possible, she wasn't sure she'd survive it. River was a good man. The kind of man you built a life with. What if she built her life with him, and it all crumbled? Would she be like her mother?

Because that was Georgie's biggest fear—that she'd become her mother, the person she'd loved most in the world—and if all the other ugly thoughts didn't make her a monster, that one surely did.

She took a step back and stared up at him, grateful for her new resolve. River may not have included himself in the list of people who were there for her, but he'd just proven he was. She didn't have to lose him. Look at River and Maisie. It was obvious she was in love with him—took one to know one—yet they were still friends. Georgie could manage it too. She just needed to push through. It would get easier with time.

"You're a great friend, River, and I'm grateful to have you in my life. Thank you for being here for me."

Something flashed in his eyes, but it was gone too quickly for her to read it. He smiled. "Of course, Georgie. You're not alone, okay?"

She nodded and stuck out her hand. "Friends?"

He lowered his gaze to her hand as he took it, his warm fingers enveloping hers. "Friends."

As he turned and walked away, she couldn't help thinking she was letting go of the very best thing to ever come into her life.

Maybe she was her mother after all. Choosing to stay in a loveless marriage. Or letting the love of your life go. What was the difference when they both caused so much pain?

In the end, choose business, her head reminded her.

So why did it ring so hollow?

CHAPTER
Thirty

It had felt like Beau was answering him, Georgie showing up like that. And then, for a few brief moments, she'd let him hold her the way he'd been itching to do. It had felt like the sun was shining on him after a long day of darkness. It had felt like coming home.

Back when he was a kid, River and his mother had traveled so much it had been his norm. Esmerelda would answer the call to some far-flung place or other and drag him along as if he were a suitcase. She made jewelry—beautiful pieces with hand-woven metal and stones acquired on their travels—and sold enough for them to live cheaply and on the fly. Sometimes they stayed in communities with other kids, and he'd get to play with children his age, but he'd never been put in a traditional school. She'd homeschooled him, or so she said, but really she'd just given him the books and let him guide his own education, something that had put him embarrassingly behind once he started public school. It had been lonely much of the time, but every so often Esmerelda (she'd never let him call her Mom) would bring him to Asheville, to Aunt Dottie, and it would feel like he finally had a place to plant his feet. Like he had somewhere he could belong. Like he had someone to belong with.

It was the way he felt with Georgie in his arms, and given the way she'd melted into him, he'd thought she felt it too. Only she'd retreated from him. Again. It was starting to seem like she was as good at pulling away as she was at running a business.

He'd thought he was going to head home. Hops surely needed to be let out soon, and if he waited too long, he'd come home to more shredded toilet paper or maybe a mauled book. But whatever desperation had driven him to seek out Beau earlier was driving him to Aunt Dottie now. (Surely she'd have something to say about that.)

Her house had always reminded him of the candy cottage in Hansel and Gretel. It was a small three-bedroom bungalow, painted a bright pastel purple with yellow trim. The yard was separated into planting beds and featured a random assemblage of sculpted animals—bears sitting with frogs. He pulled into the driveway behind her car, his heart in his throat, and made his way to the door, his feet planting on her welcome mat.

He heard voices inside, even though her car was the only one in the drive. He started to pull away, not feeling fit for company, but Aunt Dottie opened the door before he got a single step closer.

"How'd you know…?" he started.

She just gave him her *I know things, dear* look, but he caught sight of the open front shades and realized she'd probably seen the car's headlights. Although still a bit too early for darkness to fall, it was a hazy, murky day, veering toward dusk, and the lights had turned on automatically.

"I was starting to worry you wouldn't make it," she said. "The others showed up an hour ago."

"The others?" he asked in confusion.

She tsked. "You didn't get my text?"

Truthfully, no. But he'd been checking his phone only once or twice a day to avoid the Jezebel spam. Not that he wanted to admit to dodging those messages. His aunt studied them as carefully as a detective interpreting clues to a grisly crime.

"I must have missed it," he said. "What's the situation?"

"Come in, come in," she said, gesturing for him to come inside.

He did, only to find Lurch, Josie, and a couple of current Buchanan employees sitting around the dining room table.

Each sat in front of a large pad of drawing paper, and a mass of colored pencils lay in the middle.

Was this some sort of art happy hour? It wouldn't be the first time.

There were two empty places—one had obviously been Aunt Dottie's seat given the intricate drawings on the page, and the other had apparently been left open for him.

"Oh, good, you're here, River," Lurch said. "My idea is to mix five different kinds of beer together—some of them limited release—and have a competition to see who can name all five. If they win, they get to drink it. What do you think?" He grinned as if expecting approval.

"Um, do you think anyone would want to win?" he asked.

Lurch twisted his mouth to the side and then shrugged. "To each their own."

"There's food in the kitchen," Aunt Dottie said brightly. "Grab a plate! We've got a lot left to do."

"Why don't you come with me?" he suggested. "There's something I wanted to talk to you about." He nodded to

Josie, and the employees who were still, well, employees, and led the way.

The kitchen table was crowded with platters of food, arranged in front of a little chalkboard sign reading *Inspiration Eats!*

He sighed, but that didn't stop him from grabbing a plate and helping himself. He hadn't eaten since that muffin with Maisie, which he'd counted as a late lunch, and Aunt Dottie was a great cook when she wasn't trying to make all the food black or brown. "Are you planning the employee party behind Georgie's back?"

He settled into the far chair, next to an empty patch of table, and set down his plate. Aunt Dottie took the chair opposite him.

"I would *never* do that," she said as if mortally offended. "I'm just helping her so she doesn't need to worry about all of the nitpicky details. I want Georgie to be able to spend her time on more important things."

He nearly choked on a bite of mac and cheese.

"I think she very much wants to spend her time approving those details. In case you've forgotten, you nearly burned down her house."

Aunt Dottie waved a hand dismissively. "Oh, I think we're well beyond that."

"It happened a week and a half ago."

"Nearly two weeks, dear. And although I love our Georgie girl, I think she needs to let herself have more fun." She paused, tilting her head a little as if he were a work of art she were studying. "Something happened to you today."

"It's almost like you're psychic," he said, the corner of his mouth ticking up.

Another hand wave. "You know what I mean. Something *earth-shattering* happened to you."

He set down his fork with a clatter, feeling a quake inside of him. "I guess I came here to talk to you about that. I'm not sure I would have come if I'd known you had company—"

"How about a balloon-popping contest?" someone asked loudly, to which Josie replied, "How about bubbles? I've gotten pretty good with those."

He was going to have to tell Georgie about this, wasn't he? It was what a *friend* would do.

A friend. Those words had poured salt into his wounds, especially after that hug. Not that he would have dreamed of turning her away.

Aunt Dottie got up and closed the door, then rummaged through one of the cabinets for something before joining him at the table.

"I can tell it's time to give this to you," she said, handing him a black, leatherbound case across the table.

He flipped it open and sucked in a breath. It was Beau's watch, gleaming brightly back at him.

"I didn't know you had it," he said. "I was going to grab it at Beau's house a couple of weeks ago, but I guess I got distracted."

"I guess you did," she said, staring at him in that way of hers, making him feel as transparent as plastic wrap. It could be slightly infuriating, being known by someone. Being seen by them. "I told Georgie I wanted to be the one to give it to you."

He perked up a little at that. They'd arranged this?

"You know," she said slowly, "Beau would have given you his house if I weren't already giving you mine."

"I don't want to—"

Think about you dying. Because it sent a sort of panic through him, even as he felt a comforting glow at the notion

281

that Beau had thought enough of him to consider it. He was glad Georgie had the house instead—and maybe a little annoyed that her brothers and sister were on the title too—because as difficult as all of this was, he still wanted her here. Still wanted her close.

She smiled softly at him. "Beau gave you this watch for a reason, River. Not many people know this, but he wasn't the biological son of Prescott Senior. His mother was pregnant with him when they met, and they married quickly. But Prescott never treated him as any less of a son for it. The split between Beau and his son was painful for him, but when you came to live with me, he felt like he had another chance to be the kind of man his father had been."

River's hand tightened around the box, his throat feeling clogged with emotion. He hadn't known any of that. And he had a feeling the Buchanans didn't know either. Prescott would probably have an existential crisis if he found out. Part of him wished Beau had sat him down to talk about this, but the most Beau thing of all was to arrange for Aunt Dottie to convey the message instead. Well, he'd come here for some sort of grounding, and he'd gotten it. It would have to do.

"Thank you, Aunt Dottie. It's big of you to say so." He pushed his plate back, no longer feeling so hungry.

"What happened today?" she asked.

And here he'd thought he might be able to get away without talking about it.

"I went to see Beau"—he could see her practically glowing as he said it, thinking about things like kismet, him going to the grave, her knowing to give him the watch, but he kept on talking—"and Georgie showed up while I was there."

"Beau sent her," Aunt Dottie said, repeating his errant thought as if it were an absolute, ironclad fact.

"Well, if he did, he enjoys messing with my head," he snapped. "She pushed me away again. She's not going to change her mind. It's time for me to just accept that."

But his aunt was already shaking her head. "The Buchanans are nothing if not stubborn—you should know that from Beau—but I see the way that girl lights up every time you're in the room, River. You just have to be patient. The pink crystal will work its magic."

"We'll see about that," he said, wanting to believe it but not so sure he did anymore. "She was upset about her sister, by the way. Sounds like Adalia isn't coming this weekend."

Aunt Dottie frowned. "I was sure she would. I'm worried about that girl, River. She may need our help more than any of them."

Our help? Was that what this was about for Aunt Dottie? Helping Beau's grandchildren? If so, she might have her work cut out for her with the other three. He somehow couldn't imagine Junior allowing Aunt Dottie to read his tea leaves.

"I don't know any details," he said. "Just that she was crying when Georgie called this morning. Georgie was really upset to find out she wasn't coming this weekend." And that had cracked something inside of him. Because the look on her face, the loss, the loneliness, the feeling of being left—he knew all of those things and didn't want her to suffer them.

"Thanks for this," he said, shaking the watch container. "I should get back to the loft before Hops destroys everything."

"You don't want to help with the after-party planning?" She looked a little crestfallen.

"No, I'm not sure that's the best idea," he said. "Plausible deniability, and all that."

They left the kitchen together, River holding the watch box as if it were a lifeline.

"What about a trampoline?" one of the employees said. "I know a place where we can rent one at a discount. There's plenty of room for it out back."

And even though he'd said he wouldn't get involved, River found himself channeling Georgie.

"In the dark? When people are tipsy or drunk? Let's table that one."

His aunt just patted him on the back and sent him on his way.

By the time he got home, Hops had, indeed, escaped his kennel. But he hadn't destroyed anything this time—he'd just dragged his favorite sandal to the front door and cuddled up on it, as if waiting for River to come home. It was almost like he'd sensed it had been a bad day, and that cleaning up detritus from the apartment would only make it worse.

River spent the rest of the evening walking the dog, watching mindless TV, and steadfastly ignoring his phone. One look had been enough. In addition to his aunt's message, there'd been a paragraph-long text from a woman who was certain Jezebel was poaching birds and leaving them on her porch as a threat.

He fell asleep on the couch, and he dreamed of Beau. In the dream, River found himself in Beau's house. He walked out onto the back porch and found Beau in his usual chair, Jezebel curled up next to him, showing rare contentment in a patch of sunlight.

"Mighty fine watch you have there, son," Beau said, grinning at him. And, indeed, River looked down to find he was wearing it.

"A pretty okay old man gave it to me."

"Care to raise a glass with me?"

He sat down beside him, and suddenly, in the way of dreams, they both had pint glasses of beer.

"I miss you, Beau," he said, because he did. "Things have gotten strange without you."

"Yes, I suppose they have. You've fallen in love with my granddaughter."

And although River was distantly aware of it being a dream, he glanced around to make sure no one else had heard them. Jezebel just looked at him as if to say she knew everything.

"Yeah, I have," he said. "But I'm pretty sure nothing's going to happen on that front."

"I wouldn't be so sure." Beau paused, looking him in the eye. "You know, I had a feeling about you two, River. Maybe it was Dottie rubbing off on me after so many years together, but when I met her, I knew."

Shock rippled through him. Had Beau really thought he was good enough for his granddaughter? Or was his subconscious just messing with him too?

It was then a knock on the door woke him up. He roused to a dark room, lit only by the TV screen saver. Hops jumped up from his position at River's feet and scampered toward the door. River followed him, still feeling strange from the dream, and opened the door without bothering to ask who it was.

Georgie Buchanan rushed into his arms.

CHAPTER
Thirty-One

Georgie woke in her hotel room to her ringing phone, instantly alert when she read the time on the digital radio next to her bed—1:13.

The number on her cell phone screen had a New York City area code, but she didn't recognize it. She was apprehensive when she answered. "Hello?"

"Georgie?" Adalia asked with a sob.

Panic made Georgie light-headed, and she pressed the heel of her hand to her temple to ground herself. Her sister hadn't talked to her in that tone—so unguarded, so scared—since their mother had died. "Adalia? What happened?"

"Georgie, I really screwed up."

"Are you okay? Are you hurt?"

"I'm not hurt, but I'm in trouble."

"Whatever it is, we'll fix it. What happened?"

"I got arrested, Georgie. I'm calling you from NYPD's fifth precinct." She paused, then added, "I was arrested for vandalism."

Georgie couldn't stop her gasp of surprise. "Okay. It's okay. That's not too serious."

"It's a felony. It was nearly one hundred thousand dollars in art."

Georgie's heart sank. It *was* serious, very serious, and she had more questions than she could count, but Adalia didn't need a lecture, or at least she didn't need one yet. She needed her big sister. "So this is your phone call?"

"Yeah." Her voice broke. "I'm supposed to be arraigned first thing in the morning. Then I'll find out how much bail will be."

"What do you need, Addy? Money for bail? An attorney? Just tell me, and it's yours."

"I need *you*, Georgie." She broke down into sobs.

Georgie was already out of bed and dashing to the dresser. "I'm coming, Addy. What time's the arraignment?"

There was so much to do for the parties on Saturday, and she worried that Dottie would be like a runaway locomotive in her absence, but surely River would help supervise her.

"It's early. Eight o'clock," Adalia said through her sniffles. "You'll never make it in time."

"Then I'll be there when you get home."

"Thank you," Adalia said, breaking down again. "But when you go back to Asheville, can I come with you? I can't stay here anymore. My life here is over."

"Of course," Georgie said without hesitation. "And don't worry about bail. I'll get the first flight out of Asheville. I think there's a direct flight that leaves around six, so I can be in the city by ten or so."

"Thank you, Georgie."

"Time's up," a woman said in the background, her tone harsh.

"I have to go," Adalia said. "But please don't tell Lee or Dad. *Please.*"

They were going to lose it when they found out. Because while Georgie and Adalia could keep it from them for a time, they would eventually find out. It was hard to keep a secret when it was a matter of public record. But Georgie planned to buy her sister as much time as she could. "Of course. It's our secret."

"I love you, Georgie."

"I love you too." Then there was a click on the line. Adalia was gone.

She stood in place, her mind racing at the thought of everything she needed to do.

"I need a ticket," she muttered to herself. But a quick look online revealed it was too late to purchase one electronically. She'd have to go to the airport, but first she needed to talk to River. The easy thing to do would be to call him, but the thought made her throat clog. Maybe she'd stop by his loft on the way to the airport.

She sat on the edge of the bed. It was now one twenty. She had hours to go before anything could happen. There was no way she'd be able to sleep, so she packed an overnight bag, her mind racing all the while. If she left later this morning, she could possibly still get back to Asheville in time for the events on Saturday evening, but she had no idea how long it would take to clear up Adalia's mess.

What if they didn't let her out on bail?

Of course they'd let her out. It wasn't like she'd murdered anyone. No, she'd just murdered art.

What in the world had Adalia been thinking? Her baby sister could be flighty, but other than smoking pot in high school and college, she'd never done anything illegal. Georgie couldn't imagine what had driven her to destroy art. Adalia was a creator. She preserved art. Revered and respected it. Not destroyed it.

Her stomach was in knots and her anxiety was through the roof. She felt lost and helpless, desperate for someone to help her, to hold her hand through this. No, not just someone. *Him.*

She told herself it was wrong to disturb him in the middle of the night. Still, she didn't want to be alone, and she and River had agreed to be friends. They'd even shaken on it. Wasn't this what friends were for? Being there in good times and bad?

She threw on a pair of yoga pants and a T-shirt, then tossed her cosmetics bag and an extra business skirt and blouse into her already packed carry-on. Bag in hand, she headed out of the hotel room before she could change her mind.

She nearly turned around multiple times during the drive. This was crazy. It was two a.m. She couldn't just show up on River's doorstep, but all the logic in the world couldn't quell the overwhelming need she felt to be with him. She couldn't stop thinking about the way he'd held her at the cemetery—how his comfort and his strength had seeped into her. How she craved more of it.

Did that make her weak? Or needy? But she told herself that if she were back in Boston, she'd call Meredith, albeit not until morning, but still…

When she pulled up to his building, she drove around looking for a parking space. But just as she started contemplating whether the lack of a spot was a sign, one opened up a few feet ahead. The timing gave her chills, and Georgie wondered if she'd spent too much time with Dottie. Steeling her resolve, she parked and grabbed her bag out of the back seat so she could change before heading to the airport in a few hours. As she walked to his front door, she realized it was presumptuous to assume she could just stay there, but she knocked anyway. She heard yipping first, then the sound of the lock clicking over.

Play this cool. Don't fall apart.

When he opened the door, bleary-eyed and with tousled hair, her resolve to not fall apart evaporated, and she threw herself at him.

He instantly enveloped her in his arms, holding her tight. "Georgie. What's wrong?"

Tears stung her eyes. *Relieved* tears. It felt so right to be in his arms, like she'd been created to fit River Reeves's body.

"Georgie?"

She heard the panic in his voice and felt foolish. She knew she should pull away from him, yet she wasn't ready to let him go yet. "It's Adalia." Then she realized that he was probably assuming the worst. "She's not hurt. But it's pretty bad."

He loosened his hold and looked down at her, waiting for her to explain.

"She was arrested for vandalizing a hundred thousand dollars' worth of art. Because of the high value, it's a felony."

Shock covered his face, and she briefly wondered what he thought of her and her family now. If word got out, it would tarnish the Buchanan family reputation.

Oh God. Would it hurt the brewery too?

He looked past her and saw her bag. Releasing her, he fetched it, then brought it inside and shut the door, engaging the deadbolt.

For some reason, knowing she was locked inside with River made her feel more comforted, as though nothing could happen to her here. It was a ridiculous, fanciful thought—Georgie didn't do fanciful, yet there it was anyway, and since she was letting herself be a stereotypical clingy woman, she might as well go for broke.

Was this how it had started with her mom? One concession at a time?

"Let me make you a cup of tea," River said, wrapping his arm around her back and leading her to the sofa.

A throw lay in a heap at one end, and Hops leaped up next to it, looking up at her as if to accuse her of not petting him.

Once she sat down, River picked up the puppy and handed him to her. "Here. Maisie says there are very few emotional pains that cuddling puppies can't ease or cure."

She took the furball, and Hops snuggled into her chest. "Maisie is a wise woman."

"Usually…" He grabbed the electric kettle from the kitchen counter and started to fill it up with water. "Tell me everything."

So she did, starting with Adalia's strange behavior and the fact that she and Lee, who typically weren't close, had become chummy. But it was Georgie whom Adalia had called from the police precinct, and she'd asked to come back to Asheville with her too.

River listened attentively, and by the time she'd finished, he'd carried two mugs of tea into the living room, carefully handing her one and keeping the other as he sat in an armchair next to the sofa.

Georgie felt a prick of disappointment, but sitting apart was probably a good idea. The need she felt to feel him close to her, by her side, told her that.

"So, first of all," River said, leaning forward, the mug still in his hand, "if Adalia wants to come to Asheville, you can skip flying to New York and just have her catch a flight here. She can get released from jail, pack a bag or two, and head straight to the airport."

"But what about her bail? I need to go pay it."

"We can find a bail bondsman to do that. If her arraignment's at eight, the bondsman will likely be able to get her out faster than you can. We just need to contact one."

"I never would have thought of that," she said, full of gratitude.

He grimaced. "Let's just say I've bailed out a few friends before." Then he added, "In my lost years."

"After your mother left you," she said quietly.

His eyes widened in surprise, but it quickly faded. "Aunt Dottie."

"I don't know anything really. Only the bits and pieces you've told me, and then Dottie confirmed what I already suspected."

His lips pressed together, and he stared into his steaming mug. "So you don't know any specifics about what Adalia did?"

"No."

"I guess you'll just have to wait until you see her this afternoon."

"Yeah."

He set his mug on the table and got up, heading for his bedroom. She briefly wondered if he'd had enough of her Buchanan family drama and decided he was going to bed, but he returned seconds later with his tablet and cell phone in hand.

"Since using a bail bondsman never occurred to you, I suspect you don't have a preference about which one to use," he said as he sat in the chair and booted up the computer.

She released a short laugh. "No, and let's hope this is a one-and-done situation."

"Any chance you have that pad and pen with you?" he asked, giving her a little smile before he started typing.

She produced them from her purse, and when she walked over to hand it to him, she realized he was searching for bail bondsmen.

"Oh, River. You don't have to do that. That's not why I'm here."

He stared up at her, searching her face. "Why are you here? Because you needed a friend?"

"Yes," she whispered, but it was more than that. She had to admit she liked letting someone take care of her for once. She was so used to taking care of everyone and everything else. To being the one who stepped up, whether people asked her to or not.

But that wasn't why she'd shown up on his doorstep in the middle of the night. She was here because he made her feel like everything would be okay. When they were together, her frantic soul quieted, and she let herself just *be*. There was nothing to prove. No one to impress. River liked her just the way she was. It wasn't safety she craved from him, it was peace.

"Then let me be your friend," River said, reaching for her hand and squeezing. "You're an expert at whipping breweries into shape, and I happen to be an expert at acquiring bail bondsmen." A self-deprecating smile spread over his face. "Maybe I shouldn't be bragging about that one."

She smiled, feeling like maybe everything *would* be okay. "I have my strengths and you have yours. We make a great team."

He laughed, looking more at ease. "Yeah, we do."

She realized they were still holding hands about the same time he did, and they both pulled their hands abruptly apart.

With nothing else to do, she sat down on the sofa and curled up with the throw. It smelled like River, filling her with

that sense of peace again. That sense of home. Hops climbed onto her lap and she felt herself getting drowsy. Soon she was fast asleep.

CHAPTER
Thirty-Two

She'd come to him. This thing with Adalia had rocked her to her core, and she'd come to *him*.

River couldn't stop thinking about that as he made the calls, securing the services of someone called Barracuda Bob, who had, despite the name, come highly recommended. Presuming Adalia posted bail—and the man seemed confident she would—she'd be free to go by 9 a.m. Georgie just needed to call in with her credit card number in the morning.

He checked the flights from New York to Asheville and found only one seat left on a three p.m. flight connecting through Charlotte. He should probably check with Georgie before doing anything, but the next flight wasn't until Saturday night, and he figured that would be a stressful situation for the sisters. Better for them to have time to connect before the closing parties. So he took a chance and booked the flight, using his own credit card. Hopefully it would be one less thing for Georgie to worry about.

He'd gone to his office to make the calls, not wanting to wake her, but he returned to the chair he'd vacated—the one he'd chosen because he would have been tempted to scoop her into his lap if he'd sat next to her—and watched her for a moment. She looked so peaceful, Hops snuggled up next to her, and although he knew he should wake her, he wasn't quite ready. He liked seeing her here in his home, at rest, as if she belonged here. Because it felt like she did, and if he woke her up, she might feel the need to leave.

But she mumbled a little in her sleep, as if restless with bad dreams, and he told himself it was time. He went to her and crouched beside the couch. Touching her arm gently, he said, "Georgie."

"Hm," she said, stirring. "River." She reached for him, as if the last two weeks hadn't happened and they were still in bed together. As if he hadn't signed those forms. And although he loved the partnership of working with her, a deep part of him wished that were true. If not being with her was the cost of working at Buchanan, it wasn't worth it.

He took her in his arms because he couldn't not do it, when she was reaching for him like that, but then he pulled away.

A painful awareness had surfaced in her eyes, the dreaminess of moments ago drifting away.

"Adalia?"

"I found someone who'll help," he said. "He'll be there in the morning. He seems confident it'll work out. I told him you'd be in touch with your payment information between 7:00 and 8:00." He paused, wondering if he'd overstepped, then added, "I checked the flights from New York to Asheville. The only seat available before Saturday night is on a three p.m. flight tomorrow evening—or tonight, depending on how you look at it. I went ahead and booked it. I realize it might not end up working out, but I figured it was worth doing." He paused, hesitating to reveal he'd bought it, but he also didn't want her to think he'd rummaged through her things to find her card. "I used my card."

She sat up abruptly, looking at him in a way he struggled to interpret, and Hops squeaked a small complaint that might have been a bark from a bigger dog and walked off, curling up on what River had dubbed his special sandal. River went to sit in the chair again, but Georgie stopped him, her hand wrapping around his bicep.

"Sit with me," she said.

And he did, sitting close enough that their thighs touched, every point of contact searing into him. She took his hand and looked into his eyes.

"Thank you for doing that for Adalia."

"I did it for you," he said honestly.

"I know," she said.

They stayed like that for a moment, the silence between them intense but somehow not uncomfortable. In that silence, there was a universe of possibilities. Of different paths they could take, but his heart only led him down one.

She spoke first. "I have a lot of regrets about the past, River." Another pause, but the fact that she didn't pull away kept him from wondering—or asking—if he was one of them. "My father might not have been a good husband, but my mother grounded him in some way. He became a hundred times worse after she died. It was horrible to live in that house. He was so judgmental. Cold. Cutting. And I left Adalia there with him. I could have gone to college in New York, but Harvard was my top pick, and I was so happy I got in." She tucked a lock of hair behind her ear, keeping her other hand entwined with his. "Truthfully, I think it was my top pick because I wanted to *leave*, although I didn't think of it that way at the time. Adalia begged me to stay, but I told myself that she didn't need me. That Lee would look after her until I got out of school."

"This isn't your fault," he said, turning a little to face her. Needing her to see that he meant it. "You're not to blame for whatever's happening with her."

"But I *left* her, River," she said, her voice thick, "and things haven't been the same between us since. If anything, they keep getting worse. When she got into art school, she called me before she told my father, and I messed up. I knew what he was going to say, how cruel he would be, and I warned her that he probably wouldn't pay for it. That he would never consider art a career. My mother taught art history, and he always treated it like a hobby. Like it was something cute that she did." She lowered her face as if she couldn't bear to look at him. "And, to be honest, I kind of felt the same way about Adalia. I figured it was just a phase. So I have no right to be surprised that she's kept her distance. That she hasn't told me about her shows, her life. It's my fault."

He reached over and tipped her chin up slightly, so their eyes met. Hers were brimming with tears.

"I'm telling you it's not," he said firmly. "The only way of fixing something you feel you did wrong in the past is by acting differently in the future. By being there for her now. By owning up to how you feel."

"How can you be so understanding?" she asked. "I *left* her."

He understood what she wasn't saying. His mother had left him like she thought she'd left Adalia, except it was a false equivalence.

"If you're talking about Esmerelda…my mother," he clarified, in case Dottie hadn't confided his mother's name along with the rest of his personal history, "then you need to understand the situation was completely different. She was an adult, and you were still a child when you left home. A grieving child. You can't beat yourself up about decisions you made before you had the perspective to understand what you were doing. Besides, it's not like you disappeared off the face of the earth. I'm sure you called and texted." He felt himself grin a little at that. "Probably more than she would have liked."

She smiled back, but it had to be the saddest smile he'd ever seen. "I guess I did." She paused, looking conflicted, then shook it off and added, "I'm so sorry that happened to you, River."

"I'm not," he said, and to his surprise, he somewhat meant it. "The best thing she could have done was to leave me with Aunt Dottie. I think maybe she knew that. She's not a very happy person. I don't think she ever really wanted a child or knew what to do with me. She didn't even know what to do with herself. We moved every few months, but I don't think she ever found what she was looking for."

"I didn't mean to make you talk about this," she said, but he could tell it was because she worried about making him uncomfortable, not because she didn't want to know. And he found himself surprisingly okay with letting Georgie in. With spilling his secrets to her.

Because she's already in your heart, a voice whispered.

"It's okay," he said, squeezing her hand. "I'll tell you anything you want to know, but I don't want to shift the focus off you right now. This is about you and Adalia. And you should consider the fact that your sister called you when this happened. Not your father. Not your brother. You. That means everything in the world."

The look in her eyes changed then, something fierce flashing in them.

"And I came to you," she said.

"You did," he said, his soft tone belying the sudden pounding of his heart. "And you always can, Georgie. *Always.* But I have to know why."

She looked down again, and for a moment he was afraid she was going to pull away, but if anything she tightened her grip on his hand. When she looked up again, her eyes were full of purpose.

"Because all the reasons we're supposed to stay away from each other don't feel so important anymore. When I'm around you, I can't seem to remember them. I came here because when I'm with you, I feel like everything's going to be okay, not in the sense that you're going to fix it, but because you're there with me."

Something bloomed inside of him, a warmth like he'd felt earlier at Beau's grave. The sense of coming home. But he didn't pull her into his lap like he wanted to, because he had to know for sure. His heart needed it.

"Georgie, if you change your mind about us, I need you to mean it. It can't just be for tonight, or because your sister is in trouble."

She spanned the short distance between them and kissed him. It was soft and exploratory at first, almost as if she were asking a question, but the passion between them— banked for days—ignited in an instant. He shifted the angle to take the kiss deeper, their tongues twining, teeth knocking together as they tried to get closer, to take it even deeper. Almost as if they wanted to consume each other. She started to tug on the bottom of his shirt, but he didn't want this to happen here in the living room. Not tonight. He wanted her in his bed.

So he pulled away and, in response to her soft complaint, lifted her off her feet and carried her into his room.

CHAPTER
Thirty-Three

Georgie had a hard time concentrating at work in the morning. She'd only slept a few hours after receiving Adalia's call, and despite having talked to her sister after she was released (she'd agreed to come straight to Asheville on the flight River had arranged), she was a mess of worry. Didn't help that she couldn't stop mooning over River. Dottie noticed something was off right away, and she barged into Georgie's office midmorning with a sage stick, determined to drive the bad energy away because she sensed some really great energy radiating from Georgie.

Was it obvious to everyone that Georgie had experienced the best sex of her life only hours earlier?

It was hard seeing River in the office, where the current employee manual insisted they could not engage in any fraternization, when all she wanted to do was kiss him. He showed up in her doorway around noon, leaning his shoulder into the doorframe.

"I think we should take a field trip for lunch," he said with a sexy smile.

Her stomach fluttered at the thought of eating lunch with him, but they'd agreed to keep their relationship on the down-low for the moment. She needed to find a way to tell her siblings, and she figured she'd start with Adalia first. But she hadn't told her yet—it was a conversation best had in person, and her sister had just been released from jail, after all.

"This is work-related," River said with a glimmer in his eyes. "I thought we'd drop by Eye of the Tiger Brewery so you could try their porters. They make some of the best in Asheville. We might consider adding one to the winter line."

"Yeah," she said, smiling at him, relieved that she wouldn't have to turn him down. "Testing some out would be the responsible thing to do."

"How soon will you be able to leave?"

She glanced at her computer, then back at River...

It felt so good to be able to let her eyes linger, to know she had a right to look at him, even if she couldn't make it obvious until their relationship went public.

"I can go now," she said.

"I was hoping you'd say that."

They were the same words he'd said to her that first night in his apartment, before their shower. Which made her think about showering with him, their bodies slick against each other. He'd promised to learn every inch of her, and he had. He'd insisted on swiping the cloth over her from head to toe, slowly enough to drive her mad, and then...

She was at the office, where she should absolutely not be thinking about any of this. She felt her face grow hot. The grin on his face told her he'd done it on purpose, and she scowled at him a little as she gathered her things.

They left together, acting like it was no big deal, but as soon as River pulled his car into a parking space at Eye of the Tiger, he leaned over and kissed her.

"I've been wanting to do that for hours," he murmured against her lips.

"I guess good things come to those who wait," she said, and kissed him again, letting it linger a little before she pulled away. "Are we really here to taste porters?"

"No reason we can't mix business and pleasure."

"I like the way you think," she said, looking into his eyes. She liked what she saw there too. They were alight with pleasure, with happiness, something that had largely been missing the last couple of weeks, and she felt no small amount of wonder that he was happy because of *her*.

Once inside, they ordered a flight along with some appetizers. They discussed what they liked and didn't like about each of the beers, and what qualities they should reach for with their own version, River taking notes on his phone. She glanced at his screen, smiling at what she saw: *Georgie plus chocolate=happy, in beer and in general; Georgie plus bitterness=only if balanced; Georgie plus coffee=not too heavy.*

"I'm okay with coffee in the morning," she said in an undertone. "Plenty of coffee. Maybe you should add that to your list."

"Maybe I will," he said, looking up at her. "I like to make my boss woman happy. Now, about that porter…"

She was still such a beer novice, but he took her feedback and advice so seriously, as if it were as important as his own. She loved that, loved how excited he got over the whole process. It made work feel *fun*, which it never really had before, she realized. Fulfilling and rewarding, yes, but never fun.

At the end of their lunch, a big burly man with a beard came out of the back to greet them, heading straight for River. He pumped his hand almost aggressively and thanked him for coming in. He was the owner, it turned out, and River introduced Georgie as one of the new owners of Buchanan Brewery.

"She has great things planned for Buchanan's future," River said, beaming. "I'm excited to be part of it."

"I heard about Big Catch," the owner said. "You did the right thing, jumping ship. Finn let us all down, inviting those sharks into town."

River looked a little conflicted about that, like maybe he thought he should defend Finn, but he just shrugged. "I was lucky the opportunity at Buchanan opened up when it did."

"Truth be told," the owner said, running a hand over his beard, "I always figured you'd be the one to inherit Buchanan." As if realizing what he'd said, or rather whom he'd said it in front of, he turned to Georgie. "No offense, it's just common knowledge that Beau taught River the ropes about brewing—it's kind of a local legend—and Beau never talked about his family much."

Georgie felt like she was going to throw up. She'd almost forgotten about the will, or maybe she'd let herself forget. River still didn't know, but she'd have to tell him now. The sooner she did it, the less of a betrayal it would be.

Not yet, she told herself. *Not until you sort everything out with Adalia, Jack, and Lee.*

She forced a smile. "Grandpa Beau was full of surprises. All I know is we're very lucky to have River."

"It was great seeing you, River," the man said, clapping him on the back. "Glad to hear you're staying in Asheville."

"Me too, man. I wouldn't leave for the world."

Georgie's guilt amplified. What if her brothers tried to enforce the no-fraternizing policy and the noncompete?

But she was being weak, thinking like that. It was time for her to show her brothers that *she* was in charge of things.

⊨═⊨

Georgie left the brewery at five to meet the contractor for her walk-through. Adalia would arrive at the airport at seven thirty, so she had a little time to move in and get settled before her new roommate arrived.

It looked like a different house than the one she'd walked into two weeks prior. The living room had been fastidiously cleaned and freshly painted, and it looked great despite being completely empty. And the new granite counters, appliances, and freshly painted cabinets in the kitchen gave the house an updated look.

After the contractor left, Georgie went upstairs to prep her sister's room. She'd just started changing the bedding when she heard a knock on the front door. Jezebel was still missing, so she knew there was a possibility it could be one of the neighbors. She went down to answer the door with no small amount of trepidation.

But it was River, standing there with a pizza box in hand, a bottle of wine under one arm and Hops squirming under the other. "Thought you might like some help putting the house back together."

With a grin, she grabbed his shirt and pulled him through the door. She'd told him her plans for the evening, so she hadn't expected to see him until tomorrow. Was it crazy that she'd missed him?

She took the pizza box from him, mostly because she wanted to kiss him, and she didn't see it happening without something falling from his hands or out from under his arms. River was skilled in a lot of things, but as far as she knew, he didn't know how to juggle. Pizza in hand, she leaned in and kissed him, inasmuch as they could manage with the box between them.

When Hops released a mewl of protest, she stooped down and kissed his head.

River grinned as he lowered the puppy to the floor.

"I really am here to help," he said, taking the box back from her and heading for the kitchen, "and I figured you probably hadn't picked up anything for dinner."

"You know my habits all too well," she said as she walked with him. "Although I admit I'm surprised by the wine."

"I remember you mentioning you drank wine before you got caught up in brewing beer. And I figured you might be in the mood for something different. Should be enough time for you to have a glass before you need to leave for the airport."

"Well, thank you."

"Are you hungry?" He set the pizza box on the counter and glanced around, his mouth parted. "Wow. This place looks *great*."

"But it doesn't look like Beau's house." She wondered belatedly if that would bother him. Hops was wandering the floor as if doing his own walk-through, his little tail wagging.

He shrugged and turned to face her. "But it's not Beau's house anymore. It's yours. And you don't have as many memories here, so there's no nostalgia for you. Just a clean slate." He made it sound like a good thing, but she still felt a little guilty. According to Dottie, Beau had considered giving River his house too. Georgie suddenly felt like Beau's grandkids had taken everything from him. Like *she* had taken everything from him.

Would he see it that way too?

"Hey," he said, wrapping an arm around her back and pulling her close. "Adalia should be on a plane by now. She'll be here before you know it."

She buried her face into his chest, feeling even worse. How could she ever make it up to him? The only thing she knew to do was stick to her original plan and buy out her siblings in a year so she could make him an official partner.

But even so, she had to tell him before that, didn't she? How else would she live with the guilt?

He held her and gently rubbed her back. "Do you want to eat or work? Or just stand here and let me hold you?"

What she needed was to get herself together. Leaning back, she cocked her eyebrows. "What kind of pizza?"

"I wasn't sure what you'd like, so I got a half cheese and half pepperoni."

"I say you open that bottle of wine while I open the pizza." Then, with a dramatic flourish as though her task was as hard as his, she opened the box and pulled out a slice of pepperoni. She took a bite and moaned. "This is *so* good."

He grinned. "Well, if that impresses you, wait until you get a look at what I got for Jezebel."

"So you brought both of your girls some treats?"

His wink sent a bolt of lust and remembered pleasure through her. "I promise you're my favorite."

Turned out he'd brought some groceries too—some milk, coffee, eggs, another bottle of wine, along with some cheese and bread, and a few tins of sardines to lure Jezebel. Georgie put her pizza on a plate and helped bring them inside.

"I can't say I approve of this plan," she said, scrunching her nose. "It's going to smell terrible if we leave that out."

"And that awful aroma is sure to draw her home," he said with a grin. "Beau used to give her these for a treat. It's the devil cat's version of catnip."

"If this is such a slam dunk, why didn't you try it before?"

He made a face. "I was worried she might show up and attack the contractors. As you've seen, she doesn't take kindly to finding people in 'her' house."

Which surely didn't bode well for Georgie and Adalia.

Soon they were sitting out on the back porch, like they had that first night, eating pizza and sipping wine. A feeling of peace stole over Georgie. It felt like this was how it was supposed to be all along, like she'd spent the last two weeks fighting herself for no good reason at all.

"I didn't know you drank wine," she teased, nudging his shoulder. "Isn't that kind of sacrilegious?"

He nudged her back. "You're right. It's sacrilegious for either of us to drink it. I guess I should bring the other bottle home with me."

When they finished eating, River set out an open can of sardines on the back porch. Georgie had given him permission to try it once, with the agreement that he would be the one to remove the smelly fish if Jezebel (or worse, something else) didn't get to it first.

"Maybe the neighbors will stop texting me at all hours," River said. "The latest rumor going around is that Jezebel is a black panther escaped from Beau's backyard exotic zoo."

After cleaning up their dishes, they went upstairs and started changing the beds together, Georgie more than a little tempted to pull him onto one, but she checked the time and realized she had to go to the airport.

"You go get your sister," River said, leading her to the bedroom door. "I'll finish up here."

She hesitated. While she absolutely loved that he'd dropped by to help, she didn't want him to be here when she brought Adalia home. She and Adalia had too much ground to cover, plus she needed time to tell her sister about him first.

He grabbed both of her shoulders and held her gaze. "I promise that Hops and I will be gone when you get back."

She looked away, feeling ungrateful. "River. I'm not ashamed of you."

"I know. But this isn't the way to tell your sister. You need to focus on her and what happened. We have time." He gave her a soft kiss. "I'm not going anywhere." Then he smiled. "Except for tonight, obviously."

She laughed and rested her hand on his chest, savoring the feel of him.

Maybe love itself wasn't toxic at all. Maybe her mother had just picked the wrong man.

She left River on Beau's front porch, but not until after he kissed her so thoroughly her body ached to stay with him and finish what they'd started. He gave her a wave while Hops chewed on his shoestring, and then the two of them went back inside.

What would it be like to come home to River?

The thought caught her by surprise. But it was even more surprising how right it felt.

When Georgie got to the Asheville Regional Airport, she waited outside the security exit, nervous about seeing her baby sister. While she'd talked to Adalia twice during the day, both calls had been short, and they hadn't talked about anything of substance. The unspoken understanding was that they'd do all their sharing once they saw each other. Besides, there'd been plenty for Adalia to do as she packed and squared things away to stay in Asheville for the indefinite future.

A group of people began trickling out of the doors, and then Georgie saw her. Adalia's short blond hair was a mess, and she had red puffy eyes underscored with dark circles. She carted a rolling carry-on suitcase behind her, and something about her gaze searching for Georgie in the crowd made her look like a lost child. As soon as Adalia saw her, she took off running, barely stopping before she threw her arms around Georgie and began crying.

Georgie stumbled backward a few feet, absorbing her impact, then held on tight, her worry for her sister growing exponentially by the second.

"I'm so sorry," Adalia cried into her shoulder.

"Hey," Georgie said as she pulled back and smoothed the hair off Adalia's cheek. "We're gonna fix this, okay?"

Adalia looked up at her with hazel eyes so wide with hope Georgie couldn't help but wonder what it was she'd done.

They collected her two large suitcases and wrestled them into the back of Georgie's Lexus—which had been delivered a few days prior—then headed back to Beau's house.

Five minutes of silence ticked away before Georgie asked the obligatory *How was your flight?* question, and Adalia announced she'd sat next to someone with terrible B.O. Finally, her sister asked, "Aren't you going to grill me about what happened?"

Georgie started to answer, then stopped, darting a quick glance at Adalia before returning her attention to the road. "You'll tell me when you're ready."

They got home, and each of them rolled one of the suitcases to the house. Georgie had learned her lesson after the disaster with Josie. Thank God, River had saved so much of her stuff. A smile came to her lips.

"Who is he?" Adalia asked with narrowed eyes.

Georgie's heart nearly leaped out of her chest, but she managed to hide it, she thought.

"What are you talking about?" she asked as she unlocked the front door.

"Okay, I'll let it go for now," Adalia said as she followed her in. "But expect an interrogation later. Just like I'm waiting for mine."

Georgie stopped and turned to her sister. "There will be no interrogation from me later. I meant it, Addy. You tell me when *you're* ready. I'm just glad you're here."

They carted the bags upstairs, and Georgie showed her the bedroom she'd picked out for her, a room whose windows looked out onto the backyard. River had turned on a lamp on the bedside table, giving it an inviting look.

"It reminded me of a tree house. I remembered how you always wanted one when we were kids," Georgie said, now feeling foolish—then horrified when Adalia's eyes filled with tears. "We can exchange rooms, if you like. Or you can have one of the other two."

Adalia shook her head. "No. I love it."

Relief rushed through Georgie's body and she sagged against a dresser. At least she'd gotten this one thing right. "Okay. Good."

Adalia set her suitcase down at the end of the bed and stared out the window. "Why aren't you yelling at me? Or telling me what a screwup I am?"

"Because you are *not* a screwup," Georgie said insistently. "You made a mistake. We'll fix it."

"Dad would be furious. *And Lee…*" She released a sob and sat on the bed, still looking out the windows. "He knew what was happening, but he would never understand this."

Georgie bit back the urge to ask why Adalia hadn't come to her before, but she must have had her reasons and Georgie's hurt feelings had no place here. Besides, River was right—when it had mattered, Adalia had come to her. "Well, I'm glad you noticed I'm not like Dad or Lee," she said with a small laugh. "We may all be in business, but I handle things very differently than they do."

Adalia turned back to face her with bloodshot eyes. "I know. I realized that when the three of us had breakfast. You were so passionate about the brewery. Dad and Lee might be good at what they do, but they're never passionate about it. But you…" She cringed and her gaze lowered to the vintage white chenille bedspread, her fingertips rubbing absentmindedly over the bumps. "I figured you were like Dad, all cold and businessy. I guess I was wrong."

Georgie couldn't suppress her laugh. "Businessy?"

Adalia looked up with a grin. "You know. Like you have a stick up your ass."

Georgie nodded, still laughing. "Okay." She sat on the bed next to her sister. "You usually see me when I'm with Dad and/or Lee, and I guess I'm different when I'm with them. I act like I think they want me to act. That's not the real me. It's maybe who they want me to be."

As she said the words, she knew they were true. How had she never realized that before?

Adalia reached over and took her sister's hand. "That's sad, Georgie."

"I know," she whispered.

"Seeing the light in your eyes when you talked about the brewery made me realize you were much more like Mom and me than I gave you credit for."

Georgie's eyes flew wide. "You think I'm like Mom?"

The thought made her equally elated and terrified. Her mother had been warm and open, the kind of person people gravitated toward. She'd also become their father's doormat.

Adalia nodded. "More than I realized. I'm sorry."

Georgie shook her head. "No. I tried to be the kind of person Dad would find impressive, but it doesn't fit me well."

"So maybe you should stop trying," Adalia said. "Just be you and to hell with what anyone thinks."

Didn't she know it. She was getting there, but it was so much easier said than done.

Adalia turned serious. "You're still not going to ask me what happened?"

Georgie rubbed the back of Adalia's hand with her thumb. "No. You'll tell me when you're ready."

"I'm ready," she whispered.

"I'm listening."

Adalia poured her heart out. Alan Stansworth, her mentor from art school, had invited her to work in his large studio since she had limited space in her small apartment. Soon after she started working in his studio, he started taking a special interest in her mixed media sculptures. They worked together and eventually slept together, and the closer they got, the more controlling he became.

It was then some of her pieces started disappearing. He told her that space was so limited in the studio, he'd had them moved to his storage unit. He was doing her a favor. Why was she picking a fight when he was just trying to help her? It continued for a couple of months, until Adalia was missing over twenty pieces of art. She'd sought advice from Lee, who had been helpful and encouraging, but he'd told her that he couldn't really help unless she ended things with Alan. She'd tried, but their relationship had become a vicious cycle, just like their parents' marriage had been. Alan would fall all over himself to apologize to her, then he'd shower her with gifts and attention, until a few days later he'd shift to being berating and controlling. He'd cut her off from her friends in New York and had pitched a fit when she'd come to Asheville for the funeral, saying she was losing precious time she should spend focusing on her art.

"Oh, Addy," Georgie said through her tears. "I'm so sorry. I had no idea."

Adalia shook her head, wiping her face with the back of her hand. "Alan had gotten a showing at Michael Roe, a very coveted gallery. He was so secretive about the whole thing, and I had no idea what he was showing. I hadn't seen him work on anything of note in months. So on a whim, I stopped by to visit the gallery yesterday evening while they were setting up for the opening tomorrow night." She choked on a sob as she looked up at her sister. "They were *my* sculptures, Georgie. He'd stolen *my* art and put his name on it."

"Oh, Addy!" Georgie gasped, her mind reeling. "We'll get an attorney and file an injunction. We'll stop him from—"

Adalia's eyes went dead inside. "There's no point, Georgie."

Then the horrible truth dawned on her. Adalia had vandalized her own art. She scooped her sister into her arms and held on tight. "Addy, I'm so, so sorry."

How had it come to this? To Adalia destroying the very thing she'd loved?

Adalia began to sob. "He told me that I could protest all I wanted, but who would the art world believe? Me, a flighty, twenty-something art school dropout—"

"Wait. *You dropped out of art school?*"

"—or a well-known, revered artist? He said I had no hope of winning. That I should just be grateful he'd thought my work worthy of exposure."

Georgie grabbed her sister's upper arms and leaned back to look at her. "Go back to the part about you leaving art school."

"I had over a hundred thousand dollars in student loans. I couldn't afford the last year."

Georgie felt like she was going to be sick. That was partially her doing. If she'd stood up for her sister, her father might have relented. She'd pay off those loans in an instant, but she knew Adalia wouldn't let her. That suggesting it would be akin to pushing her away. "I'm sorry."

"You keep saying you're sorry, but you have nothing to be sorry *for*," Adalia said, sounding exhausted. "You're not the one who threw paint all over *Alan's* exhibits."

"You threw paint on them?"

A wicked gleam filled her eyes. "Every last one."

Georgie squeezed her arms, then released her. "As your big sister, I *know* I should be telling you that we should have handled this legally, but part of me wants to say good for you, except they were *your* pieces, Addy." Then a new thought hit her. "Over one hundred thousand dollars?"

She'd always semi-dismissed Adalia's art, but it was obvious she was *very* good. She felt gutted by her own shame.

Adalia shook her head. "It doesn't matter. And I'm not sorry. Not for one second. They weren't mine anymore. They were tainted after Alan claimed them." She sobered.

"Just like *I* am. I can never go back to New York. My reputation is ruined."

Georgie's heart broke for her. "But what about your art show? The one you were telling me and Lee about?"

"A lie Alan told me," she said, tears filling her eyes again. "To keep me too busy to notice what he was doing."

Georgie was going to find the best lawyer to destroy Alan Stansworth, but she couldn't do it until tomorrow. Tonight she was going to baby the crap out of her sister. "I think we need wine. And I have some leftover pizza."

"Wine?" Adalia asked with a wry grin. "Shouldn't we be drinking Buchanan Beer?"

"About that. There's plenty I need to tell you too, starting with what really happened in this house after the séance."

Adalia's eyes lit up, like she knew she was about to be the recipient of some high-quality gossip, and they both slid off the bed. But they didn't get very far before the high-pitched screech of a cat came from the backyard. "Jezebel!"

"Jezebel?" Adalia asked. "Do I want to know?"

There was more screeching and the sound of metal clanging against something.

Georgie made a face. "Something tells me you're about to find out, whether you like it or not."

CHAPTER
Thirty-Four

Part of River wanted to text Georgie, just to make sure Adalia had gotten in okay. He felt anxious for her, knowing how badly she wanted things to work out with her sister. He took out his phone to turn on the ringer, something he habitually kept off now that his number was common knowledge, and saw there were several texts from Finn.

He ticked his hand against the phone, thinking about ignoring them like he had the others, but it had occurred to him earlier, at Eye of the Tiger, that things might not be going so well for Finn. That maybe he was having a hard time too. And sure, he was the one who'd made the decision to sell, but even so...

He clicked through.

River, I know you're mad, man. But I need to tell you something. I think you'd want to hear it from a friend.

OK, I could practically see the expression on your face when you read that. But I AM your friend, like it or not.

Holy shit, I just saw Jezebel.

Another text came through while he read that last one: *I'm on the move. Still have that crate from when Maisie suckered me into fostering that tiny dog with the bladder issue. Stay tuned.*

Leave it to Finn to write a book while chasing a cat. Well, there was no ignoring that. Or at least Aunt Dottie would never forgive him if he did, and Beau would probably start showing up in his dreams for not-so-encouraging reasons.

So he put Hops in his crate and headed over to Flint Street for the second time that night.

His phone buzzed again on the seat beside him, and when he checked it at a red light, he saw Finn's latest text: *I think she's heading to Beau's. Plan is to intercept once she gets there.*

Which meant River would have to go there too. Finn didn't even know Georgie had moved back in.

Should he warn her?

Absolutely, yes. The one party crasher guaranteed to ruin a heartfelt reunion was a pissed-off cat who'd gotten accustomed to a life of freedom. Well, he could only hope the sardines would pacify her.

He clicked Georgie's number just as the light changed, putting the call on speaker, but it rang through to her voicemail.

Hopefully that wasn't because she was busy chasing Jezebel—or hitting Finn over the head with a cast-iron frying pan. Sure, he was pissed at the guy, but he didn't want him injured or dead.

He pulled up in front of Beau's house later, parking the car behind Georgie's—at least she'd gotten home safely—although perhaps it would have been better if she and Adalia had gone out somewhere. He'd only just set the emergency brake when he heard someone bellow in the backyard, followed by a familiar atonal shriek.

He bolted around back, pausing a second to take in what he was seeing.

Someone had flicked on the outside light, giving him an all-too-clear view. Finn had climbed up the back porch, stalking Jezebel, and apparently he'd managed to get the open canvas pet carrier over and around her, like putting a glass jar over a spider. Only now it was bucking around as if she truly were a miniature panther, spraying sardine oil everywhere, and Finn didn't have a great hold on the carrier, or her, because Adalia had just attacked him with some sort of projectile. Was that a crystal?

He wasn't sure, but he started running toward the porch. If Jezebel got out of that bag right now, things were unlikely to go well for any of them.

Georgie was running toward them too, pulling Adalia back.

"It's okay, Addy, he's a... I know him. And the cat." At the same time, Finn started saying, "Sorry, I didn't know you were here."

But he hadn't tugged the bag down hard enough, and Jezebel tore free, her green eyes full of vindictive heat. She jumped in the air, claws extended, and hissed. Another jumping hiss drove her closer to Adalia, who cringed back in horror.

Then, much to River's surprise, she simply padded past Adalia and Georgie and entered the house, her pace as slow as you please, tracking sardine oil everywhere.

River made it up to the porch and clapped Finn on the shoulder. He had a goose egg on his head, but he looked like he was probably fine. "Hi, Adalia," he said. "Like your new cat?"

Adalia's eyes went wide, and at first he thought it was a natural reaction to finding out that she was expected to coexist with a creature like Jezebel, but instead she looked back and forth between River and Georgie.

"Oh," she said. "I see. You're the mystery guy. Of course you are."

Which meant Georgie hadn't yet gotten around to telling her, but she'd figured it out nonetheless, from the situation maybe, or the energy between them. He was okay with that. He wanted people to know. Keeping things on the down-low made sense for the moment, but he didn't want to sneak around with Georgie, and he felt pretty sure she didn't want that either.

Finn cleared his throat, and Adalia's gaze shot to him.

He was still rubbing at the bump on his head, cringing every time he did, which begged the question of why he kept at it, but there was a strange look on his face, like maybe he was at a loss, something not typical for someone who always seemed to know how to charm people.

"Sorry I scared you," Finn said. "And for"—he motioned to the mess of sardine oil and the cloth pet carrier, which now had claw marks scored down the sides. "I know River and Dottie have been looking for her, and I figured I couldn't risk letting her get away. Not that I helped much, I guess."

"You didn't *scare* me," Adalia said. "I've lived in New York City for years. I know what to do with an intruder."

"Hit them with a crystal?" Finn asked, giving her a wry smile. "That seems more like behavior reserved for people who have a close, personal relationship with River's aunt."

"Hey," Adalia said, shrugging, "she gave it to me before I left and suggested I keep it on me. She's a lady who knows what she's doing when it comes to crystals. And apparently she was right."

This didn't seem to be going anywhere fast, so River figured it was time for him and Finn to make their exit.

"We should both probably go," he said. "It's late. I didn't mean to drop in on you either"—he met Georgie's eyes, silently apologizing—"but Finn told me he was on Jezebel's trail, and I didn't want either of them to catch you off guard."

"Oh, no, you're not leaving us with that cat," Adalia said. "I expect protection." She shifted her head to grin at Georgie. "And so does my sister. Come in. You guys can have some of this wine Georgie bought."

Finn made a rude sound, and River and Georgie exchanged a glance. She smiled at him and nodded, telling him it was okay. Maybe she didn't want to be alone with Jezebel either, which, fair enough. He'd have to tell Aunt Dottie she'd made it home. She'd spent the last week knitting Jezebel a welcome home sweater, but he figured he could convince her to hold off on the inevitable trauma of attempting to put it on her by reminding her, gently, that it was summer.

"And you are so cleaning up whatever horrible fish thing is now sprayed all over our porch," Adalia added.

"Fair enough," River said, following them in. He wondered if Finn was going to leave, but instead he trailed them into the house, which made River wonder what, exactly, he had to say. It had to be pretty compelling if he was willing to drink wine with a stranger who'd just clocked him over the head.

When they entered the house, Jezebel was stalking slowly through the downstairs, taking in the new—and very empty—landscape.

"Oh no," Georgie said, glancing back at him with something like horror, "what if she's mad that I changed it?"

And because Adalia apparently already knew about them anyway, he stepped forward and took her hand, squeezed it, while they watched the cat stalk around.

Jezebel returned to the kitchen from the living area, pausing in every corner and examining the new appliances, the painted cabinets. Finally, as if passing judgment, she leapt atop the refrigerator and settled into a contented ball.

"I think she approves," River said.

"Why, exactly, are we treating this cat like a deity?" Adalia asked.

A fair question, and one he thought it best to let Georgie answer. Except Finn hadn't gotten the memo. He'd been looking around the house, something hard about the set of his lips, but he shifted his gaze to Adalia at that comment. "Because this was Beau's house, and Jezebel was his cat. Take the house, respect the cat."

Hell, when had he last seen Finn with such a chip on his shoulder?

Adalia just sniffed and took out some wine glasses.

"Dude," River said. "Tone it down. We both know Jezebel is a creature of evil. Beau himself called her that. He just happened to like her that way."

"Didn't hesitate to make yourself at home," Finn said, ignoring River's comment and shifting his glance to Georgie. Something ugly played in his gaze.

"What the hell?" River said, tugging Georgie a little closer. "You don't have any call to talk to her that way. In her house, no less."

"Yeah," Adalia agreed. "I might have to rescind your part of the invitation. More wine for us."

Finn sighed and ran a hand through his hair, a nervous gesture that suggested something was preying on him. His eyes had circles under them too.

"Sorry. You're right. I'm going to head out... It's just...River, can I talk to you for a minute before I go? There's something I need to tell you." His gaze lowered to River and Georgie's linked hands. "And I'm starting to think it really can't wait."

"Whatever it is, just say it," River said. "You can talk freely in front of them."

"I really don't think I should."

Adalia had been pouring wine, only three glasses now— she'd dramatically pushed the fourth away—but she stopped, watching them.

"Well, I'm not leaving right now," River said, sick of being jerked around. "So if you want to talk to me, this is where it's happening."

"Just remember that you're the one who made that call," Finn said, fidgeting a little as he stood there.

Georgie's hand suddenly felt clammy within his, and a feeling of foreboding stole over River. It occurred to him that maybe he'd made a mistake, that they shouldn't talk about this here, in front of Georgie and Adalia, or maybe it would be better not to talk about it at all, but it was too late, Finn was already opening his mouth to speak.

"Look, man, I'm not happy to be the bearer of bad news, but I've been using Henry Manning's office to look over the Big Catch papers, and someone connected to the office—not naming names here—told me something you deserve to know."

A little gasp escaped Georgie like a sudden exhale of air.

"Turns out Beau was going to leave it all to you—the brewery, even the house—before your girlfriend here showed up in Asheville and convinced him not to. And there's a clause in the will that gives the brewery back to you if Buchanan doesn't place in the top five at Brewfest next spring."

River felt a pit open in his gut, each of Finn's words tearing into him like an actual missile. What. The. Actual. Hell. Could that be true? Had she known all of this and kept it from him? Had she thought he'd, what, sabotage the brewery if he knew?

One look at those beautiful hazel eyes, swimming with tears, told him all he needed to know. He let his hand slip away from hers.

"You didn't know that, did you?" Finn asked, his tone softer now, his gaze beseeching. "I didn't think so."

"You should go now," Adalia said from somewhere behind him. "Unless you want to get clocked with another crystal."

Dimly, River registered that Finn did leave. And the sound of footsteps indicated Adalia was making herself scarce too.

All he could think was that he needed to leave too. The safety he'd found with Georgie, the feeling of home—it had all been a lie. She'd only let him into her world under *her* rules. The fraternization clause. The noncompete. This. She and her brothers, or at least Jack, had known about the will all along.

It made it worse that Beau himself had arranged this. That he had played them like they were pieces in some sort of twisted game. Sure, Aunt Dottie had made Beau skew toward eccentric toward the end, but this kind of manipulation was something he'd expect more from the son than the father. This was a side of Beau he hadn't known well, and one he was ashamed to realize he didn't much like. It felt wrong to think ill of the dead, when Beau couldn't do a thing to explain himself.

"River?"

He realized it wasn't the first time she'd said his name, and her voice was shaking, with tears running down her cheeks.

In a weird way, he still wanted to comfort her, to trace those tears with his fingers and hold her, even though he was the one she'd hurt.

"I didn't convince him to do any of that, River," she was saying. "I didn't know what he was planning. I wanted to tell you when I found out, I really wanted to tell you, but Jack was adamant. He wouldn't have agreed to work with you if you knew, and—"

"When did you find out?" he asked, his voice sounding funny and flat to his own ears. "How long have you known?"

Her face, which had gone pale, lost even more color. "The day Jack and I signed the papers," she said. "I've known since then."

"That's what I thought," he said, but the truth drove the knife deeper. "Were you going to tell me?"

"Yes! Of course! I was trying to figure out a way to make it right. I figured I'd buy out Lee and Adalia after Brewfest, if we win, and make you partner. And if we don't, you'd have control anyway."

"You were going to wait that long?" he asked, anger threading into his voice now. "You were going to wait nearly a year?"

"No"—she reached for his arm, but he pulled away. "No," she added in a smaller voice. "I just wanted you to know what I was planning. That I had a way to make it right."

There was that phrase again: *make it right.*

Was there a way to make it right? If so, he didn't see it. Here he'd thought he and Georgie were a unit, that they were in this together—the brewery, their relationship—but she'd known about this and kept it from him. She'd *deceived* him. Beau had used him as a pawn. And Jack clearly didn't trust him (and now he knew why).

He was done with the Buchanans. Some things, once broken, could not be pieced together. Glue didn't hide the cracks or fix them.

"You think I'm perfect, but I should have told you before…I'm not. Not even a little," he said, hanging his head. "I can't do this. I'll be there Saturday night, so you don't have to tell anyone yet, but you're going to have to find someone else for the job." And though it felt like he was ripping himself apart, he added, "I quit."

With that, he turned and walked away. He left through the front door, and Georgie didn't try to stop him, but Adalia called to him from the side of the porch.

"Excuse me for saying so, but your friend is kind of a jerk."

He didn't know how to respond to that. *He's not my friend anymore* didn't feel precisely true, and he actually wasn't pissed at Finn for telling him, or even for the way he'd told him. (River had put him into a corner.) So he just shrugged.

"I don't know what happened," she continued, completely serious for a change, even as she sipped her wine. "But you're making a mistake. I've never seen my sister look at someone the way she looks at you. You belong together. To hell with the rest of our family."

Only it wasn't Jack or Lee who had hurt or wronged him, not really.

"Good luck, Adalia," he said. "I'm glad you and Georgie are here for each other." *That* he could say and mean. And after he did, he walked away.

CHAPTER
Thirty-Five

Georgie watched River walk out the front door, and it felt like her life had just walked out with him, which was ridiculous. They hadn't known each other for long enough for her to feel this devastated.

Yet she was. Her heart might as well have been ripped to shreds by Jezebel's deadly claws.

Tears streamed down her face as she wondered how to fix this, but the sound of his car starting made her realize they were over…and they'd barely just begun.

"Georgie?" Adalia said, walking through the front door with a glass of wine.

Georgie heard the worry in her sister's voice, but she didn't answer, just stared at her sister in shock. Fifteen minutes ago, she'd been consoling Adalia. Now she was the one who was broken.

"We're cursed," she whispered. "Mom. You. Me. We're cursed in love."

Adalia's lips pressed into a tight line. "I don't know about that." She grabbed another glass of wine up off the counter. "Here. You need this."

Georgie absently took it, her heart breaking a little more at the sight of the third full glass. "I've lost him."

"If he's willing to just walk out like that, then maybe it's for the best," Adalia grumbled. Her eyes narrowed on her sister. "You should sit down. You look like you're going to pass out."

Georgie shook her head in dismay, still in shock over what had happened. How quickly it had all gone wrong. "I should have told him."

"*Sit.*" Adalia gave her sister a tiny push into the chair Georgie had sat in the night of the beer tasting, that night she'd first realized River was different. Special. He'd gone out of his way to put her at ease and make her laugh. She'd never felt so comfortable with another man...and now...

Tears welled in her eyes. "I have to call him. I have to explain."

"I don't think that's such a good idea, Georgie," Adalia said softly. She'd gone back to the counter for the bottle of wine and carried it over by the neck before sitting in the chair across from Georgie. "At least not *yet*. He needs to cool down first. In the meantime, how about you tell *me* what's going on." Adalia poured more wine into her glass. "How did this thing between the two of you happen? I'd like to hear the other stories you mentioned too, if you don't mind."

Georgie ran her free hand through her hair, which reminded her she had a perfectly good glass of wine in her other hand. She took a generous gulp. "I started falling in love with him here at Grandpa Beau's house. At this very table. Over beer."

And she realized it was true. She'd heard of people falling in love that quickly, practically at first sight, and thought it was ridiculous. Nonsense. But River...everything about him had broken all of her rules, all of her notions about life. And now she had lost him.

A sob bubbled up, but she swallowed it back down. She couldn't let herself fall apart.

Adalia narrowed her eyes again. "Okay, I'm not sure which topic to focus on, so I'll pick neither and jump to the giant elephant in the room. What was that guy talking about with Grandpa Beau's will?"

"This was supposed to be River's," Georgie said with a soft cry, her heart twisting in torment, not just over her loss, but at the knowledge of how betrayed River must feel. By her. By Beau. By his own aunt. "The house. The brewery," she choked out as she broke down. "He was supposed to inherit it all, but then Grandpa Beau invited me to visit, and after I left, he changed the will." She looked at her, pleading. "I didn't know, Addy. I swear."

Pity filled Adalia's eyes, and she reached over and covered Georgie's hand with her own. "I know that, but apparently River's asshole friend didn't."

"Finn," Georgie said.

"Excuse me?" Adalia asked with bugged-out eyes. "Like a fish? No wonder he's an asshole with a huge chip on his shoulder. Probably lived his entire life having to deal with stupid jokes about his name and it's made him bitter and resentful of love." She took a sip of her wine in a dramatic flourish to punctuate her assessment of River's friend.

Georgie stared at her, mouth partially open, then shook it off and took a sip of her own wine. "I found out about the stipulations when Jack and I went to sign the papers, but Jack was worried that if River knew, he'd purposely make us lose the competition so he could inherit it all anyway. I barely knew River, but I was sure he would never do that, because it turns out that sometimes you meet a person and you just know them."

Tears filled her eyes again.

"Or in my case, you don't clue in until it's much too late." Adalia took another sip of her wine. "But you've always had a pretty good bullshit meter when it comes to everyone who isn't Dad and Lee, when he's acting like Dad's mini-me."

Georgie gave her a scowl.

Adalia held up her hands in mock surrender, still holding the wine glass in her right hand, and a splash of wine sloshed over the rim and onto the floor. At another moment, Georgie would have hastened to wipe it up. Now, she didn't much care. "It's true. Sure, you've dated assholes in the past, but I always knew why."

While Georgie could admit that she'd dated less than promising guys, she'd never purposely selected a dud. "What are you talking about?"

"Come on, Georgie. It's plain as day, and it's twofold." She twisted her mouth to the side and stared at the top of the cabinets from the corner of her eye. "Or maybe it's all one and the same." She shook herself. "In any case, you usually date men like Dad."

"*What?*" Georgie screeched in horror.

"It's true," Adalia said with a shrug. "Lots of women do it, but usually because they adore their father and it's subconsciously imprinted on their brains that he's the ideal man."

A shudder rippled through Georgie's body. "That's disgusting. Our father is *not* my ideal man."

Adalia lifted her glass. "Cheers to that. But the truth of the matter is that, for better or for worse, you have dated men like Dad—devoted to their careers. Aloof. Detached. Emotionally unavailable. Indifferent."

"You do realize those are all adjectives that describe the same thing?"

Shrugging, Adalia said, "I had to make sure I drove the point home." She leaned closer, over the table. "You dated men who treated you the way Dad has treated you your entire life, because one, that's been your experience of how a man treats women, and two, it was *so* much safer. If *they* were indifferent and aloof, you could be too. No attachment. No heartbreak."

Georgie stared at her in shock. Was Adalia right? It fit with what she'd realized about her fear of becoming like her mother.

Her sister took another sip of wine, then said, "I wish I had my phone on me so I could take a photo of your face right now. Georgie, the woman with all the answers, in shock and clueless."

Georgie rested her arm on the table, suddenly weary. "I don't have all the answers, Addy. Right now I don't feel like I have any of them."

"No one does. But you sure do a good job of convincing everyone you do. You and Lee are a lot alike in that way." A look crossed her face like she'd said too much, but then she tilted her head to the side. "Now why don't you fill me in on what a Brewfest is and why we need to win it."

Georgie told her the rest—how she'd signed without reading the fine print, thinking the signatures were simply a formality, and they now stood to lose the brewery if they didn't place fifth or higher in the Brewfest Competition next spring.

"That's why we need River," Georgie said, sounding resigned as she finished her second glass of wine. "We can't win it without him, yet if we lose, he gets it."

Adalia pursed her lips. "And you're sure he wouldn't purposely throw the contest to get the brewery?"

"I am. That's not why I didn't tell him… It's just, I couldn't imagine how hurt he'd be once he found out."

"From the looks of it, pretty hurt," Adalia said.

Tears welled in Georgie's eyes again. "To make matters worse, River just quit and Jack and Lee insisted on that stupid noncompete, which means River can't get another job within a two-hundred-mile radius. If they don't back down, he'll be forced to leave everything he loves." A sob broke loose.

She was being weak again. She'd have to take a stand and make her brothers rip that agreement up so River could work wherever he wanted. Except she knew in her heart that the only place he wanted to work was Buchanan. Georgie had no idea how she could restart the brewery without him, let alone win Brewfest. Maybe they should just concede and give River everything now, yet she didn't want to do that either. She felt like she belonged at Buchanan Brewery too. The two of them together. But he'd never trust her now.

Maybe she really had lost everything.

Adalia was making a face like she was concentrating too hard and giving herself a headache. "Why in the world would you let Jack tell you what to do?" she finally asked, starting to get irritated. "You never let *any* man tell you what to do."

"Because I felt bad for him, Addy. We ignored him all these years, and this was finally something from the Buchanan family he could have for himself…something he could be included in."

"For the record, I could spout an earful about how you and Lee kept this from me," Adalia grumbled. "But for now, I'll focus on his desire to be a Buchanan, because come on…" She shook her head. "Why on earth he would *want* to be one of us is beyond me."

"That's a very good point, but he did, and he wanted it badly. So I went against my better judgment and caved," she finished with a sigh.

"And what lesson did we learn here?" Adalia asked in a high-pitched voice.

"Not to trust men?" Georgie asked with a hint of a grin.

Adalia's upper lip curled and she gave a brisk nod. "That too, but our other lesson is not to compromise our principles. For anyone."

Her voice broke, and Georgie knew she was talking about her own hard-learned lesson too.

Reaching across the table, Georgie grabbed Adalia's hand and squeezed. "I have a lot of regrets, Addy, but one of my biggest was losing you along the way."

Tears filled Adalia's eyes. "You didn't lose me, Georgie. I was always there."

"Then I underappreciated you." She squeezed her hand tighter. "I know what's important now, Addy. River taught me that."

Sadness filled Adalia's eyes. "Maybe you haven't lost him, Georgie. Maybe he just needs some time."

Georgie shook her head. "No. Too many people have betrayed him, and I was one person too many."

And that was what hurt her most of all.

CHAPTER
Thirty-Six

River had tried to run away once, after he'd gone to live with Aunt Dottie—been *left* to live with her. He'd bought a bus ticket to Savannah with the allowance money she'd given him for helping with her energetic necklaces. Savannah was the last city from which Esmerelda had sent him a postcard. But he hadn't known what to do when he'd arrived. He was still just a kid, even at thirteen, and he felt every bit of his youth as he wandered around the city. After a few hours of going around to different souvenir shops and asking about her, learning nothing, he'd called his aunt. (The phone number he had for Esmerelda had been disconnected months before.) She'd left immediately to get him, and Beau had skipped the rest of his workday to come with her.

Neither of them had yelled or carried on—they hadn't even tried to make him feel guilty by telling him how much they'd worried. Instead, they'd taken him out to dinner, like they'd *meant* to come to Savannah in the middle of the week, but when Aunt Dottie went to the restroom during dinner, Beau had told him the truth.

Those postcards he'd been getting from Esmerelda every few weeks had all been written by his aunt's hand. She'd wanted to make him feel better—to make him believe that his mother cared enough to reach out. But Esmerelda hadn't. She didn't. He knew she was alive. Every so often, he'd find something online about her jewelry, something that proved she was still out there, somewhere, but it was as if River had ceased to exist for her.

That had made him feel screwed up inside for weeks afterward. Months. Years, even. But that was nothing compared to what he felt now.

After leaving Georgie's house, he drove back to the loft, but he couldn't bring himself to go in, so he just walked for hours, walked until his legs got tired. He saw a few people he knew—something that always happened if he walked downtown—but he couldn't summon the energy to do more than nod. When he finally got home, Hops had broken out of the crate, and there was a mess on the floor. Torn-up paper and pee. Worse, his water was empty and so was his food bowl. The puppy whimpered at his feet, pawing at them.

What had he been thinking, taking in a dog? He couldn't take care of a puppy. He'd have to leave Asheville anyway, wouldn't he? After all of this, he'd have to leave, and not just because the noncompete he'd signed ensured he couldn't work in the field. He couldn't live here, near Georgie, surrounded by memories of how life had been and his ruined dreams about how it might be.

He'd have to channel his mother and uproot himself. It had always been so easy for her to leave a place behind, a *person* behind, or at least she'd made it seem that way.

He brought Hops out, fed and watered him, and then proceeded to down the majority of a bottle of whiskey. Sometimes beer just wasn't enough.

He woke up past eleven the next morning to Hops pawing at him, whining, and another mess. His head feeling like it had been hit with an anvil, he brought the little dog out, feeling a swell of worthlessness—how long had Hops been trying to wake him, anyway?

It felt wrong to be home. He felt like he should be at the office, preparing for the events. The messed-up thing was that he felt *guilty* about leaving it all to Georgie. About abandoning her when she needed him.

She betrayed you, he reminded himself. *She lied to you. They all did.*

So why wouldn't the guilt go away? Why couldn't he stop wondering what Georgie was doing? How she was feeling?

Why couldn't he stop wanting to ease her pain?

Because you're a fool.

Hops whimpered again, and River gave himself a mental shake. If nothing else, he could get Hops sorted. He could help him find the kind of home he deserved.

He'd shut his phone down last night, but he turned it on now, ignoring the missed texts on the home screen, though he did notice the names. Aunt Dottie. Finn. No Georgie.

Which only made him wonder again what she was thinking.

He sent off a quick text to Maisie: *I need to bring Hops back today. I can't take care of him anymore. This isn't working.*

Her response was immediate: *Meet me at the clubhouse at 3. No Hops. No excuses.*

Huh. Did that mean she knew what had happened? Had Georgie told people?

No, it had to be Finn. Finn couldn't shut his mouth if world peace depended on it.

Part of him wanted to tell her no, but he needed to see a friendly face, and one that had no connection to the Buchanans and their manipulations and the love he begrudgingly bore for them.

And she'd mentioned the clubhouse, which he hadn't thought about in years. Her dad had built it for Maisie and her sisters, but no one had really used it other than River and Maisie. It wasn't much—little more than room for a table and a couple of chairs. Some books and games. But it had felt like a safe haven. Like a place where he didn't need to worry about being the new kid, or the stupid kid, or the kid who'd gotten left behind. Somewhere he could just be River. As far as he knew, she only used it for the foster dogs now.

OK was all he said in response.

It felt a little weird when he got there, walking past Maisie's house and out to the clubhouse. Like maybe he was trespassing, or like fifteen years had been erased, and he was that lost teenage boy again. But he'd seen her car in the drive, so surely she was there.

He knocked on their door, and she called out, "Use the code, doofus," and he smiled—actually smiled—as he used their knock.

She opened the door, and he was surprised to see she looked like she hadn't gotten much sleep either. Was the fundraiser going that badly?

"Is everything okay?" he asked. "You look tired."

"You're saying that to me?" she said with a smirk. "You should look in the mirror, bud." She waved behind her. "Come in. Take a seat."

It looked just like he remembered it. Hell, from what he could tell, she even had the same furniture in there, although everything smelled powerfully of dog.

"I'm not so sure I want to," he said, wrinkling his nose.

"Oh, don't be a baby. I'll leave the door open."

She did, and he sat on the old upholstered window seat, and she sat across from him on a rickety old chair. It was only after they'd taken their seats that he realized their positions mimicked those of a therapist and patient. Appropriate enough.

"You're not bringing Hops back," she said. "I refuse."

He looked away, ran a hand through his hair. "I can't take care of him anymore, Maisie. I had to quit the brewery. I found out…I found out Beau was going to leave it to me. He changed his mind, but he left a crazy clause in his will. If the brewery doesn't place in the top five at Brewfest, it goes to me anyway. Georgie knew. We…we decided to give it a try. Being together, working together." His voice took on a ragged edge he didn't much like. "But she's known for weeks, and she didn't tell me."

"I know," she said, not that he was surprised. "You'll be annoyed to hear that Finn called an emergency breakfast session with me and Dottie this morning."

He let out an exhale that was somewhere between a sound of annoyance and a laugh. "Sounds more like something Aunt Dottie would do."

"What can I say? I guess she's rubbed off on all of us." She held his gaze, something intense in her eyes. "River, Dottie's pretty upset. Finn too. Neither of them think Georgie was playing you. In fact…" She cleared her throat. "Dottie says she's positive Georgie's in love with you."

Something warm unfurled in him, but he shut it down quickly. "I didn't think she was playing me…she's not like that. It's just…she didn't trust me. I told her that I didn't want us to start anything unless she was sure, and she still didn't tell me."

"Which is shitty," Maisie said softly. "No one's saying otherwise. But don't you think she was maybe worried you'd react just like you're reacting?" She paused, tilting her head a little, and then said words that drove a knife into him. "Do you think you're the only one who's afraid of being left?"

A feeling akin to horror passed over him. Was that how Georgie felt? Like he'd left her? Like he'd decided she wasn't good enough? He thought again of those postcards. He'd looked at them after the drive back from Savannah, comparing them to one of his aunt's grocery lists, and sure enough, they'd been in her writing.

"Why are you so sure that's why she didn't tell me?" he said through numb lips. "They needed me to help make the brewery competitive. Jack thought I would tank them if I knew about the will."

"Yeah, Jack thought that," she said. "But who the hell is Jack? You don't know him, and from what Dottie said, Georgie doesn't really know him either. Why should his opinion matter that much to you?" She looked away for a moment before meeting his eyes again. "Do you honestly think Georgie distrusted you?"

And that was the real question, wasn't it?

"No," he finally said. "No, I don't. But this hurts like hell, and I hate that Beau put us into this mess. I…it makes me feel like I didn't know him at all."

She rose from her chair then, and came to sit beside him. "You knew him, River," she said softly. "But he wasn't a perfect man. He also wasn't a *psychic* man. I don't think he had the first idea you'd end up leaving Big Catch. If he'd thought you would end up taking a job at Buchanan, he never would have arranged things that way."

She was right. Everything she'd said was right. And it penetrated the wall of hurt that had built up inside of him. Something long pent up let loose, and he felt tears course down his cheeks for the first time since Beau had died.

"I messed everything up, Maisie. I'm not sure how to make it right. I wonder if I even can."

She took him in her arms and held him, just held him, for a moment, letting him cry. Then she pulled back and wiped his tears.

"You can, and you will. Do you love Georgie?"

The answer was so easy, it made him feel even more foolish for treating her the way he had. For walking away like she meant nothing to him.

"I do."

She nodded, as if that was what she'd expected, but she looked almost sad about it.

"Then you're going to get your girl back. And your job, obviously."

"It's not that simple."

"Oh?"

He told her about the contract he'd signed—the noncompete and the new fraternization clause—and she scowled as if she'd eaten a lemon.

"Her brothers sound like controlling douchebags," she said, "especially the one who knew about the will. You should have taken Georgie's advice and had Finn look at it. He never would have let you sign that."

He sighed. "I know."

"And you also know what you have to do, right?" She took a dramatic pause. "Give that controlling douchebag a call."

"Ugh," he said, feeling his head ache again through the pain reliever he'd taken. "I hate that you're right about that too."

She grinned and pointed to herself. "You can't go wrong if you stick with this controlling douchebag."

"Har-de-har-har." He motioned to the space around them. "Why here, Maisie? Why not at your office or my apartment?"

An almost wistful look passed over her face. "It just seemed right," she said. "It was always a safe place for us, wasn't it? I hoped it would be one for you now."

He hugged her again, holding on tight, bolstering himself for what was to come, and as soon as she pulled away, she said, "And no matter what happens, that's an absolute no about Hops. In fact, I already filled out the adoption paperwork for you."

"You *are* a controlling douchebag," he teased, stepping back as she fake-swatted him. "Are you coming tonight?"

"No," she said simply. "I don't think so. But you're going to tell me everything."

<hr />

Back in his car, he checked the rest of his texts. Finn was worried and apologetic. Apparently Georgie's reaction had convinced him that she hadn't deviously plotted the whole thing, but he still thought it was a bad idea for River to get involved with his boss. He couldn't help but smile a little at that—even Finn's apology texts were paragraphs.

Noted, he responded. *After all of this is over, let's get a beer or make one.*

Aunt Dottie's messages were frantic enough that he thought it best to call her.

She answered on the first ring, and he could hear the Buchanan tasting room in the background. He felt an odd pang at that.

"River, where are you?" Aunt Dottie said, and the guilt he'd felt toward Georgie doubled. Tripled. She'd worried he would leave. That he would just drive off the way her niece always had.

"I'm okay," he said. "I'm at Maisie's. She just talked some sense into me."

A relieved gust of air made him pull the phone away from his ear. "Oh, thank heavens. Are you coming over to talk to Georgie? She's had the door of her office shut all day, but I heard her crying in there, poor dear."

And if that didn't make him feel terrible...

"Not yet," he said, "I have to talk to Jack first. I want to be with Georgie, but I don't like all this closed-doors business. All of these lies and misunderstandings. I know she doesn't either. I need to clear the air."

"Speaking of misunderstandings," she said, "I hope you don't think Beau did this to spite you, or because he didn't believe in you. When you told him you were happy at Big Catch, he didn't want to get in the way of that. The way he structured the will—he did it because he wanted to make sure his grandkids took it seriously. Those Buchanans have competition running in their blood, he said, and he figured it would fire them up. I also think he wanted them to get to know you. It was his way of ensuring it. I wonder now if it was a mistake."

"Let's hope not, Aunt Dottie. I'm going to do everything I can to make it right."

When he got home, he hugged Hops to his chest.

"I guess you're sticking with me, buddy," he said, and the little dog licked him. And then he picked up the apartment, so as not to look like an insane person, and video-called Jack.

Jack picked up on the first ring.

CHAPTER
Thirty-Seven

"He's not coming," Georgie said, scanning the room for the hundredth time.

Adalia put her hand on Georgie's arm and squeezed. "I know this is easier said than done, but try to enjoy the party. All of these people are here to celebrate Grandpa Beau and *you*, Georgie. They're excited you're rebuilding his legacy."

"Not anymore," Georgie said, fighting the urge to cry.

A twenty-something man walked up and extended his hand, one of about a hundred in the last hour, or so it seemed, whose faces had all blended together. "I hear you're Georgie Buchanan."

"That's right," she said, forcing a smile as she shook his hand. "And this is my sister Adalia."

Adalia took his hand next. "Call me Addy."

The man's smile grew bigger. "Call *me* Ned. Are you part of the family business too?"

"Sure am," she said with a flirty look. "The Buchanan sisters are taking the Asheville brewing world by storm."

He laughed.

"Along with our brothers," Georgie added.

The man kept his gaze on Adalia, making it clear he didn't give a hoot about their brothers. Georgie felt a little prick of protectiveness, but at the same time, she felt lucky her sister was around to butter people up. She currently felt about as charming as a cardboard box.

"They're more like silent partners," Addy said with a wink.

Adalia had come into work with Georgie that morning, and Dottie had given her the grand tour (Dottie's words). She'd come back to Georgie's office practically glowing with positivity—this was something Georgie ascribed to the Dottie Effect, a little-studied phenomenon about what happened when people drank Dottie's Kool-Aid.

"She's right about one thing," Adalia had said. "It has good vibes. I feel weirdly at home here."

Georgie had smiled at her, but with tears in her eyes. "I felt that way too."

"We'll talk sense into him, Georgie. Dottie says he just needs a little bit of time."

Georgie hoped so, but she also knew how badly she'd messed up. There was a chance River might forgive her, but he likely wouldn't forget. And even if he agreed to come back to work, she wasn't sure she'd be able to handle the pain of seeing him every day, knowing how much he despised what she'd done to him. Knowing what could have been if she'd only been stronger.

"I want to be part of this, Georgie," Adalia had said earnestly. "I want to help reopen Buchanan Brewery."

That had choked Georgie up—how much would she have loved to hear that two weeks ago?—and she'd fought tears to reply with a straight face and clear voice. "I don't know if there will *be* a Buchanan Brewery."

"Dottie said not to worry," Adalia had said, waving that off. "She thinks fate has a way of working things out."

Maybe so, but who was to say fate was on her side? She was beginning to doubt she had any luck at all.

"Is River around?" Ned asked, his gaze darting around the packed tasting room. "I'd love to offer him my congratulations on landing at Buchanan. You know, we always thought he'd inherit the place."

And didn't that just twist the knife.

Addy gave him a sweet smile. "River's currently detained, but I'm sure he'll be here any moment."

"Georgie," Dottie called out as she pushed her way through the crowd toward her. "One of the TV crews is here."

"Great," Georgie said. "Tell them to make themselves at home and get whatever footage they need."

Dottie's face turned serious. "They want to interview you first." Then she added in a lowered voice, "And River."

Another twist of the knife. River had said he'd be at the party, but no one had seen or heard from him all day. What if he'd decided he might as well leave Asheville now since he'd have to start over eventually anyway?

Dottie squeezed her arm. "He'll show up, dear."

Georgie pushed her way through the crowd, pleased at the turnout, despite everything. It seemed like most of Asheville had shown up. She'd put out a lot of press releases and had personally invited news channels, entertainment websites, and magazines to be a part of Bury the Brewery, and quite a few had shown up. River had purposely held back the last of the reserve beer to make sure they were prepared for the party, but now she wasn't sure how far it would stretch. Not only was the tasting room full, but there was a long line weaving outside the building.

Turned out everyone in Asheville wanted to be a part of the end of Beau Buchanan's era. Everyone except for River.

Not that she blamed him.

The interview went off without a hitch, and if she looked less than miserable on camera, it was only thanks to Adalia, who'd applied cold compresses to her eyes to help take down the swelling from crying all day. A couple of days ago, River had gently suggested she wear something other than a business suit, which would mark her as an outsider, and she was grateful she'd taken his recommendation to heart. The light blue sundress she'd worn made her feel like less of a sore thumb. Her hair was loose and full of waves thanks to the French braids Adalia had put in it the night before. She'd be lying if she didn't admit that she'd dressed with River in mind, but as they counted down the last pulls, anticipating the last of the tap, he still hadn't arrived.

Which meant he wouldn't.

Dottie was behind the main bar, and when she held up a glass, announcing that it was the last of the keg, her voice broke as she said, "And that's the end of an era."

The room hushed and a lump filled Georgie's throat, the first all day that wasn't directly River-related.

"To Beau," someone called out, holding up a glass, and the chorus went round the room. "To Beau."

Georgie felt closer to Beau this evening than she ever had. So many people had come over to tell the Buchanan sisters stories about their grandfather. Many of those stories had featured Dottie, and several had also involved River. Those were the ones she cherished most, but they also tugged at her heart, reminding her of the pain she'd caused him, leading her to a conclusion her father would consider ridiculous. Infantile. *Female.*

Buchanan Brewery belonged to River more than it belonged to Georgie and her siblings, and she was going to find a way to give it all to him, no strings attached. Consequences be damned.

To hell with what her family thought. Georgie was done with trying to make everyone else happy. She should have defaulted the brewery to River as soon as she found out he was supposed to have originally inherited it. It would have been the right thing to do.

It was too late to change what she'd done, but it wasn't too late to make things right.

Of course, the brewery legally belonged to her siblings too, but she was sure none of them would want to step forward to run it. If she forfeited her share, they'd likely default too since there would be no one to manage the business. Yeah, Jack claimed he wanted to be a part of it, but he still refused to come back, he couldn't manage it remotely, and she couldn't imagine him willingly sharing the leadership with River after everything that had gone down. If he forced the issue, Georgie could insist he pay her back the hundreds of thousands of dollars she'd invested within thirty days. It was an asshole move, but River deserved it more than Jack. She'd find another way to form a bond with her half-brother. If he ever forgave her.

As for the money? It was just money. She'd put this down as a lesson well learned.

After the last drink was served, the energy in the room seemed to evaporate, as if they really were burying the brewery. The atmosphere turned melancholy, and the remaining guests soon left, hugging Dottie and the other staff, wishing Georgie and Adalia well with the reopening come fall. And soon it was just the sisters and the staff…and no River.

A couple of the tasting workers came out of a back room, passing around the last of the reserve in small Dixie cups—Beau Brown, which River and Georgie had thought would be fitting. The plan had been for Georgie to address the staff, thanking them for their support and hard work, for embracing the future with her, but she couldn't do it, because it was a lie.

She would have no part in Buchanan Brewery's future, and that broke her more than she'd expected. Turned out she'd fallen in love with her grandfather's legacy too.

Dottie seemed to sense that Georgie was too distraught to follow through as planned, so she took charge, which felt more fitting anyway.

"Beau would have loved this evening," Dottie said with a bright smile but with tears in her eyes. "He would have loved the energy. He would have loved the stories." A chuckle ran through the room. "He would have loved the community." Dottie turned and held Georgie's gaze. "And he would have loved the sense of family. He always said the employees at Buchanan Brewery were family, and Georgie Buchanan is keeping that same philosophy alive and well. She's embracing Buchanan's past and bringing it into the future, all while keeping the employees in the fold with her generosity and enthusiasm. Buchanan Brewery *needs* Georgie Buchanan, and she will lead us into the future." She lifted her Dixie cup into the air. "To Georgie."

The employees enthusiastically shouted, "To Georgie!"

It was too much.

Georgie fought to keep from breaking down, while Adalia wrapped her arm around her sister's back and whispered in her ear, "Don't despair. True love always wins, Georgie."

Not always. A fact Georgie had on some level known since she was a little girl, even if she hadn't understood her parents' relationship yet.

Adalia excused herself to help the tasting room staff clean up, but Dottie rushed over and pulled Georgie into a tight embrace before leaning back and staring into her face. "I know what you're planning to do, but it's not what Beau wanted. He knew what he was doing, Georgie. Trust in that. Buchanan Brewery really does need you."

How could Dottie know what she was planning? She couldn't, which meant the older woman probably had some other crazy idea in her head. "Thanks, Dottie, but I intend to set things right."

Dottie gave her a long look. "Don't make any decisions yet. Just come to the after-party and then sleep on it, okay?"

Georgie shook her head. "I think I should just go home, Dottie. Besides, it's for the employees, people who knew Beau, and I'm just the estranged granddaughter who came in and stole everything."

Tears swam in Dottie's eyes. "You are so much more than that, Georgie, so much more. Just give him a bit of time, okay? Because not only are you exactly what Buchanan Brewery needs, you're what my nephew needs too."

Georgie shook her head more vehemently. "No. He needs someone he can trust. Someone who won't lie to him and take advantage of him. He needs someone who won't let him down."

"Oh, Georgie," Dottie said, cupping Georgie's cheek. "That person doesn't exist. No matter how much we try, we will *always* let down the people we love. It's human nature. But it's how you come back from it that matters." She leaned closer and whispered, "Just give him more time." She pressed something into Georgie's hand and then walked away, calling over her shoulder, "And you *will* come to the after-party. Not a single one of us will take no for an answer."

Georgie opened her hand to see a two-inch, smooth, bright blue, striated stone with a small slip of paper. Dottie had written:

Blue Lace Agate—good for communication and purification. Just rub your fingers over the stone. All will work out in the end, Georgie. Have faith.

Love, Dottie

Georgie only hoped Dottie was psychic too.

With a sigh, she helped the staff shut everything down. Turned out she was going to the party after all.

CHAPTER
Thirty-Eight

All of that, and he wasn't going to make it.

River had spent an uncommonly long time getting ready for the closing party, especially since he'd ended up choosing exactly the sort of outfit he always wore, a short-sleeved button-down and khakis, Beau's watch tucked into the pocket of the pants. Georgie had encouraged him to be himself, and he couldn't be himself and also wear a suit. But he'd walked out of the room to find Hops with melted chocolate all over his fur. For a moment, he'd thought the dog had had a massive accident that he'd maybe rolled in, but then he'd found the chocolate wrapper by the couch. Turned out his aunt had hidden a dark chocolate bar for him at Easter—*Easter*—without telling him. Which might have been a nice surprise if he'd found it in April.

He'd panicked and immediately called Maisie, who'd walked him through what to do, which had involved giving Hops hydrogen peroxide to throw up. He'd needed to repeat it a couple of times before Hops actually vomited out the chocolate, and by then both of them were a mess, and slightly hysterical too. He'd changed his clothes and dropped

Hops off with Maisie, who was at the shelter, not wanting to leave him alone after what had surely been a traumatizing experience. (Or at least it had been traumatizing for River.)

As a nice bonus, one of Hops's sisters had been back at the shelter. She hadn't worked out with her foster family owing to some antagonism from a cat who sounded a bit like Jezebel, so she was temporarily staying with Maisie. But he hadn't stuck around to watch the big reunion. One glance at Beau's watch told him all he needed to know—he wasn't going to make it. Or if he did, it would be too late for him to pull Georgie aside so they could talk privately.

Aunt Dottie had texted and called him half a dozen times. (So had Adalia, whom he'd talked to after his call with Jack.) Georgie hadn't said a thing, although no doubt she had to be assuming the worst. He had a pit in his stomach at the thought of what she must be thinking, and he also felt the ache of having missed an event he'd helped plan. The end of an era.

He texted his aunt: *I had a situation with Hops. Please, please, please make sure she goes to the after-party.*

She responded with a golden ring icon, which made him cringe a little.

We'll see. Most couples don't get married after two weeks. Some don't even get married after twenty years. ;-)

Not that he'd wait twenty years, or even one, if Georgie forgave him. But he wasn't about to encourage Aunt Dottie.

He sent a quick text to Adalia too, repeating the story about Hops and the request that she encourage Georgie to show.

Roger, she responded. *But, oh boy, you better turn on the charm. You owe me one.*

As if his stomach weren't already in knots…

His call with Jack had been awkward, the way video calls usually are when they're with near-strangers. Especially near-strangers who didn't like you. But a phone call wouldn't have cut it, because he'd needed Jack to see how much he meant it when he said, "I'm in love with your sister."

That's the way he'd answered Jack when the guy had asked if anything had gone wrong with the party planning, and then, after glancing around the loft, where River was calling him from.

Jack had looked pissed at first, understandably.

"Did you not read the addition to the employee manual?" he'd asked. "Or did you just fail to understand it?"

"Oh, I understood it, and we both know why you insisted on making that addition," River said. "But I'm pretty sure she's in love with me too. I know about the will now, Jack, and you need to know that I would never, ever sabotage Buchanan Brewery." He swallowed. "Not just because it's Georgie's, but because it was Beau's." And because River would never do something like that anyway, but Jack struck him as a guy who liked solid reasons for things.

"You didn't know all along?" Jack asked, looking at him as if he were a human lie detector test.

"I didn't have a clue. We'd talked about his will before, and he knew I didn't expect anything from him. He gave me more than enough while he was here." And as he said it, he knew it was true. Whatever faults Beau had, he'd come by them honestly. He wouldn't have intentionally made River feel used or disposable, not after all he'd done for him. "He was important to me. That means all of you are important to me too."

"But especially Georgie?" Jack asked with that same hint   of   humor.

"Especially Georgie."

Her half-brother studied him for several seconds before nodding. "What do you want from me?" A corner of his mouth ticked up. "My blessing?"

"I don't want to hide that your sister means something to me, and I know she doesn't want that either. I want that clause about fraternization to go away so we can be together out in the open. No more secrets."

He'd chosen the words intentionally, knowing that Jack and his mother had been Prescott Buchanan's dirty little secret, and it was clear they'd made their mark. He saw the emotion flicker across Jack's face.

"My father will never accept you, you know."

The way he said it made River wonder just how well the son knew the father, and vice versa. Had they met in secret? Had they had a relationship of some kind? But really it was none of his business, so he simply said what he knew to be true. "I don't care."

Jack nodded, and he thought he could see the glimmer of respect in his eyes. "I'll do what I can," he said. Silence hung between them for a moment, and then Jack shrugged, as if to say, *My bad.* "I'm sorry I misjudged you. I hope we can get to know each other better when I get back."

It was on the tip of River's tongue to ask when that might be, but Jack had continued speaking. "Lee and I talked about the provision, so you'll probably need his okay to strike it. Maybe I can get Adalia to talk to him. They seem close."

There was a tinge of bitterness in his tone.

"I'll talk to her," River said. "She's here in Asheville."

Surprise flickered across Jack's face, and it was clear he wanted to ask how that had come about—that maybe he was more comfortable talking to River about it than his own siblings—but someone called out his name. A woman, her voice thick with annoyance. And Jack quickly said goodbye and hung up. Although the quick sign-off had intrigued River, he hadn't taken any time to think about it—he'd picked up his phone and called Adalia.

He had a key for Aunt Dottie's place, but there was no need to use it. The door had been propped open, surrounded by bright paper lanterns that surely posed a fire risk, and there was a huge sign next to it that promised *Art and Eccentricities*. Another sign, reading *Libations and Games,* featured an arrow pointing out back. Aunt Dottie had a large yard, flattish for Asheville, and apparently they'd come up with some way to use it. Hopefully it didn't involve drunk trampoline jumping.

Maybe he should have stayed for the planning meeting after all. How were he and Georgie going to find a private place to talk in what would surely be a madhouse?

"River?" a familiar voice called out. Josie stepped out of the door, decked out in a fairy costume complete with wings. "It's me, Josie," she said unnecessarily. "I'm wearing this to help create a sense of wonder. Dottie's letting me do fortunes tonight, but don't worry, she made me agree to a seventy-five-percent rate of positivity."

God help the other twenty-five percent.

"You're here early," she commented. "The only other person who's here is Lurch, and he's out back setting up the cups for his mystery brew game."

Ugh. They'd gone through with the weird beer mixtures.

"Yeah," he said, "I had a situation with my dog."

My dog.

Weirdly, he liked the sound of that. Even with everything that had happened this evening, he didn't regret his decision to keep Hops—okay, he didn't regret Maisie's decision to strong-arm him into the adoption. It felt right. Just like this felt right.

But he found himself remembering Adalia's text. What had happened with Georgie? What if she'd changed her mind about him? About them? What if it was too late after all?

"Don't you look all broody," Josie said. "I need to channel that look."

"Trust me, you don't," he muttered. "Do you need help setting up?"

"Nah," she said. "We finished everything up with Dottie earlier. But come in and take a look."

He did, feeling a pang of uneasiness as he remembered another night, another party setup.

And a couple of details were reminiscent of the night of the séance. The Beau statue stood in the middle of the living room. He had on a merch shirt, one of the old ones that looked like an explosion was imminent, and someone had added a pair of Bermuda shorts. An empty can of Beau Brown was wedged into his hand. Or at least River hoped it was empty. From a distance, it looked like it could be a *Weekend at Bernie's* situation.

A large box of crystals sat by the door, along with a sign that said, *Take One. Or Two! Find the Crystals that Speak to You.* Luckily, the pink crystal dick had not been left out as the recommended method of selection, although he was certain it was hidden somewhere within the house. Small blessings.

The big dining room table had been set up with pads of paper, colored pencils, and even some paints (which were liable to get all over the place if things got really raucous).

Honor Buchanan as it was. Imagine it as it will be, the sign said. There was a box for finished pieces.

Another sign advertised fortune-tellings, the arrow pointing toward the room that had been River's. *Find out your future...if you dare*, the sign said. In smaller text beneath that, it read, *At least ¼ may learn something devastating.*

He followed the sign and discovered a small two-person beach tent that had been set up within the room, taking up nearly all the available space. Although he knew it to be a fortune-telling tent owing to the scarfs that had been chaotically cast over the top, the ends brushing over the open side facing one of the house's rear-facing window, it didn't much look like one. It had a design of waves on the side and the slogan *Ride the wave*, with a little handwritten sign taped up next to it reading *of fate*. Any larger employees would have to crouch to fit into it.

For a second, River just stood there and took it in. Then he turned and smiled at Josie, who'd followed him. "This is perfect."

"I knew you wouldn't mind that we put it in here," Josie said. "Dottie said it was your old room."

And his old tent, it looked like.

"No, I don't mind at all."

"Your aunt suggested it might be a good idea to allow for privacy. You know, in case someone learns something they don't like. Wait until you see out back!" she said with a grin.

He headed over to the plate glass door at the back of the living room and looked out. More of those paper lanterns were everywhere, and he had to admit it looked kind

360

of nice beyond being an obvious fire hazard. There was a tub of tiny flashlights just beyond the door, and he could tell they'd been bedazzled with a generous hand.

Take one. Make your inner light an outer light, the sign read.

Lurch stood by a large table of drinks and refreshments—which were luckily not limited to earth tones—making his mixed beers like Frankenstein had his monster, and setting them out on a small side table in red plastic cups. Seeing him, Lurch waved and grinned. He must've been sampling what he was pouring, because he'd drawn a smiley face on his bald head with a Sharpie.

While there wasn't a trampoline, someone had gotten a giant bouncy castle, which was surely just as questionable. There also looked to be some sort of raffle station, with prizes laid out with buckets in front of them.

His grin grew wider. This was crazy. This was magical. This was Aunt Dottie, through and through, and not the darker side of her that had been on display that night at the séance. Tonight was about celebration. He put his hand in his pocket and felt the watch. Remembered what his aunt had told him about it. "You guys really went all out, huh? This is going to be the best party Asheville has ever seen."

If Georgie came.

"Just wait until the donkey gets here," Josie commented. "Aren't you going to pick your crystal?"

He reached into the box and picked a pink one, sending up positive wishes as he pocketed it.

"Can you do me a favor?" he asked, and Josie lit up as if he'd offered to do one for her.

CHAPTER
Thirty-Nine

Dottie had tried to get Georgie to leave for the after-party with her, before everyone else took off, but Georgie had dug in her heels. She was still digging them in, although Adalia had taken over where Dottie had left off. There'd been an actual look exchanged between the two as Dottie left, as if she were passing on the baton. But Georgie could be stubborn when the situation required it. She didn't want to go to the party in the first place, and if they were among the last to arrive, then surely they could leave that much sooner. "I need to straighten up my office."

"*Please*," Adalia groaned dramatically. "Your desk is so clean you could lick ice cream off it. *Let's go.* I'm dying to see the crystal statue in person."

Georgie's brow lifted. "He's supposed to be wearing clothes now, but with Dottie, there's no guarantee."

"Well, I should hope *not*," Adalia said. "I want to see it in all of its glory."

Shuddering, Georgie said, "Do I need to remind you that it's a naked statue of our *grandfather*? I saw it in person and my retinas are probably permanently scarred. I'm not sure you should risk your art career."

Adalia's smile fell.

Georgie felt awful for being so flippant. "Sorry, Addy. Your career's not over, you know."

With a weary exhale, Adalia said, "This isn't about me. It's about you." She made a face. "Wait. This *is* about me. I want to see the crystal dick sculpture, and I need you to make it happen."

So Georgie grudgingly agreed to leave, knowing she wouldn't be able to keep stalling for long. Most of the staff had already left.

———

The street was lined with cars and Dottie's entire purple house was lit up. K-pop music boomed from the backyard, seeming wildly incongruous with the location, and the front was filled with paper lanterns—total fire hazard—and a mini Stonehenge, made with three-foot-tall stones and a small water garden in the middle.

"Is that what I think it is?" Adalia asked as they walked toward the driveway.

Georgie gave her the side-eye. "If you're asking if we can time travel to seventeenth-century Scotland by touching the stones, then I find that an acceptable alternative to attending this party."

Adalia rolled her eyes. "And I thought that *I* was the dramatic one. You're supposed to be the voice of reason."

And ordinarily she would be, but she'd held it together for hours, and all she wanted to do was go home, open a bottle of wine, and drown her sorrows. Of course, the only bottle of wine she had in her possession was the second bottle River had left, which made it even more bittersweet.

She stopped, then took a slow step backward. "I think I'm going to just head home."

"No," Adalia cried out. "You're already here. You should at least come in and make an appearance."

Georgie cringed. "No...I think it would be better if I just go."

"Don't be ridiculous, Georgie. Just come inside." Adalia grabbed her arm and started to tug.

"Georgie!" Lurch shouted from behind her, and she turned to see him riding on a donkey down the center of the street. "It's your turn for a ride. You can enter the party like Jesus."

Georgie squeezed her eyes shut before opening them again, worried the stress of the day was causing her to hallucinate, but sure enough, Lurch was sitting on top of a donkey while a man in a cowboy hat tugged on the reins, leading them both.

Bursting out laughing, Adalia exclaimed, "This party just keeps getting better and better. How could you even *think* of missing this?"

Ignoring her sister, Georgie scrambled to get out of the way just as she realized what Lurch had said. "Oh, no, no, no, no." She shook her head vigorously. "I'm not getting on top of that thing."

"She really can't," Adalia said. "She has to go inside. I've heard the statue of Beau is in there, and I need to see it."

The man led the animal to the side of the driveway.

"Not yet," Lurch said, sliding over the side of the pack animal, but his foot got caught in the saddle. He hung precariously sideways while the animal handler watched in fascination.

Without giving it a second thought, Georgie rushed over to help. "Oh my goodness! Are you okay?"

Just before Georgie reached him, Lurch fell to the ground in a heap, landing in a bed of flowers. "I'm okay!"

But the flowers weren't. Especially after the donkey dug his back hooves in as if to say, *I thought that guy would never get off.*

Adalia's eyes narrowed and she pointed to Lurch. "Uh…why does he have a smiley face drawn on top of his bald head?"

"I have no idea," Georgie said under her breath, although she wasn't exactly surprised. There was just no end to the crazy when it came to Buchanan Brewery. Edging closer, she asked, "Lurch, are you sure you're okay?" She resisted the urge to wave her hand in front of her. He reeked of sweat and beer.

"Yep," he said as he struggled to get to his feet. He grabbed her arm for help and nearly tugged her over on top of him.

"Whoa," Georgie said, bracing herself to pull him up.

Once on his feet, Lurch fell sideways and pressed her back into the side of the donkey, which, unbelievably, stood stock-still.

"You're the best, Georgie," Lurch said, his face in front of hers, blowing out a cloud of beer breath. "You're gonna be great at Buchanan."

"Um, thanks," she said, trying to push him away, but the next thing she knew he was shoving her up onto the saddle, his hand on her butt.

"There you go," he said. "Upsy-daisy."

"Addy!" Georgie called out in a panicked voice. She was straddling the donkey with her dress hiked up high on her thighs, nearly showing her underwear. "A little help?"

Adalia started to say something, then stopped and grinned. "I don't have any experience riding donkeys, but I think you kick them in the sides to make them go faster."

"Not that kind of help!"

"She's right," Lurch said, staggering in place. "Like this." Then he grabbed Georgie's leg and pushed it hard into the donkey's side.

The donkey released a loud bray of protest, then took off running—or at least skipping really fast—toward the gate to the backyard, leaving its handler behind.

Georgie shrieked as the donkey ran through the open gate, tearing a paper banner that read, *Enter at the risk of excitement!* which had been strung across the opening. Tearing through the paper sent the animal into overdrive.

Once they were in the backyard, the donkey ran around the periphery of the fenced space, knocking over a metal tub of beer cans. A few people shouted in surprise, which scared the donkey even more.

Georgie leaned forward and snagged the reins as the donkey raced toward the bounce house. Bounce house? When had Dottie added a bounce house? Heck, when had she added a donkey? She tugged the reins as hard as she could, and the animal came to an abrupt stop, sending Georgie tumbling over his head and into the inflatable structure.

She flew head over heels, sprawling out on her back on the bounce house floor, staring up at the ceiling strung with white Christmas lights and streamers. Sparkles filled her vision. Had she hit her head? Did she have a concussion?

"Oh, my God, Georgie," Adalia called out breathlessly in the opening. "Are you okay?"

"I think so." But she remained spread out, trying to catch her breath and thanking the stars overhead that no one else had been inside.

Adalia crawled in and knelt next to Georgie, her eyes wide. "Seriously, Georgie. Are you okay?"

"I think so. How's the donkey?"

"The donkey seems fine. Dottie's begonias, not so much."

Georgie still lay on her back. "That's good. And everything else?"

"A few cans of beer may have perished, but the video I plan to upload to TikTok should make up for it."

Georgie's eyes flew wide. "*You wouldn't.*"

"Calm down," Adalia said with a chuckle. "I was too busy running after you to dig out my phone." She heaved a dramatic sigh, part Scarlett O'Hara, part Gossip Girl, and said, "And I'm sure that will be the biggest regret of my life…"

The word regret reminded Georgie of the well of it she carried inside her, and tears sprang to her eyes. "I want to go home. Can I go home now?"

Indecision wavered on Adalia's face. Without a word, she grabbed Georgie's hand and pulled her to a sitting position, then tugged her to the opening.

Once Georgie's feet hit the ground, Josie burst out through the back door. She was wearing a pink tulle ballgown along with small pink gossamer fairy wings, a large tiara on her head, and a wand in her hand. "Oh, drat! I heard you went flying, Georgie, but it looks like I missed it."

"Sorry," Georgie said, looking down and realizing she was missing a shoe.

Josie reached for her hand and started to drag her toward the house. "You have to come in and have your fortune read."

Shaking her head, Georgie said, "No. I already know my fortune. I'm going home."

"Here," Lurch said, handing her a red plastic cup. "This'll help."

Without thinking, she accepted the cup and took a big gulp...then spit out the liquid all down the front of her dress. "Oh my word! *What is this?*"

"That's the point," Lurch said with a hiccup. "You're supposed to guess."

Adalia took a sip, then made a face. "This tastes like cat pee."

Georgie shot her a suspicious look. "And how would *you* know what cat pee tastes like?"

Twisting her mouth to the side, Adalia grimaced. "Some things are better left to the imagination."

Georgie wasn't so sure about that. Her imagination hadn't been good to her lately. "I'm going home."

"But Georgie..." Josie protested.

"I'm going home," she said more firmly, starting to limp toward the gate.

"You're going to disappoint Dottie," Adalia said, running over to her. "And I think your shoe might be in the bounce house. And I still have to see that statue. We're already here, so can we just go in and see it? Please?"

"You go in and I'll wait in the car."

"No!" Josie and Adalia both said in unison, and Georgie had to wonder why they wanted her in the house so badly. What new horror awaited her inside?

Adalia took her hand and walked backward, dragging her sister with her. "Let's just go inside for a minute,

Georgie, *please*. And then if you still want to go home, I'll chauffeur you. You can sit in the back and everything. But please come with me."

Georgie knew Adalia wanted to see the statue, but this was borderline obsessive. "You promise we can go home after you see it?"

Adalia nodded her head enthusiastically. "Yes. Cross my heart and hope to die." She made an X over her chest with her fingers.

"Fine," Georgie grunted. "I'll give you five seconds, then I'm leaving, even if I have to walk home with one shoe."

Adalia pulled Georgie through the back door while Josie followed closely behind, as if to make sure Georgie didn't escape.

A few employees congregated in the kitchen, talking and grabbing snacks from the kitchen counter. They stopped and stared at Georgie with open mouths.

"Oh Lord," Georgie moaned. "Why are they looking at me like that?"

Coming to a halt, Adalia grimaced, then tugged the hem of Georgie's dress out of the back of her panties.

"Oh God...have I been flashing everyone *my underwear?*"

"Calm down," Adalia said, reaching up and trying to smooth Georgie's hair. "People see worse at the beach."

"Excuse me," one of the men asked, rushing through the back door. Ted from packaging, if she remembered correctly. "My wife is wondering where you purchased your underwear."

Georgie stared at him in disbelief but found herself answering, "Moon Goddess."

His face brightened. "She thought so, but she was wondering if it was from the Neptune or the Venus line?"

Could this night get any worse?

She plastered on a smile. "Neither. The Athena."

Ted nodded, his head bobbing like a hand pump. "Okay, then. Thank you."

"Do you think Buchanan will sell underwear like that?" Josie asked in her breathy voice as Ted rushed out the back door. She sounded hopeful.

Georgie reached up to cover her face with her hands, but her fingertip touched something thin and metallic on her forehead. When she pulled her hand away, she found a quarter-inch, circular piece of silver glitter. It was then that she looked down and realized she was covered in it.

"Where did the glitter come from?" she asked, looking Adalia in the eyes.

Her sister's brow shot up while her mouth tipped up in an apologetic smile. "The bounce house."

"It floats when you jump," Josie said. "Just like in a fairyland."

"Of course it does."

"You really should try it," Josie said. "We could both go right now." She grabbed Georgie's hand and started to drag her toward the back door.

"While that sounds fun," Adalia said, intervening, "I think Georgie should go back to the fortune room and take a moment to collect herself."

Josie's eyes flew wide with excitement. "Oh! I can read her future."

Adalia's head tipped to the side. "Let's let Georgie handle her own future." She steered Georgie past the sculpture, which was fully clothed and holding an empty beer can, and down a short hall, past a line of people.

Did all of these people need to pee already?

Stopping in front of a closed door with a sign in front of it that read, *Find out your future...if you dare. At least ¼ may learn something devastating*, Adalia stopped and plucked a piece of glitter from Georgie's cheek.

"No cutting in line!" someone called out.

"You want your fortune?" Adalia asked in a threatening tone. "I'll give you your fortune—your entire career depends on this woman, and if she wants to go first, you'll let her."

Georgie shook her head. "But I don't want to go first."

"Trust me, Georgie, You do."

"What are you doing, Addy?" Georgie asked, nearly too weary to care.

"Trying to make you more presentable." But then she surveyed Georgie and shook her head. "There's no coming back from this."

"What?"

Adalia shook her head, grabbing her upper arms and giving her a grim smile. "Trust your heart, Georgie. I swear it won't let you down."

The door opened then, as if the person inside truly were psychic, and Addy shoved her into the room.

CHAPTER
Forty

River hadn't thought he'd actually have to tell people's fortunes. Josie had promised to bring Georgie to him straightaway, and since she wasn't the most reliable person in his acquaintance, he'd texted Adalia to tell him where he was waiting.

You owe me, she'd written back. *I think I'll take an art lesson with Dottie as my payment.*

Your funeral, he'd replied.

So when the first person knocked, his heart leapt in his chest, and he jumped off the bed, nearly tripping over a tent pole in his haste to answer.

He opened the door, ready to let all the things he'd been feeling pour out. Ready to tell Georgie the fullness of what he felt for her, but he only got two words out—"I love"—before he realized it wasn't Georgie at all, but Blanche the brewery accountant. Blanche, who'd openly ogled him every time he came over to see Beau, even though her twin sons had been two years ahead of him in high school. She'd been one of the first people to congratulate him on getting the job.

She beamed at him, fluffing her bouffant of peroxide-blond hair.

"—telling fortunes," he finished lamely.

Her face fell a little, but then her gaze landed on the tent setup. He'd turned on the twinkle lights Josie had used to line the edge of the tent and switched off the overhead light, thinking it would create a more romantic atmosphere. He'd set out two large floor pillows on either side of Josie's crystal ball.

"Ooh, that looks cozy," she said with a wink. "Why don't we take a seat?"

Perhaps he'd been too successful.

"Um, I can already see your future," River said, waving his fingers through the air as if pulling back the celestial curtain. "You're going to have a grandchild within the year."

He'd thought it a pretty innocuous thing to say—one of the twins' wives looked so pregnant she was probably on her way to the hospital—but she gasped as if scandalized.

"I knew it, the little hussy," she snapped. "I told her this would happen if she didn't stay away from the brewery." Which was when he remembered she also had a twenty-one-year-old daughter. "Which one of 'em did it? Huh? Was it Daniel?"

What in the world had he gotten himself into?

"Uh...the future is too hazy for me to see anything else."

"Can't you try the ball?" she asked, gesturing to it.

"The reception isn't great in here." He gestured to the walls. "You know what it's like with these old houses. Thick walls."

She pouted, and it seemed like she was on the verge of saying something else, but someone knocked on the door.

River practically lunged for it, but it wasn't Georgie.

"River," Tom said with surprise. "Why weren't you at the party earlier?"

Blanche pursed her lips and stomped off. River had a feeling Daniel was about to get an earful.

"Thank God it's you," he said, pulling Tom inside. He saw the long line of people waiting to have their fortunes read. Should he just leave? Call Georgie so they could have this conversation over the phone?

But if Josie and Adalia really followed through on their part of the bargain, this would be the best place for him to talk to Georgie tonight. They certainly weren't going to get a moment alone anywhere else. Even from this room, he could hear the shouting and music—was that K-pop?—from the backyard. He lifted the curtains and glanced out the window, hoping he'd get a look at her, but all he saw was Lurch riding a donkey.

"This is a disaster," he groaned, running his hand through his hair and closing the door.

By the time he turned around, Tom was sitting on one of the floor pillows, patiently waiting as if he actually expected River to read his fortune.

Since he'd rather sit with Tom than with any of the other people in line, River sighed and pulled the second pillow next to the twin bed before sitting.

Tom looked at him expectantly, and River peered into the crystal ball.

"Um. You'll find great love and meaning within the next year," he said. Tom was a single widower in his sixties, and he seemed on the lonely side, so River hoped it was true.

"Thanks, River," Tom said, beaming back at him. "I surely hope so."

The grin he gave River made him fleetingly grateful he'd been in the tent instead of Josie—the last thing Tom needed was to be told he'd be eviscerated by wolves or would die alone in a vat of his own tears. But the next person who came in was Daniel, who was (understandably) pissed about the whole Blanche thing. He also complained that River didn't look enough like a fortune-teller, which River waved off, but by the time the fifth person came in, River had tied a sparkly blue scarf around his head out of pure boredom.

When the sixth person knocked, River was about ready to give up. He scrawled a sign on an old sheet of paper from the desk drawer—*Closed due to curse*—and opened the door ready to post it, but he dropped it when he saw her. Or, more accurately, when she was nearly shoved into him.

Georgie's light blue dress was soaked with something that smelled like beer, huge pieces of glitter clung to it in places, and she only had on one shoe.

She'd never looked more beautiful.

Her eyes lit up when she saw him, then landed and lingered on the scarf, which he immediately tugged off, his ears burning.

"Nice look, River," Adalia said with a laugh. "Or should I call you Madam Mysterio?" She stooped to retrieve his sign before shutting the door, so hopefully they wouldn't be bothered every two minutes by relentless knocking. Turned out the people of Buchanan Brewery were aggressively interested in psychic readings.

"What happened to you?" they asked at mostly the same time.

She laughed, a little nervously he thought, and he took her hand—grateful when she gave it to him—and led her over to the cushions, which he pushed into their original configuration.

"I'm sorry about earlier," he said as they sat next to each other, her heat pressed to him. "Hops ate a chocolate bar, and I had to make sure he was okay. I wouldn't have missed it otherwise. It felt awful not being there."

Something in her expression loosened at that, like she'd been carrying a weight he'd just eased.

"Is he all right?"

"Yeah," he said, rubbing his thumb against her hand. "He's going to be okay."

"River." She looked into his eyes. "I'm so, so sorry. I didn't handle any of this well. The brewery should be yours. I'm going to sign my part over to you in the morning, and I'll do everything in my power to convince my sister and brothers to do the same. It's not right—"

She stopped, as if finally registering he was shaking his head.

"I don't want that," he said. "And Beau didn't want it either. He wanted you and your family to be a part of what he'd made. I'm sorry for the way I reacted yesterday… I felt blindsided, and I didn't stop to think about what all of this was doing to you. You were backed into a corner, and instead of offering you a hand, I turned my back on you. Which is something I never, ever want to do again."

He took her other hand as he said it, and she let him, looking at him with something like wonder. "Georgie, I want to do this *with* you. All the way. I've never in my life felt more fulfilled than working with you. Being with you. And I don't want to hide what we have."

She cringed a little at that. "I know. I'm sorry about my brothers. But I'll take care of it. I promise."

"You don't need to worry about that anymore," he said. "I talked to Jack, and he agreed to back off. And from what I understand, Adalia made a lot of headway with Lee."

Shock radiated from her. "You did that for me?" A pause. "I feel like this has to be an incredibly vivid dream. *Jane Eyre* was my favorite book in high school, and you *are* pretending to be a fortune-teller. Don't think Adalia's the only one who noticed that scarf earlier."

"Oh, there was no pretending," he said with a chuckle. "I gave readings for five people, and I stuck to Josie's one-fourth rule. It was brutal for poor Kevin in sales."

"So what happened in *Jane Eyre*?" he asked, pulling her closer. "I can't say I've ever read it."

She pursed her lips. "Well, the man Jane loved pretended to be a fortune-teller so he could say things to her he wouldn't say out in the open."

"Huh. That's messed up."

"Yeah"—she arched her brow—"he had to be careful because his crazy wife was living up in the attic." She glanced up dramatically.

River huffed a laugh. "And this was your favorite book?" He pulled one of his hands away, but only so he could gesture toward the window. "Don't worry. All my crazy is out in the open, and if you still want to be with me after seeing all of this..." The donkey wandered by, chewing on some of Aunt Dottie's flowers, as if to punctuate his point. "...I'm all yours."

She kissed him then—a soft kiss that quickly turned fierce, and by the time she pulled away she was panting.

"I love you, River."

The surety with which she said it, the fire in her eyes...he'd never felt happier and fuller than he did in this moment. Than he did with this woman.

"Hey," he said, running his fingers down the curve of her cheek, "I was going to say it first." Then he sucked in a breath, bolstering himself for the words he'd never said to a woman before, other than his near brush with Blanche. "I love you, Georgie."

He kissed her first this time, savoring the taste of her, the closeness, knowing he never wanted to pull away. He tugged Georgie the rest of the way onto his lap, hands on her hips, her curves, any part of her he could touch, and she slid a hand under his shirt, running it across his abs.

He went to take it off, which was when he saw Lurch giving him a thumbs-up from outside the window.

"Um, I think we should probably get out of here," he said to Georgie, pulling back a little.

Her gaze shot to the window, and she jumped a little in his arms. "Yes, please. Immediately."

"Should we look for your other shoe?"

She glanced down at her foot and shook her head a little. "No. Let's not chance it. Maybe Josie will find it." A side of her mouth ticked up. "She's good at collecting my clothes."

He stood up and pulled her up with him, Georgie's eyes widening as he lifted her into his arms.

"I'm pretty sure there's probably at least a dozen abandoned crystals on the floor out there," he explained, "and I don't want you to hurt your feet."

She tipped her head up and kissed him at that, and he almost forgot Lurch was at the window, and there were people outside the room waiting for fortune readings, and this whole party was a massive disaster unfolding around them. But when he edged back toward the bed, she poked him.

"No, we need to get out of here before it's too late. If we don't hurry, there's going to be a fire or a flood, or who knows what, and we'll never have the chance."

He opened the door, ready to sneak out—although how he was supposed to do that with the boss in his arms, he didn't know—only to find everyone gathered in a semicircle at the end of the hall, Aunt Dottie standing next to the Beau statue, Adalia grinning at them from Beau's right-hand side, in front of an enormous cake. It had been decorated with surprisingly accurate renditions of Georgie and River.

"Surprise!" Adalia said. "Dottie spent *hours* working on it. It was my idea! Want to make the first cut?" She held out a knife, and it was only then River caught sight of the computer set up in the corner, Jack watching everything unfold with a look of fascinated horror, as if wondering what he was in for if, or when, he did move to Asheville.

"Sure," he said, because why not.

He exchanged a look with Georgie, who said, "You better not cut off my nose."

The moment was weirdly, wonderfully perfect. He had a feeling they'd remember the day Buchanan Brewery closed down for years to come. That one day they might tell heavily edited versions of this story to their kids.

He leaned down to kiss Georgie again, in front of everyone, and they all whooped and cheered.

EPILOGUE

"Oh, my God," Adalia groaned. "If I'd known you two would be so disgusting, I never would have orchestrated getting you back together."

Georgie and River were sitting hand in hand in the wicker chairs on the back porch, watching Hops romp around in the backyard. Jezebel, who was surprisingly tolerant of the puppy, sat in a dry bird bath watching like a prison yard guard.

Laughing, Georgie said, "From what I heard, Dottie had a lot to do with it too."

River raised his free hand. "I'm pretty sure I should be included on that list."

Georgie shot him an ornery grin. "Of course you were." She turned to her sister, who stood in the open doorway. "And we're not even doing anything."

"You're holding hands."

River chuckled, shaking his head as he turned to look at her. "You've never struck me as a puritan, Addy."

Georgie smiled to herself. River had taken to Adalia's nickname almost immediately, as had most of the staff at

Buchanan, but Dottie was quite adamant about calling her Adalia, saying her name fit her too well to alter it.

Adalia shuddered. "Gross. Why would you insult me like that?"

Georgie turned to face her sister, a huge grin on her face. "I'm confused as to why you're upset."

"You're like an old married couple, content with just sitting together. Watching your dog. It's gross."

Amusement lit up River's face. "So what would you have us do?"

"You can start by coming inside. I have something important to show you. You know, before you officially give up the ghost and check yourselves into an old-age home."

Georgie glanced at River, and she saw something knowing in his eyes. He had some idea of what Adalia intended. Interesting. Well, she was grateful for whatever had caught Adalia's interest. So few things did, lately.

Adalia had become a near hermit, something completely unlike her. Other than the parties two weeks ago and going to the brewery, she hadn't ventured out at all. Her sister wouldn't even give in to Dottie's persistent coaxing to "make something fabulous with her."

Georgie wasn't sure what to do or how to help. She'd already cornered Alan Stansworth into dropping the legal charges against her sister. The Monday after the party, she'd called him up and coldly informed him that Adalia had photographic proof that she had created the sculptures he'd appropriated, and unless all charges were dropped, she would be hiring the very best attorney the Buchanans could find to ensure the art community knew exactly who he was and what he'd done. The charges had been dropped that very afternoon.

When Georgie called Adalia into her office to tell her as much, Adalia had said, "Georgie, I don't *have* any photos of me making those sculptures."

Georgie had given her a conspiratorial grin. "You know that, and *I* know that, but apparently *Alan Stansworth* doesn't know that."

"You bluffed him," Adalia had said, gaping at her. "I never knew you had it in you."

Georgie had winked. "Did I mention that I considered going to law school? There are a *lot* of things you don't know about me."

"So I'm finding out." Adalia had given her a rare serious look. "Thanks, Georgie. For everything. I honestly don't know what I would have done without you."

Georgie had gotten up from her desk and given her a hug. "That's what sisters are for. I'm here, Addy. I'm not going anywhere."

And apparently neither was Adalia. Which meant Georgie would have plenty of time to figure out how to draw her out. She'd hoped that making the Stansworth problem go away would do it, but what had happened obviously left scars.

So of course she would do Adalia's bidding.

She shot her sister a look. "Okay, I'll bite. But only if you do the dishes from dinner."

River laughed. "I love your devious side."

She leaned over and kissed him. "There's plenty more where that came from."

Adalia lifted her hands in front of her face. "Now you're *really* being gross. Are you going to leave Hops back here, at Jezebel's mercy?"

"He'll be fine," River said, glancing at her over Georgie's shoulder. "He knows better than to mess with her, and if anything she's happy to have a minion."

"Which seems fitting since they're the new mascots for the brewery," Georgie said. It had been her idea to use Hops, who was surely cute enough to sell beer, and Adalia's suggestion that Jezebel would be an inspired choice to market the sours River was making. "Speaking of which, are you still good with handling the photo shoot next week, Addy? We'll need to buy a thousand sardines for Jezebel."

An emotion Georgie couldn't name flickered in her sister's eyes, but it passed just as quickly. "I've got it covered. Now, get inside before I have to lasso you. I really don't feel like watching a YouTube tutorial right now."

Georgie laughed at that, but that look weighed on her. She'd been seeing variations of it for weeks.

Adalia preceded them inside, and Georgie got up before River did and held out her hand to him. He grinned at her as he accepted the boost. "I love it when you go all knight in shining armor on me."

"I know you know what this is about," she murmured, without any heat. She liked River's surprises, the side of him that was a little more like Dottie than he realized. Just last week, he'd given her a long silver necklace with a beautiful pink crystal pendant. Made, he told her, from the pink crystal she'd thrown at his head that first night.

When she stepped inside, hand in hand with River, it took her a moment to understand what she was seeing on the kitchen table. Adalia stood in front of a six-pack of bottled beer, which was something of a mainstay around her house these days. But when she took a closer look, she gasped…

The label had an artistic rendering of Hops on it in bright, almost psychedelic colors, and it read, *Hair of Hops, Buchanan Brewery*. It was eye-catching, it was gorgeous, and it was 100% Adalia. Except that name…

River squeezed her hand, his eyes alight with pride. "Your first beer," he confirmed. "Adalia helped make it special. I thought we could try it for the first time together."

"What he means is that I did the most important and vital part," Adalia teased.

"You haven't tried it yet?" Georgie asked in bewilderment, looking up at River. "Not even when you were bottling it?"

"No," he said, "which felt extremely weird, I won't lie, but I wanted to do this with you. It's our first collaboration beer." A slow smile stole across his face. "It's the beginning of an era."

"Which will really be a bummer if it sucks," Adalia said. She grabbed one of the bottles and nodded to the porch. "I'm going out there to puppysit my nephew." A pause. "And also because I have a feeling some PDA is going to come out of this."

"Oh, you're right about that," River said, gazing at Georgie as he said it. That look was all heat, and it sent tingles through her, but she snagged her sister into a hug as she walked by. "Thank you," she said in a low voice. "It's beautiful, and I know the rest of them will be too. I'm so glad you're here."

"So am I," Adalia said, and from the emotion in her voice, it was obvious she meant it. "Now go have your beautiful moment with your perfectly adequate boyfriend."

"Aw, Addy, I knew you liked me," River said. He hugged her too, though, and Georgie felt the gratitude of knowing that at least one person in her family had accepted him with open arms. Lee and her father were furious, and Jack didn't necessarily approve, but he'd been pacified by whatever River had told him. She was surprised by how little it fazed her. Her family had a long history of toxic relationships, but *she* was breaking the mold.

After the door shut behind Adalia, River went to the table. Georgie assumed he'd gone to get the bottles, but instead he started up a drumroll, just like he'd done the day they made the beer. Funny how it was obnoxious when her father did it and perfectly charming when River did it.

"The moment of truth approaches," he said in an announcer's voice.

"I suppose this means I have to open them?"

"I suppose so. I can one-handed drink, but only Finn can open a bottle that way," he said, continuing with the drumming.

She sighed dramatically as she popped two of the bottles open and handed him one. The smell was right, but she didn't let herself hope too much. She'd liked the smell of certain beers and hated the taste.

River stopped the playful drumming and clinked his bottle to hers.

"What if it's no good?" she asked, suddenly worried. Obviously, anything River made would be good, but she was the one who'd gone through the steps for this one, and then there was the whole issue about the possible hair contamination.

"Impossible," he said, his tone absolute. He put his bottle down and pulled her to him. Setting her own beer down so quickly it nearly splashed, she wrapped her arms around his neck. He kissed her, deep and passionate, as if she were something to be savored, and when he finally pulled back, she wasn't thinking about the beer, or her worries about the brewery reopening, or about anything other than River.

"We made this together," he whispered in her ear, "and that means it's going to be the best beer ever. Until the next one, and the next one, and the next one. Because we, Georgie Buchanan, are meant to be together in all things."

He pulled back, his eyes gleaming, and grabbed the two bottles, handing one to her.

This time, they both took a sip at the same time, their eyes on each other.

The flavors were in perfect balance, the carbonation at an ideal level, the beer utterly drinkable.

"The perfect balance," she said, feeling the happiness fizz through her. "Just like us."

River set his bottle down, and she did the same, and they were reaching for each other just as Adalia called out from the porch. "Um, guys. I thought this was a twist top. Can you come help a girl out?"

And because River really was the perfect man—perfect for Georgie—he pocketed the bottle opener with a flourish, grabbed the beers in one hand, and put the other around her.

"I think this means we might have to put dog hair in all of our beer," he whispered.

And somehow it was the perfect thing to say.

Acknowledgments

My heartfelt thanks to Denise, for being my kind of crazy. I LOVE all of our collaborations, and our friendship most of all. Working on this series with you has been the experience of a lifetime.

Thanks also to my sister, Jennifer, who read this book in short installments and provided some much appreciated cheerleading. To my parents, for being super fans, and to my husband, Devin, for bragging about it shamelessly. You're a pretty good crew—I think I'll keep you.

I'm also grateful to everyone who helped make this book happen, including our copyeditor, Carolina Valdez Schneider; our proofreader, Shannon Page; and our audiobook narrator, Joy Nash.

—*Angela*

I've written so many books in such a short period of time that writing had become a chore. But then I started writing with Angela, and it was fun and exciting again. Thank you, Angela, for bringing the pure joy of writing back into my life. I'm so grateful for this experience and hope we co-write many more books together.

Thanks to my kids, as always, for putting up with my crazy schedule and my "just one more minutes" that turn into an hour. I've been trying to do a better job of being present—I hope you think so too.

And also, as always, many thanks to the people behind the scenes who make my books shine—Carolina Valdez

Schneider and Shannon Page. You two and Angela are my team. I couldn't do this without you.

And I say this every time, and I mean it just as much— thank you dear reader, for choosing OUR book to read. There are millions of books out there, yet you choose this one. Thank you.

—*Denise*

ABOUT
the Authors

A.R. CASELLA is a freelance developmental editor by day, writer by night. She lives in Asheville, NC with her husband, daughter, two dogs, and a variable number of fish. Her pastimes include chasing around her toddler, baking delicious treats, and occasional bouts of crocheting. *Any Luck at All*, co-written with *New York Times* bestselling author Denise Grover Swank, is her first book.
You can find out more at www.arcasella.com

DENISE GROVER SWANK was born in Kansas City, Missouri and lived in the area until she was nineteen. Then she became a nomad, living in five cities, four states and ten houses over the course of ten years before she moved back to her roots. Her hobbies include witty Facebook comments (in own her mind) and dancing in her kitchen with her children. (Quite badly if you believe her offspring.) Hidden talents include the gift of justification and the ability to drink massive amounts of caffeine and still fall asleep within two minutes. Her lack of the sense of smell allows her to perform many unspeakable tasks. She has six children and hasn't lost her sanity. Or so she leads you to believe.
You can find her at denisegroverswank.com

Made in the USA
Columbia, SC
16 October 2020

22952998R00233